RESURRECTION OF THE EXPS

BOOK 3

Alexander J. McCarty

Art by: William McCarty

RESURRECTION OF THE EXPS BOOK 3 Sellum. Copyright © 2017 by
Alexander J. McCarty.

ISBN 978 1 943733 05 7

Published by Sphere of Compassion, Inc.
authoralexandermccarty@gmail.com
alexanderjmccarty@facebook.com (Updates with excerpts and art).
alexander_j_mccarty@instagram.com
of_the_Exps@twitter.com
oftheexps@tumbler.com

Cover design by William McCarty

Books from *Of the Exps©* Series

Rebellion Arc
1. *Exp 8*: Rebellion of the Exps

Resurrection Arc
2. *The Hero of Sel*: Resurrection of the Exps

3. *Sellum*: Resurrection of the Exps

4. *Destruction, Creation & Absence*: Resurrection of the Exps
   (coming Summer 2018)

Rise Arc (Coming 2018)

Table of Contents

Part 10: Aftermath & War

Part 11: The Knight of Sel

Part 12: The King of Sel

Part 13: Elysium Asylum

Part 14: Apotheosis

Part 15: The Portal to Earth

Acknowledgments

First and foremost, I give a continuous and reverent thanks to my brother for bringing my characters to life with his art, helping me plan and flesh out scenes, providing feedback whenever I need it, and brainstorming with me to create new characters and hone old ones. I give thanks to my loving and supportive parents. I thank Luis Garced who read this book back when I first began writing it. I thank my family and friends who read any part of this book either digitally or in manuscript form, particularly Gabriel, Ivan, Ken, John, Jesus, Tatiana, and Val who have all supported my book series for years.

Shout out to Dr. Steve Vose and Iqbal Aktar for answering questions I had about religious traditions and sacred architecture. Special thanks to my wonderful editor, Rosemi, who, with her vast knowledge and research, has helped make this book more accessible and more real to my readers. I am grateful to the creators of clever, innovative, and thought-provoking anime, manga, videogames, scripture, and other visual literature.

As always, I thank my id for keeping me vital and driven, my ego for keeping me positive and critical about my work, and my super ego for directing my creative energies toward a better world for all living beings. Lastly, I thank you, the reader, for purchasing this book. I hope you enjoy the story/characters, reflect on the themes, and continue to support me in my future works.

Thank you! =(:3)*   (That's a bunny, by the way.)

This book is dedicated to those searching for solace in a society where their kind has been deemed an outcast. Outcasts are attributed little or no moral value by their oppressors. May we all welcome people of all cultures, creeds and species into our sphere of compassion and work toward a world that celebrates diversity and openly engages in cultural syncretism.

Introduction

While getting Exp 8 and the Hero of Sel prepped for print I have been diligently working on this book. Originally Books 2 and 3 were a single book, but in order to get a more in-depth view on the traditions and politics of Sellum, I split the second volume into two books. Looking back at it now, I feel I made the right decision (first advised to me by my editor).

To my surprise this book has even more battles than Book 1, though I feel these fights are more intense and compact. I am very happy with how this book turned out. With six parts instead of four, it moves at a much quicker pace and sets the groundwork for the final book of the Sellum Arc (coming 2018).

I'm currently working with my brother on setting up a YouTube channel called McCarty Bros for information on projects we are working on as well as our reflections on various media. The two of us have also tabled at local anime conventions and have had great success doing so.

I hope you will follow me on Facebook, Instagram, or Tumblr and feel free to message me. My Facebook group, Alexander J McCarty, updates often with quotes, excerpts, and character art from my book series. Please spread the word about my series, take a moment to give the first two books a review (on Amazon or Goodreads), and enjoy. =(:3)*

In the Last Volume:

Book 2,

The Hero of Sel: Resurrection of the Exps

Deceivant, the charming skeptic with a passion for youth and science was murdered by an anomaly named Demonica. When next he opened his eyes, he was lying in the grass and gazing at the clouds. Before long he met up with the other Freedom Forcers, most of whom he had presumed dead, and was told that he was in a place called Lum. Putting aside the absurdity of this being true, he ventured with his wife Ada to a vacant realm where he inspired Devlin, his spiteful though remarkably talented son, to break free and rescue the cutest assassin ever. After helping a zealot through a spiritual breakdown and making an alliance with a Sikh militia, he and his allies were sent to Absence by the so-called goddess Efil. Here, they met up with Devlin, Exp 8, Kaity, and Demonica. The team met with the Sinful Sorority after a temporary leave from Absence. With the Ultimate Exp's assistance, he protected Deerg from his greedy son's malicious intentions. After breaking out of Absence by defeating the guardians of the realm, they arrived in Lum. Here he came across a gruesome scene. He rescued a young girl from the bloody mess and entrusted her to Efil. While in Lum, Deceivant and his less intelligent compatriots were also confronted by Etaf. After hearing the tragic story of her youth, she sent the charming inventor and his allies to Sel. Once the Freedom Forcers defeated Etah's forces, the self-proclaimed God of Hate appeared and forced the team to relive his vengeful son's rebellious past. Thankfully, the misunderstandings were cleared up and Devlin directed his aggressive energy at Etah. After an intense battle against the young scientist's super-weapon, the mythical tyrant fell. Whether or not the skeptical scientist and his followers will survive this fanciful dilemma and make it back to Earth has yet to be determined.

Deceivant's Notes on the 'Afterlife'

FREEDOM FORCERS

Sought to free Exps from slavery. After a devastating loss, they seek only survival.

Deceivant Kagaku: Leader
Bio: Diligent scientist; Child at heart; Skeptic; Enjoys the company of little girls
Abilities: Focused and able to think abstractly; Capsule locater; He is a born leader
Relations: Ada (wife); Devlin (son); Kanasta (son); D.S. (son); Likes all little girls
Developments: Cured Violet of a religious breakdown through logical reasoning
Current Status: Alive in Sel (fearing for the lives of those he holds dear)

DECEIVANT'S EXPS

Ada: Exp 03; Mediator
Bio: Adorable loving wife whose kindness transcends scientific understanding
Abilities: Creates holograms; She can cheer up allies and reason with enemies
Relations: Ada (wife); Devlin (son); Kanasta (son); D.S. (son)
Developments: Forgave her murderous son; Reasoned with Efil for escort and aid
Current Status: Deceased (I will never forget her)

Destructus Supplious: D.S. for short; Exp 04; Bodyguard
Bio: Childish (takes after his father) and loves learning; Dependable and brave
Abilities: Giant scissors; Staple gun; Super strength
Relations: Ada (mom); Deceivant (dad); Kanasta (brother); Violet (BFF)
Developments: Learned about morality from Pharma and distrusts Lum
Current Status: Alive in Sel (ready to defend his family)

Devlin Kagaku: My greatest (though definitely not cutest) creation
Bio: Rebellious; Ungrateful; Hot-headed; Creative genius; Hopeless romantic
Abilities: Wires that can slice through metal and flesh; Creates Exps
Relations: Ada (mom); Deceivant (dad); Kanasta (brother); Kaity (beloved)
Developments: Battled the 'God' of Hate after learning I didn't do anything wrong
Current Status: Fighting the 'God' of Hate (he told us to flee and we did)

DEVLIN'S EXPS

Nina: Exp 3; Survivalist
Bio: Self-absorbed (due to my expert programming) but dependable in a pinch
Abilities: Seduction; Explosives; Gravity; Speed; Mental manipulation
Relations: Devlin (creator); Ada (teacher); Kaity (fan); Fatima (new fan)
Developments: Made a deal with Allah's Jannah; Battled Kanasta and lost
Current Status: Alive (wants to return to Lum so she can get back to Earth)

Riufen: Exp 10; Samurai
Bio: Expert Swordsman; Honor bound (will bend morals if ordered to by Devlin)
Abilities: Immortality; Complete control over body; Wields spinal cord as a sword
Relations: Devlin-sama (shogun); Bob (rival); Kanasta (venerable uncle)
Developments: Denounced loyalty to Devlin before hearing his past; Killed Bob?
Current Status: Having sworn allegiance to Devlin, he readily enters the battlefield

Violet Gold: Exp 7; Astral Warrior
Bio: Skeptic in training (under my tutelage); Still devoutly holds illogical beliefs
Abilities: Astral projection (energy manipulation in laymen's terms); Swordplay
Relations: Devlin (creator/god); Deceivant (rival/teacher); Worships Lum 'gods'
Developments: Recovered from religious breakdown after I soothed her with doubt
Current Status: Lumian; Recovered from injury through prana (energy) restoration

Exp 11: Opti/Pesi; Morale Buffer
Bio: Opti: fun-loving and helpful; Pesi: volatile and cruel; Both are simpletons
Abilities: Flight; Boost morale; Influences reality
Relations: Devlin (creator); NoOne (friend) Opti is Pesi's nemesis and vice-versa
Developments: Convinced NoOne to leave sheep; Wants to find NoOne's beloved
Current Status: Survived surefire death (connection to Influence artifact is strong)

VIPER SQUAD

Kanasta: Assassin Boss
Bio: Cold-hearted (a detestable son who would kill a little girl if paid to)
Abilities: Various gadgets and weapons; Gorilla-like strength; Keeps calm
Relations: Deceivant (dad); Ada (mom); Devlin (bro); D.S. (bro); Riufen (nephew)
Kaity (daughter); Reflector (target/client) Imam (target); Viper Squad (family)
Developments: He fought Deerg (I hope she's okay)
Current Status: Alive in Sel (on paid retainer from Devlin)

Kaity: Sniper
Bio: Kanasta's apprentice; Able to prioritize; Kitty tail and ears; Adorable
Abilities: Expert marksmanship; Magnetism (with artifact); Super hearing/reflexes
Relations: Kanasta (boss/papa); Sefiwah (love); Nina (crush); Deceivant (grandpa)
Developments: Brought team together after loss of our previous leader
Current Status: Alive (thankfully); Defeated Edirp when partnered with Nina

BoneSaw: Robot
Bio: Little robot (would make a great toy for kids if you remove the saws)
Abilities: Near indestructible due to magnetism; Deploys saws and chainsaws
Relations: Kanasta (creator); Kaity (playmate)
Developments: Kanasta has been upgrading it since we arrived in Lum
Current Status: Missing (Etah tossed it so it's still somewhere in Sel)

FALLEN COMRADES
Tempo: Died against Needle (not much of a loss honestly)
Sefiwah: Killed by the Forces of Hate (poor Kaity)
Ego: Fell during a battle against Yvne (was like a brother to Kaity)
Pharma: Defeated Karson at the cost of his own life (died a hero)
Kawai: Murdered by Etah (she was too young to die, far too young)
Atatasuki: Died fighting Etah (he's with Kawai now)
Anthrax & Matteria: Killed by Etah (a great loss for children worldwide)
NoOne: Killed by Etah (fought bravely till the very end)
Ada: Vanquished by Etah (but our love lives on)

LUM

Divided into three sections
Femina: contains female visitors
Masculino: contains male visitors
Complex: contains visitors who are neither male nor female

Important Locales
World Tree: The intersecting point between all three regions
Lotus: Islamic rebel base in Femina
Refuge: Sikh rebel base in Masculino
Prison: Location unknown, likely in Masculino

LUM 'GODS'
Devout followers of a leader who logically can't exist.

Efil: 'Goddess' of Life
Bio: a self-proclaimed 'goddess' who acts on the behalf of all life (or so she says)
Abilities: Ages living and non-living things; Highly skilled with dual sword style
Relations: Lum (absolute god/commander); Etaf (fellow 'goddess')
Developments: Sent us to Absence for our protection after failed negotiations
Current Status: Tending to Fatima and fighting against a sudden 'demon' ambush

Evol: 'Deity' of Love
Bio: A ball of love who is incapable of understanding negative ideas
Abilities: Unknown (seems to know everyone through its bonds)
Relations: Lum (commander); Violet (dear friend)
Developments: Met with us soon after we arrived; Escorted Ada and I to Absence
Current Status: Unknown

Etaf: 'Goddess' of Fate
Bio: A cold warrior angel who feels cursed and no longer believes in good and evil
Abilities: Slices target despite distance; Redirects projectiles; Stops momentum
Special Weapon: **Destiny Sword**-focuses her ability and allows her to direct it
Relations: Efil (dear friend); Lum (leader); Eoha (past life lover)
Developments: Shared the tragic story that shaped her into a cold-hearted goddess
Current Status: Gave us an opportunity to escape; Likely fighting 'demons'

Napkin: Not a Lum 'god', but joined us due to an ability from Etaf's shield
Bio: White kitten with frazzled fur; Easily startled
Abilities: It has claws but doesn't use them; Harmless
Relations: Kaity (friend); Opti (friend); Etaf (matchmaker)
Development: Bonded with Kaity (I'm a bit jealous)
Current Status: With Opti (hopefully cleaning his wounds)

REBEL FACTIONS
Deceased (homo sapien) visitors who have decided to make Lum their home.

ALLAH'S JANNAH
An Islamic all-female rebel group dedicated to claiming Lum for humanity.
They are stationed in Lotus (a mosque located in Femina).

Imam: Leader of Allah's Jannah
Bio: The stay at home head of Allah's Jannah; Distrusts all 'goddesses'
Relations: Thunder (main commander); Nina (potential ally)
Developments: Found Nina snooping around and imprisoned her
Current Status: Nearly killed by Kanasta; Orders to kill her people are on pause

Heaven's Thunder: Head Commander of Allah's Jannah
Bio: The Imam's most trusted warrior; rough around the edges; protective
Relations: Imam (Leader); Nina (potential ally)
Developments: Lost against Kanasta
Current Status: Likely recovering from a recent angel attack

Fatima: Orphan taken in by Allah's Jannah
Bio: Cute teenage Islamic girl who has grown fond of Nina
Relations: Nina (role model)
Developments: Horrifically injured in attack from Etaf's merciless forces
Current Status: Taken in by Efil (Please let her be okay)

REFUGE OF THE PEOPLE
An all-male rebel group of Sikhs intent on ending Lum's religious mandates
Located in Refuge (a Jain temple in Masculino)

Rambir: Leader of Refuge of the People
Bio: Friendly warrior who fights for the sake of minorities and the oppressed
Relations: Atatasuki (friend): Sees everyone as a teacher
Developments: Showed Atatasuki around and gave him a sword
Current Status: Unknown (likely deliberating with angels for religious inclusion)

ABSENCE

ABSENCE 'GODS'

Dedicated to remaining neutral despite Etah's intervention on Earth and Lum

Eil: First Guardian; 'God' of Annoyance?
Bio: Obnoxious talking skull that torments residents with puns and riddles
Abilities: Unknown
Relations: Neutral (leader); Needle (guard)
Developments: Told us about the ticket system (which turned out to be a lie)
Current Status: Cowering back in Absence while we're stuck in Sel

Needle: First Guard; 'Deity' of Needles?
Bio: Doesn't speak but loyally follows orders; Capable fighter
Abilities: Ejects needles from body, can trigger them to explode
Relations: Neutral (leader); Eil (guardian)
Developments: Possibly teleported Exp 8 to Absence on orders from Etah
Current Status: Back in Absence, offering us no assistance

Void: Second Guardian; 'Deity' of Nirvana?
Bio: Rock adorned with devotional symbols
Abilities: It's really heavy; indestructible
Relations: Neutral (leader); Occupy (devotee)
Developments: Nearly defeated Anthrax in battle
Current Status: Back in Absence; meditating?

Occupy: Second Guard; 'God' of Occupation?
Bio: Dutiful monk who became a 'god' to aid spiritual development in Absence
Abilities: Incredible strength and agility; Remarkable durability; Insertion
Relations: Neutral (leader); Void (guru)
Developments: Fought alongside Riufen and helped with Etah's downfall
Current Status: Went back to Absence to convince more 'gods' to help us

Plagiarism: Third Guardian; 'God' of Plagiarism
Bio: Chameleon skull who has lost comprehension of many concepts
Abilities: Copy-right (becomes the target and makes them into a bastardization)
Relations: Neutral (warden); Crystal (guard)
Developments: Defeated by BoneSaw after taking over its image
Current Status: In Absence (not providing us any assistance)

Crystal: Third Guard; 'God' of Crystals
Bio: Crystalline downer who begrudgingly follows Plagiarism's orders
Abilities: Crystal manifestation and manipulation; Impenetrable body
Relations: Neutral (leader); Plagiarism (obnoxious boss)
Developments: Aided Kanasta with fighting Deerg and gave him a new suitcase
Current Status: Convincing Absence 'gods' to join our cause

Loyal: Fourth Guardian; 'God' of Loyalty?
Bio: Proud 'dragon' (mythical nonsense) who works alongside a knight
Abilities: Flight; Fire breath; Durable hide; Strong tail
Relations: Neutral (leader); Limit (guard/comrade)
Developments: Battled against Riufen and lost
Current Status: In Absence (not providing us any help at all)

Limit: Fourth Guard; 'God' of Limitation
Bio: Chivalrous knight who enjoys battle; Fights for the glory of Absence
Abilities: Precision and power; Places clear weights on opponents
Relations: Neutral (leader); Loyal (guardian/comrade)
Developments: Stayed in Absence despite promising to help us
Current Status: Occupy and Crystal are convincing him to help out

Separate: Fifth Guardian; 'Deity' of Separation
Bio: Giant amoeba
Abilities: Divides itself; can multiply endlessly
Relations: Neutral (leader); Spin (guard)
Developments: Kanasta battled it due to a gamer grudge; It was beaten by Kaity
Current Status: Not here in Sel where we need the help

Spin: Fifth Guard; 'Deity of Spin'
Bio: Looks like a cute girl but is really just a bunch of ladles
Abilities: Makes objects spin, including entire landmasses
Relations: Neutral (leader); Separate (guardian)
Developments: Fought against Exp 8's team and lost
Current Status: Fighting with us in Sel (not really, she's in Absence)

Htols: Retired 'Goddess' of Sloth
Bio: Lethargic 'goddess' who abandoned her family for a quiet life
Abilities: Unknown
Relations: Sinful Sorority (family)
Developments: Convinced by Violet to leave the Sinful Sorority
Current Status: Basking in the lack of responsibility she has in Absence

SEL

Sel is divided into seven different regions (based off the seven deadly sins) and each demon lord owns a certain section of their respective region

Important Locales

Traitor's Trench: Contains the Sinner's Fury rebel base
Respite: Princess of Insight's hometown and a city saved by Exp 8
Crimson Coliseum: Blood-soaked stadium where Exp 8 fought Etah
Trickle Down Tower: Mineral-laden tower owned by Deerg

FORCES OF HATE

Armies and demon lords who follow the 'God' of Hate's whims

Etah: The God of Hate
Bio: My father (no joke); A ruthless tyrant who tormented my son
Relations: Deceivant (son); Devlin (grandson); Bob & Demonica (minions)
Developments: Destroyed the Hero of Sel after shaping him into a rebellious icon
Current Status: Battling my son (after taking away many of our comrades)
Abilities: Fiery aura; Turns souls into weapons with emotional properties

ETAH'S REPURPOSED SOULS

Misery Mace: Spiky mace that repurposes souls into weapons
Agony Axe: Fleshy axe with a bony tip that puts victims in unbearable agony
Wailing Whip: Pink whip with gold spikes made from Kawai's soul
Searing Sword: Rusty copper sword made from Atatasuki's soul
Appalling Arrow & Bashful Bow: The souls of Anthrax and Matteria repurposed as a moldy arrow with a plus sign tip and a rainbow bow with a pink string
Unknown what weapon NoOne was turned into

Demonica: The 'Goddess' of Death (also called Htaed)
Bio: Etah's second in command (it seems); Unpredictable; Sadistic
Abilities: Shape-shifting; Flight; Blood manipulation; Liquefaction of targets
Special Weapon: **Death Scythe**-can instantly kill 'demon' lords
Relations: Etah (lord and master); Devlin (obsession); Sinful Sorority (family?)
Developments: Involvement in Devlin's separation from his family
Current Status: Claims to love Devlin (despite what she did); Member of our team

Captain of Carnage
Bio: Armored ferret 'demon' lord; Loyal to Etah; Rides on human steeds
Abilities: Bladed armor; Zipline; Small blades for scaling opponents; Blunderbuss
Relations: Etah (lord)
Developments: Appeared when we were fighting Etah's army and attacked us
Current Status: Lost to Matteria and Nina before being carried to safety

VANQUISHED TRAITORS

Karson: Killed by Pharma at the cost of his own life
Bob: Killed by Riufen after being revealed to be Etah's minion (I wouldn't believe it but considering his spectral minions suddenly vanished, he should be dead)

SINFUL SORORITY
Contains the Seven Deadly Sisters (united by their ideals) and Demonica
(Unclear if they are wholly loyal to Etah or have their own agenda)

Tsul: The 'Goddess' of Lust
Bio: Self-taught leader of Sinful Sorority; Seems to hate Demonica more than me
Abilities: Creation of chains (or was that Demonica?); Whips; Sensation
Relations: Demonica (rival/nemesis); Seven Deadly Sisters (beloved sisters)
Developments: Bested by Demonica; Fled after her sisters failed to vanquish us
Current Status: Recovering from Violet and D.S. attacks (most likely)

Edirp: The 'Goddess' of Pride
Bio: Superficial, haughty, and hideous creature; Doesn't know when to shut up
Abilities: Fires arrows laden with insults that debilitate enemies
Relations: Sinful Sorority (family)
Developments: Fought Kaity and Nina in a city filled with 'demons'
Current Status: Killed by Kaity and Nina (is what I'd like to say, but she's a 'god')

Yvne: The 'Goddess' of Envy
Bio: A pitiful creature who covets the traits of allies and enemies alike
Abilities: Shape-shifting; Flight; Enlarges to thirty times her size
Special Weapon: **Fan of Envy**-a fleshy fan that uses air to slice enemies?
Relations: Sinful Sorority (family)
Developments: Killed Ego and devoured his body (according to NoOne)
Current Status: Decapitated by Devlin (I doubt she's dead)

Regna: The 'Goddess' of Anger
Bio: Furious 'demon' with a short fuse and sadistic tendencies
Abilities: Detaches and detonates segmented body; Regenerates limbs; Anger aura
Relations: Sinful Sorority (family)
Developments: Turned the cyber siblings against each other (but still lost)
Current Status: Hopefully dead (but seems unlikely)

Deerg: The 'Goddess' of Greed
Bio: Adorable little imp; Dollar bills for hair; Childish curiosity; Golden coating
Abilities: Shoots gemstones; Reinforce little body; Controls hard assets (money)
Relations: Sinful Sorority (family)
Developments: Battled against my son (Kanasta) and lost
Current Status: I hope she's okay (but I'm afraid to ask)

Ynnotulg: The 'Goddess' of Gluttony
Bio: Giant monstrosity of lard who sees everything as food
Abilities: Grow mouths on any part of body (including body fat)
Relations: Sinful Sorority (family)
Developments: Fell into a lava pit after Bob tricked her
Current Status: Trapped under lava (possibly dead)

REBEL FACTIONS
'Demons' who have decided they benefit from opposing the tyrant King of Sel.

SINNER'S FURY
Led equally by 'demon' lords who supposedly opposed Etah (but certain members recently fought alongside the Forces of Hate); Stationed in Traitor's Trench

Duke of Deception: Envy 'demon' lord
Bio: Manipulative lord who wants to martyr the hero (according to Exp 8)
Abilities: Special strings that are nearly invisible and highly durable
Developments: Wrapped Exp 8 in metal threads after poisoning him
Current Status: Unknown (likely scheming something)

General of Genocide: Wrath 'demon' lord
Bio: Hot-headed and volatile lord who wants to kill Exp 8
Abilities: Control over fire; Launch fireballs; Turns into a living mortar
Developments: Attacked our forces alongside the Daimyo of Death (now dead)
Current Status: Recently ran in fear from Demonica (possibly still fleeing)

Duchess of Desire: Gluttony 'demon' lord
Bio: Indulgent lord who wants Exp 8 to be her servant
Developments: Tried to eat the Prince's heart before being attacked
Current Status: According to Exp 8 she's not much of a threat so it doesn't matter

Prince of Pleasure: Lust 'demon' lord
Bio: Manipulative and sultry lord with an obsession for the Princess of Insight
(the Princess is a mute sloth 'demon' lord under the spell of his love)
Abilities: Poison that can paralyze his enemies
Developments: Poisoned Exp 8 before the hero arrived at the Crimson Coliseum
Current Status: Unknown (wanted Exp 8 publically executed to put Etah in a bind)

HERO'S MILITIA
Inspired by Exp 8's valor and virtue, they now fight alongside us against the Forces of Hate (third member is unknown)

Fuhrer of Fortune: Greed 'demon' lord
Bio: Self-indulgent leader; The sole 'demon' lord in Greed region of Sel
Abilities: Leaks gold; Mechanized throne (possibly for combat use)
Developments: Wanted to use Exp 8 as a bargaining tool against Etah
Current Status: Leading the Hero's Militia against the Forces of Hate

Baroness of Blades: Pride 'demon' lord
Bio: Battle-hungry lord who prefers to fight for a cause; Serves the Fuhrer
Abilities: Various weapons impaled in her; Ignites blood to superheat blades
Developments: Joined the Hero's Militia after being moved by Exp 8's valor
Current Status: Fought the God of Hate (was sliced in two by her own weapon)

Part 10
Aftermath & War

Chapter 89: Survival

Bodies were strewn across the scorched earth, jets of flame brought the clashing of metal and flesh into sharper focus. Etah, the God of Hate, was suspended in the air, his body broken, bloodied, and in tatters. Despite the tyrant king's fall, the pitch-black sky remained.

Deceivant was on his knees, weeping the loss of his lover. Kanasta held Kaity in a protective embrace and knocked away any demons that came too close. Riufen was giving Opti a blood transfusion while Nina kept the remnants of the fallen god's army at bay. Napkin, trembling with his paws over his eyes, was seated on Opti's chest. D.S. was shaking the hands of residents who were still a part of the ground. Demonica was collecting blood from all over the battlefield.

Violet looked to the sky with hands folded and a relieved smile.

Devlin's body was covered in dark energy.

Violet rushed to his aid, the wounds from her fight against Etah already mended. The dark energy expanded, completely covering her living god.

The black energy was gradually rising, ever so slowly lifting up the vengeful boy within.

Violet's aura reached into the muck. She quickly pulled away and sliced off the energy hand before it was promptly consumed by the dark energy.

An armada of demons still loyal to Etah formed a circle around his body and fought off the ever-growing horde of demons who sought his demise.

Violet ran off in the confusion, avoiding any encounters till she met up with her allies.

Nina was the first one to approach her. "Where is he?"

"He is beyond our reach," said Violet, visibly shaken up.

"Why didn't you leave when he told you to?"

"I had to protect him."

"Devlin values his life and he is no fool. He knew he was able to claim victory. I have total faith in him," said Nina, catching Devlin's creation as she collapsed.

The drained devotee looked up at her helper. "You're acting so differently."

"Save your energy." Nina tore off part of her shirt and wrapped it around Devlin's devotee's wounds. She turned to Devlin's brother. "Keep her safe. I'm going to get reinforcements."

Kanasta took Violet from Nina and set her down.

The dutiful ninja rushed through the battlefield and approached the neutral party. "We are just up North. We need your aid."

"Etah has fallen. We must return to Absence. No doubt there will be repercussions for our actions today," said Limit, forming an Absence portal and entering it.

"We need to retreat. I'll round my allies up and you create the portal," said Nina, pointing at the monk.

"Neutral only permitted us to help dethrone Etah. Farewell. We may never meet again. It has been an honor to fight for your cause." Occupy left the realm of Sel.

"Back to the mundane world of triviality," said Crystal, dragging his feet as he left the dark world.

Nina hurried back to her team, perking up as she noticed a new ally.

The Baroness of Blades had formed a perimeter around the Exps with her own personal battalion. "Until Etah's head is separated from his body, this battle is not over," she said, taking on three demons at once with a single sword.

"Who's in charge?" asked Nina.

"With Exp 8 dead and my brother missing, we have no leader. For the time being, I propose the team follows my command," said Kanasta.

"What happened to Devlin?" asked Opti, slowly sitting up.

"Violet said he vanished, but she doesn't know where," said Kanasta.

"Hey, that's not necessarily a bad thing. Maybe he got his teleport artifact working. My sticky artifact didn't work at first," said D.S.

"Then why wouldn't he help us escape?" asked Kaity.

"For now we will assume he is safe. We must focus on our own survival for the time being," said Kanasta.

"What are your orders?" asked Kaity, perking up.

"BoneSaw was sent further up North. We should get moving," said Kanasta.

"What's the point? Even if we find your invention, we are still trapped in this place," said Deceivant.

"We better go somewhere. Those guys look angry." D.S. pointed to the hillside.

Demons of various shapes and sizes had broken through the perimeter and were fast approaching.

"I can't shoot them all. Way too many," said Kaity as she fired into the approaching crowd.

"I can take them all on," said Demonica.

A thick black energy erupted from her body and collected in her grip. After solidifying, her crimson aura climbed up the pole. The aura hardened and shaped the weapon into a dark red scythe.

"I am the Goddess of Death, after all," said Demonica, rushing toward the attackers.

"We must cut down our enemies until we find an exit," said Riufen, unsheathing his spine and decapitating a sword-wielding demon as one motion.

Machine gun fire sprayed in their direction.

Kanasta rushed in front of Deceivant, taking the bullet spray in his stead.

Opti rose to his feet, scars and burns still coated his body. "There has to be a way to escape. We won, right? There's no way we can lose now."

"That sort of thinking is completely unrealistic," said Deceivant.

"Oh, I know! *OPTIMISTIC BURST*!"

Opti's hope emitted as a white aura from his body and blanketed the Freedom Forcers.

"He's right. I can't die yet. I am still unfulfilled," said Deceivant, standing up. "Kanasta, do you have any spare guns?"

"Take what you need." Nina opened her shirt, revealing a stash of pistols, machine guns, and grenades.

"Wow," said Kaity, gawking as she pelted the enemy.

"Thanks." Deceivant grabbed a machine gun and fired into the incoming crowd of gun-armed demons. His lab-coat fluttered as a powerful gust of wind emitted from a four-legged demon. He fixed his short black hair and readjusted his rectangular glasses before emptying the clip into the demon's belly. His golden eyes softened as he noticed a short demon girl behind the wind-manipulating demon.

The small demon raised its arm and fired a crossbow into the scientist while he reloaded.

Deceivant gripped his double helix necklace. "What are children doing in this horrible place?"

"The denizens of this realm aren't hell-spawn. They weren't born here. They are the trapped souls of living beings," said Demonica, taking out an incoming horde with the blood of their comrades.

"What kind of god sends children to a place like this?" asked Deceivant, opening fire on an adult demon who entered his range. He turned to his son. "I suppose I should thank you for the shooting lessons," he said in a charming, relaxed tone outlined with philosophical skepticism.

"Your gratitude is well received." Kanasta slammed his crystalline suitcase into the bulky wind demon, causing it to topple backward into its comrades. He leaped through a pincer attack, his skin-tight suit shielding his body. After landing he turned to face an approaching enemy. Blood splattered on his slicked back checkerboard-style hair after he blasted open the demon's head with a revolver before hitting its body aside with his metal suitcase. "I'm getting paid by the hour, so there's no need for me to kill you. It's your choice," he said in a deep, fear-invoking voice as his blood-red eyes scanned the approaching demons.

Kaity somersaulted as she fired with her feet, piercing the ground with her plasma claws to quickly change direction. She pushed off the ground and put away her side-arms. The skilled assassin raised her rifle and took out six gunner demons before landing. "I feel more like a mercenary than an assassin right now," she said with a soft but energetic voice. Her robotic cat ears perked up. She leaped off the ground before it burst open.

A massive demon, with a drill welded onto its head, burst out from beneath her followed by wretched screams.

Kaity pelted the enemy before she was plucked from the air. Her jade eyes with crosshair pupils scanned the target for a weak point. She opened fire on the target's knees and slipped out of its grip as it collapsed. Her light purple skintight bodysuit glowed as she spun up the target's arm with her plasma claws before cleaving it off. She ducked under a punch and sliced open the second arm. Drills burst out from the target's stub and bore into her side.

D.S. slammed his scissors into the drill, slowing its movement. "Are you okay, kitty-girl?" he asked in a deep but childlike voice, looking down at his friend who was hurt really bad.

"I'll live. Can you take it from here?" she asked, holding her side as she stood up.

"Uh-huh! Leave this guy to me!"

"Will do. You may dress like a kid, but you're as skilled as an assassin," said Kaity, looking up at her ally with a big grin.

"Hey, you can't talk. You're a kid too," said D.S., adjusting his school uniform.

"Yeah, I guess you're right," said Kaity, patching up her wound.

"Hey, drill-face, this is for hurting my friend!" D.S.'s muscles pulsed as he slammed his scissors into the side of an incoming drill, knocking it off its trajectory. He leaped back with his awesome light-up sneakers as a third drill shot out from the big guy's chest. "We're both bald. We shouldn't be fighting," he said, holding out his scissors.

Ten tiny drills burst out from the demon's chest.

D.S. leaned back to dodge but ended up falling backward when a drill from below pierced into his leg. He rolled back up to his feet, readjusted the correction tape on his face, and then rushed at the bad guy. All the while, his light blue eye kept watch for sneak attacks.

D.S. parried three projectile drills and then split his scissors to deflect two drills at once.

The demon fired a drill at the warrior's neck.

Rather than trying to dodge, the ultra-cool bodyguard opened his mouth to catch the drill. His sharp and pointy teeth spun around like a pencil sharpener in an opposing rotation, stopping the drill.

"Catch me if you can," said D.S., sticking out his tongue as he sprinted away.

Near the north end of the defensive line, Riufen used blood bullets to take down a group of purple poisoned demons. His empty white eyes widened. "Wait, this is dishonorable." He ended the long range assault and continued slicing through the enemy forces with his spine.

A demon lord with multiple swords coming out of each arm was fast approaching.

Riufen cut through a line of demons as he approached the swordsman.

"Stand aside. The Baroness of Blades has already chosen this one as her opponent," she said, unsheathing a sword from her gut.

Riufen bowed. "I apologize, but I have already decided that I will be the one to battle this demon," he said in a strong, devout and stoic voice.

"Perhaps it would be best if you decided who will fight me through combat," said the demon lord, sitting down to sharpen his blades on his whetstone kneecaps.

Riufen stood tall and firm. "He is right. We cannot bicker amongst ourselves at a time like this. My steel against yours," said the immortal samurai, raising his spine to the Baroness.

"This fight is meaningless. I'll end it quickly," she said, taking a step forward.

Their swords clashed.

Riufen's spine was sliced in two. His topknot wrapped in bones fell to the ground.

The Baroness sheathed her blade and paced around the warrior, looking for the next opening. "You've lost your weapon. Now you'll lose your life. IGNITION."

Riufen slid back to dodge the incoming slash.

The heated metal sliced his rock-like skin and removed one of his bony shoulder guards.

Before she could sheathe her blade, the samurai gripped it.

"You're rather strong." The Baroness twisted the sword, slicing his hand and sliding her blade out of his grip.

Riufen dodged her rapid strikes as he reached for his spine. The samurai unsheathed his spine and dragged his hand up it, hardening his blood around it. "CRIMSON COATING."

The Baroness' next strike was parried.

The blades wrung and reverberated as the warriors paced around each other.

"Your entire body is a weapon. Then those bones you wear are your own?" she asked, looking up at his faceplate. "What do you fight for?"

"Honor," said Riufen, tapping the kanji on his headband.

"I fight for fun. But I prefer to fight for a cause," she said in a raspy but proud womanly voice. The Baroness tossed her shroud aside, revealing her body was held together by a ring of heated gold around her waist. She unsheathed and slashed with one sword after the next, pushing back the samurai. When receiving a powerful counter from her opponent, one of her swords was knocked out from her hands. She leaped back, suffering only a surface wound in the process. After pulling out two daggers, one from her elbow and another from her knee, she held her ground against the samurai's relentless assault. "Each strike has power and direction. But it's more than that. You wield your blade with firm intention and purpose," she said, catching the blade between her daggers.

Riufen thrust his blade at her head.

The Baroness caught the sword between her bladed fangs. She dropped her daggers and flicked her wrist. Blades came out from her fingers before piercing into the samurai's throat. She tore out his jugular and then leaped back as his ribs shot out. The prideful demon lord removed a handful of arrows from her back and threw them at the warrior.

Every single arrow hit.

Riufen looked down at the arrows and sheathed his blade. "I was mistaken." His neck wound healed. "Your name implies that you only use blades and yet you use projectiles. I thought you were an honorable warrior. Do as you wish. I cannot continue this fight," he said, turning away.

"Very well, so you're my opponent. We once fought on the same side. I always wondered which of us was stronger," said the demon lord, holding his eight swords out with crossed arms.

The Baroness unsheathed her blade, igniting it with her blood. The sword sliced through all eight of the rival lord's swords and removed his head. "I am." The sword master cut the rest of his body into slabs of flesh before sheathing her blade in her chest. "Obviously."

"Riufen! What were you doing? I can't keep all these demons back on my own," said Deceivant, running and gunning from a bloodthirsty horde of demons with retractable claws.

"Apologies. I am rather disappointed at the moment," said Riufen, speed walking while haphazardly slicing down sword-less demons.

"I'll handle it," said a firm voice with subtle apprehension. Nina came from behind Devlin's father and rushed through a line of demons. She pulled out double blades from her lavender thigh-highs and sliced open every enemy in her path. Blood tinted her purple clothes and lightly tanned skin as her sword built up a greater number of kills. The ninja's light purple lips spit out the murky demon blood into the face of her enemy. "No need for this." Devlin's warrior removed her lilac shirt and covered the demon's face with it. She cut through the fabric and lobbed off its head. Another demon gripped her knee-high skirt and pulled her toward his blade. The slim and flexible warrior jabbed the demon's blade into his own neck and then tore off her skirt. "Deadweight," she said before tossing two kunais to blind her closest enemy. The devout weapon rushed up, tore out the kunais and sent them flying, using her plum satin scarf as a ramp. The explosive tags she attached to the kunais burst, annihilating four incoming enemies. She pulled down her black latex gloves, revealing hidden shurikens all the way up her arms. Each shuriken found a new home in the legs of the approaching enemies.

Two particularly fast demons rushed up after masking the area in smoke.

The two swords stopped in her grip. "It's good to be alive." The skilled weapon hopped into the air, slicing off two heads on the uplift. Despite her long dark eyelashes, her amethyst eyes located three demons below and flung ten shurikens off her leg into them. Before touching the floor, she kicked off the head of another demon with her powerful legs, leaving an explosive tag on his face. A wire wrapped around her hand then pulled another six demons into the oncoming blast. Nina rode the blast and propelled herself to the next group with a kick.

"Good work, Exp 3," said Deceivant.

"Looking sexy," said Kaity, speeding by and eyeing Nina's zip-up tank top and torn skirt.

"Nina, you don't have to kill them! They are just following orders!" yelled Violet.

"As am I," said Nina, gripping her blades with her toes and running across a line of demon heads while keeping her long purple hair out of her face.

"Oh yeah, we're not supposed to kill them," said D.S., his scissors pierced through four demons. "Sorry about that," he said, slowly pulling out his scissors.

"Of course we're not! I don't understand this at all. We defeated Etah. There should be a celebration, not a slaughter," said Violet, tears rushing down her light blue cheeks.

A projectile zoomed by, slicing her rags.

"Ah, I see you aren't as bulky as your clothes made you seem," said the Captain of Carnage in a high-pitched and excited tone, turning around and firing out the thin blades at his side.

Violet turned around to run, but the blades still pierced her back.

Within seconds the Captain was on her shoulder.

The ferret demon lord was clad in spiky armor and an iron helmet. A blunderbuss was situated on his back. "Hmm, this looks like an obvious weak point," he said, putting his blade up to the dot on the enemy's forehead.

"Why are you attacking us? Etah has been defeated," said Violet, speaking through her veil in a wispy voice filled with love.

"Your people took down my leader," said the Captain, looking into her amethyst eyes. "Etah was once hailed the Hero of Sel. When our realm was abandoned, Etah was the one who kept it from sinking into the lava below. The Swordsman of Sin, the Fortress of Fury, and I, the Captain of Carnage, are all obedient to Etah for reasons other than fear. We have loyalty. It's something you dolls could never understand," he said, running up and down her body while slicing it up with finesse.

Violet grabbed the armored devotee. "Please, stop this. Your god is dead. Killing us won't change that."

"I was enslaved before Etah rose to power! He saved me! I won't stop until all of you are dead!" yelled the Captain.

"Very well then." Violet lifted her long golden hair. "Let me atone for my creator's transgressions against your god. I offer my life. But only if you swear to abandon your vendetta against my allies."

The Captain stopped in place. "I am fortunate to meet such a devoted warrior on the battlefield. I accept your offer. Your blood shall satiate my revenge. But I'm going to need a lot of it," he said, slicing into her wrists.

"Leave my friend alone!" Opti grabbed the fluffy villain and pulled him off his blue-skinned buddy.

"Calm down. If my life can end his revenge, then I will gladly die. I can save all of you and lighten the burden of karma on his soul," said Violet.

"Who is going to save you?"

"I don't need saving. I don't deserve it. I've partaken in this war for my own selfish reasons. What besides more violence will my future bring?" she asked, peering into the light blue pupils in the center of his white, pure eyes.

"What about Devlin? What about your friends? I've lost too many people I care about today. I won't lose anyone else!" Opti slammed the fluffy ferret to the ground.

"Please stop. Hasn't there been enough violence already?" asked Violet in tears.

"I'll do what it takes to protect my friends. If we die fighting, then so be it, but I'm not going to let you just throw away your life!" Opti dodged a blade as it shot out and then kicked the adorable little enemy. "Napkin! He's all yours!"

The white kitten with frazzled fur let out a ferocious mew and then ran behind the man with the white mask.

"That was cute. Was that supposed to scare me? Pathetic." The Captain jerked toward the cat but was unable to move. "What is this? Is my body afraid? Of what!? Move, damn it!"

"Oh yeah, a peaceful victory!" cheered Opti, before falling down. The light blue tips at the ends of his long white hair were less vibrant, as was his ghostly pale skin. The drama mask covering his face had dents and burns around his heart-shaped eyehole and the permanent black half-smile beneath it.

"Are you an angel or a weapon?" asked the Captain, looking at his opponent's white garb and blue-tipped wings.

"I'm just a good friend," said Opti, his voice cheerful as always.

"Stay still. I'll do my best to heal you," said Violet, pouring prana into his body.

Napkin rubbed up against her leg.

"You have won through peaceful means. I welcome you to the team with open arms," said Violet, putting a bracelet around her fellow being's neck.

"More and more are breaking through. Not sure I can handle them all," said Nina, gripping a sword in each hand and drenched in blood.

"Isn't there any way to stop the fighting?" asked Violet, helping Opti to his feet.

"Etah kept things in place. Until there is a new God of Hate, there's bound to be a bit of anarchy. **Blood Spike**," said Demonica, her blood shooting out and hardening to pierce through her gold-plated attackers.

"Fall back!" yelled the Baroness, having her forces recline while continuing to fight.

"Incoming!" D.S. ran through the advancing line of demons, having them get torn up by the drill-headed demon lord following him.

The blood left over from the onslaught shot out as a spike and pierced straight through the drill demon.

"I'll handle whoever breaks through the east line." Demonica created a wall of blood spikes that pierced through an entire battalion of gunner demons.

Deceivant fired at the few demons who managed to avoid the spiked wall.

"I appreciate the covering fire, but it's not necessary," said Demonica with a breathy, bewitching voice that trailed off at the end of each sentence.

31

With a single wave of her scythe, the dark goddess sliced four demons in half. Her black-and-red mane swayed side-to-side as her sickle pupils struck terror into her next victim.

The terrified demon covered his face before being eviscerated by her scarlet fingernails.

"Oh my, blood really brings out my complexion," said Demonica, dragging her hands over her sleek purple figure and down to her powerful wide hips.

Four toxic demons charged her, their skin dyed by the poison within them. "I prefer killing angels, but this is still fun." She spun around, piercing the demons with her dagger stilettos. The corrosive blood that splattered on her iron dominatrix outfit jutted out and pierced through twelve demons.

"We can't keep killing for our own selfish reasons. What makes our cause better than their own?" asked Violet, pushing aside four-legged enemies with blasts from her energy body.

"What cause? This is self-defense. What we are doing now isn't an affront against nature. It's just a reaction to it," said Deceivant, guarding Opti's back with a spray of bullets.

"Even with all our friends helping us, they just keep coming," said D.S., cutting off the legs of a demon whose feet were held in place by hands protruding from the ground.

Demonica's serpentine tongue popped out and licked the blood off her cheek. "Well, well, looks like another demon lord broke through." Her wings spread before she slammed into the wall-shaped demon.

Some lackeys seated on the demon lord's shoulder fired a volley of flame arrows at the traitor.

"You dare look down on me? I'm a goddess," she said, caressing the six sharp horns erecting from her crown. "**Blood Bath.**"

A stream of blood shot out from her palms and sprayed onto her attackers. They collapsed into blood and dripped down the body of the wall-shaped demon lord.

"I have come with a message," said the demon lord.

"For me?" asked Demonica, perking her misty purple lips.

"Yes. The Dark One has returned. He has summoned you."

"Wait a minute! Demonica, you got into Absence on your own. You can get us out of here, can't you?" asked Deceivant.

"That's right. In just a moment we'll all be out of here."

"Fantastic!"

"Everyone, gather together!" yelled Demonica.

Kanasta, having fitted his metal suitcase inside his more valuable crystal suitcase, approached his team. He lifted Deceivant and Opti onto his shoulders and rushed to Demonica's location. "BoneSaw, we are leaving!"

Violet pushed a frenzied demon to the ground before running to Demonica.

BoneSaw popped out of the ground. The small metal box of an assassin engaged its circular saws, tore through the bodies of ten injured demons and then rushed over, taking the occasional detour to kill more demons.

"Waiting for the proper moment, as expected," said Kanasta, lifting his mechanized son off the ground.

"Sorry. Change of plans. You're on your own." Demonica hopped into a Sel portal before it vanished, leaving them stranded.

"We never should have trusted her," said Kanasta, keeping the poisonous demons at bay with well-timed shotgun blasts. "I'll take care off the wall." He rushed ahead and slammed his fist against the demon lord's fortified metal body. "Damn it! If I can't break through this, I'll never be able to complete Reflector's job. I have to grow stronger!" The assassin boss punched through the iron layer, then his fist stopped.

Beneath the iron was a thin layer of diamond.

"Go ahead and try. None have bested the Fortress of Fury!" exclaimed the demon lord.

"If I can punch through diamond, I can break anything!" he yelled, repeatedly slamming his fists into the wall.

"Everyone, the Prince of Pleasure has made his move," said the Baroness of Blades, pointing at the approaching army coming out from a pink haze.

Chapter 90: Sinner's Fury & Hero's Militia

The Prince's forces, all lust demons, rushed out from the fog and quickly engaged the enemy lines heading toward the Freedom Forcers.

"Thanks for all the help. Why have you decided to aid us?" asked Kanasta before slamming into the wall demon.

"The Hero's Militia was inspired by your leader's heroism. His death in no way diminishes our morale. As long as we stand, you will be protected," said the Baroness, deflecting wind blasts from the four-legged demon lord.

"Are they here to help too?" asked Kaity, pointing to the approaching army behind them.

"No. They are here to destroy you. Once we've set up a defensive line, we'll do our best to relocate you to a safe zone. Hold your ground until then," said the Baroness, losing hold of one of her blades after being blasted by a sudden gust of wind.

A mortar shot out from the rival army and crashed into a large gathering of ally troops. The scorched fleshy ground let out a wretched scream.

Fire shot out from the mortar after it landed, burning everything within six meters.

"The traitor is dead! Why are you all still fighting? What the Sel are you even fighting for?" asked the General of Genocide, the fire coating his body shooting up like a pillar.

"We are fighting to survive," said Deceivant, loading his gun and aiming it at the demon lord.

"Well then good news. We don't want you dead. Exps have shown they are strong enough to fight the gods. Come to our side and we'll end this battle here and now," said the General in a harsh, cracking voice, incinerating the attackers who came within range.

"Then join you we shall," said Violet, her eyes alight with hope.

"Let's not be so hasty. We must weigh our options first," said Kanasta, standing atop the wall-shaped demon lord.

"Screw that! I'll make it really simple. Join us or I'll kill you all right now!" yelled the General, aiming at Deceivant.

"I won't let you," said Nina, standing in front of Devlin's father.

"Stand down, General!"

The General of Genocide lowered his hand.

A misshapen mess of a living creature that was neither male nor female emerged from the enemy lines. Half a woman's face was sewn onto the demon's fleshy head and bare breasts were seared onto its charred chest. It had arms instead of legs and had the Sinner's Fury flag—a bright red flag with a burning skull as its icon—as a cape. "Greetings, I am the Duke of Deception. I have come to offer a compromise and put an end to this unsightly battle."

"It's a blessing to meet you," said Violet with a bow.

"Why would we trust someone with 'deception' in their title?" asked Deceivant, aiming his gun at the hideous woman.

"Whoever is cut down has to withdraw their forces. How is that for a compromise?" asked the Baroness standing atop the now headless wind demon lord and gripping her sword.

The Duke walked past the Baroness. The envy demon lord stepped up to a bulky demon with a golden belly and the flag of the Hero's Militia—a blue flag with Exp 8's fist as its icon—attached to his mobile throne. "Would you like to hear my offer, Führer?"

The only demon lord of greed was an obese blob in a velvet bed. The bed was made mobile by four pointed metal legs. A crown was fused into the demon lord's head, and the rest of his body was adorned in jewelry. Heated gold leaked from the demon leader's belly button giving his belly a rich coating. "You are in no position to make comprises. I am the only demon lord in my region, unlike you. And with the Goddess of Greed unable to lead, all her forces fall under my command. Not that the incompetent little gremlin was ever fit to lead anyone. But I digress. You were useful for a while, but now I fail to see what purpose Sinner's Fury could have. I created that group in order to form a coalition of elite demon lords so we could increase the land under our control. It was a political ploy, but one that has run its course," said the Führer, with a regal, boisterous and flamboyant tone.

"Then Sinner's Fury has gained a life of its own. It will continue to grow with me as its leader. Other than adopting a martyr as an icon, what purpose does Hero's Militia have?" asked the Duke.

"To unify all of Sel. Exp 8 entrusted me with this mission. To fight us is to fight freedom itself. You seek unity through hatred and despair. We seek it through love and hope. I see no reason why there should be two rebel groups; it will only keep the people divided."

"Eheheh. You're the one who left Sinner's Fury."

"Fate decided it was time for the group to break apart. The dice chose the Princess of Insight as the leader for that day, breaking apart the false equality our group appeared to have. If you had all chosen to stand with the hero rather than hold on to outdated modes of thought, our forces would be unified."

"You never realized that the Mediator was never in control. She was indeed a neutral party, but every single dice roll was determined by me and my strings. I chose the Princess of Insight at the most opportune moment," said the Duke, making an image of the enemy commander's shocked face with its prized strings.

The Führer growled and then composed himself. "You have no faith in fate. Neither do I. Still, I never believed in the leader of the day system. I'll make this very simple, Duke. Either surrender and raise your fist in respect to the hero or perish along with every member of your army," he said, tapping together his jewel-encrusted fingernails.

"Exp 8 wouldn't want that. He sought peace, not war," said Violet.

"Yes, my dear. But by annihilating outdated, warmongering, weak-willed demon lords, we clear the way for a glorious age of peace," said the Führer.

"Duke, I've decided. I will come with you. Who will join me?" asked Violet, looking out at her allies.

"Before deciding, realize that by joining your idealistic friend you are agreeing to live the rest of eternity trapped in a shredded body. You will not die, but you will also never reincarnate," said the Duke, signaling the Baroness.

"You're just using Exp 8's memory. He would have gladly risked going into harm's way if it meant a greater chance of ending this violence," said Opti, walking to the Duke's side.

"Kill them both before any other gems decide to throw away their lives," said the Führer.

Nina stood in the Baroness's path. "My mission is to keep them safe. Don't make my mission more difficult," she said, placing her sword to the Baroness' throat.

"The hero believed in me and sought to avoid conflict whenever possible. I won't lie and say that we are acting on the hero's wishes. Regardless, I am a warrior. I have no interest in peace." The Baroness removed the dagger with the crimson grip that was deeply imbedded into her head. With nothing holding it up, her cowl fell back.

The Baroness' eyes were red and boiling. Scars covered her face and her hair was made up from chakrams imbedded in her scalp, all layered on top of each other. "I'll put my faith in the Führer's cause if only to imbue my blade with purpose."

"I'll handle her." Nina leaped back as the dagger lunged at her throat.

The Baroness jumped in the air, engaging the enemy in midair combat.

Nina parried each strike but was unable to advance.

After landing, she flung shurikens at the Baroness whilst defending herself from the rapid dagger strikes.

After detaching two chakrams from her head, she spun them around to deflect the projectiles.

Nina rushed in and lashed her sword at the enemy.

After deflecting three swipes, a chakram caught the katana.

Nina released her sword and sent a shuriken out from under her sleeve.

The projectile pierced the Baroness' eye.

Nina swiftly took advantage of the opening by reclaiming her sword and jabbing it into the warrior's side. She pulled out her now superheated blade and sliced off the hand wielding the other chakram.

The Baroness rapidly tossed throwing knives from below her arms as she backed away.

Nina dodged most of the knives and blocked the ones she couldn't.

"What is going on here? Ladies should never fight," said the Prince of Pleasure in a suave, sultry voice that almost masked his dark tone, taking a seat on one of his soldiers.

The Prince was tall, slender, and had a contorted grin. The seductive demon lord was wearing a suit of skin with a still-beating heart pierced on the lapel.

"Silence. Baroness, you are the greatest warrior of all the demon lords. Why are you losing?" asked the Führer.

"She is faster than me," said the Baroness before rushing back into battle.

Nina retreated, leaving a trail of explosive tags that became stuck to her attacker's feet.

"And far more cunning. She will serve our forces well," said the Duke with a wide grin.

The Prince leaped in the middle before the Baroness could draw her blade.

"I will not lose!" yelled the Baroness.

"You already have," said the Prince, pointing to the line of explosive tags now coiled around her legs.

"I always thought you were one of the smartest demon lords, Prince," said the Duke.

"Most handsome, yes, and certainly the most passionate. Sometimes my passion causes me to do dangerous things," said the Prince, removing the tags while running his hand down the Baroness' legs.

"You never had faith in the hero. After all, it was with the help of your poison that I captured him and sent him to die at the Crimson Coliseum. Why stand with Hero's Militia when you sold out their beloved hero?" asked the Duke, tapping its fingernails together.

"Explain yourself this instant!" yelled the Führer.

"The Duke misread my actions. I sent Exp 8 to the Crimson Coliseum because I had faith in him. After seeing him fight to defend that city, I knew he was the only one who had a will strong enough to conquer Etah. Such a shame he died. Perhaps once this is all over, I shall be the new hero," said the Prince.

"You shouldn't have left Sinner's Fury until you got hold of your beloved. The Princess of Insight is under our custody. Withdraw your forces or she will suffer," said the Duke, signaling the gluttonous demon lord to break formation.

"Will the Prince's love falter once his dearly beloved's eyeballs have been scooped out?" asked the Duchess of Desire with a slobbery and deranged voice oozing with desire, while pressing her spoon fingers to the hostage's eyes.

The sluggish princess struggled in the greasy grip, gnashing her sharp teeth at her captor from beneath her long locks of hair.

"She'll never be as hideous as you are," said the Prince, looking at the Duchess' muscular build, bulging eyes and pot belly with disdain.

"I doubt you want your fiancée to suffer for your lack of cooperation," said the Duke.

"Hahaha! What fiancée? The Princess has yet to accept my proposal," said the Prince.

The Princess reached out to her beloved with tears welling up.

"Fiancée or not, you love her more than your own vanity. Mmm, what a tasty little thing she is," said the Duchess, stabbing the Princess' cheeks with her fork fingers.

"The previous demon lord of her city was poisoned. Every enemy and rival she had was broken either politically or physically. There is nothing special about her. I choose her because she was pitiful. Having a princess who couldn't even walk without assistance was the best way to expand my influence into the region of Sloth. Her precognitive powers are a total farce. She didn't predict any deaths or political shifts. I merely told her what to say and then made her words a reality," said the Prince, shifting the heart on his suit.

The Princess mutely screamed.

The Duchess dropped the eye in her mouth and rolled it around with her tongue.

"None of that changes that you still love her! Her pain is your pain!" yelled the General.

The heart popped in the Prince's grip. The seductive demon lord approached his damsel in distress and pushed his fingers into the holes in her throat. "Who do you think removed her vocal cords? I needed her dependent on me. I was the only one who would love the voiceless Princess. You're all so ignorant." He pulled away. "I have no sexual desire whatsoever. It is the control aspect of sex that captivates me. Imposing my will on others makes me feel alive," he said, tearing open his shirt and revealing his bare purple chest.

The Prince's male and female lust demons licked the poison sweat off his bare chest.

The Princess screamed inaudibly as she reached for him.

Nina ducked under the Baroness' sword and rushed up to the Prince.

"You're despicable! She loves you! How can you abandon her now?" she asked with an intense glare.

"The Führer has promised me the entire region of Sloth. I have no need for her now," said the Prince, pushing his minions away before buttoning his shirt.

"Ignore him, Nina. We mustn't get involved in this. Our only priority is survival," said Deceivant.

"He is right. We have no way of leaving this place. We must avoid conflict with the residents," said Kanasta.

"You have such a strong spirit. It would be a pleasure to break you. But, the Baroness has chosen to kill you herself. And who am I to intrude upon a lady's wishes?" asked the Prince, blowing the Baroness a kiss with his glowing purple lips.

Opti opened fire on the Duchess. "Run away, Princess!"

The Princess took one step with her broken leg and then fell flat on her face, sobbing into her long black hair.

The General rushed to the downed hostage.

"Stop. She is useless now," said the Duke.

The Princess crawled to the Prince and cried against his knee.

The Prince kicked her off. "Mute and deaf? I used you! I never loved you!" he yelled into her ear.

Nina looked away in tears.

"Stand down, Baroness. There's nothing to gain by having you risk your life battling that woman. She and the others who stand against me will—" The Führer stopped. A bullet bounced off his forehead.

"We all oppose you! We oppose Hero's Militia and Sinner's Fury! None of you stand for what Exp 8 stood for, what he died for!" yelled Kaity.

"Forgive her; she is but a child. I take full responsibility for her actions," said Deceivant, stepping in front of his adorable ally.

"Kaity's right! You guys are evil! You're super bad and not in the cool way. You're just mean!" yelled D.S.

"You claim to represent a people who you only seek to profit off of. Your dishonor is unconscionable," said Riufen.

"Shame. I would have liked to have kept at least a few of you alive. You could have done great things for this world. But you fear change and deny my merciful offer. I'll waste no more time. Anyone who threatens the hope we offer must be destroyed. Our founder lived by this principle when he swore to dethrone Etah. In the name of the Hero of Sel, I deem you all traitors! Dispose of them!" yelled the Führer.

"Does that mean you declare war on Sinner's Fury?" asked the Duke, batting its eyelashes.

"Yes! Hero's Militia officially declares war on Sinner's Fury!" yelled the Führer.

The Duke tapped its fingernails together excitedly. "Yes! Yes! You've played right into my hands, Führer. Predictable as ever," it said, snapping its fingers.

"In what way does killing you and your forces benefit you?" asked the Führer, patting his golden belly.

Demonica emerged from a puddle of blood and fired crimson chains at the Führer. "It gives me the authorization to intervene. Sel gods can only kill their own people during a war," she said with a crazed look.

Chapter 91: The Duke's Agenda

The blood chains bore into the Führer's glossy skin.

"You've sided with the enemy. Is there nothing you won't do to achieve victory?" asked the Führer, struggling to break free.

"Enemy is entirely a matter of one's perspective," said the Duke, caressing its feminine cheek.

The Baroness sliced the chains of blood. "Retreat, my lord. I shall keep you covered," she said, holding her blade out.

Deceivant approached Demonica. "I'm not quite sure what's going on, but we need to get out of here. Name your price," he said with an outstretched hand.

"I have everything I want already. It's best if you stay out of this. I'll deal with you and the other Freedom…hmm…well, I suppose you aren't Freedom Forcers anymore, are you? Not with your leader dead and Devlin missing, that is," said Demonica with a smirk.

"You know where he is, don't you?" asked Nina, her mouth now covered by a blue cloth.

"I might. But you shouldn't worry about that right now. I'm here to destroy Hero's Militia. If you don't get in my way, you won't get killed," said Demonica.

"Wait. Surely there is a peaceful way to solve this dilemma," said Violet.

"Perhaps there is, but I gave up on peace a long time ago," said Demonica, walking past the blue-skinned devotee.

"Duke! What in Sel's accursed name is she doing here? She serves Etah, in case you forgot!" yelled the General of Genocide, trembling in terror.

"I did not forget. Hmm. I suppose I should tell you the reason I joined with the Führer to create Sinner's Fury. It's nothing as idealistic as a revolution or as selfish as the Führer's reasons. I am eternally loyal to Lord Sel. I co-founded the group to bring all those who spoke against our ruler in the shadows into the light. That's why I needed a demon lord from each region to join Sinner's Fury. Demonica was kind enough to sponsor the group and give me the necessary resources to bribe and secure weaponry for Sinner's Fury. But that was just another part of the plan. Weeding out the traitors was my sole mission," said the Duke.

Four black portals appeared behind the Duke.

Tsul was the first to emerge. The dark pink-skinned demon was slender and curvaceous. Her own tentacles were worn as clothing. Red wax dripped down her sides, stopping once it reached her feathered legs. The self-sufficient sin moved her black whip-like hair away from her face and looked out at the warring demons with sadness. "When will we stop fighting amongst ourselves? Still, we can't just allow outward rebellion to go unpunished. Prepare for battle," she said in a composed and commanding voice, her breath coming out as a pink puff of smoke.

Demons rushed out of the portal and quickly created a perimeter around the portals.

A gooey green blob came out from the second portal. It grew deer horns and silver hair. The goop solidified into the large and wrinkled green-skinned goddess. Yvne's small pupils glimmered with longing. "I'm not sure which side to root for," she said in a curious voice, almost like a whisper.

Edirp held her head high as she emerged. Her body was firm like a pillar, boosted by her stiletto boots and made extra steady by her bone corset. Her dark purple skin radiated from within. The beauty of the goddess' gray hair was accentuated by elegantly arranged peacock feathers. The Queen of Sin's disproportionate breasts gave her elegance an otherworldly dimension. Black smoke brought out the color in her eyes just as the blood on her lips gave it an alluring glow.

"There are three armies, Yvne. Sinner's Fury, Hero's Militia, and the Forces of Hatred. Now, tell me which one you think we are here to aid. Honestly, I don't know how you don't know already. You best put forth more effort or we'll find ourselves a new Envy. And yes, we most certainly can do that," she said in a fast paced, haughty and narcissistic voice.

"Sinner's Fury, right…because we are Sins?" asked Yvne.

"No. That's wrong. We must help the Forces of Hate. Got it?"

"Understood." Yvne looked out at the battlefield.

"So which is which?" she asked.

"You don't even know that much. Do you pay any attention when Tsul is teaching us?" asked Edirp.

"Sorry. I get distracted. Look at the sky. It's so dark. I wish I was dark too." Yvne's body turned black. "Oh look, I am now. Yay," she said with mild joy.

"Pay attention! Each group has a flag bearer to keep them from getting confused while in combat. The red flag is Sinner's Fury, the blue one is Hero's Militia, and our flag, belonging to the Forces of Hate, is the black one with the lava plume. Don't attack the demons near the lava plume flag bearers. Everyone else is an enemy of Sel."

"But other than the flags, they look so similar. They're all demons, aren't they?"

"That's always the case with civil wars."

"Yvne, might I ask who gave you permission to kill Ego?" asked Demonica.

"It was his fault! He was so big and powerful! I couldn't live in a world where someone that great existed," said Yvne, growing in size.

"Wait a minute. Where is Regna? Edirp, wasn't she with you?" asked Tsul.

"She was with me at Ynottulg's grave, but when I told her about our mission, she ran off," said Yvne.

"We all made the portals together. She can't be too far," said Edirp.

"There's something I don't quite get. If the Sinful Sorority sponsored our side, then why are they telling Yvne to attack us?" asked the General, turning to the Duke.

"Incidentally, all the leaders of Sinner's Fury, excluding myself of course, are to be done away with. As is every member of its army," said the Duke, retreating behind the Sinful Sorority.

"Blessed miracles! This is absurd! I won't go down without fighting!" yelled the General, his voice breaking out into a high-pitched squeal.

Regna ran out from her portal, piercing the living ground with each step. The goddess had an athletic build and red skin with veins visibly pulsing magma inside. Two clear horns protruded from her crown, and like the rest of the spikes on her segmented body, they were alight with a swirling inner flame. Her hair was long, messy, and a blend of orange and red. The wrathful goddess flashed her shark-like teeth. "Why in Sel's name are we fighting demons? We should be rallying our forces against Lum!" she yelled, her disdainful seething voice boiling with rage.

"Until the rebel problem has been dealt with, we can't assemble against Lum's army," said Demonica.

"You're driven by bloodlust! I don't trust a word you say!" Regna's eyes pulsed with rage, shifting from a lighter shade of red to a darker one.

"These orders come straight from the Dark One. I may not approve, but I will not oppose the will of this world," said Tsul.

"Then I'm only going after the demon lords. He's an enemy, right?" asked Regna, pointing to the flaming demon lord.

"Only the Duke and our own lords are to be spared," said Demonica.

"I didn't ask you. Hey, you ready to die?" asked Regna, raising her spiked fingers.

"Why is this happening? I swear I'll kill the Duke myself! Where is he or she, where is it!?" yelled the General.

"That's it! Scream! Fun time!" exclaimed Regna, bouncing up and down before rushing in.

"Our forces have already gathered around Etah. The Exps and their allies are to be captured; unless they become a problem, you're not permitted to kill them! The Forces of Hatred will triumph! All the rebels will be eradicated!" exclaimed Demonica, shooting blood out from her arms before shaping them into scythes.

"BoneSaw, cover our escape," said Kanasta.

Smoke blew out from BoneSaw's sides, blanketing members of both armies, the Exps and the Sinful Sorority in a thick fog.

Violet hoisted the Princess of Insight onto her shoulders and then joined her team.

Reinforcements for the Forces of Hate emerged from hidden pits. The massive vehicular demons unloaded fifty soldiers each, which quickly engaged their enemies.

"Now that we outnumber them, I'll make sure none of the rebels escape! Prideful Presence, Burst!" exclaimed Edirp.

The ground rumbled and screamed before free falling two-hundred feet.

The forces of all three armies and the Exps had nowhere to run.

The Führer patted his belly. "Taking out the Gods of Sel was a much later part of my plan. I suppose my conquest will come much sooner than predicted. Do not lose faith! The hero himself rallied his forces against these gods. Gluttony, Sloth, and Greed have all fallen due to our hero's actions. To win this war we must defeat the remaining gods!" he yelled, raising his fist.

Yvne landed in front of the Führer. "I wonder what it's like to have hope in a hopeless situation," she said, her arms becoming blades.

The Baroness rushed in and engaged the jealous goddess.

Tsul turned to Demonica. "Killing our own people when we should be fighting the angels...are you sure this is what our leader wants?"

"He has his reasons. If it doesn't sit well with you, then just capture the Exps. I'm going to have some fun," said Demonica before piercing through a living shield and slicing the demons cowering behind it.

"There were no civil wars when Etah was leading us," said Tsul, turning away.

"I'm sorry did you say something?" asked Demonica before eviscerating a group of demons with crossbows for arms.

"I'll capture the Exps," said Tsul.

"No. I don't think you will," said the Prince, standing in her path.

"You're a member of my own kingdom. I'd rather not end you," said Tsul.

"Well that's too bad. You see, I've been waiting for an opportunity to break you. Having a goddess, particularly the Goddess of Lust, beneath me is something I deeply desire," said the Prince, sizing her up.

"I think I understand now. Allowing demon lords to exist has created great conflict in our realm. You and your kin are responsible for turning our people against us," said Tsul, thrashing her whip at him.

The Prince leaped to the side. "Ah. I've got you interested. Now I just need you to be dependent on me," he said, carving into his bare chest with his fingernails.

Tsul cracked her whip again, but the Duchess rushed in, getting hit in the Prince's stead.

"Control is such a wondrous thing," said the Prince, having the Duchess, ravenously lick the purple blood off his fingers.

"You've intoxicated her. I'm impressed," said Tsul, retracting her whip.

"No. By eating the Princess' eye, she got a taste of my most desirable fluid. She isn't merely intoxicated. She is addicted to me," said the Prince, signaling the Duchess to attack.

Edirp looked down from her two-hundred-foot pedestal. "Damn. Using my powers now would cripple my allies as well as my enemies. Hmm. Tsul seems preoccupied. I'll take care of the Exps."

The platform joined the ground and Edirp took a leisurely stroll to her enemies, flooring any troops that stood in her path.

"Though my loyalties to this realm never faltered, I did ask for something in return," said the Duke.

"Complete control over the region of Envy?" asked the Führer, patting his belly.

"Eheheh. It's much more modest. I asked to be the one to kill you," said the Duke, holding its metal strings up.

"This won't be the first assassination I've stopped," said the Führer, his golden belly heating up.

Chapter 92: Conflicting Worldviews

The Baroness rushed in and sliced off the goddess' head.

"Such skill. Such power!" exclaimed Yvne's severed head.

The sword master attacked the headless goddess with the blades in her feet, but each strike was parried.

"Commander, we will do our best to hold her back. We will not lose you here," said a sword-wielding demon.

"I do not fear death. I will not run. Nor will I ask for assistance," said the Baroness.

"How did you do it? Working alongside the other demon lords as equals?" asked Yvne.

"Sinner's Fury gave me a reason to draw my sword, it offered me purposeful combat," said the Baroness, lunging her sword at the goddess.

Yvne's body contorted to dodge each strike. "Not why? How?"

"I've got a question. How can you support a system that needlessly exploits the people who give it life?" asked the Baroness, launching the throwing knives beneath her arms.

After the first knife hit, Yvne's skin became armored like a crab.

"It's not uncommon. Most don't care about those outside their group. Though I am jealous of Sel's power, it is my own sisters I am most envious of. Those in close proximity, with similar social status, are those with which we compete against. Make sense?"

"*Metamorphosis Frenzy!*" Yvne's fingers became spears and pierced the Baroness' legs. After shifting into snakes, they coiled around her body.

"I understand. The Führer's words finally make sense." The Baroness kicked off and stabbed at the snakes while the goddess approached. "Without hope we become emotional parasites. Your pitiful nature is proof of his theory."

"I do feed off of the joy of my sisters. Perhaps I am a parasite." Yvne's hand transformed into a spiked club before slamming into the skillful warrior.

The Baroness parried the bullet assault that followed the attack. "Your region has created more problems than all the others with its monopoly on technology and weaponry. Ending you will end the gap in technology. Peace can come from death. I understand now," she said, leaping out of the way of a rocket.

"You're nimble and very pretty. I'll like you much more once you're no longer able to move," said Yvne, firing out razor-sharp scales from her arm.

The Baroness blocked four scales before one sliced into her leg. After falling to her knees, the other scales cut her up.

Yvne became a leaf, soared behind the powerful fighter, and then transformed into an elephant.

The Baroness rolled past the elephant's foot and kicked off the ground. She sliced into its leg, getting sprayed by acidic blood.

The trunk shifted into a bastard sword once it hit the Baroness, piercing straight through. The elephant then morphed into an iron maiden.

The Baroness pressed two daggers against the sides, struggling to keep the doors from closing. "This fight is so exhilarating!" The Baroness dropped her dagger before unsheathing her blade. "*IGNITION!*"

The iron maiden was sliced open and then it became muck.

"How do you find joy in violence? I've never felt happiness. Is it warm?" asked Yvne, shifting into a ten-armed warrior with a sword in each hand.

"It's blisteringly hot!" yelled the Baroness, rushing into a rapid sword assault. She spun her blades around, deflecting all strikes, and then stabbed her foot into Yvne's body. "*DUAL IGNITION!*" The Baroness unsheathed two swords at once, slicing through the goddess' blades and delimbing her arms.

"There is nothing that can stand against your heated blade. It's best if I improvise," said Yvne, transforming into her own version of the Baroness, with two extra arms and extra hot blood.

Yvne tore a sword out from her stomach but the Baroness dodged. The next two strikes came at once. The Baroness leaned back, slammed the hilt of her weapon against the swords and unsheathed her prized katana, lobbing off Yvne's head.

The goddess became a puddle. "Fighting you is pointless. I can't win." She went into a group of chain-wielding demons and started fighting them.

"I was barely able to keep up. If not for her weak will, I would have surely perished," said the Baroness, sheathing her sword in her chest.

"Burn! Burn! Burn!" The General tossed a volley of fireballs at Regna.

"Heehee! That tickles," said Regna, blushing as she was assaulted.

"Goddess or not! Nobody can survive my *FLAME CANNON!*" The General put both hands together and emitted a pillar of flame.

Regna screamed as she was engulfed.

"That's what you get for underestimating the General of Genocide!"

Regna wobbled around before falling to the ground. "That was…phew…rather hot," she said, holding her chest.

"Why aren't you dead?! *FURIOUS MORTAR!*" The General shot into her like a fireball. "I'll blast you into oblivion! *AZURE INCINERATION!*" Blue flames erupted from his hands and exploded into the goddess.

Regna landed in front of him, breathing heavy. "You've flipped my switch!" she exclaimed, her body now flickering.

"What the!? Stay away from me!" yelled the General, jumping into a geyser of flame to recharge.

"Aw! He's shy!" exclaimed Regna, firing off her hand.

The hand pierced into the General's chest.

He yanked it out, but the fingers stayed in place.

"The whole treat others as you would want to be treated, the supposed Golden Rule, doesn't make sense to me," said Regna.

"Nothing you say makes any sense!" yelled the General, clawing into his flesh to pull out the explosive fingers.

"I mean, if one person follows the rule and another doesn't, then there will be a conflict. I propose a new Golden Rule. Treat others the way they treat you. You've given me your enflamed passion! I'm giving you mine!" she exclaimed, shaking her hips.

"I refuse to die!" he yelled, yanking out one of the fingers.

"You know, I could talk to the other Sins. Maybe we could work something out," said Regna, rocking back and forth.

"What are you going on about now?"

"Haha! You're so cute! I always thought that sisterhood was all I would ever have! But now…after meeting you, something deep within me has stirred. How about instead of killing you, you become my steamy, sexy, and fiery boyfriend? How does that sound?!" she asked with a big smile.

Flaming demons rushed up and grabbed Regna, holding her in place.

"I only get enjoyment out of one thing: burning my enemies to cinders! *SUPER FLAME CANNON!*" yelled the General, redirecting a superheated geyser into the goddess once it shot out beneath him.

The demons holding Regna were reduced to ash.

"And that's a wrap! Yeesh, why would I want an ugly girl like her as my girlfriend, anyway?" he asked with a shrug.

"Ugly? I'm ugly?" asked Regna, her body no longer flickering.

"Ugly and obnoxious! I thought I killed you!" yelled the General, tossing extra hot fireballs at her.

Regna rushed up to him and stabbed her fingers into his throat. "You really shouldn't say such mean things to nice girls!" she yelled before ripping out his throat. She whined and wailed as she tore his body to pieces. "Men are all jerks! Never again! Sisterhood is all I'll ever need to keep me warm." She crouched over his body. "**CORPSE GRENADE**."

The bully's limp body was turned into a bomb.

Regna picked up the corpse and tossed it into the wall-shaped demon lord, blasting him to bits. "I'm really pissed right now! Time to vent!" she yelled, heading into battle as she cried liquid magma.

Edirp's leisurely stroll ended once she arrived at the remaining Freedom Forcers.

"We took her down before. I thought she was dead. I should have made certain. Her head was busted open, right?" asked Kaity, turning to her partner.

"Yeah. I recall something like that," said Nina, scratching her knuckles.

"None of the Seven Deadly Sisters of the Sinful Sorority –the goddesses of Sel, whose powers stretch beyond your comprehension–who you should be eternally grateful to even be in the presence of…none of us were allowed to kill you. Our orders were to keep you all alive," said Edirp.

"That makes sense. Tsul hardly seemed interested and she said she wasn't allowed to kill us," said Violet.

"No! She's lying. One of them killed Ego! Explain that!" yelled Kaity.

"I owe you absolutely nothing. In fact, it's absurd for you to make any demands of me. I'm a goddess; you are a mere mortal, and a child at that. Still, though not because you asked, and certainly not due to the rude way in which you asked, I'll explain. Yvne, my darling sister, doesn't know how to hold back. She, rather like Regna and Ynnotulg—may she rest in peace—is swayed by her emotions. I, however, am not. Though that sniper bullet did hurt, I was not defeated. All of you should rejoice at this opportunity. I, Edirp, Queen of Pride and the destroyer of armies, will display my true power."

"Does she ever stop talking? She reminds me of someone I am not fond of," said Nina, raising her katana.

"Opti, please keep her safe," said Violet, setting down the Princess of Insight.

"I'll protect her too! Wow, a real life Princess!" exclaimed D.S., bouncing in place.

The Princess rubbed the nice man's bald scalp.

"Let's keep our distance for now. We don't know what she is capable of," said Deceivant.

"She attacks with arrows imbued with insults to weaken her opponents. If we don't get hit, then there's no problem," said Kaity, aiming her rifle.

"Prideful Presence."

The ground beneath Kaity screamed as it dropped. Her shot missed and she fell into a pit.

The assassin's plasma claws shot out and she climbed up the wall.

"You do realize we aren't soul-less monsters right? All of us gods were once living beings on Earth. Htols loved to spend time with her sisters. Her laziness is a product of love. After all, longer working hours equates to less time spent with our families! She loved us dearly and you took her away!" Arrows imbued with insults emitted from Edirp, each one aimed at a different enemy.

The team opened fire on the arrows, but the bullets passed through.

"Oh you're used to my physical arrows, aren't you? Well these ones are a bit harder to destroy, and by that I mean they are impossible. Face it, you stand no chance at...."

Nina picked up Napkin and rushed into the arrows, having each one enter the white kitten.

"What are you doing to Napkin!" yelled Kaity.

"The only way to stop the arrows is to get hit by them. This cat is the weakest member and therefore the least valuable to the team. Seemed like using him to deflect the shots was our best option," said Nina, tossing kunai with explosive tags attached at the enemy.

The ground beneath the goddess rose, getting blasted in her stead.

"It hurts so much." "The pain!" "Save us!" wailed the living pillar.

"You raise your hand against a system as old as death. Why? Are you really naïve enough to believe your weaponry is enough to change this realm?" asked Edirp.

A second volley of arrows came out; this time their target was Nina.

The nimble ninja leaped up the shattered rock fragments as she navigated through the arrow storm.

"We're not like Exp 8. We're just fighting to survive!" yelled Deceivant, aiming his rifle.

Edirp was assaulted by bullet fire before Nina's katana slammed into her neck. The katana bounced back.

"Condemning Curse."

Twenty arrows fired out from Edirp's sides and into Nina, sending her crashing to the ground.

"Useless. Weak. Pathetic. Unlovable," said Nina in tears.

The ground beneath the ninja warrior plummeted and released wretched screams.

"I'll rescue her!" yelled Kaity, tossing her gun aside and going down the pit on all fours.

"Where is Deerg?" asked Kanasta.

The ground rose up to Edirp who was in midair. "She was unable to fight. Wait. It was you, wasn't it? Where is my little sister's head?" asked Edirp, firing out a massive arrow with *MURDERER* written on it.

"I have it, right here," said Kanasta, lifting up his suitcase.

He stood his ground as the arrow crashed into him.

"I am an assassin, not a murderer. If you're going to insult me, at least use something that makes sense," said Kanasta, pulling the physical arrow out and shoving it in the ground.

"You decapitated a little girl! Give her that precious child's head back immediately!" yelled Deceivant, reaching for the suitcase.

"She's a goddess, likely older than you. And she is Devlin's enemy. Even without her head she's still alive, just not functional," said Kanasta.

"If we give you her head, will you leave us?" asked Violet.

"I don't make bargains with mortals! I'll get her head back once I've killed him!" yelled Edirp, her aura pooling into her hand.

The aura shimmered and then solidified into a scepter. The scepter was a pillar of flesh adorned with luminescent compliments. The top of the scepter was shaped like a hand and held a reflective ball in its grip.

"Behold and tremble in fear; my true weapon has been summoned!" she exclaimed, pointing it at Kanasta.

Deceivant opened fire on Edirp, but the bullets simply bounced off.

Kaity leaped out of the pit with Nina hoisted over her shoulders.

"How splendid! She will make the perfect example! Behold the power of the Scepter of Pride!" Edirp aimed the scepter at Nina.

Purple energy coated Nina. The nimble warrior's body slammed into the ground, crushing Kaity beneath her.

"Heavy with her own self-loathing. Kanasta, get the scepter out of her hands this instant!" yelled Deceivant, standing in front of Nina in a failed attempt to weaken the scepter's power.

"Understood." Kanasta leaped off the ground.

"I don't think so. **Imperial Atmosphere**!"

A purple wave of energy emitted from Edirp, sending Kanasta back to the ground and the rest of her enemies down to their knees.

"It takes so much energy just to stand up," said Riufen, taking a step with trembling legs.

"I order you to bow!" yelled Edirp, firing an arrow, laden with the insult *weakling*, at the samurai.

A ball of spiritual energy exploded the insult before it could connect.

"We can't get up to her; we'll have to bring her down to our level. Edirp, you shall learn that in essence, all are equal. *ASTRAL PROJECTION!*" Violet's astral body left her.

"You run quite the risk bringing your energy body out into the open. My attacks affect the emotional body, thus weighing down the physical body," said Edirp, firing ten arrows out at once.

"Devlin warned me of a coming apocalypse. Even though I know the end of all the world as I know it is fast approaching, and there is no way to stop it, I won't let it end here. All of us are going to face the inevitable apocalypse together!" Violet's astral self fired energy shots, taking out three arrows. The other seven hit her and then bounced off.

"What apocalypse? The souls here no longer reincarnate. The sinful don't get a second chance. This system has done its part in sustaining the Earth," said Edirp.

"My spiritual fortitude cannot be swayed." The astral body ran up the pillar and punched the goddess.

The Sin of Pride gripped tightly onto her scepter as she fell back.

Rather than hitting the ground, the floor beneath her went up to catch her. As it rose, the bodies of the residents infused with the ground split apart.

"Your aura strengthens based on how much higher you are than your opponent. Kaity and Nina must have beaten you when they were on equal ground," said Violet's astral self, kicking the Devi's arm.

"I'm a goddess! You can't defeat me," said Edirp, grinding her teeth.

Parts of the elevated ground shot up into Violet's energy body, assaulting it like a machine gun.

"No more!" "Stop!" "It hurts!" cried the living pillar.

"I must end this for their sake." Violet kicked off the air and placed herself directly above Edirp. "I wonder if your aura weakens when you are beneath someone," she said, changing her hand into an energy blade.

"I won't lose! *Prideful Geyser!*" Purple energy erupted out of Edirp like a fountain, sending Violet flying forty feet in the air.

"It doesn't matter how high you are if you can't touch me!" yelled Edirp, sticking out her tongue.

Violet flung her bladed energy at the dark goddess.

"My sisters are counting on me! *Condemning Curse!*" Twenty arrows erupted out of Edirp's body and shot toward the energy blade.

The blade cut through each arrow, undeterred.

Edirp rolled on her back, raising the ground as soon as she reached its edge. "You won't hit me!"

"I have full control over every part of my astral body."

The blade changed its trajectory and careened into Edirp's right arm.

The energy connection was severed.

Edirp's beloved staff fell out of her limp grip and tumbled out of her reach.

"It's my energy! I can just summon it again!" yelled Edirp.

The scepter dispersed into purple energy.

Edirp's aura pooled into her hand, but it did not become a weapon.

"Even the gods are not without limitations. It seems we are indeed trapped by our karmas," said Violet's astral body as it soared toward Edirp.

Holding her hand out in the gesture of restraint, Violet's astral body pressed against Edirp. "*ASTRAL DISCHARGE!*" A powerful energy burst out.

Edirp fell limply to the floor.

The ground around them erupted in cheers.

Violet's astral body fell backward, unable to make the trip back home.

Kaity pushed Nina off her and held her chest. "Are you okay?" she asked, wincing in pain herself.

"I…I can't move my legs," said Nina, barely able to raise her arms.

The arms of the protruding residents passed Violet down to her allies.

Kanasta hoisted Violet over his back and climbed up the scorched pillar. Once atop, he set her down on her energy body. The two bodies fused and Violet awoke.

"Is everyone safe?" asked Violet weakly.

"Yes. Thanks to you," said Kanasta with a nod.

"Thank goodness," said Violet, closing her eyes.

The Duchess flung her hooks at the Goddess of Lust.

Tsul gasped in delight as her flesh was pierced.

The Prince patted his shirt. "Hmm. Yes, your heart will do just fine. I'm in need of a new boutonnière," he said with a smile.

Tsul cracked her whip again.

"The Führer believes it is money that moves humans and demons to action. Let's find out if he's correct." The Prince spit on the ground.

Demons came out from the crowd and rushed in to drink up the spittle, incidentally protecting the Prince.

"I've placed my fluids in their pools, the water they wash with and the blood they ritualistically consume. Once they've had a taste, the mere pheromones of my fluids are enough to make them do anything," said the Prince.

"Is that so? Prove it," said Tsul, readying her whip.

"I will. Hey, you want more, right? Then kill her," said the Prince, licking his fingers.

Tsul whipped the demons as they rushed up to her.

"So, do you agree? Does money really make the world spin?"

"If he is correct, if money moves demon and human societies, it still does not benefit the world as a whole. It is lust that populates the Earth. Without lust, neither those who seek sin nor those yearning for virtue would even exist. And if a species overpopulates, it can lead to extinction," said Tsul as she whipped her enemies.

"You make a good point. As for me, I'm not driven by money or lust," said the Prince with a shrug.

Taken up in a mad frenzy, the demons broke apart into a violent, bloody orgy.

"Well that's new," said the Prince, examining his saliva.

"The spikes on my whip are laced with my own aura. Once my pheromones enter their veins, they are swept up in a crazed, rush of passion. Pleasure drowns out all their senses."

"Then I best not get hit," said the Prince, pulling a needle from his hair and dousing it in his blood.

"If only it were so simple. *RUPTURE.*"

The frenzied demons bloated until they burst, spraying flesh and blood in all directions.

Though the Duchess stood in front of the Prince, some of the blood still touched him.

"You can expand your aura?" asked the Prince with wide eyes.

"Yes. I condense my lusty aura into droplets. The droplets then expand until they pop. I am the leader of the Sinful Sorority. Without me, all the Seven Deadly Sisters would have been engulfed in their own passions. I helped them wrestle their passion till it transformed into their power," said Tsul, whipping the ground.

The Duchess tore the hooks out of Tsul and flung them into the Prince.

"Turning my toys against me, very clever! To think I am fighting against the head of the Sinful Sorority. That makes this even more exciting! Let's see if my fluid is more intoxicating than your poison," said the Prince, tearing at his side.

His shimmering purple blood was soon lapped up by the Duchess.

"Good. Now kill her as I asked if you want more," said the Prince.

The Duchess stabbed her hooks into the Prince, lapping up the blood as it gushed out.

"Your fluids aren't strong enough. They leave the victim in a conscious state," said Tsul.

The Prince stabbed a needle into the Duchess' neck and kicked her off. He then removed the hooks. "Damn! It wasn't easy getting her under my control!" he yelled, standing up.

"Looks like it's already beginning to expand," said Tsul.

The areas on the Prince's body that were hit by the blood from the frenzied demons were bloating.

The Prince tossed a handful of needles at Tsul.

"So different parts of your body have blood with different attributes…interesting. What was that you hit me with, something to sedate me?" asked Tsul.

"No. I've changed my mind! You're too dangerous! It's deadly toxin!" yelled the Prince.

"You do realize I'm immune to poison," said Tsul, sweating out the purple toxins. She leaned over, face-to-face with the toxic boy.

The Prince covered his lips in purple blood and then locked lips with Tsul. To his surprise, the goddess kissed back, lapping up all the blood. She sucked out his air as he struggled in her grip.

The bulges on his body shrank.

Tsul broke out of the kiss and rubbed under his chin. "I don't like to kill. I may have overestimated you, but you are still fairly dangerous and very handsome. I'll keep you as a plaything. Though I don't need anyone to reach the peak of pleasure, sex is always better with a willing partner," she said, snapping a collar around his neck.

The Führer removed superheated golden chunks from his belly and flung them at the Duke.

The two-faced demon lord sliced the heated projectile with a metal string but was still burned when it grazed its skin. "Let's be honest, Führer. Neither of us is fit for battle. We are leaders, not warriors," said the Duke, walking around its enemy in a circle.

"Indeed. Most of the greed demon lords don't fight at all. I took over their domain through bribes and compromises. I use this corrupt system in order to enhance my reign," said the Führer, coating his body in heated gold.

"And yet you stand against the system now! Despite all it has done for you," said the Duke, moving toward its nemesis.

"I hit the ceiling. Without breaking the rules I would be unable to expand my kingdom. Sel has great conflict not because it is made up of sinners…the widespread turmoil exists because it is compartmentalized. Demons stick to those who sin in a similar way. But I know the truth. Oftentimes demons are placed in specific regions due to a vacancy, not due to their conduct while in the world of the living. They flock with the ones in close proximity, not necessarily those with like-minds," said the Führer, his body now fully covered in gold.

"And you find that reason enough to betray our benefactor, our God?" asked the Duke, lashing metal strings at the Führer.

Demons with animal parts grafted onto their bodies came out from behind the Führer and were sliced in his stead.

"I do indeed. Demon lords have no power when it comes to realm-wide policy. Our only purpose is to keep the demons of our domain in line. What is a politician that cannot represent his people? The system itself creates rebels. Look at the size of our armies. That is the cry of the people. The people need a voice," said the Führer, signaling explosive demons to rush the Duke.

The Duke sliced two demons and then slammed their halves into the others, blowing them all to bits. "The people need to learn their place. I am a demon of envy. Whether or not I was placed there due to my own actions or merely to fill a vacancy, I have thrived and taken up my sin with dignity."

"Demons die for me, but even those who battle for Sel do not offer you so much as a cheer. You are alone," said the Führer, signaling more demons to attack.

"The lord works through me! As long as I serve my god, I am not alone! And if god put me in the region of envy, then that is where I belong!" yelled the Duke, slicing through the butcher-bladed demons and their heated weapons.

"You're missing the point. Most sinners do not stick to a single sin. Take me, an exemplary politician, for example. Yes, I am greedy, but I am also a proud demon. Though proud, I covet the land of others, and I often consume more than my fair share of decadent delights. I am a hard worker, but I'm lazy when it comes to exercise. I have quite the temper, though it's hard to upset me. And, like many men, I enjoy the company of beautiful women and lose track of time when they tend to me. They love to rub my belly and call me the good luck Buddha, haha! I'm a sinner of all colors! Take a moment and think about your sins. Is envy all that drives you, or are you far more complex than this realm deems you to be?" asked the Führer as his archers assaulted the Duke.

"None of that matters! Sel is my god! It is our god! Who are we to question it?" yelled the Duke, shielding the lady portion of its face from arrows.

"Living beings. We are brought into this world as empty shells, our souls encrusted with karma whose causes we have no recollection of. This world is without purpose. We don't reincarnate. We merely suffer and then we are asked to risk what remains of our so-called life in battle against Lum. What exactly is it we are fighting to protect?" asked the Führer as the vehicular sloth demons rammed into the Duke.

The Duke leaped up, catching the living automobiles in threads. The demons crashed into each other and exploded. "You and your kind are whiny and arrogant. What does it matter why our Lord makes us suffer, has us risk our lives? All that we own…all that we are comes from the mercy of our god. You bite at the hand that crafted your very soul!"

"Should every child bow to their parents' will? Should every construct be at the mercy of its constructor?" asked the Führer, calling in his beast tamers.

The Duke's strings severed the leashes and allowed the furious beasts to attack their oppressors.

"Any analogy to our relationship with our Lord falls short. Children were not en-souled by their parents. Slaves are not beloved by their masters. Sel has deemed you an enemy. Who am I to question the all-knowing?" asked the Duke, pulling a single string.

The intricate pattern the Duke had laid out during the entire battle came together all at once.

The Führer was trapped, every limb perfectly wound up. "You've questioned your own sex. There was a demon who was so badly burned it didn't know whether it had been male or female. It tried to do gender-specific activities but found it enjoyed some from one category and others from the other. Unable to discern its identity, the demon would locate the prettiest girls and the most handsome of men to find the perfect face, the smoothest legs, and the most fitting bosom. Once it found an adequate combination of stolen parts, the demon wanted to be recognized. And so it took down one of the demon lords through threats and gossip. It then took his place. Despite your faith, your god never even had the decency to tell you what you are. Even now, after bringing every insurgent into its vision, the truth is hidden from you. Why do you serve such an ungrateful god?" he asked as his body was slowly sliced.

"It's all part of my karmic path. Each moment of suffering, of fear, of struggling with the pain of not knowing has brought me closer to Lord Sel. One day, I will leave behind this body and join back with the lord as pure essence," said the Duke.

"Sooner than you may have expected. End it," said the Führer with a grin.

A black orb pressed into the Duke's back before exploding.

A figure wrapped in a shroud approached the Führer and released him from the strings.

"I had hoped I could sway him to my side. I suppose a priest and a politician hold conflicting worldviews. Those who accept pain and despair are truly beyond my reach. Now that you're here, we can change the tide of this war," said the Führer, closing his wounds with heated gold.

Chapter 93: The Battle of Heroes

Demonica stopped her vicious assault against her own people and took flight. She landed in front of what was left of the Freedom Forcers.

"We're not afraid of you. Your annoying sister lost!" yelled D.S.

"Just leave us alone," said Kaity with her beloved hoisted on her back.

"I can't fight her. I've failed Devlin," said Nina, her tears becoming vapor after crashing to the ground.

"Nothing has been lost yet. I can take her," said Kanasta, tossing a canister of angel feathers at her.

Demonica's blood shot out and liquidized the feathers. "It's so cute how you all are getting so worked up. Didn't you hear what I said earlier? I'm just here to capture you."

"And what is our fate once we've been captured?" asked Riufen.

Demonica smirked. "Oh, that hasn't been decided."

"Then we will stand our ground and fight," said Riufen, hardening the blood around his spinal sword.

"And what are you planning to do to the Princess?" asked D.S., shielding the grief-stricken girl.

"Well I've got to kill her. All demon lords who opposes the system must be dealt with," said Demonica.

The puddle behind the Princess shot into the young maiden as a spike.

"Stay away from the puddles!" yelled Deceivant, firing at the traitor.

"Oh and what are you going to do about the blood on your bodies?" asked Demonica, holding her chin.

Opti screamed out.

Deceivant turned to see his ally's own blood pierced into him like stakes.

Demonica's legs were severed by high-propulsion saws. They reconnected as soon as the blood splatter hardened.

Kanasta fired a shotgun blast into Demonica's face and then rapidly assaulted her body with punches.

"**Blood Spike!**" The death goddess' body jutted out, piercing into the assassin's chest.

Riufen's blade pierced straight through her heart.

Demonica's body hardened. Once her head regenerated, she smiled at the samurai's attempts to dislodge his weapon.

Riufen leaped back and pulled out another spine from his back. The sword spun around to deflect a spray of blood bullets.

Kaity set Nina down and blasted Demonica's head open. "She can't aim if she can't see."

"Take this," said Nina, handing Kaity a grenade.

"Grenade!" Kaity flung the explosive behind Demonica, having the blinded goddess back up right into it.

"We die for the hero!" yelled the ground before being blasted.

Kanasta grabbed Riufen and took cover, keeping relatively blood free.

Demons from all corners of the battlefield cheered.

"You see it too, right?" asked Deceivant, pointing to the sky.

A wrecking ball-sized black orb floated above the battlefield.

Opti grabbed his cheeks as his eyes teared up. "He's alive!"

A cloaked figure stood atop of the pillar formed by Edirp. His arm was raised to the skies.

The Führer's voice echoed throughout the war-torn scorched battleground. "The Hero of Sel has returned from the realm beyond! Freedom is beyond death! Take hold of the hero's will within you and use that hope to claim victory against the Forces of Hatred!"

"I should have known the Ultimate Exp couldn't be so easily destroyed," said Deceivant.

Demonica rose out from a puddle near Deceivant. "How in Sel's ignoble name did he survive Etah's attack?" she asked, liquefying her head for an instant to avoid Kaity's bullet.

"Heroes never die! Justice prevails! My friend is alive!" cheered D.S., punching the air each time he heard an orb burst.

Demons with wolves on collars came from behind the team, accompanied by a blue flag bearer.

"We'll tend to your wounded," said the demons, surrounding Nina.

"I surrender my life for the hero!" cheered an explosive demon before slamming into Demonica and blasting her to pieces.

Kamikaze demons stood by the blood puddle in proximity to the hero's allies.

"It's an honor to meet you all," said a flag bearer, bowing to each member.

"Any hero worth idolizing wouldn't approve of you throwing away your lives to buy us some time. Place these near the puddles instead," said Nina, offering a roll of explosive tags.

Kaity took the explosive tags and tossed them into the puddles. "How will you trigger them?"

"They will activate if there is enough movement in the area. We have her pinned down for now," said Nina, patting a wolf as it healed her leg.

"With her stuck, how many of the Sinful Sorority remain?" asked Deceivant.

"Last I saw Yvne, she was devouring the Duchess of Desire. Regna has been taking out the demon lords and is currently fighting the hero himself. Tsul is rushing across the battlefield, spraying her power enhancing pheromones on her allies. Even with the hero fighting with us, we would have been decimated if not for our temporary cease-fire with Sinner's Fury," said the flag bearer.

"And we would have been taken hostage by Demonica if not for your assistance," said Deceivant.

"We'll win this. We beat Etah, after all," said Kaity, giving supporting fire to her demonic allies.

A corrosive beam shot into the orb from the cliffside overlooking the battlefield. The orb burst.

Despair took a sudden hold of the rebel armies.

A massive figure slid down the cliffside, engaging into combat as soon as it landed.

A fleshy axe with a blade of sharpened bone tore through a demon commander. His soul was promptly consumed by a spiked mace with rows of teeth inside.

"I won't let all I've done be for naught. As long as I live, my empire stands!" The twelve-foot figure summoned up the new soul—now a spear—and plunged it into the throat of an approaching enemy. Seeing another attacker to his left, he transformed the impaled demon into a sword and decapitated his foe. Five demons rushed him and shattered their swords against his molten body. With pulsing muscles, the figure knocked them aside. "These souls are weak. But I am too tired to summon up my strong ones. These will have to do for the time being," he said in a deep and rough echoing voice.

The figure plunged the mace into his foe's chest and formed the soul into a shield to block the incoming arrow assault. "You dare attack your ruler!" The God of Hate rushed through the enemy line, his swirling dark red eyes solely focused on the resurrected hero.

Kamikaze demons rushed toward the battle-worn Lord of Hate.

"I've never felt such fatigue. **BASHFUL BOW**!" The bow tattoo on his arm lost its glow once the Deva materialized his weapon. The dark god rushed into his enemies, swiftly crushing them, changing their souls into arrows and firing those arrows at the approaching kamikazes from by releasing the pink string from his rainbow-colored bow.

A line of archers took aim, but were decapitated by an armored ferret.

The furry creature rushed up to the tyrant king and bowed. "Welcome back, my Lord. The hero is just up ahead. Once he is crushed, victory is assured."

"I destroyed him. Every fiber of his being!" yelled Etah, clenching his fists.

A line of demons took cover.

A speedy orb zoomed over the crowd before being knocked aside by Etah. Their eyes met.

The God of Hate filled every wound on his body with his red energy.

The hero rushed up to Etah, firing orbs at any enemy soldiers in his path.

"How are you alive?!" yelled Etah.

The hero's arm emerged from his cape. It was sleek, metallic, and had an orb coming out from its palm.

"So be it, then," said the god with heavy breaths.

The hero swerved to dodge a blast of the god's aura.

The orb burst prematurely, masking the hero's next move.

"I saved this world! Without me, Sel would have sunk into the lava below! To defy me is to defy every demon!" The god rushed forth, stepping on an orb placed on the ground.

"I die for the hero!" cheered a protruding head before bursting.

Etah's thin aura shot to his leg but was unable to deflect the explosion.

Once the god had been lifted off the ground, a volley of ten orbs shot out and sent him flying in the distance.

A combined battalion of Sinner's Fury and Hero's Militia soldiers rushed at the downed god.

The hero raised his arm and fired a massive orb, signaling his warriors that his will had triumphed over hatred itself.

The explosive tags on the puddles liquidated and joined the puddles. Demonica rose out and sliced two grenades thrown her way. She spread her wings and took flight, avoiding the explosive demons below.

"She's probably going after the hero. I'll stop her," said Nina, standing before falling abruptly to her knees.

A demon commander, wielding a scepter, broke through the defensive lines around the hero's allies and was quickly attacked by BoneSaw. She defended against his strikes with the steel plates adorning her body.

"We can meet up with him once everyone is healed. We don't even know what this…" Deceivant froze up. "Kanasta, order BoneSaw to stand down."

"What?"

"Order that thing to stop!" yelled Deceivant.

Kanasta called BoneSaw back.

"You, do you recognize me?" asked Deceivant, staring into the woman's brown eyes.

The crossbow on the commander's arm engaged, hitting Deceivant's leg.

"Is he under a spell or something?" asked Kaity, bringing the demon to its knees with her sniper shots.

"You're Vanessa, aren't you? Why am I asking? I know who you are, even if you don't. And you're here. But of course you're here." Tears poured out of the scientist's eyes and down his cheeks. "I'm in hell."

Deceivant shot the woman's arm as she raised it to fire. "I can't believe this is happening." He wiped away his tears, leaving only conviction. "I have wanted to tell you something. I just never thought I'd actually get the chance! Haha! Screaming to the skies doesn't quite have the same effect as saying it to your face." He gripped his chest. "After you died, I found true love. I found out who I really am. It changed my life in ways you couldn't even imagine." He walked up to her and raised his shotgun. "Why can't I pull the damn trigger?"

"May I?" asked Kanasta, placing his hand around his father's.

"No. I have to do it. She won't believe it otherwise. I won't believe it." Deceivant closed his eyes and pressed the gun against her forehead. "I thought I needed you, but I don't. Never did."

Her head was blasted open. The limp body fell.

Deceivant turned to face his allies, unaware of the bits of her brain on his cheeks. "Sorry about that."

"Who was she?" asked Kaity softly.

"It doesn't matter anymore," said Deceivant, sobbing in his hand.

"Do you know?" asked Kaity, looking up at her papa.

"I have a guess," said Kanasta, turning away.

"Dad, are you okay?" asked D.S.

"Yes, son. I'll be fine. I just realized that I'm really in hell. Haha!" he exclaimed, grabbing his head.

"Not for long," said the flag bearer.

A demon fully clad in a gimp suit was by his side. A trail of saliva came out from its ball gag. Other than grunts, it made no noise.

"He looks different than the gimps used by that crazy guy," said Kaity.

"He is. This is…well, it's complicated. Let's just say you can leave when ready, and I suggest sooner rather than later," said the flag bearer.

A white portal appeared on the floor in front of the gimp.

"Come on, team! Onward toward Heaven!" cheered Deceivant, entering the portal in a daze.

"Thank you very much," said Kaity with a bow before lifting Nina onto her shoulders and rushing into the portal.

"What about Exp 8?" asked Opti, holding Napkin in his arms.

"Yeah, and what do we do with the Princess?" asked D.S.

"Taking her to Lum would no doubt put her in more danger. As for Exp 8, he is not alone." Kanasta crouched down to the gimp. "Bring him to our location once he's done here."

"Understood. We will also protect the Princess of Insight," said the flag bearer as more reinforcements joined the blockade.

Opti picked up Violet in his arms. "You sure you guys don't need our help?"

The Baroness came out from the crowd. "You've done more than enough." She turned to Riufen and offered him a sword. "It was left behind on the battlefield. It's unlike any blade in Sel. It belongs to you, right?"

Riufen shook his head. "It belonged to a brave warrior, but I shall brandish it and carry on his legacy," said the samurai, hoisting the slanted sword.

"Next time we fight I won't use arrows," said the Baroness with a grin.

"Then I look forward to our next encounter," said Riufen with a bow.

"Thanks for all the help. After you," said Kanasta, gesturing BoneSaw to enter the portal.

"Your leader, the hero, really is something else. I feel as though his willpower has affected me," said the Baroness.

"You're really cool too! You agree, right, Riufen?" asked D.S.

"Yes. I mean, she is a proud and incredibly skilled warrior," said Riufen.

"You'll keep the Princess safe, right lady?" asked D.S.

"With my life. Despite what the Prince said about her, I feel she is indeed a special demon," said the Baroness.

"Fight hard, but don't die. We must fight again," said Riufen before vanishing in the white vortex.

"As I am now, I cannot complete Reflector's mission. Regardless, I must focus on what I can do. I still have a job to complete in Lum. Once that job is completed and I am reunited with my brother, I will return to this place," said Kanasta.

"Well I'm okay with not coming back. The zombie people are cool, but it's so hot," said D.S.

"Till next we meet," said Kanasta with a salute.

"Bye, blade lady!" exclaimed D.S. as he and Kanasta exited to Lum.

A black beam shot into the sky and obliterated the Hero's orb.

"That energy? Has he returned?" asked the Baroness.

Chapter 94:Child of Darkness

Devlin awoke, surrounded entirely by darkness. Spurts of flame sporadically erupted out in the distance, but never enough for him to get a clear image of where he was.

The young inventor cringed in pain and writhed around as the darkness around him filled his insides.

A pitch-black cloud, somehow darker than the rest of the area, steadily approached.

An ominous low voice came out from the cloud. "You have proven yourself most worthy."

Darkness hardened around Devlin's body, enveloping him in a heavy material.

The energy climbed up his neck and covered his head. It solidified into a black helmet with a row of sharpened teeth. The helmet covered everything but Devlin's golden eyes.

"Looks like I finally got your attention," said Devlin, his voice deepened by the helmet.

"Don't be so modest. By dethroning the God of Hate, your grandfather, you have earned the right to become a god! You've surpassed my expectations."

A bright red light gleamed inside the black cloud.

"Then you're the one who did it. You gave the orders. You ruined my life," said Devlin, his eyes like a blade.

"Etah's soul yearned for power. That made it easy to manipulate him. But you were quite the tricky one. The only way to make you follow my wishes was if you believed them to be your own. By isolating you from your family and identity, I bent your beliefs. Ever so slowly, you became my pawn."

"You planned for me to kill Etah?" asked Devlin.

"Etah was certainly useful. But his soul could never be bent to my will. If he gained too much power, he would surely seek to destroy me. This made him a liability. Now that he has been beaten, he will never again be hailed as a ruler. You've created the perfect opportunity for me to reclaim my kingdom."

"Etah was just another stepping stone for my godhood. I took him out for my own reasons," said Devlin.

"Ah, that is the beauty of it. I control both sides of the chess board. I put my pawns in the proper spaces. From there they willingly follow my wishes. I needn't even speak. I simply watch as my pawns fight one another. No matter what side wins, I benefit. Each death brings me more power."

The darkness took form around Devlin's body, enveloping him in sleek black armor. The black plates moved around his body like corrosive sludge. The armor parted in the back as Devlin's tail came out. The dark energy then blanketed the tail and solidified.

"You must be pretty confident to tell me all this! News flash: I used you to become a god."

"Pretentious as ever, I see."

"I've gotten what I needed from you. I'll be back to end you once I've mastered my powers," he said, pooling his dark energy into a portal.

"You belong with me. You've always been a child of darkness. I merely set you on a path that would cultivate the darkness within you."

"That's a load of human shit! The darkness in me came from my separation from my family! It was a lie you forced on me!"

"Yes, it's all coming along splendidly. There is no longer a need for subtle manipulation. I have power over your soul. You are mine to control. From now on, you will address me as Lord Sel."

Devlin's eyes lost their fire. They were blank, like that of a corpse.

"Understood, Lord Sel."

Devlin burst out of the cocoon of darkness, finding himself above the battlefield. A dark pillar of energy had gathered beneath him.

The demons below took notice, but rather than raise their weapons, they ran in terror.

Devlin looked up at the orb in the sky. Without a thought he raised his arm and blasted the orb.

The corrosive black energy obliterated the orb without triggering it to detonate.

His golden eyes regained their vigor. "This is the power I've sought."

Four flaming mortars came his way.

Devlin hit each mortar with a black shot from his fingertips.

The mortars were dissolved before they could reach him.

"I'm unstoppable. No. It's more than that. I'm destruction incarnate!" He placed his hands on the pillar of dark energy, causing it to shoot out in multiple directions at once.

Every aerial projectile on the battlefield was utterly annihilated.

"Now then, where is Kaity?"

His eyes shifted, searching for her heat signature.

"Hmm. She isn't here. Why are they fighting? I killed Etah. There should be peace. Three flags, different colors…it all makes sense now."

Devlin gripped his head in agony. "Stop! I'll end the rebellion; just tell me what you want me to…." His eyes became hollow.

Dark energy poured out of his body like an eruption of smoke. It wasn't long before the entire battlefield was enveloped in the fog.

Even in darkness, battle cries and screams could be heard.

"Time to end it."

Tiny beams of dark energy emitted from the pillar and hit specific targets all across the battlefield.

The smoke pooled back into the figure clad in black armor.

Every flag had been destroyed. Confusion took over as friend and foe became indistinguishable.

"Etah's reign is over. I have taken his place as the ruler of Sel. This civil war is pointless. Demon-kind must stand united. As ruler I seek to unify our people against Lum. If you accept me as your ruler, then bow down. Those who insist on fighting amongst each other will be eradicated." His voice projected out to all corners of the battlefield.

Many demons dropped their weapons, if only out of fear.

The Sel energy around his head solidified, shaping into a black helmet.

"You're not the hero! The hero is here, fighting by our side! He won't stand down!" yelled the Führer, concealed by a wall of golden demons.

"The hero you follow does not exist. He is a mere pawn of the demon lords."

A speedy orb slammed into the dark figure. It was swiftly crushed in his grip.

"You will see just how weak your hero is." Sel's Knight leaped off the pillar and landed. As the hero rushed forth, the knight fired beams into the living ground.

The hero zigzagged across the area, picking up orb mines he had left and joining them with the orb on his palm.

"Stop him at all costs! He must not destroy the hero!" yelled the Führer.

Demons from all regions and even tortured angels rushed at the black knight.

"If you had any idea who you were opposing, you would be groveling in reverence," said Sel's Knight, braving bullets, flames, arrows, and spears.

The pillar liquefied, crashing on the troops like a tidal wave.

An orb the size of a beach ball pierced through the wave and slammed into Sel's Knight.

The hero then fired a perimeter of smaller orbs at the ground.

The black knight skid back a few feet before annihilating the orb.

Once the wave broke, only the tortured angels were annihilated. The demons were stuck in the muck, but otherwise unharmed.

"Angels are untrustworthy. They have no place here…not even as slaves," said the warrior clad in darkness.

"Who the hell are you!?" yelled Regna, rushing on all fours through the sticky floor at the knight.

"Your new king." The knight whacked her aside after dodging her relentless assault.

The hero rushed in with a massive orb.

"*DARK ERUPTION*." Sel's Knight turned away.

The beams he fired into the ground earlier shot out alongside screams of agony. They bore into the hero's legs before annihilating them completely.

The legless hero fell into the muck.

The people cried out in despair. Some broke into sobs.

Sel's Knight approached as the hero lifted his arm. He held out his energy-laden hand to eradicate the hero's last attempt. After firing beams into the floor, spikes jutted out and hoisted up the hero.

A single beam shot into the hero's cloak.

"Your hero is already dead."

Chapter 95: The Hero's Legacy

The cloak dissolved. Exp 8's arm was grafted onto the body of Brick, who had been modified to be approximately his height.

"And thus the dark truth pierces through the radiant light of deception. The Führer used the only part of the hero he could get his hands on and crafted a lie to rally you into following his will."

"I'll ask again! Who the hell are you!?" yelled Regna, stuck in the muck.

"The new ruler of this world," said Sel's Knight, raising his arms.

"Indeed you are," said Demonica, landing behind her fallen beloved.

"You didn't kill the enemy demon lords?" asked the knight.

"Not all of them. Not yet."

Sel's Knight turned to her and fired a Sel blast into her chest. "This goddess has played you all for fools. I didn't give the order to wipe out the rebels. Sinner's Fury and Hero's Militia were all part of a cleverly constructed plot by Demonica, Etah, and the demon lords."

The Führer was suddenly attacked by his own people. "So what if I lied about the hero being alive? I only wanted us to win the war! And the new hero is one who spoke with the true hero. Stay away from me! Stay away!"

The knight's helmet dissolved, revealing his jet-black hair and piercing gold eyes. "Exp 8, the true hero, told me to take over should something happen to him. We both co-led the Freedom Forcer's against Etah's army. The hero's legacy lives on within me," he said in a dramatic, youthful voice.

Demons from all regions bowed down.

Sel's Knight caught sight of the Führer. He created a portal and teleported up to the golden demon lord.

"You aren't the hero's ally. You're the true tyrant of this realm," he said, pointing at the black knight with a shaky finger.

"The demon lords and the gods involved will be punished." Sel's Knight waved his hand.

The Führer vanished.

The knight entered another portal and appeared behind Demonica.

She rushed at him, running right into his newest portal.

"Capture the other demon lords and bring them forth. All of them have conspired against you," said the black knight before catching a throwing knife.

The Baroness rushed in. "I won't go down without a fight! I will lay down my life for the Princess!"

Sel's Knight formed a black blade of energy and engaged her.

The Baroness parried each strike, swiftly tossing her blade aside once the corrosive energy reached the sword's hilt. After sending two throwing knives at the knight's face, she gripped two swords and removed them from her chest.

The superheated blades slid against the Sel blade before slicing into the knight's armor. They dissolved instantaneously.

Sel's Knight kneed the Baroness in the face and tore out a sword from her body. He raised the sword and then cleaved his enemy.

The two bleeding halves parted and fell into separate portals.

"Enter the portal if you accept punishment. Otherwise you will be annihilated here and now," said the Knight.

The demon lords entered the dark portals with hesitant steps.

"Then come at me! I serve only one lord!" yelled the Captain of Carnage, seated atop Etah's head.

"As you wish." The knight turned the sword into a spear of energy and flung it at the demon lord on the God of Hate's shoulder.

Etah dodged the spear and charged, his aura flickering.

The Captain fired his blunderbuss once he was within range, but every piece of shrapnel dissolved once it hit the armor.

"There is one thing Sel energy cannot destroy," said Etah, holding up his hands as the Agony Axe formed. "Souls!" The axe swooped down and slammed into the knight's arm, cutting it off. The axe vanished before hitting the ground.

Wires erupted out. "**DARK EMBODIMENT**." Black bullets fired off the knight's fingertips into the wires, giving them Sel properties.

"I am still a god!" Etah lifted up a chunk of the living ground, slowing the wires for a mere moment.

Once they had busted through, he was already out of range.

The wires turned around before boring into his back.

The Captain sliced them with his blades. The blades disintegrated. He grabbed discarded weapons along the battlefield, sliced some wires, and then threw them aside.

"Your loyalty gives me faith in this world," said Etah before leaping back to dodge a Sel shot. "Finally an opening. **CHAOS CHAIN**!"

Chains shot out from the god's arm and connected to the knight.

"Your weapons are indeed impervious to my energy. You, however, are not," said Sel's Knight.

The shot had spread across the ground and was now eating away the useless god's foot.

"I will not lose you in this battle. Captain, I order you to leave the premises. If I fall against him, I fall alone," said Etah.

The Captain bowed and then rushed off, using some daggers he had picked up to keep his foes away.

Sel's Knight fired a beam at the fleeing demon lord.

A pole materialized in Etah's grip and absorbed the Sel blast.

"You're weak from our last fight," said the knight as the God of Hate walked toward him in a daze.

"I'm tired, that's all. This weapon is known as the Painful Pole. Time to wake up!" Etah gripped the pole with both hands and plunged it into his own flesh. The dark Deva wailed out in agony.

"You're leaving yourself open," said Sel's Knight, collecting the dark energy from the ground and forming it into a spear.

Etah strafed to dodge the spear only to get pelted with dark bullets.

"Now it's only a matter of time before you are completely consumed," said Sel's Knight, reattaching his arm.

"After climbing so high, I refuse to fall!" The God of Hate ripped out his afflicted areas and tossed them aside. "This world is mine!" He rushed at the knight with new energy, swinging the Agony Axe once he was within range.

"That weapon is just a bit too slow to hit me." The knight stopped the axe in its tracks with a black energy blade.

The axe dissipated.

Sel's Knight cringed as the Painful Pole slammed into his stomach.

The Chaos Chain had been wrapped around the pole and quickly reeled the knight into a beat down.

"I'm wide awake now!" yelled Etah, knocking aside the knight's hand before he could fire.

"**OMINOUS OBSTRUCTION!**" Sel's Knight lifted up the liquid energy and formed it into a wall. "My head. Why do I feel dizzy?"

"The emotions of these weapons are channeled by the very souls that make them up. They are also amplified when used in tangent with a soul they had a powerful bond with!" Etah rushed behind the wall, striking the knight with the Wailing Whip before piercing through the armor with the Searing Sword. "How does it feel to have your own creations used against you, Devlin?"

"With enough power, all emotions can be numbed out!" Sel's Knight glowed with a corrosive black aura.

Wires shot out from below and pierced into Etah.

The tyrant god was soon blanketed in the black aura.

Sel's Knight formed a black portal on the ground behind Etah. He then rushed into the god, tumbling into the portal along with him.

Silence befell the battlefield.

A portal appeared.

Sel's Knight emerged, wearing his helmet. "And so the war ends. Edirp, if you would be so kind as to raise the ground back into its proper place."

"No! Instead I'll send you and everyone here to their end! Sel will be purged of all treachery! **Prideful Presence**!" Edirp raised the ground around her and her sisters by lowering the screaming battlefield.

The knight turned around, but Regna was no longer stuck in the muck.

"You'll die with all the rest! **Condemning Curse**!" yelled Edirp, firing arrows out at the false ruler.

Sel's Knight created a portal and fell into it. He arrived behind Edirp and lifted her up. "Demonica played you. I didn't order every rebel's death, only that of the demon lords." The knight's eyes flashed red.

"My lord, it's you," said Edirp.

"Stop this madness and raise the ground back to equanimity," said the knight, setting her down.

Edirp nodded. The ground traveled up like an elevator.

"Will this really end the war?" asked Tsul, looking up at the black knight.

"Members of Sinner's Fury, Hero's Militia, and the Forces of Hate, I ask a simple question: why war against each other? The rebellion in Sel was a ploy. Etah ordered the leaders to form Sinner's Fury to weed out traitors. Look to your fellow demons. If Sinner's Fury had not joined with Hero's Militia, they would have been decimated by the Forces of Hate. It was the demon lords, along with Etah and Demonica, who pitted you against one another and tricked the Sinful Sorority into doing their bidding, and they have been dealt with. The demon lord system has been crushed. If you believe in a unified Sel, then bow to me. If you still wish to battle, then face annihilation. Decide now!"

By the time the battlefield was at equal level with the rest of Sel, every single demon was bowing.

"Welcome back, Lord Sel," said Tsul with a bow.

The gimp demon appeared in front of the knight. In his hands was the Captain of Carnage, knocked out.

"And so the final demon lord is captured. You sent the Exps on their way?" asked Sel's Knight.

The gimp nodded.

"Then you followed my every command."

The gimp nodded with excitement.

"Hmph. Typical. Oh well. Demonica has really made quite the mess of things in my absence. No matter. The Civil War of Sel is over. Now it is time to start a new war," said the knight, vanishing along with the Sinful Sorority in a black portal..

Part 11
The Knight of Sel

Chapter 96: Memory & Loss

Deceivant, Kaity, Kanasta, BoneSaw, D.S., Opti, Napkin, Violet, Nina, and Riufen arrived in a snowy valley.

Despite the blanket of white, the trees were leafy and vital. Snow bunnies and lemmings popped out upon hearing the new visitors arrive.

"Yay, level complete!" cheered D.S., high-fiving Kanasta.

"Indeed," said Kanasta with a smile.

Violet slid out of D.S.'s arms. "There's still so much about Sel's culture I'd like to learn about. I'll go back once things have cooled down."

"Are you sure you're not too tired?" asked D.S.

"I'll be okay," said Violet, holding her chest.

"Set me down. I can walk," said Nina, hoisted on the shoulders of the girl Devlin loves.

"Uh-uh. Even if you can walk, you need to rest that leg," said Kaity.

"No. I don't want to be a burden."

"You could never be a burden."

"So, here we are. Heaven. Look at all the snow," said Deceivant in a daze.

"Hmm. Opti, pick up one of the bunnies," said Kanasta.

"No! Don't. You can't touch people if they don't want it. That's one of the rules here, remember?" asked D.S.

"Not a problem. I'll just get them to come to me," said Opti, lying on the ground.

"No time," Kanasta leaped into action and caught the snow bunny in his grip. He lifted it up. "It's a girl. That means we are currently in Femina."

"What's Femina?" asked Nina.

"It's where all the good little girls go!" exclaimed Deceivant, making snow angels.

"Why were we sent to Femina? And why this specific area?" asked Kanasta, examining the frost on a nearby tree.

Nina slipped out from the grip of the girl beloved by Devlin. "I doubt we will find the answer to that by standing around."

"We can't do anything. We're all dead," said Deceivant, gripping his head.

Violet approached him and placed her hand on his chest. "You need to pull yourself together. This place being real doesn't go against any of your cherished theories. Science has no stance on the afterlife. The reality of this realm brings many opportunities. Just as I can now experience new religions, you have before you a brand new world with unknown phenomenon to observe and undiscovered universal laws to uncover."

"You're…you're absolutely right. This is akin to the moment when Copernicus discovered a round Earth, when humans first explored the moon, when physicists found evidence of the multiverse, when I first shared a bed with Mika. Lum isn't a denial of the world; it's another layer of the universe. As a scientist, it's my duty to discover its systems and functions. Thank you," said Deceivant, hugging the wise woman tightly.

"Happy to return the favor," said Violet, hugging back.

"We need to find Devlin." Nina pulled Devlin's creation out of the hug. "You saw him last, any clues as to where he disappeared to?"

"None. Absolutely nothing," said Violet, shaken up.

"Everyone, may I have your attention?" Deceivant opened up his coat and set a small sky blue sphere on the ground.

Kaity looked away in tears.

"I think we're safe here." Deceivant tapped the blue orb. "Ada, materialize."

The blue sphere was soon encapsulated by a nude motherly figure. The holographic woman's hair appeared after a short time lag. Ada smiled upon seeing her beloved family.

"Mommy!" cheered D.S., hugging Ada as soon as she fully formed.

"Yes, son, I'm here," she said, holding her darling little boy to her bosom.

"I told D.S. that my darling wifey wasn't really dead, but I decided to keep it a secret from the rest of you. I even lied about it in my journal in case it was taken by an enemy," said Deceivant, opening his coat to show off his black notebook."

"I thought she was really dead," said Kaity softly.

"We were in the midst of a battle, so it wasn't exactly safe for her to come back," said Deceivant.

"Does that mean everyone is alive?" asked Opti, his eyes brimming with hope.

"No. The others are dead. Even Kawai, my little girl," said Deceivant, collapsing into tears.

Ada broke down as well, crying on her big boy's shoulder.

"It's okay, Mom. We still have each other. Everybody goes away eventually," said D.S.

"Where is Devlin?" asked Ada, panic in her eyes.

"He defeated Etah and then he vanished. We don't know where he is," said Deceivant.

Ada embraced her husband. "Then the fighting is over?" she asked with a tearful smile.

"I hope so," said Deceivant, combing his beloved's hair with a trembling hand.

"Why did you send her projection to fight Etah? I thought she was really dead," said Kaity with watery eyes.

"I had Ada's projection enter Etah's battlefield, expecting her to die. Staging her death was our best chance of getting an ally who could combat Etah," said Deceivant, smiling at the true Nina.

"You…what?" asked Nina, pausing the sharpening of her kunai.

"I wouldn't put in a program without a backup plan. Welcome back," said Deceivant, offering his hand to the shy warrior.

"You're the reason she exists. Don't expect any gratitude from me," said Nina, turning away.

"Fair enough," said Deceivant, lowering his hand.

"So then, you're a different Nina? I thought something was off." Kaity leaped up. "There are two Ninas!"

"Yay, more friends!" cheered Opti. "Napkin, say hi."

The kitten looked up at the scary lady and then covered his face.

"He's a little shy," said Opti, petting the kitty.

BoneSaw turned to the deadly ninja and nodded.

Nina nodded back.

"Son, I'd like to introduce you to your niece," said Ada.

"I'm confused. Are there two Ninas?" asked D.S.

"Two minds in a single body, not unlike Exp 11," said Deceivant, pointing to Opti.

"It's nice to meet you! Let's see, the other Nina is Sexy Nina. That makes you Cool Nina!" exclaimed D.S., sitting in his mom's lap.

"Selfish and Selfless are more accurate, but I suppose that works," said Deceivant.

"Nina is sufficient. The other one is only a program," she said, glaring at Devlin's father.

"Programs are real in their own way," said Ada, looking down.

"You're right. She's more of a virus," said Nina with a grimace.

"Welcome to the family, Nina," said Ada, beaming at her granddaughter.

"Think of me as a warrior devoted to Devlin, not as a member of the family. I will fight to protect Devlin's creations and loved ones," said Nina, raising her katana.

"It all makes sense now. I noticed a considerable difference in both style and skill. Welcome to the team," said Kanasta, offering her his hand.

"It's an honor to be welcomed by Devlin's brother. That said. I haven't forgotten how you tried to kill him," said Nina.

"Do not speak ill of my exalted uncle," said Riufen.

"Nina dear, that was all a dreadful misunderstanding," said Ada.

"What's misunderstood is your duty as a parent. You abandoned him," said the ninja girl with a glare.

"I understand. When Sexy Nina was in control, you were asleep, right? You weren't able to see what she saw or hear what she heard," said Kaity.

"I was only aware in the moments where she was being selfless. Only when she saw Ada's life in danger and when that girl was injured was I aware of what she was experiencing." Nina turned to Devlin's father. "Every other moment I was trapped, alone, and only partially conscious."

"So then you have no idea what's been going on?" asked Deceivant.

"Devlin killed his mother. The fake Nina died, went to Lum—which is where we are now—and then a Sel god, called Etah, killed Ada's projection. Once Nina stepped up to face him, I took control. Devlin tasked me with keeping all of you safe. That's what I'll do. I don't need to know anything else," said Nina.

"You should know that Devlin's family didn't betray him. It was all a set up by Etah. He wanted to isolate Devlin so he could manipulate him," said Violet.

"I don't trust your words," said Nina, sheathing her katana.

"It's true," said Kaity.

"I'm Exp 03. The only creations of his I was in contact with were NoOne and Karson. The Exps made by Deceivant that I know are Ada, Kawai, Atatasuki, and Bob. I don't trust Ada. And I'm assuming the others are dead."

Kaity turned away.

"The point is: I don't trust any of you. Until I hear from Devlin's lips that his family didn't sell him out, I won't believe it. I'm not saying you are lying. The only one who is a liar is her," said Nina, pointing a shuriken at Violet.

"Take that back! Violet is the mostest honest person ever!" yelled D.S.

"Enough! We shouldn't be fighting. Nina lost the only people she trusted. If she doesn't trust us, that's fine," said Kaity, taking in a deep breath.

"Glad you understand," said Nina.

"Everyone…I think we should…honor the dead. We should do a tribute to honor those who have died. Exp 8 would have," said Ada, tearing up.

Deceivant put his arm around his wifey and kissed her on the forehead. "If that's what you want, then we'll do just that."

"I agree. They all deserve a proper sendoff," said Violet, folding her hands.

"We can honor them by locating Devlin," said Nina, scratching her knuckles.

"I agree with Violet," said Opti, folding his hands.

"Yeah, me too," said D.S. with a sniffle.

"I concur," said Kanasta.

Kaity leaned into her papa and wiped her eyes.

"But only if you're up to it," said Kanasta, patting his little girl's back.

Kaity's head popped up, her eyes teary and her smile wide. "I'd love to."

"Good. Let's all...uh..." said Deceivant.

"Gather around in a circle," said Ada, grabbing her husband's hand.

Deceivant wrapped his fingers with Kaity's and then turned to his wifey. "I think it would be best if you would lead us, my darling."

"Alright. First of all, I would like to apologize on behalf of all of those we...um, killed...in order to attain victory. I'm sure you had your own reasons for fighting, and I wish it didn't turn out that way. For all the dead demons and the Sinful Sorority...we're very sorry," said Ada with a teary smile.

"Is she serious?" asked Nina with a confused look.

"We were defending ourselves," said Kaity.

"Indeed, truly we have erred," said Kanasta.

"That's my wifey," said Deceivant, gazing at her with passion.

"I'll take it from here. We come together now to honor our allies who are no longer with us." Kaity wiped away her tears. "Sefiwah..." Kaity froze up.

"She will be sorely missed," said Kanasta, lowering his head.

Kaity nodded, her tears dropping. "She means everything to me! She's the reason I've survived so long. She's the reason I'm here right now."

"She was a remarkable killer and a wise elder sister to the Viper Squad. Her influence will never fade away," said Kanasta.

"When I was apprehensive, she would steady my hands. If I needed a lover, she would make love to me. And when I needed to feel a mother's warmth, she would hold me like a child. I love her so much. I loved her more than anyone. I still do. I'll always love her. And now I've lost her twice." Kaity broke down into tears.

Napkin hopped on Kaity's shoulder and nestled her cheek.

"Sefiwah was so gentle and compassionate. I'm truly grateful we met," said Ada.

"Uh-huh. I never felt alone as long as I was in her arms. I miss her so much," said Kaity, wiping away her tears with one hand and petting Napkin with the other.

"She'll always watch over you. I know she will," said Ada.

"You loved her and she loved you. You're both so fortunate," said Nina, her gaze dropping.

"Blessings to her spirit," said Violet softly.

BoneSaw raised a saw in salute.

"Ego joined the Viper Squad soon after Tempo and I formed it. Even when things got tricky, he stayed level-headed and focused. And he found a safe way out of any situation, no matter how dangerous. Without his assistance, I wouldn't be alive today. He loved music, sports, and vehicles just as much I love money, games, and my family. His outgoing positive attitude kept the family together. Most importantly, he emotionally supported Tempo. They were like brothers. They both died fighting. I only hope my death can be as purposeful," said Kanasta.

"So if he joined when you and Tempo made the group, was Ego like a little kid when he signed up?" asked D.S.

"Ego is only a year younger than Tempo. In addition to being very fit and naturally youthful, Ego underwent corrective surgery to keep his image," said Kanasta.

"I remember when we would sit together and listen to his favorite songs. He was always able to break out of any stressful situation just by listening to music. He helped me relax. He was always fun and friendly," said Kaity.

"Sounds like a worthwhile person," said Nina softly.

"I wish I had gotten to know him better," said Ada.

"Me too," said D.S., his bottom lip pushed out.

Kaity perked up. "Ego was my big brother. He made me laugh and cheered me up when I was sad. He was someone you could always count on. We'll never be able to replace him," she said, failing to hold back her tears.

BoneSaw rubbed against his sad comrade.

Kaity picked up her little companion and held it close.

"What about Tempo, is he dead too?" asked Nina.

"Yeah. We already sent him off. He wouldn't really want to be part of a tribute anyway," said Kaity with a teary smile.

"Tempo was a great warrior and had a warrior's death. His imprint on the Viper Squad will never be forgotten," said Kanasta with a salute.

"Pharma was my nephew, even though he treated me like a cousin. He was really smart. Oh and he was a nice guy too! I don't know if he realized it, but he was a really good person," said D.S.

"I didn't know you were so close," said Deceivant.

"We bonded in Lum. Got along great. He's a nice guy. He likes to share and he's cool and he believes in equality," said D.S.

"He stood by Devlin's side till the very end. He was more dependable than Karson. Can't say I expected it to turn out like that," said Deceivant with a half-smile.

"He found contentment through intoxication. Though I do not encourage his method, he was still a powerful spiritualist," said Violet.

"I once thought he was a coward, but he chose to fight against Karson despite him knowing it would lead to his death. He died honorably," said Riufen.

BoneSaw did various gestures to reenact Pharma's battle and ended with a salute.

"That's right. You were there when he died. He must have fought bravely," said Riufen.

"Speaking of Karson. Is he dead?" asked Kaity softly.

BoneSaw nodded.

"Karson joined Etah out of cowardice. Though once an honorable warrior, he fell and is not worth remembering," said Riufen, his eyes watering up.

Kaity stepped up. "At one point he was our comrade. And many of us were once enemies of the Freedom Forcers, myself included. I think he deserves a tribute just like the others."

"Traitors don't deserve sympathy," said Nina with a dark glare.

"He was a friend," said Ada, her voice cracking.

Deceivant squeezed her hand and looked up at her with a smile.

Ada smiled back. "Karson was always so brave, and he refused to attack the weak point of his enemies. Despite being a soldier, he was friendly and loving."

"Even when death was certain, he entered the battlefield. I was fortunate to have fought him," said Kanasta.

"He understood honor. In that respect he surpassed me. But in the end, he chose to side with Devlin-sama's enemies. I cannot forgive him. That said…I won't forget his chivalry," said Riufen.

"I hope he is at peace now," said Violet.

"I'm not sure if I mentioned this, but Bob is dead," said Riufen.

"What? You said you beat him, not killed him. Are you sure he's dead?" asked Deceivant.

"I assumed you defeated him, but are you sure killing him is even possible?" asked Kanasta.

"His Jiva minions vanished once he was torn to pieces. Whatever force kept him alive must have died out," said Riufen.

"Very well, I'll have to make some corrections to my journal," said Deceivant.

"I didn't sense his soul once you told us he was beaten. Bob truly has moved on," said Violet.

"Um, so Bob is next then, right? He was…always so mean. And he was sarcastic too. He was a big jerk! Wait, my bad. Um, he was…playful?" said D.S., sucking on his thumb.

"Bob was a traitor to all. Though it pains me to say, he was also my greatest teacher. Devlin-sama was confident in my abilities, but Bob knew I could do so much more. He believed in me like no one else. And his dishonorable way of living served to strengthen my resolve to live honorably. He was my greatest enemy, yet he helped me more than anyone," said Riufen in tears.

"When Bob was welcomed to Devlin's lab, I felt uneasy. If he so easily betrayed Devlin's father, then why should he be trusted? But it was more than that...his energy was unsettling. Bob kept me on my toes at all times. I'm not surprised he betrayed Devlin. May he never return," said Nina, her hands clasped in prayer.

The group fell silent.

Deceivant cleared his throat and steadied himself. "Kawai was my darling little girl. You were too young, far too young," said Deceivant before breaking down.

Ada tried to smile at her husband through her own tears. "You always brightened up the mood! Exp 8 loved you dearly. He loved you more than anyone. Even if neither of you noticed it, it's still true."

"She gave everything her all. And she was a loving sister. Why did she have to go away?" asked Deceivant, shaking in misery.

Ada held her husband in a gentle embrace.

The married couple cried in each other's arms.

Kaity wiped away the tears on her cheeks. "Kawai didn't like me at first. She said I was copying her style or something. But I think she realized just how unique she was. Even in tough times she stayed focused on her goal. She was a sweet little sister and an admirable fighter."

"Kawai brought Devlin much joy before he created me. I am grateful to her," said Nina with a nod.

"She was mean sometimes, but I'm sure she had a good reason. I never really tried to get to know her. We lived together for so long and I didn't ever try. I'm a bad person," said D.S., crying against his arm.

"Kawai was focused on her one true love. She didn't try to make friends because she felt it would weaken her resolve. If only she knew just how strong she was, how beautiful she was," said Ada, looking up at the clouds.

"She defeated me and Kanasta. That little warrior had a resolve only rivaled by that of her cherished brother. Which brings us to the next fallen warrior." Riufen lifted up his slanted sword. "Atatasuki could only fight when he was filled with passion. His fists, alight with his own energy, had an inner power that I have yet to achieve. He was supportive of his family and was able to make allies by his genuine nature. I have deep respect for him. And I will carry his sword with pride."

"He was so brave," said Kaity.

"A bit hot-headed and jumped into battles beyond his abilities, but I suppose that was part of his charm," said Kanasta.

"He fulfilled his purpose as both a warrior and a friend," said Nina.

"I miss him," cried D.S.

Ada embraced her son. "We all do, sweetie."

"He was a living miracle. I may have helped him discover his god, but he helped me discover my strength," said Violet, her hand radiating with energy.

"Atatasuki was inspirational! And he was the funniest Exp ever! I'm sure he'll stay by his sister no matter where they are," said Ada with a big smile.

"He was really funny. And super cool!" cheered D.S.

"Exp 6 was my greatest blunder. He didn't operate properly and was poorly built. But that didn't matter one bit. Despite all my errors, he turned out just fine. He transcended his glitches and used them in combat. Truly a remarkable creation," said Deceivant with a smile.

"From what you're saying, it seems he grew a lot. You may have created him, but Devlin gave him a purpose. Devlin truly is a benevolent creator," said Nina, looking up at the clouds.

Deceivant cleared his throat. "Speaking of benevolence and inspiration, Anthrax was quite the little genius. He was an expert in his field. I respect him greatly. No. It's more than that. He made a great effort to keep his compassion despite his intellectual nature. He struggled to be present with his patients for their sake," said Deceivant.

"Anthrax always wanted to help people. He had his pride as a doctor, but the patient always came first," said Ada.

"That's for sure. When he was unable to heal people in Lum, he decided he wanted to be an angel. He was already a little angel though, metaphorically speaking, of course," said Deceivant with a blush.

"He was really nice and super smart! He was more mature than a lot of adults. Oh and he gave me candy," said D.S. with a toothy grin.

"He was a cute, caring bundle of love," said Kaity.

"He's with Matteria now. Even in death the two are one," said Ada, beaming up at the clouds.

"Together forever!" cheered D.S.

Deceivant smiled at his creation. "Once Anthrax was lost, Matteria surrendered his life so that his little lover wouldn't be lonely."

"What a fool. Dying won't solve anything. He should have lived on as his lover would have wanted," said Nina.

"You don't know the circumstances! What he did…it was beautiful," said Kaity, wiping her eyes.

"It wasn't just Anthrax. Matteria is beloved by so many people," said Deceivant.

"He supported Devlin in my absence. I can never repay that debt," said Kanasta.

"Not even turning her into a boy could change how cute and playful Matteria was. He took my forced modifications and built a unique identity. Matteria was a lot of things, but above all I saw him as a beacon of social justice," said Deceivant.

"Matteria taught me about gender norms and stuff. He made me feel more normal," said D.S.

"He was a crowd pleaser who put his fans first. No wonder him and Anthrax got along," said Opti.

"His goal in life was to unite people of all walks of life together."

"By people, you mean humans, right?" asked Nina.

"No. He tried to break all boundaries, species included. He brought Exps into a positive light. And every product he promoted was free of animal testing. He lived an admirable life," said Deceivant.

"Nothing can stop their love. Matteria and Anthrax will be together forever," said Ada in tears.

"Were they both created by Devlin?" asked Nina.

"Yes. It was after I, um, modified you that they were created. Matteria was always loyal and loving to Devlin. Had I not changed his sex, it seems likely that they would have hooked up," said Deceivant.

"They stood by Devlin's side when I was unable to. And they died before I even knew they had lived. Maybe I shouldn't be here during the ceremony," said Nina, turning away.

"You're part of the team," said Opti.

Napkin hissed at Nina.

"Hey now, she's our friend. Please don't be mean," said Kaity, petting the kitty behind the ears.

Deceivant turned to Nina. "You're one of our best fighters. Besides, you know the final member whose life was taken."

"I do?" asked Nina.

"NoOne," said Opti softly.

"Yeah, I know him," said Nina.

"Well then, why don't you start?" asked Kaity.

"What's there to say? He was lonely and scared," said Nina, turning away.

"He was also incredibly powerful! When the Freedom Forcers met him, he almost beat all of them! What he lacked in confidence, he made up for in humbleness!" exclaimed Ada.

"NoOne was always loyal to Devlin. He was so strong but never thought much of himself," said Kaity.

"Indeed. If he had been aware of his own strength, he would surely have been a force to reckon with," said Kanasta.

"Yeah and he'd be here...with us," said D.S.

"I hope you're happy, NoOne. I hope you've found peace," said Ada.

"I uh...I didn't know him very well. I keep to myself mostly. He is, uh, was very powerful though. And his loyalty, I admire it greatly," said Nina with an awkward bow.

"He found courage and died a hero. Couldn't have gone out a better way," said Deceivant.

"NoOne and I really connected in Lum. He was a friend to sheep and he was my friend too. Even though he was scared, he took a stand to protect his friends. And he had a dream too. There was a girl who looked at him with love and he...he just wanted to see her one more time. I'm going to find her! And I'm going to tell her about his dream!" exclaimed Opti.

"I'll help you!" cheered Ada.

"Me too," said D.S., pushing out his fist.

"Do you know what she looks like? Or when he saw her?" asked Deceivant.

"Not a clue! But I'm going to find her!" cheered Opti.

"Do what you want. But first, we must find Devlin," said Nina.

"Shouldn't you be more concerned about yourselves?"

The team turned around.

Demonica was standing before them, waving.

Riufen and Kanasta rushed in.

Napkin ran off before being captured by Opti.

"Calm down. I'm not here to play with you." Demonica snapped her fingers.

The gimp that had brought the team to Lum appeared out of thin air.

"I believe you are familiar with this one," said Demonica.

"You sent us here," said Deceivant, glaring at the demon queen.

"Yes, but there's no need to thank me. And you can continue your ceremony. I won't interrupt. Promise," said Demonica.

"We already finished," said Kanasta, signaling his protégé to move to cover.

"No. We aren't. Nina's right. I have been lying. Devlin didn't vanish. He was covered in black energy. There was nothing I could do. Nothing any of us could do. But, I couldn't let us lose hope. Not in the middle of a war. Devlin is dead," said Violet, her voice like a whisper.

Nina fell over and covered her face.

Ada cried in her husband's arms.

"Devi-kun was lost, scared, and confused. And a lot of people died because of him. But he always cared about his children. And he loved me so much—more than I thought you could love someone—I will never forget him," said Kaity.

"Little brother beat Etah. He can't be dead," said D.S.

"Devlin gave me life and a purpose. I will live on and spread the love he placed in me," said Opti.

"Stop it! My brother is not dead!" yelled Kanasta, slamming his fist into a tree.

The tree fell over.

"There's one last thing. Remember how Exp 8 arrived in Absence and he was missing an arm. The Hero we saw on the battlefield only fought with one arm. The rest of him was completely covered," said Demonica.

"You're trying to break our morale!" yelled Kanasta, rushing at the demonic woman.

"She's absolutely right. It's more likely that the arm was grafted onto a demon. Once Exp 8 was engulfed is Etah's energy, nothing remained. You were all there! You all saw it," said Deceivant, looking over his allies. "Both of the leaders of the Freedom Forcers are no more."

"But he's a good guy. Good guys aren't supposed to die!" yelled D.S.

"I didn't sense his presence anywhere after the attack," said Violet, lowering her head.

"We aren't the Freedom Forcers anymore. Not without him. We're nothing," said Opti in tears.

"BoneSaw, stop the clock. Erase the data. Devlin…our client is dead. We will not be receiving payment. The job is cancelled," said Kanasta in tears.

BoneSaw nodded.

"Why did you come here? Any other reason than breaking our spirits?" asked Riufen.

"Would you rather be wasting your time hoping for him to return?" asked Demonica, looking to the snow-covered ground.

"You make a good point. You're here to capture us, aren't you? That's the mission your leader gave you?" asked Deceivant, raising his shotgun.

"Etah is defeated. Besides, my loyalty lies with Devlin above all else."

"Who were you taking orders from then?" asked Deceivant.

"If Etah was defeated, I was ordered to capture all of you. But I had a change of heart and have decided to protect you instead," said Demonica.

"Etah is still alive, isn't he?" asked Deceivant.

"Even if he is, he can't see what I'm doing in Lum. For all he knows, I'm still searching for you," said Demonica.

"Thank you for giving us an escape from Sel, and thank you too," said Violet, waving to the gimp.

"Oh yeah, forgot introductions. Everyone, this is my sex slave." Demonica gestured to the person in a full body black gimp suit. A trail of saliva came out from the ball gag. Other than grunts, it made no noise.

"It's a blessing to meet you," said Violet with a bow.

"Does it have a name?" asked D.S. with a tilt of the head.

"Do you waste your time naming the dirt beneath your feet?" asked Demonica.

"Then that outfit. It's not just for show. You really are a dominatrix?" asked Kaity, looking up at the mask around Demonica's eyes.

"That's right."

The gimp looked up at its mistress through the blindfold.

"What do you want? A treat? You were late," said Demonica, stabbing her nails into its shoulders.

Another trail of drool came out as the gimp gasped in pleasure.

"Don't be so mean. You did us a true service," said Violet, patting the gimp on the head.

"I was rewarding him. Hey, hands off!" yelled Demonica, grabbing the zealot's arm.

"I meant no offense," said Violet with a bow.

"This is my possession. See?" Demonica tore off the top portion of the gimp's mask and pointed to a tattoo on the gimps forehead that read: *Property of Demonica*. "Nobody touches unless I give the okay."

"What do we do now?" asked D.S., tugging on his dad's lab coat.

"There is no 'we' anymore. I'm going to search for NoOne's beloved," said Opti, turning away.

Napkin hopped out of his arms and ran up to the cat-girl.

"Of course I'll take care of you," said Kaity, lifting the kitten into her arms.

"I have a mission to complete. We may not be Freedom Forcers, but we are still the Viper Squad," said Kanasta, grabbing his apprentice's hand.

Kaity and BoneSaw nodded.

"Nina, I saw your skill in battle. Would you like to join the Viper Squad?" asked Kanasta.

Nina swiftly wiped away the tears beneath her eyes. "Devlin left me with a mission. I will stay and protect his parents until I die."

"I shall do the same," said Riufen.

"Me too," said D.S.

"I owe Devlin my life," said Violet.

Ada grabbed her husband's hands. "I think we should move on."

"What?" asked Deceivant.

"We died. We're in Lum. We should stay together and move on together," said Ada, white tears still leaking out.

"If that is what you wish, I will not stop you. I'll keep you protected until you are ready," said Nina.

"What are you and Gimpy going to do, demon lady?" asked D.S.

Demonica liquidated into a puddle and seeped into the snow.

The gimp vanished into thin air.

Nina drew her katana and stood in front of Devlin's parents.

Angels emerged from behind the trees and beneath the snow.

"What do you want?" asked Nina, searching for an exit.

The ground troops parted and Etaf emerged. She was clad in pearl white misty armor and had a bright white hilt at her side. Her helmet had been left behind, letting her silver hair flow freely. White ritual paint colored her otherwise dark and creamy cheeks. "You've returned from Sel."

"I don't know who you are," said Nina.

Deceivant raised his hand. "Calm down. We know her. Yes, our forces took down Etah. We were victorious in our mission. In return for our assistance, I ask that my wife, myself, and the others who want to leave, are all safely transported back to Earth. I don't think that's too much to ask considering the threat Etah posed."

"He is more of a threat than we had imagined," said Etaf softly, barely opening her lightly tattooed lips.

"We lost a lot of friends. You have to take us home," said D.S.

Etaf examined the Exps and assassins. "How did you get back?" she asked, her inquisitive tone both detached and firm.

Violet took a step forward. "We were teleported by—"

"One of the Absence gods provided us a means back to Absence and from there we were brought here," said Deceivant.

"Which one?" asked Etaf, staring into the man's eyes for the slightest hint of deception.

"Crystal!" exclaimed Ada.

"Hmm. Yes. I suppose that would work." Etaf paced around them.

"It worked out splendidly. Now, I'm aware that Exps are a bit of a concern here. I think sending us all back to Earth would be the best option for us and Lum," said Deceivant.

Etaf stopped and pooled her aura into her hands. The aura solidified into a sword that was wide near the hilt but thinned out all the way down to its gleaming tip. "You're rather arrogant if you think you can lie to a god." She stabbed the Destiny Sword into the red snow.

Demonica reformed, holding her chest in pain. "What kind of sword is that?"

The angels jumped in shock and then quickly aimed at the Goddess of Death.

"She brought you here," said Etaf, her blade to the dark goddess' throat.

"Through what means? She is a Sel god through and through," said Deceivant.

"That's something I don't know. But you're going to tell me," said Etaf, signaling her troops to close in.

"Stop! It was Gimpy! It brought us here! We aren't Demonica's friends, but she did help us," said D.S.

"Demonica? You're on a first-name basis with a Sel goddess?" asked Etaf.

"That is the name she told us. As for the gimp, it had a powerful spiritual presence, akin to a god, goddess, or deity," said Violet.

"When did Sel's forces capture a Lum god?" asked Etaf, biting her lip.

"I dunno," said D.S. with a shrug. "But we told you, so you don't need to hurt us."

"Who's Gimpy?" asked Etaf.

"It was completely clad in black latex. We weren't even able to decipher its sex," said Deceivant.

"Perhaps she knows," said Etaf, drawing blood with her sword.

"As if I'd tell you anything." Demonica smirked.

The blood shot out from her wound and hit the goddess' armor.

Etaf countered a blood assault with her sword. "They are all guilty of conspiring with Sel. Capture them all! Lum will decide their punishment."

The aerial angels fired shots that intersected, culminating in a blinding burst of white energy.

Deceivant fired into the air, dispersing some of the angels.

Riufen tore out his eyes and grew new ones. Now able to see, he held back the group of bear angels on approach.

Kanasta had night vision goggles and was firing at the feet of the group of wolf angels.

Kaity was already shooting the eagle angels out of the air.

Demonica was sliced in two by the Destiny Sword. "Damn angels! **Blood Spike**"

Her blood jutted out and killed two approaching angels from behind.

"Get us out of here!" yelled Deceivant, firing wherever he heard footsteps.

"I thought she was our friend," said D.S., waving his scissors around blindly.

"I can get you out of here," said Demonica.

"The last time you said that you abandoned the team," said Nina, deflecting arrows with her eyes closed.

"You don't trust me?" asked Demonica, blocking the Destiny Sword with the Death Scythe.

"You want something in return, don't you?" asked Kanasta.

"All I ask is you don't forget my act of kindness," said Demonica, snapping her fingers.

"Great! Yeah, get us out of…here." Deceivant looked around.

Trees, birds, sunlight. They were back in the forest of Lum.

"You were saying," said Demonica with a smile.

Deceivant looked at Demonica curiously. "Your slave can travel through realms. That's rather handy, if unscientific," he said with slanted eyes.

"Why didn't you ask your friend to help us get out of Absence?" asked Kanasta.

"It's a fuck-doll not a friend."

"I'm not listening! La-la-la!" yelled D.S.

"And you can't exit Absence if your soul is bound to it. You need permission from the Absence gods. No exceptions. Period," said Demonica.

"Yeah, but we weren't really bound, remember?" asked Opti.

"I didn't know that at the time. You're free now, so what does it matter anyway?" asked Demonica, choking her gimp by yanking on the leash.

"Then that must be how you made it to Earth back when Devlin summoned you," said Kanasta.

"That's right," said Demonica.

"Then you can bring us to Earth, right now." said Deceivant with a hopeful smile.

"Teleporting the dead to the realm of the living is impossible. I should get moving." Demonica kicked the gimp to the ground. "Get me out of here!"

The gimp nodded and then vanished along with the demon goddess.

"As expected. She still has plans for us," said Kanasta.

"Well everyone, I suppose this is where we part ways," said Opti.

"Wait up! You're my little nephew. Nina is sworn to protect you too. Why not come with us?" asked D.S.

"He's right. We can still look for NoOne's beloved," said Deceivant.

Kanasta stepped up. "It's safer to travel with a group. We will break apart when the target is in sight. With the angels after us, we need to find a safe zone."

"Yes!" cheered Violet.

"What happened?" asked D.S.

Violet raised her bracelet. "We still have one place to call home."

"Good thinking. The rebel base shouldn't be too far from here," said Deceivant.

"Hey guys, since we're together, can I make up a team name?" asked D.S.

"Yes. And when the Viper Squad leaves, it will only be temporary. We will return to the group once the job is completed," said Kanasta.

"Okay. Then from now on we're the Remnants of Freedom!" exclaimed D.S., raising his arm.

"Is that supposed to cheer us up?" asked Kaity, still wiping her eyes.

Deceivant pulled his wifey in. "It's a fitting name. Just don't expect us to do anything heroic."

"Agreed. We are surviving. That's all. Which way is the base?" asked Nina.

Violet closed her eyes and held out her hand. "It's very close. Follow me."

Chapter 97: Finding Refuge

"And you're sure we will be welcomed?" asked Nina.

"That's what they said. Welcoming in guests is one of their religious duties," said Deceivant.

"We've arrived," said Violet, stepping out from behind a pine tree overlooking the rebel base. "It's heavenly!"

The temple was shiny and white like the Heavens. Grass freely grew around the perimeter of the building, and flowers sprouted on the lower walls of the structure. A winding passageway coiled around the sacred building, allowing attendees to avoid unnecessary violence by treading on the plant life. At each corner of the pathway were mini shrines, created for the sake of paying respects to great sages and deities. Four pillars came out from the top of the shrines. The tallest and most sacred of the shikharas erected out from the center of the structure. This spire served as a direct medium between the garbha griha and the gods above. It symbolized the infinite power of creation. The structure was formed with aged capstone, though historically dating it based on that would be impossible without knowing Lum's sacred architectural history. The roof of the building had several shalas built along it.

"Last one there is a slowpoke!" hollered D.S. as he ran off.

"I accept your challenge," said Kanasta in hot pursuit.

"Heehee, better hurry up," said Kaity, passing them up on all fours.

"Youth is such a wonder," said Deceivant, holding his wife's hand while looking out at the kids.

"This is it. Once we're inside we'll be safe. We'll only leave when we're ready to move on," said Ada.

"Proceed ahead of me. I'll watch your back," said Nina, ready to jump into action should something emerge from the pine forest.

"First!" cheered Kaity, stopping at the front door.

Four and a half seconds later Kanasta arrived. "Your speed is as impressive as ever."

"Aw, man. I lost," said D.S. with a pouty face, arriving last.

"Be careful who you challenge. You may get into trouble with that competitive spirit," said Kanasta with a subtle smile.

Violet was the last to arrive, taking each step with patience and reverence.

Kaity knocked three times and the door opened.

"And who might you be?" asked a young man with dark skin and a turban.

"I'm Kaity! Is your leader around?" she asked, peeking inside.

"Yeah! He's like really old!" exclaimed D.S.

"He is inside. But I'm afraid I must ask you to leave. In these troubled times we cannot allow visitors," said the young man.

"All of us were formally invited," said Kaity, raising her bracelet and signaling her allies to do the same.

"I will go speak with him. You should be careful. It isn't safe for a girl to roam around in Masculino."

"She can handle herself," said Kanasta, patting his apprentice's head.

The young man went inside and closed the door.

"Nina, can I use some of that water?" asked Violet, eyeing the bottle attached to the warrior's waist.

"Sorry. I need it."

"But it is customary to bathe before entering a gurudwar. We should all take a bath."

"I agree! Let's take a bath together!" cheered Kaity, hopping onto Nina.

"Get off."

Kaity slid off.

"Maybe the other Nina was fine with you jumping on her, but I'm not. I hardly know you."

"You're right. I'm sorry." Kaity's metal ears drooped.

"You can't reprimand her for being herself. You can hop on my back if you want," said Deceivant, crouching down to the adorable cat-girl.

Kaity looked away.

The door opened and a muscular man with thick eyebrows and an untrimmed beard stepped out. He was dressed in blue and had a turban around his head.

"It's the old guy," said D.S.

"Greetings, Rambir," said Deceivant.

"You have returned, my friends. Ah, I see some new faces."

Rambir's wide smile gradually dropped once he saw the kirpan in the samurai's belt.

"We've been through a lot. May we stay here for a while?" asked Deceivant.

"Yes, of course! This is the Refuge of the People. It is as much your home as it is mine. My name is Rambir and I shall do all I can to make your stay pleasant. Though, to be courteous, when inside the temple call me Singh," he said with a big smile and a wise, friendly voice.

"I'm Nina. We thank you for your hospitality," she said with a firm bow.

"My name is Riufen, and your kindness will never be forgotten, Singh-san," he said, bowing down.

"This is Napkin." Opti picked up the kitty's paw and waved. "And I'm Opti for optimism."

"Kanasta. The one behind the bushes there is BoneSaw," he said pointing.

"Kaity Rin Rainbow Viper. But you can call me Kaity!"

"I'm Ada. Thank you for taking care of our forgetful friend."

"My name is Violet, and it is a blessing to meet you. There aren't any gurudwars where I live, but I've seen many in my travels."

"It's a pleasure to meet all of you. Come in, friends. Dinner will be served shortly. Oh, and this is for you," said Rambir, offering the sky-clad woman some clothes.

"Oh. Thank you very much," said Ada, getting dressed with her husband's help.

"Your sword is magnificent," said Riufen, staring at the slanted, jewel-encrusted blade.

"When I arrived in Lum, I was naked. I had nothing except this kirpan and my karas. They are truly a part of my identity," said Rambir.

"Um, is there a bath nearby? We're all rather sweaty and dirty. We wouldn't want to disrespect you or the temple," said Violet.

"Ah, I heard about you from your friend. It is a special privilege to meet you," said Rambir, lowering his head.

"I, oh, it's a divine gift to meet you as well," said Violet with a blush.

"It's not a problem for us to come in, even though we are female, is it?" asked Ada, looking over her feminine friends.

"It is only a crime for a woman to cross into Masculino. Once there, there aren't additional repercussions for entering any buildings. Now, why don't I escort you all to the communal bath? Once you're all cleaned up, I'll show you around the rest of the temple. Come inside." Rambir opened the door and led them through the communal hall. "No need to worry. These are my friends."

"Nina is injured. Can you show me where the infirmary is?" asked Kaity.

"I'm fine. Honestly, I think a nice warm bath is the best medicine for me at the moment," said Nina, watching for any suspicious movement.

"Can I scrub your back?" asked Kaity, waving her hips side to side.

"I'm fully capable of tending to myself," said Nina.

"Oh, okay."

Rambir led them down an arched hallway and into the bathhouse.

There were two baths: one in the middle, cut out in the shape of a sword and filled with hot water, and one on the outside, with a circular shape and cold water. Together the baths made the symbol for the Sikh religion. Everyone in the baths turned when the strange visitors arrived.

"Oh yeah, it's boys only. No cute little girls in Masculino," said Deceivant with a sigh.

Some of the kids got out of the bath.

"Whoa! Look at the statue! It moves!" cheered a boy, beaming at Riufen.

"That sword looks really sharp," said another boy, reaching for the ninja lady's katana.

"It's sharp enough to cleave a man in two. Don't touch," said Nina.

The kid backed away.

"Oh, don't mind her. She's just shy. You shouldn't try to grab someone else's things, right?" asked Deceivant.

"I just wanted to see it," said the kid with a look of disappointment.

"You can look at my sword," said Riufen, removing his spine and flattening its tip.

"Whoa!" "How are you not dead?" "What are you?" "So cool!" exclaimed various kids.

"Why are the young men staring at me?" asked Ada, covering her chest.

"It's likely been a lifetime since they've seen a woman," said Rambir.

"Wow, your skin is so beautiful," said a young man, stepping up to the blue-skinned woman.

"Why, thank you," said Violet with a smile.

"We have important things to discuss, and I can't bathe with all these people staring at me. Can you ask them to leave?" asked Nina.

"I suppose it will take some getting used to. Everyone, our guests would like to be alone. Please leave the bathhouse," said Rambir.

The humans reluctantly got out of the bath, never looking away from the newcomers.

"Thanks," said Nina.

"Enjoy," said Rambir before leaving.

"Come on in, everyone!" exclaimed Opti with a wave, already in the steamy bath.

"Yes, we have a lot to figure out," said Deceivant, helping his darling wifey undress.

"Kaity, keep your suit on," said Kanasta sternly.

"C'mon. The sweat is sticking to me," said Kaity with a frown.

"Son, Kaity has been through a lot. We all have. It would be best for all of us if she bathes naked," said Deceivant with a firm tone.

"Your presence here is but one reason she should stay in her suit," said Kanasta, entering with his suitcase placed on the side of the bath.

"Stay here, Napkin. You and BoneSaw can guard the area," said Kaity.

BoneSaw saluted and stood by the side of the closed door, ready to ambush anyone who entered.

"I'm going in the cool pool. Sel was waaaay too hot," said D.S. before jumping in the outer bath.

"I'll join you," said Violet, dropping her clothes before stepping in the bath.

"A warrior must harness their inner heat," said Riufen, setting his armor in a neat pile before entering the warm water.

"Let's cool off first," said Deceivant, holding his beloved's hand as she stepped in. He set his glasses down next to his clothes and plopped in.

"What's wrong, Nina? Having trouble deciding what bath to use?" asked Kaity.

Nina turned away. "I'm used to bathing alone. Either alone…or with Devlin," she said, smiling through the cloth.

"The other Nina liked to bath alone too. It was one of the few things I didn't like about her," said Kaity with a frown.

"Oh. I suppose I'll go in the cold bath, then," said Nina, stopping her strip when she noticed Devlin's crush ogling her.

"This is good enough." Nina leaped in, still wearing her underwear.

She landed in front of Deceivant and stared into his eyes.

Kaity popped out from behind her.

"Is there something on my face?" asked Deceivant, washing his cheeks.

"Devlin's eyes," said Nina, staring at the beautiful golden irises.

"If anything, Devlin has my eyes," said Deceivant.

"Can I have them?" asked Nina, her hands stretching out.

Deceivant pulled back. "No. They're mine."

The ninja pulled back her hands. "My apologies."

"You're so funny, Nina," said Kaity, peeking over her crush's shoulder.

Nina covered her chest. "Do you hate me?"

"What? Why would I hate you?"

"Either you hate me for taking away your beloved Nina or you're lying to yourself by thinking I'm the same as her."

"That's enough of that," said Deceivant, stepping in between them.

"Not a word out of you. Do you have any idea how much I want to make this bath run red with your blood?" asked Nina in a cold, detached tone.

Opti's eyes darkened and became red. The white portion of his mask became black. His skin became black as his wings molted and blackened. The friendly pacifist's white hair spiked up as it darkened. Sharp fingernails rose out from the once gentle hands. The smile on the mask shifted into a jagged frown. "Did someone say blood?" asked Pesi, sticking out his tongue.

"Is he an enemy?" asked Nina, ready to strike.

"He's mostly harmless," said Kaity.

"Why should I trust anything you say?" asked Nina with a glare.

"Lighten up on Kaity. She's been nothing but kind and hospitable to you," said Deceivant.

Nina glared at the thieving girl. "I despise her. If it weren't for Devlin's orders, my katana would be pierced through her throat. As she struggled in her final moments, I would slowly turn the blade."

"Ooh! You're my kind of woman!" exclaimed Pesi in a raspy, furious tone while flailing his fingernails.

Kaity ran out of the bath, covering her face.

Kanasta leaped out and rushed to her. He gripped his little girl in a fatherly embrace.

"You're not Cool Nina. You're Mean Nina! You made my friend cry!" yelled D.S., standing up in the bath.

"Her misery won't hurt Devlin. He's the only one I care about. And…he's gone." Nina broke down into tears.

"Oh, you poor thing." Ada held the sad girl to her bosom.

Kanasta entered the warm bath with Kaity, holding his daughter close to him.

"Alright. I think it would be best if we discuss strategies," said Deceivant.

"We can't discuss anything with him around." Nina turned to Pesi. "Go back to where you came. Give Opti back his body or I'll carve into you until you no longer recognize yourself," said Nina, gripping the virus' face with one hand.

"Pesi isn't like you. Opti and Pesi share one body. There is no true owner," said Deceivant.

"Either way, I don't trust him." Nina turned to the mind thief. "Should I start by breaking your arms?"

"I like you a lot!" exclaimed Pesi with a crazed grin.

"Do you like having the ability to speak?" asked Nina, gripping his tongue.

Pesi nodded nervously and transformed into his wimpy half.

"Now can we discuss our plans?" asked Deceivant.

"Yeah, like how are we going to find NoOne's beloved?" asked Opti.

"About that. What makes you think she is in Lum?" asked Deceivant.

Opti fell silent.

"She probably saw him at Devlin's lab. But I have no idea which girl it could have been. Either way, she is most likely alive and on Earth."

"You're so smart. It's a good thing it wasn't at my hubby's lab. So many young ladies have visited," said Ada with a smile.

"I guess I was a bit too hasty on trying to leave the team. Sorry, everyone," said Opti.

"No worries, buddy," said D.S., lifting up his pal's hand and giving him a high-five.

"Now, let's talk about the angels and what they want with us," said Deceivant.

"If it weren't for the misunderstanding, I'm sure Etaf would have been very happy to see us," said Ada.

"No. You're oversimplifying it. If you recall, in the midst of our battle with Etaf she said that Lum was no longer watching. She told us to run away. Either she is trying to gain our trust or trying to make us not trust Lum. It's possible she is on our side but Lum isn't. Do you all recall when Efil listed our crimes?" asked Deceivant.

"Yeah. There were a lot," said D.S.

"She was missing one. Back when I first arrived at the World Tree, I scraped some moss off for examination. And if you all remember, after the assassins were whisked away to Absence, she decided not to list their crimes."

"Perhaps there were too many to list," said Kanasta with a smile.

"Ah, but she listed Tempo freezing Violet and every crime committed by an assassin before they entered Lotus. I believe the reason these crimes were left out is because the angels were unable to see what transpired inside," said Deceivant.

"You love the sound of your voice, don't you?" asked Nina, rolling her eyes.

"You're over-thinking it. Efil just didn't want to waste time. After all, Etaf's forces were on their way to eliminate us. When we were spending time in Absence, Efil was likely arguing on our behalf," said Violet.

"Even if what you say is true, it doesn't disprove my theory. The goddesses may have a large surveillance network, but they are not omniscient. It seems very probable that Lum is also not omniscient or at least not at all times. Though we can't say Lum even exists. It's just as likely that a goddess or multiple goddesses are posing as Lum."

"Efil is wholly devout to Lum. I have faith in Efil, so I believe in Lum," said Violet, folding her hands.

"Are you feeling better now?" asked Ada, patting Nina's head.

"Why are you treating me like a child? I'm fully capable of dealing with my own emotions."

"Friends offer each other support."

"I have no friends." Nina turned away.

"Anyways. Given that Lum isn't omniscient, it can be tricked," said Deceivant.

"That reminds me. When I cornered the Imam at the Allah's Jannah base, Selfish Nina mentioned a portal to Earth. If Lum is distracted, perhaps you all can enter the portal," said Kanasta.

"You're not coming?" asked Riufen.

"As I said. I have a job to do here," said Kanasta.

"Okay! We'll help you with your errands. Then we can all go together," said Ada.

"I appreciate the concern, mother, but the Viper Squad is more than capable of finishing this."

"I don't know if I can help," said Kaity, leaned against her papa.

"Of course you can. One day, you will surpass me and lead the Viper Squad."

"I don't even have my rifle. And I promised Sefiwah that I would move on after she left. I'm no longer a part of the Viper Squad," said Kaity, before submerging her face underwater.

"I will complete the job on my own then." Kanasta's hand moved in a flash and tore a circular saw out from the air. He looked up at BoneSaw who had its other saw poised in salute. "Splendid. We will complete the job together."

BoneSaw caught the saw once it was sent back its way.

Nina approached Violet. She looked her up and down. "You're very beautiful."

"Thanks," said Violet with a blush. "You're absolutely gorgeous yourself."

"I wasn't complementing you. Why would Devlin create someone so beautiful? Were you made to replace me? Did you make love to him?" asked Nina, leaning in uncomfortably close.

"Violet was created to help Devlin on a spiritual path. It's escapism through the denial of reality. Sadly, it's more common than you may think," said Deceivant.

"That's not entirely true. Devlin was very lonely. He missed his mother. I think he made me to be his surrogate mother. There were many times I would hold him in my arms like a child. Sometimes he would even call me his mother. I tended to him out of devotion. Devlin is my creator, my god, the mussawir of my embodiment. He brought out the divine motherly love deep within me. He was almost like a baby Jesus or maybe more of a mischievous little Krishna," said Violet with a soothing smile.

"But then why would he make you so beautiful?" Nina turned and sized Devlin's mother up. "Oh, that's why. It makes sense now."

97

"What? Are you making fun of me?" asked Ada with a scrunched forehead.

"No, my dear. Nina was giving you a compliment," said Deceivant, patting his wifey's head.

"Oh, that's sweet. Thank you," said Ada with a nod.

Nina turned away.

"One day, Devlin stopped coming to me. I think he felt that my warmth and love threatened his desire for revenge. He was so afraid to stop hating his parents. I'm glad he let go of his resentment before he moved on," said Violet, folding her hands.

"I still don't know if that's true. And I never will," said Nina, covering her eyes with her palms.

Deceivant scooted in. "Let's continue discussing Lum's intentions. The arrival of Exps in Lum seems to be the moment that Etah was waiting for. Perhaps the gods believe that Exps will tip the scales in favor of Sel or Lum, depending on which realm we choose to side with. After all, before we left Lum, the Forces of Hate had breached and were attacking. And, as far as we know, the only way for them to get to Lum is from Demonica's gimp. The forces were likely sent to capture us, or perhaps they were sent to distract Lum. I have no doubt that their intervention is what distracted Lum when Etaf told us to flee the area."

"So then we were saved by the Forces of Hate?" asked Riufen.

"It may very well have been a coincidence, but that does seem to be the case. However, that is only true if we assume that Etaf wasn't lying to us about Lum no longer watching us," said Deceivant.

"What are you going on about? We fought Etah. We helped the good guys out. They think we're friends with Demonica. Wait! What if Demonica showed up to make us look like the bad guys?" asked D.S.

"That's an incredibly likely possibility. Breaking us apart from the angels and the goddess' would make us more likely to join the Forces of Hate. If nothing else, it would bunch us all together, making it easier for them to round us up."

"Very true. Once Etah was defeated and Demonica reappeared, she ordered her sisters to capture us. They want us alive. It seems both Etah and Lum don't want to kill us," said Kanasta.

"Doesn't Etah only want us alive so he can kill us himself and mold our souls into weapons?" asked Riufen.

"That's most likely the reason, but there may be more to it," said Deceivant.

"Hey, if we kill Etah, do you think they'll come back?" asked Kaity, leaning over the side to face the cold bath group.

"They will be unable to move on until he is vanquished. That is all we know," said Riufen, holding his spine and focusing on it.

"The truth is we have no idea whether we can rescue our allies from Etah. That's what pains me the most," said Deceivant, gritting his teeth.

Nina looked up. She swam to Devlin's father and placed her hand over his hairy chin.

"What are you doing this time?" asked Deceivant, his back against the side of the bath.

"Just checking something."

Opti stood tall in the bath. "If you ask me, I think Lum and the angels want what's best for us. Either way, there are lots of people here, belonging to many different species. I will use my strength to protect them. I won't go back to Earth until I know Lum is safe."

"You have no responsibility to this place. Why bother?" asked Nina.

"It's the right thing to do," said Opti.

"I agree completely," said Kaity.

"Ah, Kaity, that reminds me. When we talked to Efil she said the angels turned you over to Etah because you were under a Sel hex after your marriage with Devlin was completed."

"What!" yelled Nina, swiftly grabbing her katana before leaping at her enemy.

The blade was placed right to the girl's throat.

"You had best think of your next action carefully," said Kanasta, looming behind the attacker.

"M-M-M-Married to my D-Devlin?" asked Nina, her eyes in a daze.

"I only married him so I could get him to put an end to his crazy plan. Once I got control back, we agreed that the marriage didn't count. I don't love Devlin, okay?" asked Kaity.

"Nina, put the sword down," said Deceivant, placing his hands over hers.

The jealous ninja pulled away. Her cheeks were flushed.

"Are you alright?" asked Kanasta.

"Fine," said Kaity with a smile.

"Thank goodness. So Kaity, how did you die? You were alive when I died on Earth, so I honestly have no clue," said Deceivant.

"I didn't. Devlin said he teleported me to Akihabara. I don't remember it though. When I was under that hex, I was unaware of everything that happened."

"I know the feeling," said Nina, setting her sword down.

"The goddesses can't be trusted," said Deceivant under his breath.

"What makes you say that? Efil has done so much for us," said Violet.

"The only way Kaity could have made it to Lum was if she was taken there by a goddess. From there she was sent to Sel. Hmm, seems there was some sort of underhanded deal between one of the Goddesses and Etah."

"You're being too narrow-minded. Demonica made it to Earth, right? Maybe they sent some angels to escort her to Lum where she would be safe," said Violet.

"And then they realized she was under a spell and handed her over to Etah? Seems very unlikely," said Deceivant.

"Well what if...what if...."

"Look, all I'm getting at is we should be careful before we trust what the Goddesses say, including Efil," said Deceivant.

"Do as you like. I have faith in them," said Violet.

"Dad's got a point. Efil says Lum is a good guy, right? Well when Pharma and I talked, he said that the ones claiming to be good aren't the good guys. So like, if I say you're evil, then I'm the one who's bad. I know, it's confusing," said D.S.

"It's best to be wary, that's all I'm saying. I wouldn't claim Lum or any of the Goddesses to be evil, but their intentions for us might not be what we ourselves desire," said Deceivant.

"Why am I wasting my time here? I'm all washed up. It's time to visit the temple," said Violet, stepping out of the bath.

"We've been here long enough. We should gather information from Rambir. He's been here much longer than we have," said Kanasta.

"I've said what needed to be said. We can get out now," said Deceivant, helping Ada out of the cold tub.

Nina grabbed his leg. "I want to talk with you. Alone."

"No way! You said mean things to him. He'd be crazy to stay with someone who wants his blood," said D.S.

"It's fine. Nina is sworn to protect me. I am in no danger. I'll catch up with you all in a bit," said Deceivant with a dismissive wave.

"BoneSaw will stand guard in case she does try to attack you," said Kanasta.

"Yeah and Napkin too!" cheered Opti.

"Nina was just venting. She would never hurt us. See you later, my love," said Ada, blowing a kiss.

The Remnants of Freedom left the bathhouse, leaving Nina and Deceivant alone.

Chapter 98: Subtle Erosion

The Remnants of Freedom left the bathhouse to meet with Rambir and gather information.

"I miss the old Nina. We were finally starting to bond…and now she's gone," said Kaity, lowering her head.

"This Nina is a superior warrior. And she is dedicated to my brother. We are fortunate to have her on our side," said Kanasta.

"Singh!" Violet waved at the head of the temple.

"Ah, I see you're all washed up now," he said, approaching his new friends.

"May I visit the main temple now?" asked Violet.

"I'll come along too," said Ada.

"I've never been to a temple before. Should be fun," said Opti.

"Is it alright if you send someone to escort them? I have some questions I'd like you to answer," said Kanasta.

"That is fine. Singh, go and show them around the temple," said Rambir, signaling the cheerful young man who greets people at the door.

"It will be my pleasure," said the young man.

"I'll see you later, Mom. I want to stick with the funny beard guy," said D.S.

"Wait up. I'm coming too," said Kaity, joining the temple group.

Rambir looked up at Kanasta. "You may ask me anything."

"We left to Sel and have only recently returned to Lum. Has anything notable happened?"

"Lum sent angels out to kill any and all rebels. Thankfully that order was rescinded before any harm came to my people."

"Why would she kill people? That's really bad," said D.S.

"The real question is: why did she take back the order?" asked Kanasta.

"Rumor has it that it wasn't Lum who made the order at all. It was false information spread by an extremist angel. I'm not convinced that's really the case. Soon after the order was given, demons appeared in Lum. I think that is the real reason the order was taken back. I do not know how the demons crossed over. It's a rather unsettling affair," said Rambir, stroking his beard.

"In Sel we fought Etah's army. We thought we had beaten him, but he still lives," said Riufen.

"I think I know where they came from. I found something peculiar in the basement of Lotus. At the time, I thought they were tortured humans. But after going to Sel, I realize they are definitely demons. I believe the Imam sent out the demons once the angels began slaughtering her people," said Kanasta.

"The Imam will do anything to achieve victory. But still, that doesn't explain how the demons arrived here in the first place."

"Gimpy! It must have sent them here. Gimpy is Demonica's um…play doll," said D.S., turning away with embarrassment.

"Are you certain there is a demon that can bypass the Light Wall?" asked Rambir with an intense gaze.

"When we were cornered in Sel, Gimpy sent us to Lum. Demonica is likely planning something," said Kanasta.

"You mustn't concern yourself. You are safe here. Many warriors live within these walls. They will keep you all safe," said Rambir, before opening the door in front of him. "You may enter." He beckoned his new friends inside.

Small mats had been placed all along the ground. Boys and men with injuries were sprawled throughout the room, being tended to by doctors and holy men.

"What happened to him?" asked D.S., looking down at a man who was kinda see-through.

"For some it happens sooner, but we all must move on. His memories left him and his body is fading. We are doing our best so he has a smooth transition into his next life," said Rambir.

"I had heard you were rebels. Yet it appears you are aiding the angels," said Kanasta.

"Refuge is a home, a sanctuary, and a place where souls move on. We rebel against Lum forcing her religion, Allah's Nur, on unwilling people. Otherwise we are at peace with our lives here." Rambir kneeled down and placed his hand on the clear-bodied man. "It is almost time for him."

"Is he going to die?" asked D.S.

"We are all dead. He is ready to move on."

The man's body faded, leaving only a light blue soul. The soul passed through the wall.

"Are we going to go 'poof' too?" asked D.S.

"Some say it is a subtle erosion of thought. But to me it seems that the light of this world buries our memories under bliss and eventually our identity fades. Wearing something over the head is supposed to deter it, but I'm not certain that this is true. Either way, moving on here is as inevitable as death is on Earth. But it is nothing to fear. It is a chance for a new beginning."

"Where is his soul going?" asked Kanasta.

"To Samsara, the place where the Portal to Earth is. Once there, the angels will examine his spiritual development, and then his soul will choose its next incarnation."

"Let's say I went 'poof'. Can I come back as a T-Rex or something even cooler?" asked D.S.

Rambir smiled. "The soul must bind itself to an existing entity. You cannot become something that is extinct."

"I guess that makes sense."

"Are you thinking of reincarnating?" asked Riufen.

"Yeah, but only if Mom is doing it too. I won't leave her behind," said D.S.

A blob came out from beneath the door.

"Eww, it's all green and yucky," said D.S.

"It's an enemy," said Kanasta

"Evacuate everyone, immediately," said Rambir, addressing the doctors.

The blob expanded and took form. It became a slightly shorter replica of Ego. "How's this? Do I look familiar?"

Kanasta whipped out a shotgun and blasted the imposter's head open. "Ego is dead. That's the only thing you two have in common."

Plasma claws shot out from the muck and sliced into the assassin's side.

When Kanasta turned, he saw a replica of Kaity with discolored hair.

"Stop pretending to be our friends!" yelled D.S., rushing in with his scissors ready.

Guns came out from the sides of the replica's arms and opened fire.

D.S. shielded his face, but most of the bullets were deflected by Kanasta's diamond suitcase.

Riufen engaged the enemy and sliced off its arms. "If you can alter your shape, then become a swordsman and battle me."

"Should I go find Mom?" asked D.S.

"Kaity is with her. She will keep Ada safe. No doubt she went with them in case such a situation occurred. The day she will surpass me may come sooner than I predicted. We must focus our attention on the enemy here. Yvne is the one who killed Ego. We best be on our guard," said Kanasta.

"*Jealous Metamorphosis!*" Yvne transformed into the Baroness

of Blades, though with fewer swords imbedded in her body. "*Ignition!*"

Riufen dodged the superheated strikes before tossing his spine.

Yvne jumped back. Before she could land, Riufen pierced a new spine through her head. "I'm not here to kill. Only capture. But being told to just

103

capture…it makes me want to kill. Maybe killing just one of you is okay," she said, blasting the samurai with her shotgun arm.

D.S. dropped from above and sliced off the bad lady's head.

Riufen's wounds closed before he brandished the slanted Sikh sword. He raised the blade and then sliced his opponent in two.

Yvne's two halves shifted as they split apart.

"Not sure if we can kill her," said Kanasta.

"*Yin Yang Metamorphosis!*" Yvne's two halves joined together as a strange fusion of Pharma and Karson.

"Hmm, is it Pharson or Karma? Hey wait, was she watching all of us fight?" asked D.S.

Riufen blocked against the nicotine sword. "Her posture and skill is different. Pharma was a complete novice with a sword. She cannot copy their fighting style." The samurai leaped back to avoid the shotgun blast.

"Doesn't it bother you to fight your friends? To kill your friends?" asked Yvne, parrying D.S.'s scissors with well-timed shotgun blasts while keeping the swordsman at bay with Nicky.

"As long as they have a sword, I welcome it," said Riufen, dragging his blade down and slicing off her medical needle fingers.

"Too many enemies. Must improvise." Yvne's head turned into Karson's.

"*Desire Duping!*" The head multiplied itself by three and then shot off as missiles. The missiles headed to the back of the room, where the doctors were evacuating the patients.

Kanasta ran to the back of the room and jumped into the wall. He kicked off, grabbed a missile, and tossed it into the other. After being pushed back by the explosion, he took aim and fired his shotgun at the final missile.

Riufen sliced the enemy to ribbons. "The battle is won."

"It is now! **SOLDIER'S LEGACY**." D.S. sprayed liquid nitrogen on the gooey blob, freezing it in seconds.

"This victory belongs to you," said Riufen with a bow.

"No. It belongs to Karson," said D.S.

The gun shifted in his grip, morphing into a snake. It smacked D.S. and left the room.

"I'll get it!" hollered D.S., swinging open the door.

An explosion erupted out from down the hall.

"Don't bother. We must regroup with our allies. Nina may be fighting an opponent beyond her abilities," said Kanasta, motioning Riufen to follow him.

Previously: Violet, Ada, Opti, and Kaity joined the young Sikh man for a tour of the temple.

"So this place was built by Jains?" asked Violet.

"It was originally a Jain temple; a Jain monk called for its construction. The builders used discarded parts from other temples and other dead matter to build it. This place was built by many people though, mostly Hindu architects. There are small shrines outside. A few of them have a symbolic footprint of where the maker of this temple once stood. To the Jains who come here, those shrines hold the greatest importance," said the young man.

"Wow, Singh, you know so much," said Opti.

"I only know what my teachers have shared with me. What is your religion? Are you a Jain as well?"

"Oh I…I don't really have a religion. But I'm a good guy. I like helping people, especially fluffy or furry ones."

"Then it is my duty to make you a Sikh, like me."

"Opti is learning and growing at his own pace. He lives in an agnostic present, like a curious child," said Violet.

"Aw, you're so sweet," said Opti, hugging his blue-skinned buddy.

"Can you tell us more about this place? You said you learned from your teachers. Is there a school here?" asked Ada.

"There is indeed. Students of all ages and backgrounds come together to learn. Sometimes we have visitors from other temples come by, and they share their wisdom with us."

"There are more temples? Can you show me where?" asked Violet.

The young man reached into his pocket and pulled out a map. "Lum is a very large place. It is much bigger than Earth." He handed the blue-skinned princess a multi-paged map. "You should probably try to go to the Femina temples." He turned a few pages. "These temples will gladly welcome a female guest."

"Thank you, Singh," said Violet, bowing before shifting her attention to the map.

"Could I teach at the school? I'm a certified K–12 teacher back on Earth," said Ada.

"Everyone is welcome to teach. After all, we each know something that someone else doesn't," said the young man.

"Wonderful!" exclaimed Ada.

"So there's a temple, a school, a bathhouse. Anything else?" asked Kaity.

"There is the dining hall where we all sit together. The simple design replicates the frugal life of the guru. There are also individual rooms for guests to stay at. I will take you there after dinner."

"When can we see the other temples?" asked Violet.

"Another time. Shall I show you the shrines outside?" asked the young man.

"Please do," said Violet with a glowing smile.

The Sikh led them down the hall to an exit door. He pointed to the pathway that seemed to go around the entire structure. "This path is for followers to circumambulate the temple."

"I'd rather run along the grass," said Opti.

"This is a Jain temple. There is life in the grass. It is a home to many creatures and is alive itself," said Violet.

"Good point."

"Even on a concrete pathway we must be careful not to step on our fellow five-sensed beings," said Violet.

"Wait. Something odd is going on. The angels are leaving," said the young man, seeing a group of birds fly off together.

"Something's coming out from between the trees," said Kaity, peering through her sniper scope.

"You can lower your gun. The guards have already left to investigate," said the young man, pointing to the group of six warriors with swords at their sides moving up the hill.

Kaity's eyes widened. "It's Demonica!"

"Hi! Thanks for helping us!" hollered Ada, waving excitedly.

The guards lifelessly toppled down the hill.

"Alert everyone inside! I'll try to keep her busy," said Kaity, rushing to a better vantage point.

Previously: the Remnants left Nina and Deceivant alone in the bathhouse.

Deceivant looked up at the ninja girl. "So, what is it you want to—"

Nina gripped his hands. "These are the hands that created Devlin."

"Heheh. Indeed they are. And these are the hands made by Devlin," he said, rubbing the tops of her hands.

She pulled away and turned around. "Would you wash my back?"

"How can I say no to such a pretty girl?" asked Deceivant, grabbing a bar of soap from the side of the bath.

"Pretty? I'm pretty?"

"Yes. Though you're more cute than anything. So shy, almost like a child."

"Enough like a child…or not enough?"

"I don't quite understand."

Nina turned around, looked away and scratched her knuckles. "Would you…make love to me?"

Deceivant's eyes popped. "I…uh…well…uh."

Nina pressed up against him. "I want those eyes. If you die, can I pluck them out and keep them?" she asked with a tiny smile.

"W-What?"

"Do you think Devlin would hate me if I made love to you?"

"No. He loves you dearly. Though it would likely increase his resentment for me," said Deceivant, backing up into a corner of the bath.

"Love or hate. It doesn't matter anymore. I need him to have strong feelings for me. Indifference is the only thing I can't handle. But none of that matters anymore, does it? I finally come back and he's gone," said Nina, her eyes wet with remorse.

Deceivant put his arm around her and held the troubled girl close to him.

"You're the reason we were separated. You ruined everything!" yelled Nina, grabbing his arms and pressing him to the wall. "I want to kill you right now," she said, digging her nails into his skin.

"You have every right to hate me. I think you need some alone time," he said, hoisting himself out of the bath.

Nina pulled him right back in. "You owe me. All I want is for someone to love me. After all you've done to me, don't I deserve something?"

Deceivant placed his hand on her cheek. "It would be my pleasure to make love to such a cute girl."

Nina leaned against him. "Should I undo my wrap?"

Deceivant placed his hands on the wraps covering her boobies. "Relax."

"Oh. Okay," said Nina, turning away with a blush.

His hands went to her sides and under her arms. His fingers moved like a spider, relentlessly tickling the girl.

Nina turned to face him. "What are you doing?"

"Um, tickling you."

"I'm a warrior. My body is immune to such things."

"You say that but…." He lifted up her leg and tickled the bottom of her foot.

"Like I said, immune. As if I would have such an obvious weakness."

"Okay. Then…." Deceivant placed her on his knee and put his hand to her belly. "How about a tummy rub?!"

Nina pulled away. "You're mocking me," she said softly.

107

"But every girl loves tummy rubs," said Deceivant, searching his hands for meaning.

"I'm not a child. I'm a woman." Within a second, the ninja removed the wrap and exposed her bare breasts. "Now." She leaned in, pressing her bosom against the Devlin look-alike. "Make love to me."

"They're um…rather large," said Deceivant with a nervous grin.

"I know. Apparently Devlin likes small ones. Did he design me with these to deny his attraction to young girls? Is he that afraid of being like you?"

"Hmm. I never thought of that."

"You don't like them either, do you? What am I doing?" asked Nina, turning away. A tear fell from her eyes.

"My wifey has breasts that are bigger than yours. It's not a problem at all." He placed his hands on her overdeveloped bosom and rubbed them in a circular motion.

"Do they feel good?"

"Yes. Superb! They're um…very responsive."

"You know, you're rather handsome. Without that old man hair on your chin, you kind of look like Devlin."

"I'm not him. I'll do my best to comfort you, but I can't replace him."

"You're right. I feel nothing toward you. But we shouldn't give up just yet." Nina pressed up against him and lowered the blue cloth, exposing her lips. "Kiss me." Her cheeks turned bright red.

Deceivant moved in and rubbed noses with her.

Nina's hand gripped his throat. "What was that?"

"Butterfly kisses."

"I know what they are. Devlin calls them bunny kisses. Did you not see my lips pucker? Do you enjoy embarrassing me?" she asked, tightening her grip.

"Not at all. It's just, I usually like to play around before kissies."

"Kissies? What are you a grade-schooler?"

"Well I like to think of myself as—"

Nina pulled him in close and stared intensely into his eyes. "Kiss me. Now."

Deceivant nodded.

She released her grip.

His lips pressed against hers. He then playfully gave her a barrage of kissies.

Nina put her hand in the way. "Forget kissing. I want you to drown out my sadness with pleasure. Become one with me here and now," she said, gazing at him intensely despite her flushed cheeks.

"Whoa! Whoa! Whoa! That is something I cannot do," said Deceivant.

"You like children. I'm well aware. But what you don't know is that I'm…a virgin." She grinded against his knee.

Deceivant's face lit up once he noticed her underwear floating on the surface of the bath. He shook himself to his senses. "That has nothing to do with it. I do not penetrate. Period. I don't like it. I won't do it. End of story."

"Not even if I call you…grandpa?" asked Nina, looking to the side as she blushed.

"What kind of person do you think I am?" asked Deceivant, scratching his neck.

"What about my butt?" asked Nina, hoisting herself up so he was pressed against her bottom. "Don't you want to slide your Popsicle in?" she asked, covering her cheeks in embarrassment.

"Aww. You are so cute," he said, pinching her cheeks.

"Well are you going to do it or not?" asked Nina, her face steaming.

"No penetration. Finger sucking is okay. As is surface rubbing," said Deceivant, tweaking her nipples.

"I won't force you to do something you're against. Love making without love is empty pleasure," she said, sliding off of his lap.

Deceivant leaned in and poked her boobies. "Why so glum. Come on, smile," he said, tapping her nose.

"Hrugh! Is this how you make love to your wife? By making her feel like a preschooler?"

"That is correct," said Deceivant with a nod.

"Well I'm done with it. It just feels like you're mocking me. What was I thinking?"

"I'm not trying to upset you. Come on, smile," said Deceivant, lifting her cheeks to get rid of her frowny face.

Nina knocked his hand aside. "We're done. Devlin is dead. You're my last chance at happiness. But it isn't working out. I feel worse than before we started," she said, vanquishing her tears as soon as they were released.

"Wait, give me one more chance. Just tell me what you want," said Deceivant.

"Okay…grab my wrists and press me against the side of the bath. I'm kind of shy so…this way is best. Sometimes I imagine Devlin forcing himself on me in a rush of passion," she said while licking his ear.

"I'm not comfortable with that…even if it is just pretend," said Deceivant.

"Well I'm not comfortable with taking the initiative. I know." Nina lay on her side and stuck out her butt. "Spank me."

"Oh, uh…okay." Deceivant patted her butt.

"Come on. Get into it," said Nina, shaking her butt.

Deceivant grabbed her sides and stood her up. "There doesn't have to be a top or bottom. We can just be side by side," he said, leaning against her.

Nina perked up. "Devlin said something similar once."

Deceivant started to rub her back. "No need to rush. We have plenty of time."

"Do you get horny, like, at all?" asked Nina, sliding his hand down lower and lower.

"Haha! You're not the first girl to ask me that. Rub-a-dub-dub."

Nina crossed her legs.

Deceivant pulled his hand away. "I'm sorry. I thought you wanted me to touch you there."

"What I'm asking from you is something you can't give. You don't love me and I can't love you. I tried to find refuge in this world without Devlin. I was selfish and foolish to try to move on." She turned away. "I need to be more careful. Selfish actions give her more strength," said the warrior to herself.

"Come here. Just sit in my lap. Cry on my shoulder if you need to. I want to help," he said, patting her head.

Nina grabbed his hand. "No way. Next it will be 'here comes the choo-choo train' or time for a 'piggy-back ride.' I'm done."

"I specifically held back from both of those, mind you."

"I thought you would be mature and maybe even a bit kinky, but you're just an immature child." Nina lifted the cloth over her mouth.

"I think it's best if we get out now," said Deceivant, placing the undies in her hands.

Nina slid into her underwear and wrapped her breasts. "Not yet." She swiped the katana from the side of the bath.

BoneSaw leaped into action, firing a saw that was quickly deflected.

Nina kicked the robot aside and held her blade out. "If you ever bring back the other Nina, I will kill you. Understand?"

Deceivant nodded. "You have my word as a scientist. I will never bring the other Nina back."

She kicked BoneSaw aside once more and then lowered her blade. "Glad you understand." Nina slipped into her clothes. "Let's get going."

"Yes, of course," said Deceivant, leaving the bath and quickly getting dressed.

The door opened.

A knight clad in black and wielding a golden sword stood before them. "Come with me or die," he said, raising his sword.

Chapter 99: Bravery

Previously: Devlin was possessed by Lord Sel and ended the demonic civil war before leaving in a black portal along with the Sinful Sorority.

He awoke on a ground of solidified Sel energy. Lava flowed around the dome, kept back by an unseen force. Small lights flickered around him like fireflies in the night.

"You finally came to. I was starting to get worried," said Demonica, looking down at him.

Devlin stood up, still clad in the heavy black armor. "Where is this place?"

"Welcome to the Core. This place is wedged beneath the pool of lava under the living island. It is the very center of the Realm of Destruction. The Core is also from where Lord Sel watches over us all," said Demonica, poking one of the floating lights.

"My head feels strange. What happened? It's all so hazy."

"You won, remember? You defeated Etah and Lord Sel made you into a god. Then you stopped the war in Sel," said Demonica, running her hands down his sleek black armor.

"That's right. Hey, where's Kaity?" he asked, looking around.

"The little tease and all her friends are safe, thanks to me. Which brings us to the matter at hand, we're going to Lum."

"Is that were Kaity is?" asked Devlin, holding his head.

"Is that all you think about?" she asked with a grimace.

"When can we leave?"

Demonica leaned into him. "About that, what do you say we make it a date?"

"A date…with Kaity?"

"No." Demonica grabbed his hand. "With me."

"Okay. You helped me become a god, after all. A promise is a promise," said Devlin, grabbing her other hand.

"Fantastic!" Demonica hopped. "I'm going in first to scope out the area. Lord Sel has something to discuss with you. Meet me there," she said, bouncing in place.

"I will," said Devlin.

Demonica vanished.

A dark cloud approached Devlin.

"What god am I?" asked Devlin, turning to the cloud.

"The God of Ruin. Whatever you touch erodes until it is dust," said Lord Sel.

"What were you before you became the god of this realm?"

"I was two entities joined into one. I have no discernable beginning."

"Did you have a name?"

"Enough questions. I have a gift for you."

A golden sword with wires coiled as a blade came out from the black cloud.

"Take hold of Bravery. It is a weapon only you can properly wield."

Devlin bowed and opened his hands.

Bravery's hilt connected to his wrist as soon as he gripped it.

"Did you make this weapon for me?" asked Devlin.

"It was once wielded by the God of Courage. Even after his death, it stayed manifested."

"It bends to my will," said Devlin, elongating the blade.

"Indeed. The blade recognizes you as its new master."

"What is my mission?"

"You must go to Lum. Demonica will instruct you further once you arrive."

"Last time you manipulated me. I won't let it happen again. This time, I will stay in control," said Devlin.

"I only intervene if necessary."

Devlin arrived in a pine tree forest.

Demonica turned to him and smiled. Her eyes popped open. "Where did you get this?" The dark goddess gripped his golden sword and leaned against his shoulder.

"Lord Sel passed it on to me."

"It suits you well," she said, moved to tears.

"Is something the matter?"

Demonica wiped her eyes. "I'm fine."

"So, what is our mission?"

"We're here to recruit our old playmates. But we can kill whoever gets in our way and whoever refuses. Sound like a fun date?"

"If I had absorbed Exp 8's power, the plan was to go on a killing spree. I have the power now. It's time to celebrate," said Devlin, grabbing her hand.

"Do you know what happens to those who are killed in Lum?"

"Not a clue," said Devlin.

Demonica summoned up a scythe, radiating with her aura. With a single slash, six approaching humans tumbled down the hill. "Neither do I. All I know is: they don't reincarnate. Maybe their souls reach a state of oblivion or maybe they move to a world beyond this one."

"Do you want the next group?" she asked, pointing to the ten Sikh warriors on approach.

"Are we taking turns now?" Devlin aimed his hand and fired a blast of dark energy.

The warriors leaped out of the way of the blast. The ones who were hit quickly severed the afflicted areas.

"I meant to fire a beam. Why didn't that work?" asked Devlin.

"You had a massive source of energy nearby when you were fighting in Sel. You'll need to be a bit more conservative here," said Demonica, sending out her nails.

The Sikh warriors held out their swords and blocked the attack.

"Stop fighting!" Opti was running up the hillside, waving his hands around.

"Oooh, shall we strike him down together?" asked Demonica, biting her lip.

"There is no need to harm him. I'll convince him to join us."

"Make it quick. We are still on a date," said Demonica.

Suddenly her chest had a hole blasted through it. The dark goddess fell to her knees.

"A sniper. Is Kaity here?" asked Devlin, searching the area.

A bullet slammed into the knight's knee, knocking him off his feet.

Opti spread his wings before ramming into the dark figure. He landed on top and quickly pinned down its arms. "We don't have to fight. Just go away."

Bravery coiled around Opti and slammed him against the ground.

"I'll deal with you later," said Devlin.

"Where are they attacking from? How did it hurt me?" asked Demonica, holding her chest in pain.

"I'll take care of it." Devlin rushed down the hillside all the while searching for the cute sniper.

Another bullet came and slammed into his head.

He would have fallen if not for Bravery pushing off the ground.

"This weapon is very handy indeed." Devlin placed the sword to the ground.

The golden strands spread out across the ground and entered the cracks in the corridor.

"I know you're there. Come on out, Kaity," said Devlin.

A figure leaped out from behind a pillar and rushed at the dark warrior.

"Violet...but where is Kaity?"

Violet slammed her energy-coated hands into the servant of darkness. "You are not welcome here."

The devotee's energy was consumed by the armor.

Demonica fired chains of blood at the religious warrior. "It was her. Those bullets were laced in her aura. That's why it hurt me."

"Do you think Kaity is inside?" asked Devlin.

"Seems likely," said Demonica, deflecting Violet's sword assault with blades of blood.

"Then I leave these two to you," said Devlin before rushing inside.

The two lion statues near the door sprang to life and leaped at him.

"Why have you sided with the humans? Have you forgotten what they've done to your kind?" asked Devlin, grabbing each one by the throat.

"By becoming mawalis we have transcended our species. The humans here seek peace with the angels. We will gladly fight to defend them."

"Angels and mawalis are all domesticated animals. Where is your pride? Did you discard that too?" asked Devlin, before he slammed one of the lions into the wall.

"A pawn of Sel has no right to judge us." The lion spread its wings before it was encased in golden strands.

Devlin tossed the other lion aside and rushed into the building.

A line of guards as long as the hallway greeted him with swords at the ready.

"To think my creations would side with the humans. They have become pathetically desperate. *RUIN!*"

Devlin fired out a blast of Sel energy.

The dark energy slammed into them like a shotgun blast, toppling them all.

Devlin opened each door and checked the inside for any of his allies as Bravery protected him from projectiles and close-range attacks.

A bullet bounced off his helmet.

Bravery spread out, eviscerating the attacker.

"Humans are so pathetic. To think I once thought I was one of them." Devlin opened the door to the bathhouse.

Nina and Deceivant were a foot away.

"Join me or die," said Devlin, raising Bravery.

Three saws shot into his sides and were quickly dissolved by his armor.

Nina kicked Deceivant out of the way before drawing her katana.

Devlin gripped the sides of the door and emitted dark energy.

The energy spread out along the walls.

BoneSaw zoomed by and sliced into the intruder's leg.

The saw was partially consumed in the process.

"I'm not afraid to die!" yelled Deceivant, blasting the enemy with his shotgun.

Bravery took the shape of a shield to deflect the blast.

"Devlin left me with a mission. I refuse to fail him!" Nina flung shurikens lined with explosive tags at the knight's feet.

The tags burst before the knight could destroy them with his Sel bullets. The explosion pushed Sel's warrior back into the hallway.

"Another bad guy!" yelled D.S.

"That is a sword, correct?" asked Riufen, eyeing the golden weapon in the knight's grip.

"Um, Demonica's back," said D.S., pointing behind them.

The Goddess of Death stood in the hallway, drenched in fresh blood.

Opti flew into her from behind, getting pierced by a blood spike.

Demonica's blood grabbed his legs and flung him into his allies.

"Who is he?" asked Opti, looking up at the black warrior.

Nina came out from the communal bath and landed in the hallway, having leaped over the corrosive energy with Deceivant pressed against her.

"It's just a remnant of the Forces of Hate," said Deceivant.

"The Forces of Hate, Sinner's Fury, and Hero's Militia no longer exist."

"Then what are you here for?"

"I am Sel's servant. We are all Sel's pawns. Some of us just choose to serve it willingly," said Devlin, raising Bravery. "I will keep this very simple. Join me or die," he said, his voice deepened by the helmet.

BoneSaw jumped to the intruder, its saw gaining speed.

The knight's black aura took the form of a hand and grabbed BoneSaw.

D.S. thrust Snippy at the bad guy, but the black stuff gripped onto the scissors.

"These god powers are so cool!" exclaimed Devlin, enveloping BoneSaw in darkness.

Kanasta dropped down from above and tore BoneSaw out from his brother's grip. "What has happened to you?" he asked, the corrosive aura clinging to his skin as he wiped it off his robotic son.

"I've become a god." Devlin jabbed Bravery at his brother.

Riufen parried it with his spine. "That is quite the sword you have."

Kaity entered the hallway with Violet leaned against her. The devout Exp was covered in injuries.

Bravery coiled around Riufen's arms and then wrapped around his body.

"Kaity, I've been looking everywhere for you," said Devlin, reaching out to her.

"Did your master send you to kill me?" asked Kaity, before unloading a full clip into the enemy's forehead.

"Stand back, everyone. I will fight this dark warrior on my own," said Riufen, getting into a fighting stance.

"Fine by me. You are the perfect opponent to test my new powers," said Devlin.

Riufen charged at his new adversary, slashing furiously.

Devlin was quickly being overpowered.

Just as it was knocked aside, Bravery shot out strands that pierced through the samurai.

Devlin shaped his aura into a sword and stabbed his greatest living creation vigorously.

Black energy spread out from the wounds, further eroding the samurai's body.

Riufen leaped back, rapidly slicing away his infected body parts.

Bravery sliced through the swordsman's spine, stopping at his neck. "I'm unstoppable." The sword then pressed on, slicing the stoic warrior's head off.

Riufen's body fell to the ground. It picked up his head and reattached it. "You have beaten me honorably, but I must continue this battle. I will protect Devlin-sama's comrades."

"You don't realize who you just fought, do you?" Devlin's helmet dissolved, revealing his face.

Nina fell to her knees and cried.

"Is it really you?" asked Ada, rushing toward him.

D.S. grabbed mom and pulled her away. "He's a bad guy now."

"Devlin's has been corrupted. For now, we must keep our distance," said Deceivant, grabbing his beloved's hand.

The strands from Bravery jutted out. They pierced into the chests of the Remnants of Freedom and wrapped around their capsules. Kaity was the only one who wasn't attacked.

Nina looked at the wire pierced in her chest and cried.

"So, as I was saying, join me or die," said Devlin his voice cold and detached.

"I am sorry, everyone. Devlin needs me. He is my god. I must follow him," said Violet, bowing her head in respect. She skipped to Devlin's side. "You've accomplished your dream," she said with a hug.

"I must follow Devlin-sama," said Riufen before walking to his shogun.

"There will be plenty of enemies to kill," said Devlin, his eyes focusing on the compact murder machine.

BoneSaw slid out from Kanasta's grip and treaded over to Devlin's side.

"You still work for me, Kanasta. I have you on retainer," said Devlin.

"I cancelled that job because I thought you were dead. I cannot join your side until I have completed my assignment in Lum. You may have chosen a dark path, but you won't kill me," said Kanasta, staring into his brother's eyes.

"Don't be so sure. He murdered his mother in cold blood," said Deceivant, grinding his teeth.

"I'll join you," said Pesi, his legs shivering in fear.

"Is that everyone?" asked Devlin.

"Why are you doing this?" asked Ada in tears.

"I won't kill the rest of you as long as you don't get in my way. Enjoy your lives in Lum, but the moment you take a stand to defy me, you'll be killed. Except Kaity, of course. I'd like to have a chat with her at another time."

The strands receded into Bravery.

"Let's head back." Devlin left with Pesi, Riufen, and BoneSaw at his side and an arm around Violet and Demonica.

Chapter 100: A Place to Call Home

"Nina!" Kaity shook the ninja to her senses. "Get up!"

Nina got back on her feet.

"We have to get out of here," said Kaity, pulling on her hand.

Nina looked over her shoulder.

The dark energy from Devlin had already consumed the bathhouse and was spreading down the hallway. The corrosive sludge was nearing near Nina at an intimidating pace.

"This is the stuff that sprayed on me when I sliced Needle. What was an Absence god doing with Sel energy?" asked Kaity.

"Fantastic question, but let's stay focused. Once it takes down the foundation, this whole building will collapse. We need to leave. I'll go help evacuate the people," said Deceivant, running off.

"I'll help you," said D.S., running off to where his dad went.

"Should we go too?" asked Kaity, holding Nina.

"Our priority should be our own survival. Go after them and convince them to evacuate," said Kanasta.

"The books! I'll get the books out," said Ada before stopping. "Which way is the library?"

"Forget the books; we need to escape," said Nina, looking at the black energy creeping up the walls.

"Wise words," said Kanasta, carefully stepping around the blood puddles in case Demonica returned.

"Books are knowledge, wisdom! I'd rather die than do nothing as countless ideas are lost forever!" exclaimed Ada, opening door after door.

Napkin growled at the encroaching Sel energy.

"I admire your spirit, but it's no use," said Nina, crouching down to pick up the kitten.

The dark energy was pushed back, traveling upward rather than down the hall.

"How did you do that?" asked Nina under her breath.

"Found it!" Ada rushed into the library.

"Nina, I doubt my mother will reconsider. To an AI, information is life. May I ask for your assistance?" asked Kanasta.

"I could just knock her out," said Nina, walking up to Devlin's brother.

"Napkin has delayed the corrosion. If we are running low on time, then I will force her to vacate the premises."

"How about this? I'm faster than you, but you're stronger than me. I'll schlep books, and you get these people out of here. They're too injured to leave on their own, and it's our fault they got attacked."

"Understood." Kanasta lifted four men over his shoulder and ran to the exit.

Nina rushed in the library and joined Devlin's mother, Rambir, and four other Sikhs in moving books. "Strange. Thought you would be evacuating the people."

"I left that duty to the other religious leaders. These books hold the wisdom of many prophets, not only Sikh. Each one is more precious than the lives of everyone in the temple," said Rambir with intense eyes.

"Not sure if everyone feels that way," said Nina, already emptying half a shelf's worth of books.

"Books have only one life. Each book you find here was handwritten from route memory or was freshly created in Lum. Here, pass this on to your friend Violet," said Rambir, handing the ninja princess a luminescent book.

"Allah's Nur. What does that mean?" asked Nina.

"God's Light, or more specifically, Lum's light. This book is the scripture of Lum. At the most basic understanding, it is an alteration of the Quran. But at deeper levels, it is a new religion in and of itself. This version has an English translation. It also contains the original Lumian script. This book is the only known scripture not written by human hands."

"Is that so? Maybe I'll give it a read," said Nina, looking at the golden pages.

"I believe you'll find it illuminating. I realize that most scripture would be offensive to Exps as they often claim that human existence is transcendental in ways unlike the existence of other life-forms. That book in your hands says that all living beings are capable of deep meditation, accruing karma, and reaching liberation. Allah loves all her children equally, after all," said Rambir with a smile from ear to ear.

"Maybe I'll read it with Devlin," said Nina with a blissful smile.

A loud crash followed by smaller crashes came from just outside the room.

"The ceiling is already collapsing. Are these all the books?" asked Nina, taking hold of her wheelbarrow.

"The most important books, the sacred texts, have been collected. Sadly, we will be unable to save every book."

"Singh, the exit is blocked," said one of the Sikh men, looking at the rubble blocking the door.

"That is the only exit," said Rambir, his voice dropping into despair.

Nina tossed an explosive tag on the wall and triggered it. "Time to go."

Rambir, Ada, Nina, and the other men took their wheelbarrows out of the temple and entered the outside area.

Kaity left the group of Sikhs and rushed to her allies outside. "I was starting to get worried. Wait, where's Napkin?"

Kanasta opened his hands, revealing the shivering kitten. "He kept the energy back while I carried the injured to safety."

"Aww, that's my little buddy," said Kaity, patting the kitty's head. "You're a good man," she said, perking her head up and giving her papa a big smile.

"It was Nina who convinced me. Thank her," said Kanasta.

"With pleasure!" Kaity rushed up to Nina. "That was really nice of you to help them out."

"I'm not like Devlin. I don't hate humans. I don't hate anyone, well except one person," said Nina, turning away.

"I get it. I'll go," said Kaity, stepping back.

Nina turned and looked up at Kaity with eyes alight with joy. "You're right…I do hate you," she said, now smiling.

Kaity ran off, wiped her tears, and looked up at Ada. "How did things go on your end?"

"We saved as many books as we could," said Ada, tearing up as she watched the darkness spread throughout the back of the temple.

"And we made sure everyone got out. Not a single casualty," said Deceivant, putting his arm around Kaity and D.S.

Another crash.

The temple lost its foundation and caved in on itself.

All the Sikh's looked away, except for Rambir.

Deceivant approached him. "This happened because we were there. I was so busy thinking about our safety that I didn't think about how we were endangering the people in the temple. I take full responsibility. I'll do what it takes to make amends."

"Did you know this was the first temple ever built in Lum?"

"No. I didn't. Please, if there's anything I can do."

"It lasted for such a long time. I'm surprised it held up as long as it did."

"If we weren't here, none of this would have happened," said Deceivant, peering over his side at a group of little boys in tears.

"There is nothing we can do. It's been a learning experience really. And now they will make their move." Rambir put his hand on Deceivant's shoulder and pointed to a group of birds hovering above the temple.

The birds dived down and made a circle around the temple.

Wings of light sprouted from their backs and light energy emitted from their mouths, keeping the dark energy from spreading to the grass.

"I best get moving. I have to calm my people," said Rambir.

Deceivant saw an aura of light around the Sikh leader. He blinked and it was gone. "I'll help too," he said, following behind.

"Now you show up!" "Damned angels!" "They don't care about us at all!" "You let our temple fall!" yelled various enraged rebels.

"It's best if you leave. The angels may turn their aggression on you," said Rambir, putting an arm on the scientist's shoulders.

"No. I'm going to do what I can to help. We owe you at least that much," said Deceivant before approaching a group of rebels who were picking up stones. "Before you attack the angels, ask yourself what good can come of your actions."

"Don't you even start! You and your freak show are the reason those demons attacked us! We lost our home and you're telling us not to retaliate!"

"Those warriors stayed behind. Made sure I got out. I would have died if it weren't for their help," said a rebel, seated down and with a broken leg.

"You know the angels don't care about you, but they are bound by their laws. They want you to attack. It will give them grounds to slaughter everyone here!" yelled Deceivant.

A Lum portal appeared.

Etaf emerged. She peeked over her shoulder at the rebels and then turned her attention to the corrosive ruins. Light energy poured out from her hands, but it was not strong enough to dispel the darkness.

A rebel rushed to Rambir. "Singh, we found six guards by the Southern hills. They are all dead."

"I bear the responsibility for their deaths." Rambir clanged his kirpan against his karas, grabbing the attention of his people. "I welcomed the Exps in, knowing full well the dangers of such a decision. I would do it again without a second thought. We are the Refuge of the People. When there are those without a place to call home, we open our doors. I bear full responsibility for the temple and for the lives lost. If you wish me to step down as your leader, then I shall do so. What I refuse to do is let this incident change our purpose. When we have no option but to fight, we will fight. There is no need to cause any more harm. We've lost so much already," said Rambir, his tears dripping down to his beard.

The Refuge of the People folded their hands and prayed.

Lum energy shot down from the sky and encompassed the black ruins of the temple.

The black energy was overtaken and flowers now thrived in its place.

"Where do we go now?" asked Nina.

Etaf turned to face the Remnants of Freedom and summoned up the Destiny Sword. "Sel's forces have breached Lum. Come with me now. There is only one place in Lum where you will be safe."

"Demons, angels, you're all the same! You all want us either in your custody or dead at your feet!" yelled Deceivant, holding his wife to his chest.

"Run! I'll hold her off," said Nina.

"But you could die," said Kaity.

"Death isn't the thing I fear," said Nina, drawing her katana.

"No! I'll fight too," said Kaity, releasing her plasma claws.

"Kaity, I order you to retreat now. Nina and I will hold her off," said Kanasta, stepping past her.

"Yeah, I'll help too," said D.S.

"No!" yelled Ada. "Nobody is allowed to stay behind, okay?" She was in tears as Deceivant dragged her away.

"Chiitasare-gurus. You cannot escape fate itself," said Etaf before swiftly slicing the air.

The slash went through Nina and into Deceivant's leg.

He toppled over, falling to the grass.

Nina grabbed Kaity by the chin. "If you care about me at all, get Devlin's parents out of her range."

Kaity nodded with a face full of tears, before running off.

Nina rushed in and slammed her katana into the enemy's sword before it could cut the air.

"After the Exps, now! Don't let a single one get away!" yelled Etaf, commanding her forces.

"Cover their escape! Exps are being treated unfairly in Lum. Raise your kirpan and defend the minorities!" hollered a Sikh soldier before rushing in.

The archers fired at the winged angels while a group of thirty sword-wielders engaged the ground angels.

Nina slammed her legs into Etaf, having them climb up her body. Her legs then wrapped around the goddess' arm and straddled it.

"Go with your parents. Nina and I will handle this," said Kanasta.

"Don't treat me like a kid!" yelled D.S.

"You're my brother too. Live on!" yelled Kanasta before rushing in and slamming the goddess.

Etaf toppled to the ground before rolling back to her feet.

"You better not die! If you do, I'll cry so much and you'll feel really bad!" yelled D.S. before running off.

The Sikh angel lions approached the apathetic goddess. "Where were you when our temple was being destroyed?"

"I was busy. And that temple belongs to the humans. You forget your place," said Etaf, flinging the ninja girl off.

"The residents of that building are more angelic than you'll ever be," said one lion before his head plopped to the ground.

"Do the rest of you wish to side with these rebels?" she asked, raising destiny itself.

Kanasta jumped back as the lions rushed in.

"You're Devlin's brother. That makes protecting you my responsibility. I will keep the goddess off your back. Get going," said Nina.

"I won't."

"You may be the only one who can bring him back to his senses. You have to live," she said, fiercely throwing shurikens to offset each of the goddess' slashes.

"The same goes for you," said Kanasta, whipping out his sidearm and shooting the fingers gripping the Destiny Sword.

"I was right in front of him. He didn't even notice me. All he saw…the only one he cared about was Kaity!" yelled Nina, launching off the ground with dual katanas in tow. Once she was in range, she slammed her blades into the goddess' sword.

The Destiny Sword flew out of Etaf's grip.

The lions pinned the murderous goddess to the ground, two of them gripping her arms with their teeth.

Kanasta zoomed up to Nina and caught her in his arms before she could land. "I can't return to Kaity without you."

"I don't care about that child!" yelled Nina, struggling in his steel grip.

"Then we are at an impasse. I care deeply for her," he said, quickly finding cover.

"ⱫƐⱮƁⱢⱾⱤⱣⱫⱢⱱ!"

The Destiny Sword, still floating above, sliced the air.

The angel lions screamed out.

"They're going to die," said Nina.

"Yes. But you don't care about that, do you?" asked Kanasta.

Nina turned away.

"Why are you so eager to die?"

"I'm afraid."

"Afraid that we will never get Devlin back?"

"No. I'm afraid that we will," said Nina, her face quivering.

Protected by Sikh rebels both angel and human, the Remnants of Freedom left the temple ruins and fled into the pine forest.

Part 12
The King of Sel

Chapter 101: The Living Sword

Kanasta raced through the pine forest with Nina in his arms.

"They couldn't have gone too far," said Nina, sliding out of his grip and rushing ahead.

"May I ask a favor of you?" asked Kanasta.

"Do as you want. But I'm not obligated to agree."

"Understood. Please, be kind to Kaity. She has lost many who she cherished deeply."

"I'll have a talk with her later. Found them," said Nina, rushing into a clearing and spotting Devlin's father.

"Where is Kaity?" asked Kanasta, looking over the team.

"Scouting. She wants some space," said Deceivant, seated on a log with his hands folded.

"Should I go look for her?" asked Nina.

"Leave her be. Poor girl. She's been through so much." Deceivant looked up. "Thank you, son, for always taking care of her."

"I am all she has now that BoneSaw left us," said Kanasta with a solemn tone.

"She has me!" cheered D.S.

"And me," said Ada.

"And she has Napkin. She's with him right now," said Deceivant.

"There are only seven of us now. I feel lonely," said D.S.

"We need to keep moving. Who knows what Sel and Lum have planned for us?" said Deceivant.

"Violet has a map of all the nearby temples! We can go one by one. I'm sure one of them will welcome us," said Ada.

"Violet isn't here," said D.S., his shoulders dropping.

"There are more maps in the…Violet has the last map," said Ada softly.

"Etaf is hunting us. Going inside any temple needlessly puts others in danger. We should regroup and discuss what to do next. Till then, we keep moving," said Deceivant.

"I'll go get Kaity. We're both kids, so we understand each other," said D.S.

"It's best I stay here to protect the others. Travel carefully," said Kanasta.

Kaity was in the forest, using a twig to play with Napkin.

The kitty stared intently at the twig, arching his back up.

"You're really something you know that?" asked Kaity, smiling at the kitten.

Napkin pounced on the twig, gnawing on it with his tiny mouth.

"You get scared but you don't carry it with you. I try to be strong, but honestly I'm terrified. I've already lost so much. I thought it would be over after Etah was defeated. But now…Devi-kun…is our enemy."

Noticing the twig was no longer moving, Napkin looked up. "Mew."

"Thanks for trying to cheer me up. Hey, do you think Nina really hates me? She hardly knows me; how can she hate me?" Kaity broke down in tears.

Napkin rubbed against her leg.

"Sorry. I'm being so rude. Crying about being lonely when you're right here." Kaity picked up Napkin and embraced him.

Napkin nestled up to her and purred.

"At first I thought Etaf's wheel had a malfunction, but we really are destined to be great friends," said Kaity, petting Napkin lovingly.

"Mew," said Napkin with a little smile.

"Aww, you are so cute!"

Napkin struggled out of Kaity's grip so she set him down.

"You're right. I should go back to them," said Kaity softly.

Napkin rushed off into the bushes and Kaity followed.

Previously: Devlin returned to the Core.

"Alright, that's it! I'm tired of waiting for your boss to show up!" yelled Pesi.

"We must be patient," said Violet, seated lotus style while bouncing up and down.

"You came when he was in the middle of a discussion with his loyal pawns. It's bad timing, that's all," said Demonica, leaning against her knight in shining armor.

"Our date was cut short. We can continue when we begin our next mission," said Devlin.

"You two are dating?" asked Violet, breaking out of her meditation.

"I owe her a single date. That's all," said Devlin.

"Devlin-sama, are you being manipulated in any way? Perhaps through mind control or some form of coercion?" asked Riufen.

"Is a deity threatening you?" asked Violet.

"I'm fully in control of my thoughts. For the time being, Lord Sel's wishes and my own are the same. We are both benefiting from one another. It's that simple," said Devlin before bowing.

"Lord Sel?" asked Riufen.

A black cloud emerged from the darkness. It peered over its new pawns and then approached its prized possession.

"Splendid. You've brought your old allies to my side," said the cloud.

"Devlin, would you introduce us?" asked Violet, gazing into the black cloud.

"The angels of Lum fear the power of my true name, calling me the Dark One in its place. I am Lord Sel, the true god of the Realm of Destruction," said the black cloud of energy.

"I am not worthy!" exclaimed Violet, falling to the floor in humble submission.

Riufen walked to the dark deity and crouched down. "Lord Sel, I have done a disservice to you. Two hundred and sixty-three demons have fallen to my blade and seventeen to my blood. How can I make recompense?"

"There were barely any casualties. Decapitations, impalings, they are mere injuries. Demons are much more durable than you give them credit for. Even so, your honesty and loyalty should be rewarded. I have a sword in need of a wielder," said Sel.

"I graciously accept your offering," said Riufen, lowering himself further.

"Demonica, bring him his new sword," said Sel.

"And what sword would that be?" asked Demonica.

"The living sword, that which needs no wielder."

"And yet you think the swordsman can handle it? That weapon is more of a god than it is a blade."

"An immortal blade for an undead samurai."

"As you command." Demonica bowed and left.

"Why are you playing favorites? I want a dark evil weapon too!" exclaimed Pesi.

"Well, I don't need any gifts. Being in your divine presence is reward enough," said Violet, glowing with energy.

"Blah, blah, blah. Are we going to crack some skulls or just sit around talking?" asked Pesi.

BoneSaw raised its saws in agreeable protest.

Devlin ended his bow and stood at attention. "I'm not sure if the other Freedom Forcers will join. Either way I warned them not to intrude and informed them of the consequences should they choose to do so."

"We abandoned that name after we were told you were dead. The team is now called the Remnants of Freedom," said Violet.

"Pathetic yet rebellious at the same time. Not sure if they should be overestimated or underestimated," said Sel.

"Is there going to be some killing going on? Are we going to paint the white land of Lum crimson red with blood! If not, why am I wasting my time with you?" asked Pesi.

"I cannot discuss my plan in detail at this time. But I suppose it would be prudent for me to reveal my primary goal: the dethroning and subsequent execution of the Great Goddess," said the dark cloud, glowing red from within.

"I'm guessing there will be plenty of violence paving the path toward such a gruesome goal. Count me in," said Pesi, flailing his fingers around.

BoneSaw bounced up and down with approval.

"I swore loyalty to Devlin-sama. If he asks of me to offer my blade to you, then I shall do so without question," said Riufen, unsheathing his spine and crouching on bended knee.

"I cannot participate in the killing of any god or angel. I will stand by Devlin's side and offer him support without going against my new religion," said Violet, standing tall and proud.

"Splendid. You are all invested in this for your own personal reasons. There are several stages to the plan, and stage one will commence posthaste. The specific role you play in each stage will be made available as necessary," said Lord Sel, circling around its new allies.

Demonica's gimp appeared out of thin air. Once its ball gag was removed by its mistress, the gimp stood up and whispered in her ear.

"Well, what is the situation?" asked Sel.

"The Virtues will not intrude. They are still deliberating on how to end the coming war," said Demonica, hoisting a massive weapon covered in a black sheet.

"That makes things almost too simple," said Sel, dropping a bit.

"What are our orders?" asked Devlin.

"Riufen, BoneSaw, you two will keep the Remnants of Freedom occupied. They must not interfere. Kill them only if necessary."

Riufen turned to Devlin-sama, seeking his guidance.

"Do as he says," said Devlin with a shrug.

"Don't forget this," said Demonica, dropping the weighty weapon to the ground.

Riufen hoisted up the weapon, gazing intently at the black wraps containing the power within.

"Send them off," said Demonica, stepping on her toy's head.

The gimp approached the samurai and the killer box and sent them to Lum.

"Good boy." Demonica slammed her heel on the slave's back.

"What about the rest of us?" asked Devlin.

"For the greatest chance of success we will need Etah's assistance," said Lord Sel.

"Good luck with that. Pretty sure I killed him back when I was with the Freedom Forcers," said Devlin.

"Well you didn't. Demonica's toy took care of his wounds after I evacuated him from the warzone. The God of Hate is very much alive," said Sel.

"Is that so? Where was he when we were storming the temple?" asked Devlin.

Etah emerged from the darkness with fresh tattoos seared into his flesh. "I am a warrior. There is no glory to be won through attacking the defenseless." The God of Hate turned to his master. "Who do you want destroyed?" he asked, finishing his depiction of the Searing Sword by piercing his aura-coated finger into his skin.

"Patience. I can't send you in alone. Come on out!" hollered Lord Sel.

The minion emerged out from behind the fog. It had Uzis for feet, revolvers for hands, and a missile for a head. The rest of its arsenal was hidden beneath a sleeveless British cadet uniform. Despite his newfound loyalty, the living arsenal had the colors of Britain adorning his head. "Just tell me where to shoot," he said in a British accent.

"Karson will be working alongside you. He has proven himself quite useful as a weapon depot if nothing else. Though reviving him has become quite the tedium," said Sel.

"Pairing me up with a weak soul…you don't trust me, do you?" asked Etah, glaring at his master.

"Who are you calling weak?" asked Karson, loading up dual rocket launchers.

"Settle down. I don't want to have to revive you so soon. You both lost your battles. But loyalty is all that matters. And you both gave it your all, so my trust in you has not faltered," said Lord Sel.

"Ready for battle, Sir!" Karson walked out and went to the dark warrior's side.

"You're sending them after the Remnants as well, aren't you?" asked Devlin.

"Not quite yet," said Sel.

"They won't interfere. With Refuge in ruins, they are on the run. They will be too busy fleeing to plan any sort of offensive strategy," said Devlin.

"That is likely the case, but we must be wary. I doubt all the Remnants of Freedom have given up. If anything, seeing you may have invigorated them with a newfound desire to rescue you. One of them holds a personal vendetta against me, and I doubt he will surrender without a fight. We cannot allow the Remnants of Freedom to be captured by the angels or wait until they decide to join them," said Lord Sel.

"What do I do? How can I serve?" asked Violet.

"You and Demonica will be backup in case we run into trouble," said Lord Sel.

"Wait just one moment. Who has a personal vendetta against you?" asked Devlin.

"That's for me to know and for you to waste your time pondering about." Sel turned to Etah. "I'll inform you which ones are to be killed."

Devlin stood in between the gods. "You need to think this through. They all have potential use. Kaity is an incredible warrior—"

"Indeed she is. You can relax; she isn't on the kill list," said Sel.

"Ada poses no threat at all."

"And that's a reason not to kill her?"

"She's the only way to get to Deceivant, and he can make Exps for you."

"Hmm. You make a good point."

"And if you get them, then D.S. will surely follow. He even gave Etah trouble with his deceptive fighting style."

"You have a way with words, but I fear you are still too attached to them."

"Your mission is my mission. And the more troopers we have, the greater our chance of victory. Kanasta will protect his family as well, and he could easily be hired to kill some angels for you."

"And Nina?"

Devlin smiled. "She is loyal to a fault. Her will is mine to command. And her combat is secondary only to Riufen's."

"That loyalty could quickly become a liability should you chose to betray me," said Lord Sel.

"I have no motive to. We both seek Lum's destruction."

"Yes, our wills coincide for now. For the time being, we must assess the Remnants' intentions."

"Does that mean I can see Kaity?" asked Devlin, hope beaming through his helmet.

"Yes. Yes. And you must inform her that I have come out from the shadows," said Sel.

"Shouldn't we keep that a secret?"

"Why bother? The Freedom Forcers are more useful than they are dangerous. Oh, by the way—"

Devlin screamed out as his armor consumed his flesh.

"If you betray me, I will make you watch as I devour your beloved little kitten," said Lord Sel, a glowing red light shining from within it.

Devlin stood up, exhaled, and smiled. "What are you worried about? Pawns can only move forward and they can't attack their own king," he said with a bow.

Previously: BoneSaw and Riufen were sent to Lum to keep the Remnants of Freedom occupied.

BoneSaw tapped Riufen's leg and pointed past the ravine.

D.S. picked up Napkin who was on a tree branch over a river. "You shouldn't run off. It's dangerous here." He pet the kitty's ruffled fur. "Okay, now tell me where Kaity went."

"You distract him. I'll find the others," said Riufen, turning away.

BoneSaw hopped onto a saw, rode it to the bushes near the target and then sent it flying.

The saw sliced D.S.'s stomach, causing him to fall into the lake.

BoneSaw magnetized to the saw and flung saws as it passed by the target, getting four mini saws to connect before the assassin joined back with its saw.

"That was so cool!" D.S. stepped onto the shoreline as the killer robot sped up to him.

"**KILL**." BoneSaw revved up a massive saw before being knocked off its seat.

Rather than fall off, BoneSaw magnetized to the bottom of the floating saw. Its robot arms stretched out, sending three saws toward the target's throat.

D.S. ducked the attack. "You missed." He pulled the giant saw out from above BoneSaw and stabbed it into the robot before tossing it to the ground. "Oh yeah, touchdown!"

BoneSaw's back compartment opened as it struggled to move.

"You made me lose track of Napkin! You better apologize," said D.S., crouching down to the broken bot.

Thimble-sized BoneSaws came out from the opening and marched onto the target's feet.

"Get off!" yelled D.S., shaking his leg.

The tiny robots shoved their saws in his skin.

D.S. tried to pull them off, but they wouldn't budge without ripping his flesh. "Okay, no more games. Let go of me. It hurts. Ow. I'll say it, okay? Pleeeeease let go."

"**KILL**." "**KILL**." "**KILL**." "**KILL**." The little BoneSaws exploded one by one.

D.S. fell to the white grass with mangled legs.

131

BoneSaw backed out of the saw and magnetized back together. It dislodged the aerial saw and then sped off, searching for its next target.

Riufen sped through the forest, searching for any trail that might have been left by the Remnants of Freedom.

"That's far enough," said a muffled heroic voice.

Riufen turned around and stopped in place. Standing before him was a warrior clad in pearl-white armor with a helmet shaped like a dragon's head. In the warrior's grip was a lance.

"As the proud knight of Absence, I, Limit, will not allow you to leave," said the pearl knight.

"Last time you held back and suffered for it. Don't make the same mistake," said Riufen, pointing his new sword at the knight.

"You don't intend to fight me with a blade still in its sheath, do you?" asked Limit.

Riufen tore off the black wraps covering his gifted sword.

The massive weapon was covered in green and blue scales. It wasn't until the mouth split open and the blade emerged that it could even be identified as a sword. The weapon looked like a reptilian predator with a blade where its tongue should be. The crocodile's eyes were blood red and glistened with violent intentions.

"I've never seen such a bizarre weapon," said Limit.

"Neither have I," said Riufen.

"You are going to challenge me with a sword you've never used?" asked Limit, pointing his lance.

"There is always a first battle for a sword, but this blade is likely older than both of us."

"I accept your challenge. But first I should explain myself. You must want to know why I have come to this paradise."

"No need. Let us do battle," said Riufen, entering a fighting stance.

"Such a strange blade," said Limit, pacing around with his lance at the ready.

"It has more weight than I'm used to. Forgive me if my attacks are a bit imprecise," said Riufen, taking a step back.

"Such honesty. It will be your undoing." Limit thrust his lance at the samurai, who leaned back just out of its range.

"Even though it did not hit, my body felt the willpower behind that thrust," said Riufen, gripping his sword with both hands.

"You seek an honorable bout, but I cannot oblige. I oftentimes must withhold my sense of honor in order to be an optimal guard for Absence. 𝕴𝖓𝖍𝖎𝖇𝖎𝖙𝖔𝖗 𝕬𝖉𝖉𝖎𝖙𝖎𝖔𝖓."

Clear weights tied themselves to the swordsman's arms and legs, holding them down.

Riufen struggled and lifted his arm up three inches before it was brought back down.

"Such power. You must be thriving off your sense of loyalty as well. Let us see which of us has the greatest devotion." Limit's lance pierced into the eastern warrior's chest, carving a hole straight through his capsule.

"Dead already?" The sword slid out of the samurai's stone-like hands. It walked on all fours and impaled its wielder with its tail. It then flung him at the knight.

Limit dodged Riufen only to be bit in the leg by the sword.

The sword sped to its host and devoured him.

"What sort of tactic is this? Your technique is wholly unique!" exclaimed Limit, fending off the bladed tongue of the crocodile with his lance.

The sword jumped backward and spit the dead samurai out like a bullet.

Riufen's ribcage shot out as soon as his eyes met the knight's.

Limit planted his lance in the ground. His body then slammed down, making for an instant evasion. He grabbed the lance as he rose back up and pierced it into the samurai's open chest.

"I'm done with you!" The sword's blade-like tongue stabbed into the samurai's head. It looked up at the knight with a toothy smile. "Impressed?"

Limit tore out the lance and pressed it to the sword's head. "Your void of loyalty is a disgusting sight. I must smite you. Not for Absence, but for that brave warrior."

The sword knocked the lance out of Limit's grip. It scurried up to Riufen, hoisted him on its back and left.

"Yes, this shameful retreat suits me. How naïve I was to challenge such a warrior with a new blade. I have tarnished his great name."

"Still alive? Here I was expecting a feast," said the sword in a vicious and sly tone.

"My dishonor keeps my body indestructible. If I had true honor, that jab would have killed me, immortality aside."

"Immortality. That's quite the claim," said the sword.

"It is something I must burden. Hmm, a sword of your caliber deserves a name," said Riufen.

"Who's to say I don't already have a name?" asked the crocodile, turning its gaze to the arrogant swordsman.

"Were you named by your previous wielder?" asked Riufen.

"I am a living sword. I have no wielder."

"Yet you only became vital once you were in my grasp," said Riufen.

"Don't think you're my master. I cling only to those able to serve my purposes. I am Gladius, the epitome of swords."

"Gladius is a most suitable name. I promise you, in the next battle I will prove myself to you," said Riufen.

"I see why he chose you. You're quite the fool," said the sword.

Devlin approached the remaining Freedom Forcers, still clad in black armor.

"No need for alarm. I came only to talk to Kaity," said Devlin, raising his hands and dissolving his helmet.

Kanasta looked into his brother's eyes, scanning for sincerity. "She isn't here. She went off on her own."

"Ah yes, that's good. Mislead him," said Deceivant with a smile.

"You won't fool me, Deceivant. I don't sense her here." Devlin turned away.

Ada released her husband's hand and ran toward her son. "Please, come back to us."

Kanasta gripped his mother and held her back.

"Kaity can't be too far," said Devlin, searching the treetops.

"He'll use her to manipulate you!" yelled Deceivant.

Devlin partially looked back. "As long as I serve my master, it has no way to manipulate me."

"I get it! You allied with Sel's forces to keep us safe, right? You can negotiate to keep us protected. You can even hold back Lum's forces from capturing us without causing a rift in our relations with Lum. That's it, isn't it?" asked Ada, reaching out to her son.

Devlin smirked. "Don't get in my way." He rushed off into the trees.

"Kaity! Where are you? I only want to talk!" yelled Devlin once he was out of sight.

Something dropped from behind him.

Kaity placed her gun to the back of the traitor's head. "Go ahead. I'm listening," she said, her finger on the trigger.

"Do you not trust me?" asked Devlin, turning to face his beloved.

"Why are you doing this?" asked Kaity, digging the gun into his forehead.

"For power, of course," said Devlin with a half-smile.

"You're not in control, are you? Whose orders are you following?"

"Angels call it the Dark One. It's the entity that gave Etah his orders."

"Then you're working for Etah's master. Think about that, would you? Why would you work for the one who sabotaged your life?"

"I'm merely siphoning power off of it. The Dark One is my pawn."

"You're the pawn. You may think you're in control, but you're not."

Devlin's eyes became hollow. "How very, very true. I am a pathetic pawn who only exists because Sel allows it. I'm just another playing piece, like your father was," he said, dark energy pouring out from his feet.

"What?" asked Kaity, taking a step back.

"Do you still care for him? The man who turned you into a killing machine?"

"If you weren't in Devlin's body, I'd kill you right now."

"You couldn't even if you tried. You're as weak as your mother."

Kaity smacked his face with her gun.

"Oww! What did you do that for?" asked Devlin, holding his cheek.

"Is it really you?" asked Kaity, hey eyes tinged with suspicion.

"Who else would I be?"

"What did you want to talk to me about?" asked Kaity, turning away and crossing her arms.

"I'm worried about your safety. Lum's forces won't rest until they have your allies in their custody. I want you to leave them. If you come with me, I can guarantee your safety," said Devlin, reaching out to her.

Kaity shot his arm, pushing it aside. "I'm staying with my allies."

"I don't want Lord Sel to hurt you."

"Lord Sel…is that the Dark One?"

"Please, Kaity. If your team joins Lum, I won't be able to convince Sel to spare them."

"Why would we join Lum? After you destroyed our one safe haven, Etaf appeared. She's hunting us down right now. Our priority is survival. We're already a target as it is."

"Don't let Deceivant lead you into danger. He always has his own agenda."

"He didn't abandon you. It was Etah who broke you apart from your family. Do you still resent him so much you can't call him father?"

"I still can't find it in myself to trust him. For whatever reason, a part of me still feels he is partially to blame. But I'm not the same child of vengeance I once was. Please, keep my parents safe."

Kaity nodded.

"I'm sorry for all this. Stay strong, Kaity. This will pass and then we can all live in peace," said Devlin.

"Bye," said Kaity before walking off.

"Be safe." Devlin entered a black portal.

Devlin appeared in the Core.

"Are they are heading out to get Lum's aid?" asked Lord Sel.

"They just want to be left alone," said Devlin.

"Yet they are getting closer and closer to the Elysium Asylum. This is no coincidence."

"Perhaps it is a coincidence," said Violet.

"Perhaps, but we shouldn't be sloppy."

Riufen appeared, bowing upon arrival. "I failed in my mission."

"Limit's interference was an unseen development. You only failed because you did not probe him for information."

"The gift you gave me wielded me with greater skill than I wielded it," said Riufen, his face against the ground.

"Naturally," said Gladius with a toothy grin.

"Riufen, here's an artifact I retrieved from your world to help you in the next battle. This will allow you to learn how to use your new sword without any concern," said Sel.

Demonica's gimp offered a graphite stone to the samurai.

"Thank you for this boon. I am not worthy," said Riufen, absorbing the artifact before bowing.

"The mission was to discern the Remnants' agenda. Devlin was able to meet with Kaity one-on-one due to you keeping the others occupied. You and BoneSaw both succeeded. Now, enough of that. Whether they know it or not, they are getting closer to the Elysium Asylum. We must ambush them before they arrive. Devlin, you are coming with me."

"What's at the prison?" asked Violet.

"I get to fight this time, right?" asked Pesi, standing up.

"Yes, yes. Listen everyone; there are extra Exps in Lum. If the Remnants of Freedom get their hands on them, it could prove problematic. One in particular has the power to turn the tide. Now off you go!" exclaimed Lord Sel.

Demonica's gimp sent everyone away except for Devlin and Lord Sel.

"What is our mission?" asked Devlin.

"To kill a god," said Lord Sel, radiating with darkness.

Chapter 102: The Deity's Temple

Kaity met up with her teammates in the forest.

"Careful. Devlin is out looking for you," said Deceivant, his eyes fixed below him.

"I…I already talked to him," said Kaity with a solemn look.

"What did he say?" asked Kanasta.

"He warned us not to get aid from Lum. Is that where you are bringing us?" asked Kaity, looking over the inventor's shoulder.

"Aw, your face is so cute," said Deceivant, barely holding back from pinching her cheeks.

"Answer the question," said Kaity, knocking his arm aside.

"Sorry, I was distracted by your wittle nose. What was it you were saying?" asked Deceivant.

"She asked if you are leading us somewhere. Are you planning on having us join Lum's forces?" asked Kanasta.

"When we first came to Lum, I didn't really believe it was the afterlife. I still hold firm to my doubts, but for the time being I will continue to assume that this place is where the dead go. And taking that into consideration, I have to investigate something important. It will be dangerous, but if I don't go…then I have no right to call myself a father," said Deceivant, worry growing in his golden eyes.

"You're different than Devlin described," said Nina, popping out from behind the trees.

"Where were you?" asked Ada.

"Keeping watch. Devlin talked so dearly to you," said Nina, turning to her ally with a solemn look.

"Then you heard what he said. His parents didn't abandon him," said Kaity.

"That isn't what he said. I'm not convinced. That said, I have no reason to think any of you are lying to me. I'll try to be more amiable," said Nina, her gaze lowering.

"I have some bad news. Etah was following the orders of a greater god. It's a deity called Lord Sel."

"Etah was the king of Sel. Does that mean Lord Sel is the god of Sel?" asked Ada.

"That's what is implied by the name," said Kaity.

"Lord Sel. A being so feared we haven't heard it mentioned until now. And that's who my brother is working for, correct?" asked Kanasta.

"I'm afraid so," said Kaity.

"I've heard of it. Mika talked about Lord Sel. To think I once thought her superstitious," said Deceivant with a tremble in his voice.

"Is Devlin alright? Is my little boy being manipulated?" asked Ada.

"Sel took over him in the midst of our conversation. Seems he can lose control at the flip of a switch. As long as Devlin is in that armor, he is captive," said Kaity.

"Then we must break it," said Kanasta.

"And I know just the person for the job," said Deceivant.

"Who?" asked Ada.

"You'll find out once we've arrived," said Deceivant, patting his wifey's head.

"Oh yeah. Found our brave little warrior crying by the river. Catch," said Nina, tossing Napkin.

Kaity caught the frazzled kitty and pet him calmingly. She then turned her attention to Deceivant and swiped the object in his hand. "What are these dots on the screen? Where are you taking us?" she asked, waving the locator.

"To the Elysium Asylum, the prison of Lum. It's likely well guarded and may even be inaccessible. We aren't joining forces with Lum. If anything, Lum's forces will be hunting us down without mercy afterwards."

"Then we won't be safe anywhere."

"Can you track down Devlin with that?" asked Nina.

"His armor interferes with the tracer on his capsule. No doubt he will meet us at the prison."

"Yeah, but going to the prison puts us all in even more danger," said Kaity.

"If Etaf wants us to go to the prison anyway, then is it really a problem?" asked Ada.

"It is if we break out their prisoners," said Deceivant with a shrug.

"We are ill-equipped for another battle against Etaf. That said, we'll follow you to the prison and decide if we'll join you once we arrive," said Kanasta.

"Where is D.S.?" asked Ada.

"He's right...gone. Kanasta, Kaity, you two go out and locate him. The rest of us will travel further upriver," said Deceivant.

Kaity looked up at Kanasta. "What do you think we should do? You're the only one here fit to lead."

"Ada is a schoolteacher, and I am more than capable of leading," said Deceivant.

"Stay put. Someone is approaching from the bushes," said Kanasta, moving his protégé behind him.

138

"I see it on the radar, but I can't identify who it is," said Kaity.

D.S. came out from the bushes and limped back to his team.

"Did Devlin hurt you?" asked Kaity.

"BoneSaws. Tiny BoneSaws. My legs hurt," said D.S., leaning on his mother.

Kanasta crouched down to the wounds. "Hmm. You were able to walk after they exploded. I may need to tweak the blast to make it a bit stronger."

"Did you give it the floaty saw too?" asked D.S.

"Yes, was it useful?" asked Kanasta.

"It would have been more useful if BoneSaw used it when we were fighting demons," said D.S. with a pouty face.

"BoneSaw likely had a reason. I do not know what it was," said Kanasta.

"Maybe my boy's little bot saw you as a threat," said Ada.

"Yeah! That's gotta be it!" cheered D.S.

"Lean on Kanasta's shoulder and let's move along," said Deceivant.

"What did I miss?" asked D.S.

"The god of Sel is our new enemy," said Kanasta.

"Great another big bad guy. Haven't we lost enough friends already?" asked D.S., breaking down into tears.

"There, there," said Ada, nestling her boy to her bosom.

"He's deadweight like that," said Nina.

"So what, we're just supposed to leave him behind?" asked Kaity.

Nina tore off part of her shirt. "We should get him healed before we move on, or else we're putting everyone at risk."

"If we stay here, out in the open, we're still at risk," said Deceivant.

Napkin jumped out of Kaity's arms and ran off.

Nina leaped into action and caught the cat as he ran down the hill. "Our brave little warrior found us a rest spot! To think I once thought he was the weak link in our team," she said as Napkin bit and clawed at her arms.

The Remnants of Freedom met up with her.

"It's beautiful," said Ada with shimmering eyes.

A structure made from wispy pink energy was just down the hill. It was round like a dome and had a cylindrical winding path that was sealed off. It was as tall as the oak trees around it and was cloaked in a field of flowers of all the colors of the rainbow.

"Nice find," said Kaity, picking up her kitty pal.

"It's like a castle straight out of a fairytale," said D.S. with a wide smile.

"We can't see what's inside. Could be dangerous," said Kanasta.

"Do you want me to do some reconnaissance?" asked Kaity.

"We need to get to the prison. It isn't too far from here," said Deceivant.

"I wasn't asking you," said Kaity, sticking out her tongue.

"We're still in Masculino. If you're caught, it could get us unwanted attention," said Kanasta.

"Fine then. I'll go in. Kanasta would no doubt intimidate whoever is inside, whether he intends to or not. If they aren't hospitable, we will continue our trek to the prison," said Deceivant.

"I'll get as close as I can without alerting them," said Nina.

"If I'm not out in ten minutes, please come rescue me," said Deceivant.

"Understood," said Kanasta.

Deceivant went down the hillside and approached what he believed was the front of the structure.

"What temple do you belong to?" asked a hoarse voice behind him.

Deceivant turned to see a woman nearly completely concealed under a white garment. Only her amber eyes were visible.

"Oh, I belong to…."

"Forget it. It doesn't matter." The woman bumped shoulders as she passed by him. "I am Heaven's Thunder. I am here on behalf of the Imam."

The wall of light dropped and she proceeded ahead.

Deceivant followed, relieved to see that the pink light coating the ground was not sticking to his feet. He lowered his head once he spotted two polar bear angels guarding the entrance to the main hall.

"I'm here for the meeting," said Thunder, standing tall and firm.

"And him?" asked the angel, pointing to the man with his claws.

"He's from Refuge of the People. Can't you tell by his bracelet?" asked Thunder, grabbing the man's hand and raising it.

"Understood. Move along," said one of the bear angels.

"Is this your first time coming to Beacon?" asked Thunder.

"Yes. Is this place made from the deity's energy?" asked Deceivant.

"It is indeed. The Deity of Love set up this area near the Elysium Asylum, that way its energy can bless the prisoners."

"How very kind."

"Is it? I think the energy is a subtle form of manipulation. The prisoners are placated by it, keeping them subdued."

"You're quite the skeptic."

"And you're the scientist who was caught sleeping with a child. How did you even make it to Lum? And how did you get a kara from the Refuge of the People?"

"I assure you I in no way took advantage of Mika. As for why I am here, that decision was not mine. Lastly, I befriended Rambir and was given this," said Deceivant, tapping his bracelet.

"You don't trust the Goddesses either, do you?"

"Doubt is vital for every scientific endeavor."

"How would you like to get out of here and back to Earth? We could use the help of your creations to breach Samsara."

"You should know that a scientist is wary of meddling in religious affairs."

"So you're not interested?"

"I cannot return just yet. There is someone waiting for me here."

"Likewise. My daughter has gone missing," said Thunder, her eyes losing their intensity for an instant.

Deceivant followed Thunder through an ever-growing crowd and up to an elevated platform.

There were over thirty men and women, all seated on chairs of light.

Thunder gestured where he should sit and took her own seat between a Hindu woman and a Jain nun.

"Well this is quite a surprise. I had heard they were all but wiped out," said the Rabbi seated next to Deceivant.

"What happened? Is it true your entire temple was demolished?" asked a Buddhist monk.

"Yes, please tell us what happened," said the Jain nun.

"Sel's forces destroyed the building. I was lucky to survive," said Deceivant.

"I heard it was a massacre. You should thank the Lord you were spared," said a Christian man.

"There's an injured man with me. Can I bring him in?" asked Deceivant.

"I'm not even sure it's safe to have you here. Was there any reason the demons attacked your temple? What did your people do to offend them? Or was it just a coincidence?" asked the Christian man.

"Are they going after temples?" "What if our church is next?" "Can't anyone stop these demons?" asked the religious leaders.

Deceivant turned, noticing a little girl hoisted on a woman's shoulder. "Maybe I should leave."

"You can't leave till you tell us what you know. Look, you're the only one with a clue of what's going on. We're all scared, even the angels," said the Christian man.

"Yes, the main reason we gathered here is because we all want to know what's going on," said the Rabbi.

"I don't know why they attacked. I need to go," said Deceivant, standing up.

"Now, now, there's no need to cancel. I apologize for my tardiness."

Efil, the Goddess of Life, ascended up the stage, looking right up at the scientist.

Deceivant sat down, unsure whether she saw him or not.

Efil took her seat next to a Jain monk and a Catholic priest. "I thank you all for coming here. I assure you that Lum is doing all she can to keep the threat contained."

"How did these demons breach the Angel Wall?" asked a Rastafarian priest.

"They bypassed it somehow. They have found a rift and are exploiting it, but they are unable to move large numbers in. All the angels of Lum are currently searching for the rift. The Angel Wall has not faltered in the least. As long as the gods of Lum draw breath, it shall be unbreakable," said Efil.

"Are other places of worship in danger?" asked Thunder.

"It's best to stay cautious, but there is no reason to assume more demons will attack. Etaf informed me that the demons who attacked the Refuge of the People were completely wiped out."

"And the visitors?" asked Deceivant.

"Pardon?" asked Efil.

"Were there any survivors?"

"I tended to the injured, but they suffered many casualties. My prayers go off to their loved ones."

"Why were they killed? The whole temple was destroyed, correct?" asked Thunder.

"That is correct. As for why they were killed...."

"They were after me. The demons know I am a skilled inventor. It isn't safe for any of you as long as I am here. I must get going." Deceivant took a stand, bowed to the group and then stepped off the stage.

"I'll escort you," said Efil, swiftly moving up to him.

"There's no need," said Deceivant, walking through the crowd.

The goddess grabbed his hand. "I can get you all to safety. But I must finish up here first."

"We don't need your help."

"You still don't trust me?"

"The angels watched as the temple collapsed. They did nothing for the people they were supposed to protect."

"I'm sure that was just a misunderstanding."

"Etaf came after and tried to round us up. The Sikhs fought her to keep us protected. The demons only killed a few people. The majority of the casualties were caused by your partner," said Deceivant, clenching his fist.

"Etaf acted brashly, but she surely had reason to. It isn't safe for you to wander around in Lum. I will escort you as soon as I am done here."

"Finish quickly. Sel's forces are close by. This place will become their next target if I don't get out of here now."

"I'll do what I can to keep you safe."

"Don't bother. Just make sure to get the children to safety if this place is attacked." Deceivant moved through the crowd and exited the structure.

The charming inventor met up with his allies at the top of the hill.

"What's the verdict?" asked Kanasta.

"We need to get moving."

"Did they spot you?" asked Nina, applying water to D.S.'s wound.

"There are angels inside. They didn't recognize me, but we should still move on," said Deceivant.

"Hey, I can stand up. Thanks, Cool Nina," said D.S.

"It wasn't entirely my doing. Violet put her energy in these bottles...before she betrayed us," said Nina.

"So then, I guess we'll head to the prison for now. Which way is it?" asked Kaity.

"It's behind the building I went into, but it's best if we go around and stay hidden in the trees," said Deceivant.

"Agreed," said Kanasta.

Ada stopped walking. "Wait. We never finished the tribute. There's one person we haven't spoken of yet."

"You mean Exp 8," said Kaity softly.

"The Ultimate Exp. He certainly lived up to the name. Always brave and a great leader...it seems impossible that he's gone. He had limitless potential," said Deceivant, keeping a steady pace while he talked.

"He welcomed me to the team with a hug. I still remember it. He was always so caring," said Kaity, grabbing her papa's hand.

"He was a great guy!" cheered D.S.

"Exp 8 made sure everyone was happy. He looked out for all of us. Even though he's gone, we're going to keep on fighting!" cheered Ada.

"That's right. We aren't finished just yet," said Deceivant.

"Must have been a great leader," said Nina, walking backward at a quickened pace to urge the team to speed up.

"Uh-huh. The best," said Ada with a big smile.

"Well then, umm, that's it," said Deceivant.

"Wait. I have something to say," said Kaity.

"Of course. We're all here to support each other," said Deceivant with a smile.

"I want to apologize to Karson. I was the one who killed him, over and over. The reason he made that deal was because I was being childish," said Kaity.

"There, there, let's keep it positive. Karson was a brave and honorable warrior. He was a bit funnier than he realized too," said Deceivant.

"Yeah, he was always so serious and very proud," said Ada.

"He was way cool! Too bad he became a bad guy," said D.S.

Karson came out from the foliage and stood in front of the Remnants of Freedom.

"You're alive," said Kaity with a smile.

"Well, yeah. I am. You were talking about me," said Karson, scratching his head with his pistol hand.

"I named my new special move after you!" hollered D.S.

"Did we interrupt?" asked Violet, arriving next.

"We were honoring the dead," said Ada, lowering her head.

"They're over here!" hollered Karson.

Riufen, Gladius, Exp 11, and Demonica joined with the gunman and devotee.

"Perhaps we should come back at a later time," said Violet, turning to her allies with concern.

"These are our enemies! We can't show any mercy," said Pesi.

Etah appeared spontaneously in front of his allies and grinned. "Still some strong souls left to claim."

"The one in the cloak, he wasn't Exp 8, was he?" asked Deceivant.

"An imposter. The true hero died by my hand," said Etah, clenching his fist and releasing his aura.

"Kaity, run on my signal," said Kanasta.

"Devlin isn't here. Kanasta, make sure the people in the temple are safe," said Deceivant.

"Understood," said Kanasta before running off.

"Who wishes to join my internal armory?" asked Etah with a grin.

Napkin leaped out from Kaity's arms and ran off.

"Let him go. It's best he runs for now," said Nina.

"Please, just leave us alone," said Ada in tears.

"Split up and run. I'll distract them," said Nina, drawing her katana.

"We shall handle things from here." Occupy emerged from the bushes, along with Void, Needle, Separate, Spin, Plagiarism, and Crystal.

"Hello, Crystal, Occupy, glad to see you again, my friends," said Deceivant, nodding to them. His head darted to face the others. "Why did the rest of you abandon us when we were fighting Etah?" he asked, anger boiling in his throat.

"Calm yourself. It was a delicate situation and Neutral was acting on behalf of Absence. But things have changed now. I'll explain later," said Occupy with calming gestures.

"You'll explain now," said Deceivant.

"With the demon lords out of the picture, Lord Sel now has command over all of Sel's troops. Before it would have to request troops from each specific demon lord, and it would only receive a small portion of their respective armies since all demon lords seek to become the ruler of Sel. With the unification of Sel, Lum is now truly in danger. Sel now threatens the balance of Sellum. And it is only a matter of time before Lord Sel sets its sights on our realm," said Occupy.

Loyal swooped down from above, uprooting some trees as he landed.

Limit was proudly seated atop his comrade.

The God of Hate took one step toward the Absence gods. "Lord Sel forgave your transgressions against me. All of Absence will pay for any further transgressions. Sel's unified army will wreak havoc across your beloved land if you dare attack us. Return to your realm," said Etah, signaling with the Agony Axe.

"We cannot allow Sel to harm the neutrality of Sellum. We will defend Lum from your conquest," said Occupy.

"Mom, Dad, stay back. I'll protect you," said D.S., stepping up.

Pesi approached the thorny needle god. "I can't afford to fail. Once I win this fight, Lord Sel will recognize my power. Hmm, I wonder if I can make a pile of needles suffer."

Karson stepped up to face the knight and the dragon.

"Let's find out what kills better: guns, swords, or beasts. Haha."

Riufen set his sights on Plagiarism and Crystal and stepped up to challenge them. "It is dishonorable to copy one's being. And it is even worse to make a weak imitation of them. Gladius, I will take care of both of them alone. You can fight Nina and Kaity."

"Don't command me, swordsman. Which ones are Nina and Kaity?" asked Gladius.

"Looks like it's the two of us again," said Kaity with a smile.

"Oh, have we done this before? I'll follow your lead then," said Nina.

Etah turned his sights on D.S. "I didn't think you would survive being chopped in two. Your warrior's spirit will soon be mine."

"Then take mine as well," said Occupy.

"I will make you regret stopping me from killing Devlin," said Etah.

"Weren't you limping away?" asked Occupy.

"I will overcome this humiliation! I claim your souls for the glory of Sel!" yelled Etah, energy pooling from his hands.

Demonica flew up to Separate and Spin.

"I will teach the gods of Absence not to trifle in Sel's affairs."

Violet confronted her living god's parents. "Do not think of me as a traitor. I am a firm believer in Devlin. I will follow him faithfully regardless of his path. Prepare yourself."

Chapter 103: Preserving the Balance

Pesi led Needle to a rocky area by the river. "After I suffered a near fatal wound, almost fully killed from my dark blood loss, I unlocked the true power of my artifact. *PESSIMISTIC PULSE SUICIDE!*"

The evil bad man released his energy aura out as a dark black blast.

Needle stabbed itself with its thorny appendages. The spines from its elbow fired out and pierced into the dark mortal's arms.

"Damn you to Sel! Feel the wrath of my fist of ruin!" Pesi flew forward and punched the god's face. He screamed in pain before tumbling to the ground. The crazed sadist tore out the spines lodged in his hand, getting more furious with each one.

Needle fired a single spine.

Pesi rolled out of the way and then took to the skies. "Can't hit me now, you stupid idiot!"

Hundreds of spines came out from the god and fired into the air.

Pesi frantically maneuvered in the air, switching to Opti each time he got hit before switching back. "The agonizing pain isn't so bad once you're already pierced. I'll just dodge you till you run out!"

Needle tore out a piece of its own body and sent it flying.

The spiky ball burst once it passed by its target, showering the mortal with spines from behind.

Pesi crashed to the ground as his flight pattern was altered by agony. "Opti, keep him busy while I build up evil energy." (Switch) "You're really entrusting this battle to me?" asked Opti, slowly getting back to his feet.

Needle fired a large spike that burst into mini spikes before contact.

"Owiee! Okay, if you're not going to be nice, then I won't either. I'll use up all my energy at once and beat you with a single attack!" exclaimed Opti, closing his eyes and holding out his palms.

The spines on Needles arms stood up, spinning in place before shooting out.

Opti's eyes opened. "All your needles are now fluffy bunnies! *OPTIMISTIC BUNNIFICATION!*" he exclaimed, sending a constant stream of a powerful white aura along with his life force into the sharp god.

Needle looked at its body curiously before suddenly collapsing. Thousands of snow-white bunnies appeared in place of its body, all bundled together.

"Hooray! It's a fluffy bunny mountain!" cheered Opti, snuggling a fat brown bunny that tumbled out from the very center of the pile. "So cute." The fun-loving invention fell backward, exhausted.

(Switch) "Kehahahahaha! Now for the finishing blow. ULTIMATE PESSIMISM, MASS SUICIDE!"

Overtaken by an overflowing surge of despair, the bunnies hopped toward the river to drown themselves.

"That's how you take down a god! Kehaha!" (Switch) "No, Pesi! I won't let you! I will save them!"

The pure-hearted pacifist burst out of the psychopathic sadist's body.

"What just happened?" asked Pesi, looking at his other half rise from the ground.

"ULTIMATE OPTIMISM, HOPEFUL AWAKENING!" Opti's white aura flooded into the bunnies. His eyes lost their luster and his skin lost some of its vigor before he collapsed. "From now on. I'm me, always. Praise the bunny gods," he said before closing his eyes.

The bunnies were overcome with forced optimism, canceling out their recent affinity for suicide.

"This is real! I'm finally free of that moronic, imbecilic, idiotic simpleton! It's all because I tried to kill innocents! No more happy thoughts, no more fluffy feelings. The butterflies in my belly are being devoured by my stomach acid! Keheheh! I'm free! I am free to unleash true horrors upon all worlds!" yelled Pesi, furiously clawing at a tree.

A chubby brown bunny went up to Opti and snuggled his face. "It's you again. I'll call you Muffins! When I wake up, I'll be sure to rub you behind the ears real good."

Pesi kicked his sworn enemy. "Get up! It's time to go assist Lord Sel. Leave the bunny and let's go."

"I could never! I'm taking Muffins with me," said Opti as he picked up the bunny and struggled back to his feet. "Wait, why should I help Sel?"

"Would you rather die?"

"Yes."

"Ugh. Look, Lord Sel is a god. That means it has omniscience. I bet it can find that girl you're looking for."

"NoOne's girl?"

"Yeah, whatever. You coming or not?"

"You betcha."

Karson stayed his ground, commencing his battle with Loyal and Limit in the forest clearing.

Karson exchanged his machine gun hands for crossbows. "If I'm going to shoot down a dragon, I might as well do it the old-fashioned way," he said, locking in an arrow.

"Your soul is honor-bound. This will be a glorious battle," said Limit.

"We are both warriors of Britain; let us find out whether history favors the knight or the gunman." Karson sent arrows soaring through the sky at the dragon.

Limit tossed his lance into the air, hitting three of the arrows.

The arrows bounced off Limit's armor and were unable to pierce Loyal's hide.

Limit jumped up and grabbed his lance.

"Forget the gunman. There is something going on at Beacon," said Loyal.

Limit nodded and rushed off.

"You bloomin' coward!" yelled Karson.

"I am more than able to handle you," said Loyal, dragging his tail across the ground and uprooting some trees in the process.

Karson set his arrows alight with the flamethrower in his leg and fired through the haze of dust and wood.

The burning arrow pierced into the dragon's eye.

Loyal wailed in pain, lifting his foe off the ground with the sheer might of his lungs.

"The time of the dragons is over! Postmodern warfare makes your kind obsolete." Two rockets fired from Karson's arms.

Loyal ejected a fireball, blasting the two rockets.

Karson's head navigated through more uprooted trees and blasted into the flying warrior's chest.

The dragon god was pushed back but was uninjured by the blast.

Karson landed on his feet. His chest cannon had been gathering energy during the disturbance. "Technology was once how humans borrowed the power of the gods they idolized. They lived as prosthetic gods for over a thousand years. In the twenty-second century humans created artificial beings that embody the power of the gods!"

Loyal's eyes widened before he released a jet of heat.

"Technology has now surpassed the heavens. Exps are gods of warfare! **PARTICLE BEAM**!"

The energy beam obliterated the breath of flame and shot through Loyal's arm.

"Devlin defeated Etah. I can surely obliterate you!" yelled Karson, charging another beam while sending out a volley of rockets.

"Gods of warfare. Interesting. Let us test your claim."

Trees were torn from the earth as the dragon batted his wings.

"Come at me! Forget guns versus beasts. This is a battle to decide whether machines or gods are superior! Technology versus divinity!" yelled Karson, repeatedly shooting off his missile head each time his neck disengaged another missile.

Loyal swooped toward the boisterous mortal, staying on course despite the rocket barrage.

"***PARTICLE BEAM, GOD DESTROYER!***"

The condensed beam shot into the dragon god's chest.

"Victory!" cheered Karson.

Loyal's tail pierced the machine and lifted it off the ground.

"Where's your aura, war god?" asked Loyal with a bladed grin.

"How did you?"

Loyal's claws pierced into the man of metal. "It appears the artificial gods just don't measure up."

Karson was ripped apart by the god dragon's talons.

Riufen led Crystal and Plagiarism to an open field.

The stoic samurai stopped in place and turned around. After grabbing his sword he deflected the four crystalline projectiles heading toward him.

"I'm a guy named Crystal. I have to work with a talkative chameleon. The love of my life was taken from me. And to top it all off, I have to fight you of all people. I never catch a break," said Crystal, holding his forehead.

"Cutting through diamond is a necessary step toward becoming a better warrior. Come at me," said Riufen, planting his feet in the ground.

"What a pain." Crystal fired pieces of his arms at the swordsman.

Riufen held still and let the giant shards shoot through his body.

Crystal was suddenly pushed back. "What did you do?" he asked, forming a shield out of new minerals.

"I used the Mirror Artifact, apparently," said Riufen with a curious look.

"So whenever I hit you, I get hurt? Great, as if you weren't strong enough already."

"We can take him." Plagiarism shot his tongue at the skillful swordsman, who pierced it with his spine.

"Hmm, I wonder if I can stack targets." Riufen closed his eyes and spun his spine around. "**SAN SEPPUKU**." He plunged the blade into his skull and then his capsule.

Plagiarism had a hole through its forehead but the slice was unable to pierce his lazy guard.

Crystal set his boss on the ground. "Lum has lots of problems: compartmentalization, elitism, a religion that encourages blind loyalty, and rules that forbid lovers from becoming one." Minerals jutted out from his back. "Despite all its issues, it's a very special place to me." His body doubled in size as he expanded from within. "Most importantly, there's someone very dear to me who once lived here." He slammed his fists together, making the crystals jut out like spines on a porcupine. "I can't get fired up about protecting something as nebulous as a place or a species or even a way of life. But I'll fight for her. And I'll win." He tore off a handful of spikes.

Riufen swerved and jumped to dodge the mineral barrage. "Loyalty drives us both. Let he who fights with greater honor claim victory."

"I've already won."

Riufen leaped back into an invisible wall.

"Ever heard the expression 'the tip of the iceberg?'" asked Crystal.

The crystal spikes from below emerged from the ground, each one a miniature mountain.

Riufen's ribs burst out from his chest, breaking to pieces once they hit the crystalline structure below.

"I'd almost forgotten what fighting with a purpose feels like.

STALAGMITE STORM."

The jagged mini mountains fired shards into the air.

"Atatasuki, I call upon your fortitude, my comrade." Riufen unsheathed the jeweled blade and, along with his spine, deflected the mineral barrage.

"Did you forget what's above you?" asked Crystal.

The shards bounced off the clear barrier above and shot back down.

Riufen spun in place, slicing projectiles from below and above.

His blood sprayed on the invisible wall above as more and more projectiles sliced his flesh.

"You can't keep it up forever," said Crystal, taking a seat and looking up at the clouds.

"There is no need to." Riufen ended his rotation and was pierced from all angles.

The barrier above shattered. Riufen kicked off the side barriers and hopped out of the invisible prison. He landed in front of the god, hidden beneath a coat of mineral spikes.

"You're not done yet, are you?"

Riufen tore out the spikes concealing his face. The warrior's blood seeped back in and his skin regenerated. "You and I have much in common. Our entire body is our weapon."

"True. So how did you make it shatter?" asked Crystal, standing up.

"I didn't. You did," said Riufen, pulling out the spikes one after the next.

"Time for round two." Crystal rushed forth.

Riufen blocked the god's arm by using both blades. "Indeed."

Minerals grew out from the arm and pressed into the samurai's skin.

Riufen pushed the arm aside with both blades and kicked off the ground. "CRIMSON COATING." With both blades coated in hardened blood, the samurai sliced into the god's neck.

"You can't cut me!"

Riufen kicked off, dodging an incoming fist. He blocked a mineral shot with his spine.

The fortified spine snapped.

The mineral pierced into the warrior's chest.

Riufen tore it out and used it to deflect the incoming projectiles. "Your bones are stronger than my own."

Once he landed, the swordsman hardened his bones and rammed into the god.

"You're fighting for the wrong side. Just like I was," said Crystal before besting the warrior in the power struggle.

Riufen's feet were held in place by minerals, keeping him pinned.

"Farewell." Crystal sandwiched the swordsman between his massive fists, popping him like a tomato. "Try coming back from that."

Riufen regenerated, examining the splatter of blood and bone that was once his body. "Your attack must be stronger to rid me of my cursed immortality. Hit me with your strongest technique! It's the only way to settle this."

"All my minerals are the same. Oh, okay. I know what to do." Crystal tore out a mineral spike from his back. "This is the power of my solitude."

The god's aura climbed up the spike and coated its tip before being flung.

"It has been a glorious fight." Riufen snatched the projectile from the air and pierced his joints one after the next, ending his self-mutilation by erasing his own neck.

"What are you doing?" asked Crystal.

"Seppuku is often undertaken to restore honor to one's self. If this ability can transfer the act unto someone else, can it restore their honor in the same way? This is very interesting. Is it truly dishonorable to kill oneself in order to kill another? Under normal circumstances, no, but I am using an artifact. I need not worry until later. Right now I must meet up with Lord Sel." Riufen bowed to his opponent.

Crystal fell to pieces. "How did you do it?"

"I was only able to win because you were able to surpass your own power. The barrier was weaker than the crystal spikes, and your crystals are weaker than your aura. This victory belongs to you, but so does the defeat. Farewell." Riufen walked away, disappearing among the trees.

Nina and Kaity chased after Gladius all the way to the exit of the forest.

"So this is where it was leading us. Is this some kind of barrier?" asked Nina, looking up at wall of white light.

"Not sure, but let's make sure it doesn't get in there," said Kaity, looking around for the target.

Spikes rose out of the ground and closed in on them.

Nina pushed off the ground the moment the spikes touched her feet.

Gladius shot out of the dirt, clenching his jaws down on the ninja's meaty legs.

"Let go of her!" yelled Kaity, firing a whole round into the creature's head.

"Try to find an entrance. I'll take care of him." Nina stabbed her katana through the oni's skull. "It's over." The nimble ninja pushed herself out of his jaws and fell to the dirt. She bit off some extra bandage around her arms and applied it to her leg wounds as she rolled away from the living sword.

Gladius rushed after her, unknowingly picking up explosive tags with each step.

Nina jumped in the air and tossed a shuriken at a tag just below the crocodile's snout.

Gladius swiftly moved his head out of the way.

All the tags exploded.

Nina tossed her shirts and pants into the smoke cloud and detonated them.

Gladius was sent flying out of the cloud, his body scorched and bloodied.

Nina climbed up the branches of a tree and leaped off. She landed on the enemy and was now dressed as a kunoichi. In one hand she twirled a ninja star the size of an umbrella. She stabbed it into the enemy's back, keeping it in motion as it tore through his flesh.

Gladius thrashed his head backward, slamming into the warrior's leg. His tail then pierced her other leg.

Nina fell off his back, swiftly searching for an object to grab hold of.

Gladius' bladed tongue shot out and into her tasty thigh.

"You almost had me," said Nina, her voice above her attacker.

153

The living sword blinked and looked again. Only the ninja's clothes were stabbed by his tongue.

Nina was on top of him in only her underwear. She stabbed her fingers into the crocodile's brain, forcing him to retract his tongue and her clothing. The disciplined warrior pushed off him as she pulled out a detonator from her hair.

The clothes exploded in the crocodile's mouth.

Gladius collapsed to the ground, belly up and smoldering.

Nina swooped down with double blades at the ready.

The crocodile rolled out of the way, and Nina swiftly adjusted and sped after him. He lashed his tail, but she dodged every swipe and slapped on an explosive tag in a different area each time.

The living sword's tail exploded, sending him tumbling across the ground.

Nina matched his speed and sliced her blades into his stomach each time his belly was exposed. She then reached into her bra and grabbed a handful of kunai.

The kunai made a circle on the crocodile's stomach.

Nina gripped all the kunai and twisted them, carving a hole in the demons' belly.

Kaity leaned against the wall of light, staring in awe at the almost nude ninja.

"Did you find a way in?" asked Nina, piercing her katana through the hole as she pressed Gladius against the wall.

Kaity stared at her blankly, a trail of drool mixing with a small puddle beneath her.

"Are you possessed?" asked Nina, grabbing her sword. She flicked a pebble at Devlin's beloved.

"You're pretty," said Kaity with a wide smile.

"Did you find the entrance?"

"Oh, uh, yeah. Just walk on through," said Kaity, pushing her hand through the wall of light.

"Good enough, I'll incapacitate him." Nina reached into her underwear and pulled out a talisman. "*Gravity Bind*." She slapped the talisman on his forehead.

Gladius fell flat on his belly and froze in place.

"It won't last long. Let's move," said Nina.

Kaity drooled as her eyes went up and down the ninja's body.

Nina looked down. She closed her eyes and rematerialized her kunoichi outfit. She grabbed Kaity's shoulders and looked her up and down. She spun the girl around and crouched down to get a better look at her butt. "If he likes girls of your body type, then why did he make me like this?" she asked with a solemn tone.

"Maybe he didn't know what he found to be the most attractive," said Kaity.

"If I had been stronger…if I stayed in control, this wouldn't have happened. He wouldn't have fallen in love with you. No. I need to stay focused. Let's see what's beyond this wall," said Nina.

"You're even more amazing than the other Nina," said Kaity with a smile.

"I've been inconsiderate. You love her, don't you? She is my greatest enemy. You most likely won't see her again. You must hate me for taking her away. We'll discuss this later," said Nina, catching Gladius' leg twitch from the corner of her eye.

"**HATRED PRISON**!" Etah created a box around Occupy, Void, and Destructus Supplious with his heated aura. "Three new souls will be added to my armory."

"This guy is tough with a capital T. I'm not sure I can beat him," said D.S.

"Then I merely ask that you back me up," said Occupy.

"Hey you know, all three of us are bald," said D.S. with a grin, patting Occupy's head.

"I've never fought an Absence god. This will be interesting." The Deva ran up to the monk and slammed the Agony Axe down upon him.

"**BODHI BLOCK**." Occupy stopped the blade's descent with Void's indestructible body.

Etah's whole body shook from the impact. "My ambition will not be hindered by anyone!" The warrior lashed the axe furiously at the Absence god.

Occupy defended himself with his impenetrable mentor each time the axe hit. He slid around the next axe strike and flung his powerful guru into the warrior's foot.

Etah looked down, expecting excruciating pain, but Occupy had caught Void with his other foot.

The monk kicked Void up, crushing Etah's face and sending him flying through the air.

"That should keep him away for a while," said Occupy, looking above for his guru.

Etah crashed into a tree, his back against its trunk.

Scissors pierced through the bark of the tree and through the god's throat.

D.S. took out his giant staple gun and shot staples into Etah's hands and feet, pinning him to the ground.

Etah ripped his hands out of the staples, slicing them open. He then yanked the staples out from his feet.

Something swooped by and sliced D.S.'s face.

"I'll keep you entertained," said the Captain of Carnage, reeling his blades in.

"Yay! Now I won't be bored!" cheered D.S., slamming his scissors on the projectile fluffball.

"Not bad!" The Captain rolled and fired out his blades.

They sliced into D.S.'s shoulders.

When the childish Exp looked up, he could see the fluffy demon was zooming toward him.

D.S. raised his scissors and cut the lines.

The Captain fell and tumbled to the ground.

D.S. ran to his opponent and kicked him, sending him flying like an American football.

The hatred barrier fell before the Captain crashed into it.

"Thanks for the help!" cheered D.S. before running off.

A little deeper in the forest, Occupy was going fist to fist with the God of Hate.

"To think I almost lost a great ally. I'll track down the warrior child once I'm done here. You should know that my weapons don't merely have a connection to my soul. They are linked to one another. The karmic bonds of their souls strengthen each other. And that power is mine to command! **WAILING WHIP**!" Etah lashed the golden razor blades of the pink whip at the monk who retreated to dodge, placing his back against a tree. "**SEARING SWORD**!"

The rusty copper sword with a heated tip was thrust toward the enemy.

Void took the attack head on but was completely unfazed.

"My guru takes in the worries, pain, strife, and wishes of the residents of Absence. He burdens all of it but maintains a steady state of mind. Your emotional weapons have no power over inner peace," said Occupy, spinning around the tree before landing a flurry of kicks on the God of Hate's chin.

Etah un-summoned his arsenal and grabbed the monk's foot.

The monk kicked off the god's head, having his foot slide out from the searing hot grip.

"You're the strongest of the Absence gods, aren't you?" asked Etah, taking the battle to the air and having his massive punches redirected by the monk's palms.

"Haha. Guru Void is the strongest. Every guardian is stronger than me. And, well, most of the guards too," said Occupy, running around the Sel god's body while dodging his fists.

Etah fired a blast of his aura that was rendered useless once it hit the rock god. "Then surely you are the most humble."

"Haha. Wrong again. My arrogance is my greatest obstacle," said Occupy before Etah's fist connected.

"**CHAOS CHAIN**!" Chains shot out from Etah and coiled around the warrior monk. "This weapon attacks your mind directly, barraging it with conflicting thoughts and rendering you unable to react." The God of Hate fired another blast of his aura, hitting the monk head on.

Occupy smashed through a tree and then ran up its broken mast to disperse the momentum. "The mind is always troubled by distracting thoughts. Your prized weapon can be conquered through a healthy meditation routine."

"You should be obliterated!" yelled Etah, firing another blast.

Occupy jumped off the tree and fired Void into the angry god. "You felt it, didn't you? Your worries and pain vanishing as soon as they came into being. My teacher is the ideal I strive for."

Etah struggled beneath the rock, grabbing onto a nearby tree to escape its weight. "Such power and yet it cannot it even move. Wondrous! When I have grown strong enough, I will add Void to my internal armory!"

Occupy stood atop his guru. "Can god create a rock so heavy that he cannot lift it? This question is paradoxical in nature, yet it has me wondering…is my master that rock? Is the weight you feel the weight of your own karma, or is it Void's spiritual fortitude?"

Etah's arms sprung forth.

Occupy leaped up, lifting his master with his bare feet. "The answer is…it's neither. What you felt is the power of nirvana. It is stronger than any mountain…" the monk released his guru "and yet lighter than a feather."

Void floated above Etah.

"Insolent fool! Feel the might of the bond between soul mates! **BASHFUL BOW**! **APPALLING ARROW**!" Etah fired a white moldy arrow with a plus-shaped arrowhead at the monk.

The arrow hit Occupy's chest and fell to the ground. "Bonds are merely karmic baggage. They are as transient as life. Why would something that lacks substance be able to affect a steady mind? Anything in flux lacks a firm footing in reality."

"You dare slander the power of emotions, of bonds! Face annihilation! **HATRED ERUPTION**!" Etah's aura fired out from his palms as a constant stream. It bent around the monk until it covered him completely. "This is the attack that ended the Hero of Sel! **HATRED CONTAINMENT**!"

The aura exploded.

Occupy's burned and bloodied body fell to the ground.

"What are you?" asked Etah, taking a step back.

"I am in need of more training if I was able to be injured by something not real. How pathetic. I'm like a child burdened by nightmares. Haha," said Occupy before tossing Void.

The rock slammed into Etah, smashing him through fifteen trees.

The injured warrior god looked around to see trees every which way. He sliced the trees down with his axe but more popped up.

"Wow, you can make trees! You're totally eco-awesome!" cheered D.S., as he raced to catch up to his new bald friend.

"No, I can't make trees. Those are just copies of the trees in the area. I can occupy a given area with anything that already existed there. With my power, thoughts are occupied by the peaceful void of Absence's atmosphere," said Occupy, making a tree each time he pointed.

"I don't get it at all," said D.S.

"Okay. There's a fish in a pond. I can make more fish or more water in that pond, but I can't put a candle in it. However, if I have a candle nearby, I can then fill the pond with candles. Can't make more than one group at a time though."

"Cool. How did you get that power?" asked D.S.

"By becoming a God of Absence. My skill is necessary to keep idle minds idle."

"Are you following us to the prison?" asked D.S.

"By the recent decree of Neutral, we are to intervene in any attempt on Sel's part to kill a Lum god. That said, we remain unbiased. If a Lum god makes an attempt to kill a Sel god, we are also to intervene."

"Who are they after?"

"Well there are two gods in Beacon: Efil and Evol."

"That sucks! They're both super nice," said D.S.

"Yes, I must offer my assistance before it is too late."

"You're a peacemaker, right?"

"I'm a peace promoter and sustainer, but not a peacemaker. Peace is a state of mind and cannot be created," said Occupy, cleaning off his guru.

"You should play with Violet. She likes religious stuff," said D.S.

"Once this battle is over I must return. All the Absence gods, guards and guardians alike, are essential to the continued stability of our realm."

Demonica led Separate and Spin to a forest clearing. "Hopefully some angels will spot us. It will make things much more fun." Her hands became blood red. In a split second, her fingers shot out.

The amoeba divided and avoided the attack.

Demonica's arms fell off. "Why don't you separate this too?" she asked as her arms exploded, shooting blood all over.

Spin sped up to Demonica all the while flinging tops at her.

The tops went right through the Goddess of Death, making ripples disperse throughout her body.

"Pathetic." Demonica's stomach opened up and tentacles shot out, ensnaring the arrogant god.

Spin's skin was torn to shreds, and the human structure became a mass of tops. "*Spin, Blood.*"

Demonica's body became a whirlpool and was unable to solidify.

The tops raged forward at the Sel goddess before slipping into a puddle of blood.

"Die!" Demonica's eyes were brimming with murderous intent. She summoned up her scythe, grabbed it with one of her stomach tentacles, and plunged it into the puddle of blood.

The aura of the scythe pierced inside the puddle.

"And just like that, a God dies," said Demonica as her scythe faded away.

The puddle of blood turned into the shape of an arm and reattached to Demonica. Blood shot out from her shoulder, forming into another arm.

"There we go. Good as new," said Demonica, solidifying the blood to create new arms. "Hmm, now where's the other one?"

Tens of thousands of Separates were all around her, like dust in the wind.

"Ooh, you're quite the tricky one."

"*Crimson Shower.*" Demonica's arm shot blood into the air. It poured down like rain.

The dark goddess stuck her tongue out, tasting the blood as it crashed into the innumerous gods.

The tiny amoebas charged into Demonica, piercing through her body from various angles.

"Mmm, that's quite an attack you have. But it's wasted on me. You cannot kill death itself," said Demonica.

The Separates combined into one.

Demonica shoved her arm in the amoeba. The deity turned completely red and collapsed into blood.

The last amoeba formed an Absence portal and fled the scene.

159

"Devlin will be the greatest of all gods, and I will stand by his side as his queen," said Demonica, absorbing the blood puddle through her feet.

Violet approached Ada and Deceivant near the back end of the forest clearing.

"I won't let you harm them. Leave now. I will earn nothing from your death," said Kanasta, appearing behind his target.

"Devlin is counting on me. I won't fail him," said Violet, coating her scimitar in an astral aura.

"I told you to protect the people in the temple," said Deceivant.

"My first priority is the safety of my parents," said Kanasta.

"Then you're all that stands in my way," said Violet, pointing her weapon.

"You don't have to do this," said Ada.

"I must. I am religiously obligated." Violet rushed toward Deceivant, her blade at the ready.

Kanasta sped in front and grabbed the blade just as it turned to jab him.

Violet struggled to pull the blade out.

Kanasta snapped the blade in two and slammed his knee into the traitor's stomach.

Violet fell to the ground and took a deep breath. "Why am I still too weak to help Devlin?"

"You are fighting with doubt, not devotion," said Kanasta, holding the sword to her throat.

Violet's astral hands grabbed the broken blade and stabbed it into the killer's foot. She jumped to her feet and thrust her bladed cross at the enemy.

Kanasta knocked the cross out of her hands and tripped the traitor. He pressed his hands to her back and slammed her to the ground. "You can surrender anytime."

Violet stretched her arm out and grabbed onto the holy cross.

"*ASTRAL PULSE!*" Her energy body rammed into the assassin boss before immediately rejoining her. The devotee rose to her feet and swung the cross vigorously.

Kanasta dodged the swipes with ease. He saw an opening, grabbed her hand, and crushed it.

The cross slipped out from her broken fingers.

Violet tried to pick up her holy weapon, but her fractured hand could not support its weight.

"It's over."

Violet whipped out a dagger with her other hand and rushed up to Deceivant. She held the blade inches from his neck. "I don't understand. I did a ritual for this. I should be possessed by a warrior spirit. I shouldn't be struggling," she said in tears.

"Nina's even more devoted to Devlin than you are. If joining Sel would do anything to help Devlin, then she would have done so. The thought never crossed her mind because she knows that as long as Sel is in power, Devlin will be a tool." Deceivant pulled the dagger out from the zealot's trembling hands.

"Nina is following orders given to her. She is more devoted to his most recent commands than she is to his mission. I killed Atatasuki for him. I fought against gods for his sake. Don't think I won't fight you too." Violet slammed into the maker of her god.

Deceivant stumbled but held his ground. "Why did you abandon us when we needed you most?"

"I joined Lord Sel to uncover the truth about Devlin's loyalty. My living god is not being controlled by Lord Sel. Once I realized this, I decided to stand by his side. I will follow his will whether it leads me to Lum or Sel. I am an extention of his will. 𝘼𝙎𝙏𝙍𝘼𝙇 𝙋𝙍𝙊𝙅𝙀𝘾𝙏𝙄𝙊𝙉!" Violet's aura jumped out from her body and kicked Kanasta.

"If you truly love someone, you must do what is best for them, even if it isn't what they want," said Kanasta, deflecting each kick.

"I have faith in Devlin. His gaze goes beyond this moment. Those golden eyes have already seized the future. Why are you fighting against him?" asked Violet as her aura punched her god's brother vigorously.

Deceivant smacked the crazed zealot. "Did you forget what Devlin did to the Refuge of the People? No plan that permits such cruelty is one I will ever have faith in!"

"Devlin seeks to prevent the end times. No sacrifice is too great for the future." Violet's aura burst out from her hands and slammed into Kanasta, knocking him off his feet. Her astral body leaped up and pierced its hands into the assassin. "I don't need to kill you. But you must not impede Devlin's ascension."

"What ascension? He's been corrupted by Sel's power! He killed Ada, you know. Are you really going to follow someone who would murder his own mother?" asked Deceivant as he was being punched by the crazed zealot.

"I do not judge him. The path Devlin walks is not one I fully comprehend, but I am fully devoted to seeing its fruition," said Violet, slamming Deceivant to the ground.

"Enough!" wailed Ada. "You're our grandchild. We're all family. Why are we fighting?"

"Agreed. Surrender now and we can end this himsa," said Violet, as her astral body was slowly being pushed off the assassin.

"Sel wants to wage war against Lum. Are you really okay with that?" asked Ada in tears.

"Lum is a home for all the animals who have died. Devlin will not allow it to fall."

"And if he isn't strong enough to stop Sel, what then?" asked Ada in tears.

Kanasta kicked the astral body off.

Violet's energy body turned its hand into a blade before it landed and gripped Ada.

"Are you ready to surrender now?" asked Violet.

"Let her go," said Deceivant, desperation diluting the intensity of his gaze.

"None of us want this fight. So surrender before I have to kill again," said Violet, her eyes watering up.

"Your death will come the instant she falls," said Kanasta, his eyes scanning for an opening.

"Violet…you can't do this," said Deceivant in tears.

"I'll do what I must," said the devotee, taking a step back.

"Leave, son. We can handle it from here," said Ada.

"Are you sure?" asked Kanasta.

Ada nodded.

Kanasta sped off.

"Please release me, Violet," said Ada.

"Do you surrender?" asked Violet.

"Followers of Allah's Nur can't take hostages. Lum worship is your new religion, is it not?" asked Ada, turning to smile at the troubled girl.

"Then I shall repent in Sel." Violet wiped her eyes.

"Rambir gave Nina the book, Allah's Nur. If you join us, you can read it," said Ada.

"You can't reason with zealots. The only thing more dangerous than them is an anthropocentric misanthrope," said Deceivant.

"Violet, Devlin said he needed Exp 8 to awaken in order to prevent the end times, right?" asked Ada.

"Then you understand that this is far more important than your lives?" asked Violet.

"What if Exp 8's awakening meant the awakening of the willpower in those left behind? What if the Remnants of Freedom are the ones who will stop the coming apocalypse?"

"It has nothing to do with Exp 8. Devlin needs power to save the world. And I will help him attain it," said Violet.

Kanasta approached from behind.

"What are you doing?" asked Violet, having her aura fix its grip on the hostage.

"I'm calling your bluff."

"I'm not bluffing."

"Look at you. You're crying. You don't have to do this anymore. According to Allah's Nur, righteous actions will lead to a righteous path," said Ada, smiling at her.

"Devlin needs us. His armor is a prison, whether he realizes it or not," said Kanasta, approaching the astral body and slowly releasing his mother from its grip. "I leave the rest to you," he said before rushing off to Beacon.

Ada hopped up to her troubled friend. "Come on, Violet, dry your tears and let's go free some prisoners."

"I can't serve Devlin like this. You've all changed me. The old me would have done it, but the current me…she is riddled with doubt," said Violet in tears.

"Listen to your instincts. It's god's gift to all living beings. Instinct is the divine whisper that sets us on the path to righteousness," said Deceivant, grabbing the zealot's hand.

"Then this feeling…I should follow it?" asked Violet.

"Well I made all that up but seems possible, right? Or do you doubt your own instincts?" asked Deceivant.

"Well…maybe a little bit," said Violet, drying her eyes. "Thank you, all of you. I pray that this path leads to Devlin's enlightenment," she said with a smile.

"With that as your goal, it surely will," said Ada.

"Now that you're on our side, you must have some inside information for us," said Deceivant.

Violet's smile dropped. Her eyes widened with urgency. "Lord Sel seeks to destroy the Angel Wall that keeps his army from crossing into Lum. With each fallen Lum god, the barrier weakens. Once it falls, Lord Sel's army will storm this realm and kill the Great Goddess. These battles are just a distraction. Lord Sel sent us here to keep you from reaching the prison."

"And what about my son?" asked Ada.

"Devlin stayed behind when we were sent out. He was likely given a separate, more important mission. Lord Sel doesn't fully trust us with its current plan," said Violet.

"If he's after the gods, then Efil is in danger. She's inside Beacon," said Deceivant.

"I pray we aren't too late," said Violet.

163

Chapter 104: Protect the Temple

Previously: Devlin's allies were sent off to keep the Remnants busy.

"What is my mission?" asked Devlin.

"The Goddess of Life is in the temple. Kill her," said Lord Sel.

"As you command."

BoneSaw raised his saws, trying to get the realm god's attention.

"I believe the killing machine wants to help too. Is there a reason he wasn't sent off with the others?" asked Devlin.

"BoneSaw cannot speak and therefore cannot reveal sensitive information to the enemy. I don't fully trust your former comrades," said Lord Sel.

"And what about Demonica and Etah?"

"Limit was recently spotted in Lum. Seems very likely the other Absence gods could be lurking around."

"I mean, do you trust them?" asked Devlin.

"I know them too well to trust them completely. I'll send in backup as soon as you've landed. They'll be coming in small groups as to not bring unwanted attention." Lord Sel turned to face Demonica's gimp. "Send him out."

The gimp turned to face Devlin and the little robot.

Sel's Knight and BoneSaw arrived in Lum just outside Beacon.

"Wonder why it didn't just teleport me inside," said Devlin.

"Wait up, Black Knight," said a voice from behind.

Devlin turned to see the Führer, the Prince, and the Duke all rushing to join his side. "Lord Sel sent you? I thought the age of demon lords was over."

"We are forbidden to ever return to our home," said the Führer.

"Lord Sel has turned us into its specialized assassins," said the Duke, wearing black armor plates.

"The God of Destruction wants us all dead, but as a tactician it decided to makes use of our abilities. Still, the Dark One could have at least given us some minions. Ugh, this is truly a suicide mission," said the Prince, now with a collar around his neck.

"Any more reinforcements coming?" asked Devlin.

"More demon lords and some Sel gods will join us shortly. Lord Sel wants us out before Lum's forces arrive. No doubt an angel has already spotted us. We best make haste," said the Duke.

"You obey my orders, understood?" asked Devlin.

The demon lords nodded.

"Stay behind me at all times," said Devlin, blasting the wall of pink energy to pieces.

The entire corridor was filled with angels of various species.

"Were they waiting for us?" asked Devlin, gathering dark energy in his fist.

"It matters not. We have our mission," said the Prince, slicing his arm to coat his fingertips in poison.

"For the glory of Sel!" The Baroness, her two halves seared together both vertically and horizontally, came out from behind and cleaved through the front line of angels.

Devlin ejected his blast into the incoming light arrows. "Foolish, she almost got herself killed."

"Just what I needed." Edirp stepped atop the Führer. "Bow down to me, lowly angels! 𝐈𝐦𝐩𝐞𝐫𝐢𝐚𝐥 𝐀𝐭𝐦𝐨𝐬𝐩𝐡𝐞𝐫𝐞!"

Every angel in the corridor was floored due to the gravity of their own insignificance.

One warrior, clad in foggy white armor stood proudly. "This is as far as you go, pawns of Sel," said Etaf, manifesting the Destiny Sword.

"They sure have tightened security here," said Tsul, whipping the angels as she walked by.

The Baroness' steel slammed against the Destiny Sword. "Leave this one to me."

"You're only a demon lord. Etaf is a goddess. Edirp, I'll need your help to take her down," said Tsul.

"You heard her, move along," said Devlin, passing by the Baroness.

"Our target is further in. We will not leave this place without a battle," said Yvne.

"That had better be the case," said the Baroness, ducking under a swipe from a legendary sword before rushing to catch up with her team.

Devlin's group arrived at the main hall. Humans of various ages and faiths broke into a crazed panic once the initial shock subsided.

"It's so crowded. Hard to see if our target is even here," said the Prince.

"I'll clear it up," said Devlin, firing a blast into the panicked mess of humans.

The surviving humans dispersed, giving the team a clear view of the stage.

"There she is," said Devlin, pointing at Efil who had just stood up from her seat.

"She had better be worth my time," said the Baroness, charging forth.

Three humans hopped off the stage, drew their weapons, and approached the Baroness.

"Don't engage them. You want the goddess, correct? Leave these warriors to us," said the Duke of Deception.

The Baroness jumped over the mortals and landed on the stage.

"*ANGER EXPLOSION!*"

The side of the dome was blasted open.

"Damn this place! Couldn't find the front door!" yelled Regna, stomping her feet as she entered the blessed temple.

Napkin rushed in front of her and let out a ferocious roar. "*Mew*."

"Haha! That was adorable. Were you trying to scare me?" asked Regna, leaning over the little kitty.

"Efil, I challenge you," said the Baroness, pulling out two swords from her body.

"You will lose," said Efil, standing firm as ten angels commanders came out from behind her.

The Baroness was suddenly knocked off her feet. She tumbled off the stage.

"That's far enough. By Lord Neutral's decree, I shall not abide the killing of a god," said Limit.

"Stand up, Baroness. We shall take him on together," said Yvne.

Devlin and BoneSaw ran around to the back of the stage. "Are you ready to die, goddess?" he asked, gathering dark energy in his arms.

"If I do, then I die defending Lum," said Efil.

The three human warriors approached the demon lords.

"Had we acted differently on Earth, our roles here could be reversed. I am the Duke of Deception. To my right is the Prince of Pleasure and to my left the Führer of Fortune. We are demon lords. Tell me, humans, what are your names?"

The woman pointed her spear. "I am Heaven's Thunder, proud warrior of Allah's Jannah."

The blue-skinned naked and thin man brandished his sword. "I discarded my name. I serve Lord Shiva."

The dark-skinned muscular man with tattooed arms and legs spun his bamboo stick before slamming it to the ground. "I died defending my homeland from invaders. I am willing to do so again." He rushed at the Duke.

The sly tactician yanked some strings, sending the Prince in the path of the attack in his stead.

Each time the Prince lashed his poison-laced fingertips, he was dodged. Before he could retaliate he was knocked at his side, his head, and then his feet. The barrage continued even after he fell to the floor.

166

"Combat is not my greatest skill, but I will not be beaten by a mere human," said the Führer, countering Thunder's assault with the bladed, spider-like appendages attached to the bottom of his royal bed.

The blue-skinned man screamed as he rushed at the Duke.

"You really should watch where you step."

The man's foot was caught in a string. He was dragged across the ground and sent slamming into his dark-skinned comrade.

"Just the opening I needed. Thank you," said the Prince, jabbing his fingers into the arm of his enemy.

"You seem like an intelligent demon. Are these your minions?" asked Thunder, ducking under a pincer attack before stabbing her spear into one of the metal legs.

"I was once a great leader. But now I serve the very system I sought to destroy. I could have killed you by now, but the longer I draw this out, the less time I have to spend fighting the Goddess of Life."

"I too have had many chances to sever your head."

"Then why haven't you?"

"I seek the Portal to Earth, and I'm not above making deals with demons to attain it," said Thunder, holding back two bladed feet with her iron spear.

"Who could have guessed that such a delightful creature would find itself in Lum? Here I thought this world had only elitists and blind followers. You are a rare breed indeed."

Thunder won the power struggle and toppled the Führer over.

"Can you help me or not, demon?" asked Thunder, her blade pressed to the Führer's flabby neck.

"If no other opportunities arise, I'll forward your request to Lord Sel. May I ask what you offer in return?" asked the Führer.

"We'll keep the goddess' occupied. What more could your lord ask for?" asked Thunder.

"Straight-forward and a skilled negotiator. What fortune I must have to be given this encounter," said the Führer.

"Farewell then. If I stay any longer, I will surely meet my end here," said Thunder before leaving through the hole made by Regna.

"You let your prey escape," said the Duke, wrapping its opponent in a cocoon of string.

"Mine is still fighting. Paralyze one arm and it just uses another," said the Prince before being knocked down once more.

"Allow me," said the Duke, tugging on some string.

The tattooed warrior leaped over the trap, whacked the Prince with his weapon, and used the momentum to kick off and slam his bamboo staff into the Duke.

"It can't battle all three of us," said the Führer, rising up.

Kanasta entered, setting his sights on the golden bellied demon lord. He rushed ahead and intercepted the Führer. "Is that a gold coating, or is your belly made of gold?"

"You were with the hero, weren't you?" asked the Führer.

Kanasta slammed his fist into the man with the golden belly. "Very well. I'll find out myself," he said, snatching a sword from the cocoon.

"Why are you using slow-acting poison?" asked the Duke, redirecting the bamboo strikes with its string.

"The same reason you're not using your devotion strings. I don't want to die fighting a Lum goddess," said the Prince, slashing the warrior from behind. "Ha! Got your other arm. What are you going to fight with now?"

The tattooed warrior dropped his staff and gripped it with a prehensile foot. He then continued his assault.

"A little help here," said the Führer, using four of his legs to keep the sword from piercing him.

"It's real, isn't it?" asked Kanasta.

"You want the gold, then take it!" he yelled, flinging superheated chunks at the assassin.

Kanasta took the attack head on, not even cringing as the heated gold merged with his flesh. "Definitely real. I think I'll take it as a souvenir. I'll put it right next to Deerg's head."

"What are you?" asked the Führer with quivering lips.

The Prince dragged his fingernails down Kanasta's back. "Best not to mess around with this one. That poison is lethal. You have a few seconds left for regrets. Feel free to cry if you need to," he said, patting the professional killer's back.

"Whoa, that is rather strong," said Kanasta, teetering back and forth.

"Splendid job! Duke, keep him moving about with your strings so it seems like he's still fighting us," said the Führer, clapping his hands.

"Never thought we would see eye to eye," said the Duke.

Kanasta pulled the sword back, ducked under the bladed arms, and jabbed it into the area around the Führer's stomach.

"Get him off me!" yelled the Führer, digging his leg claws into the assassin's arm to weaken his grip on his weapon.

"Relax. He'll be motionless any moment now," said the Prince.

The Duke lashed his strings, but the assassin dodged each swipe all the while carving around the golden belly.

Kanasta tossed the sword aside and then yanked the massive golden chunk out. After jumping off and carefully maneuvering through a web of string, he landed in front of the Prince. "Why are you working with the Duke? Aren't you with the Hero's Militia?"

"Why aren't you dead?" asked the Prince, getting ready to strike again.

"What kind of ultimate assassin would I be if I wasn't immune to all forms of poison? That's a deadly mix you got there, but it's still made up of individual poisons that my body is more than prepared to fight." His fist a blur, Kanasta downed the Prince with an uppercut. He bent down and collected the special blood in a small vial.

The Duke's strings wrapped around the killer's arm. "Finally you fall into my web."

"You're very skilled with those. But you should be wary of your surroundings."

Spinning on his head, the tattooed warrior slammed his bamboo staff into the Duke's unarmored head, rattling its brain and knocking the enemy out.

"Let's get the injured to safety," said Kanasta, unraveling the cocoon and freeing the man within. He then coiled the threads and shoved them, along with his most recent trophies, in his suitcase.

Previously: Napkin let out a mew, seeking to stop Regna's advance.

"What in Lord Sel's accursed name is going on? Why am I trembling!" yelled Regna, shaking with each step she took.

"*Mew!*" exclaimed Napkin, stopping the goddess in place.

"What are you an Exp, a god, or just a really powerful angel? It doesn't really matter! You're dead!" Regna fired off her arm.

Napkin jumped out of the way but not without getting caught in the blast.

"Ha! I don't need to move to take you down," said Regna, flipping off the cat. Her middle finger shot out and pierced into the cat's hind leg. "You can't frighten my fingers. Once a piece of my body detaches, it's no longer affected by my emotions. That said, I can still will it to further segment."

Napkin bit onto the finger and tried to yank it out.

"Dumb cat. It's barbed. Once it's in, it ain't coming out. Oh, it's going to hurt so much when it bursts."

Napkin stared defiantly at the finger and mewed.

Regna's finger stopped flashing; it had been defused.

"That doesn't even make any sense! Die!" Regna's arm shot out.

Napkin ran back and jumped over it.

The hand ejected from the arm and sliced the cat. Its fingers then fired off one by one at the itty bitty kitty.

Napkin raised his back and let out a defensive mew.

The fingers stopped in midair and floated.

"What are you!" yelled Regna.

"*Mew. Mew. Mew. Mew. Mew!*" Napkin approached with a vicious assault of roars, pushing Regna out of the building.

Previously: Limit appeared and prepared to do battle against the Baroness and Yvne.

"It is just as Loyal predicted. This place is The Dark One's true target," said Limit, readying his lance.

"Such beautiful armor. I want it," said Yvne, hooks shooting out from her body.

Limit leaped over the attack and landed before the swordswoman. He advanced with well-timed thrusts but kept a watchful eye on his other opponent.

The Baroness took a step back, just barely dodging the knight's joust. She sheathed her two swords and froze up.

"Can't move your arms, can you?" asked Limit before thrusting his lance.

The lance was stopped by a steel-plated wall that popped up from the ground. "*Metamorphosis Frenzy!*" The wall collapsed into a puddle and then spun around, forming new weapons as it clashed against his steel.

"I don't need my arms to take you down!" The Baroness yanked a sword out with her mouth and lunged at the knight.

Limit slid his foot into her, knocking her off her feet and avoiding a sudden thrust from the living puddle all at once. He raised his lance, blocking an assault from ten weapons spinning together like a weaponized top.

"Such skill! Such strength!" exclaimed Yvne, increasing the power of her barrage.

The Baroness leaped off the ground like a lioness and unsheathed her weapons.

"*Absence Infusion.*" Limit closed his eyes, imbuing his lance with clear energy the moment of impact.

The Baroness' prized swords vanished as they hit the lance, as if spirited away to another world. "Such power. Your refined will is something I must conquer," she said, repeatedly stabbing into the lance.

Limit leaped back as Yvne transformed into a fleshy battering ram. "I best keep my distance.

"𝕽𝖊𝖘𝖙𝖗𝖆𝖎𝖓𝖙 𝕽𝖊𝖒𝖔𝖛𝖆𝖑!" Limit's hands rode up the shaft of his weapon.

The lance opened up and doubled in size, shifting from a light weapon to a heavy one.

Limit heaved the twelve-foot lance above his head, gaining momentum. He then tossed it at the swordswoman.

Yvne shifted into Riufen and stood in the lance's path. Her legs were quivering.

"Don't fail me now! 𝕴𝖓𝖍𝖎𝖇𝖎𝖙𝖔𝖗 𝕬𝖉𝖉𝖎𝖙𝖎𝖔𝖓!"

Clear weights with chains attached themselves to his lance just before impact, holding it in midair.

Limit ran up and roundhouse kicked the lance.

The tip of the lance, which had been coated in the knight's clear aura, tore through Yvne as it completed multiple rotation cycles.

The Baroness slid under the lance and stabbed her bladed feet into the gaps in the knight's armor. The prideful demon lowered her hood and viciously assaulted him with an onslaught of chakrams she tore out from her head. Once she got to the one's imbedded in her scalp, the heated chakrams sliced into the knight's arms.

Limit rammed into the Baroness before being sliced from behind as the chakrams retracted back to her head.

"My whole body is a weapon. I'm a living armory! 𝗜𝗚𝗡𝗜𝗧𝗜𝗢𝗡." said the Baroness, unsheathing a sword with two hands and slicing through the knight's armor and flesh.

Limit's arm plopped to the ground.

"Let us joust!" yelled Yvne, turning into a replica of Limit with thinner armor and flesh missing in various places.

Limit jumped back, grabbed his lance, and formed clear chains around the imposter's feet.

Yvne spun her lance in a circle, deflecting four thrusts before being overpowered.

"𝕬𝖇𝖘𝖊𝖓𝖈𝖊 𝕴𝖓𝖋𝖚𝖘𝖎𝖔𝖓. The tip of Limit's lance was coated in a clear aura yet again, piercing through the lance and slicing the knight in half.

"You cannot regenerate that which I have struck. You will be smited," said Limit, poking holes in the dark goddess as she transformed and retreated.

The Baroness tossed an arrow at the knight's helmet, if only to get his attention. "What do you fight for?"

"I fight to defend my realm. Your lord's mission puts all of Sellum at risk. What do you fight for, swordswoman?" asked Limit.

"I…I don't really know anymore. I'm just following orders so I won't be killed."

"Well, the dark goddess has fled. Will you stand and fight me here, or will you raise your sword alongside me and preserve the balance of Sellum?" asked Limit, picking up his arm.

"I'll fight with you," said the Baroness, using some metal string to help reconnect the knight's arm.

Previously: Etaf engaged two dark goddesses in battle.

"Lord Sel told us all about your powers," said Edirp.

"Say no more, sister. The less she knows about what we know, the better," said Tsul, gazing into the light goddess' eyes for a hint of her next action.

"What does your master think he knows?" asked Etaf, taking a cautious step forward.

"Who cares what we tell her?! We're an unstoppable team." Edirp stepped on top of a downed polar bear angel. "You have the ability to bring destinies into fruition or something. It doesn't really matter."

"You boast and yet you don't even understand my power," said Etaf.

"We know enough. After her," said Tsul, pointing her whip.

Ten of the angels she whipped had a sudden burst of energy and charged at Etaf.

With two slices the charge ended, but Tsul was now three meters closer.

"If you can't see us, you can't cut us. But you know what, go ahead and cut me," said Edirp, arrows erupting out from her back.

Etaf sliced her hair and allowed the arrows to crash into the strands.

"Who told you my secret? Was it that accursed woman, Violet!" yelled Edirp.

"Was that a secret?" asked Etaf, slicing the air.

Edirp was sliced but unaffected. "You're too lowly to harm me."

"Ah, so it's a matter of elevation then," said Etaf, changing her target to the angel beneath the arrogant goddess.

Edirp hopped off the angel before it was sliced to bits.

"Let's make this a bloodbath. *LIBIDO CLIMAX*," said Tsul.

Twenty angels went into a frenzy and tore each other limb from limb.

Tsul whipped Etaf while concealed within the crowd, swiftly dodging any slash even remotely nearby.

Having her vision blocked by the fountains of blood and flesh, Etaf's feet were pierced by four of Edirp's arrows.

"Weak-kneed, clumsy, glass-boned, and pathetic. Let's see how you handle all those insults," said Edirp, hopping off one body to the next to close the distance.

Etaf fell to her knees.

Tsul took the opportunity to wrap her whip around the Destiny Sword. She yanked the aura blade out from the goddess' hand. "She should be defenseless, but keep your wits about you."

"ZEMBLANITY."

The Destiny Sword spun in place, slicing the air in multiple directions.

Edirp slipped on the bloody wound of one of the angels and fell to the ground.

Tsul screamed out as her body was being sliced to pieces.

"You die now! **Prideful Presence**!" yelled Edirp.

The floor beneath Etaf plummeted abruptly.

"Sink into the earth!" yelled Edirp, helping her sister stand back on her feet.

Tsul wailed in agony.

Etaf appeared behind the sisters and was wielding the Destiny Sword. She collapsed to her knees but held up her weapon. "If you know what's best for you, you'll surrender now."

Tsul's wounds were filled by her aura. "The battle is over.

RUPTURE."

Etaf's eyes widened. Blood burst out from her armor. "You laced your whip with your aura, didn't you?" she asked, holding the Destiny Sword with trembling hands.

"That's right. I think we're done here. By now your precious friend Efil is probably dead," said Edirp, kicking down the arrogant goddess.

Etaf's eyes shrank. "You were distracting me?"

"Sister, I can't stand up," said Tsul toppling over.

"Her sword cuts deep. But it doesn't matter. We won," said Edirp.

"I must save Efil," said Etaf, pushing off the Destiny Sword to get back on her feet.

"*Blood Spike.*"

The puddles of blood around the light goddess hardened and pierced through her armor.

Demonica crouched down to her victim. "Stay here for a bit. I'll be back once Efil has fallen."

"Sister, it's you," said Edirp.

"Finish her off," said Tsul.

"Why don't you two get some rest?" Demonica created a portal and kicked her little sisters in.

"I beg you; let me speak to your master. I'll do as you ask. Please, don't let her die," said Etaf in tears.

"You're in no position to bargain," said Demonica.

"You want entry into Elysium, don't you?" asked Etaf, grabbing the dark goddess' hand as she turned away.

Demonica smiled. She bent down and grabbed Etaf's cheeks. "I don't care about that. The outcome of this war really doesn't matter to me. What I want is something only Devlin can give me."

"You love him, don't you? Well I love my dear friend Efil. Please, you must understand," said Etaf in tears.

"What are you worried about? Not even the Death Scythe can end her. There's only one way to kill that goddess. Make sure to invite me," said Demonica, walking off.

Previously: Devlin and BoneSaw engaged Efil in battle, determined to kill her.

BoneSaw spun behind her as Devlin assaulted her from the front side.

Efil jumped up and deflected the incoming saws by smacking them aside.

Devlin fired a Sel beam at the goddess, but she cancelled it with her own energy.

The white energy crashed into Devlin, forming vines on his body.

Efil landed and pointed at BoneSaw. "TIME LAPSE." A light green aura shot out from her fingertips but was dodged by the robot.

"You should focus on me." Devlin shot a wire at the goddess' throat.

Efil caught it between two fingers. "Everything ages."

The wire became dust.

Devlin detached the wire from his body before it could erode him. "Another obstacle for me to surpass," he said, pacing around her.

The flowers on Efil's breasts blossomed, releasing a pod of seeds.

Efil touched the ground with her fingertips just as the seeds landed. "TIME LAPSE."

Trees shot out from the ground.

Devlin ran up to Efil as she rushed toward him. His fist detached from his arm and was propelled into her face. His armored hand shot out wires that then connected to her head. Sel's Knight thrashed the wires around, slamming the goddess into the nearby trees.

The wires rusted, and Efil tumbled into the bushes.

Devlin shot a wire at the back of her head and pulled her across the ground as he reeled her in. He grabbed her throat once she was within range.

"I will not let you win," she said, her face firm like the trunk of a tree.

"You don't have a choice," said Devlin, his cords wrapping around her throat.

Efil's hand jabbed at Devlin's chest but was caught by his wires. Her other hand was pressed against his helmet. "TIME—"

Devlin broke free of her grasp by kicking her off. "Whoa! That was way too close. I better finish this up quickly."

Dark energy flowed out from his armor, coating him in a thick black fog.

"You were the one who destroyed the Refuge of the People. I will not let you leave here alive!" exclaimed Efil, forming a sword from her light-green aura.

"Heh. Your angels were watching the whole time. You should thank me," said Devlin, firing out wires from various directions out from the black fog.

Efil deflected the first seven with swift slices. One wire pierced her leg and three more bore into her side. "LIFE BARRIER." The goddess formed a shield of her energy, making the rest of the incoming wires turn to dust. "Did Sel send you here to kill me?"

"That's right. And I can't fail now." Devlin raised Bravery.

The golden strands jutted out. They shot through Efil's aura before piercing her chest.

"Why aren't they aging? It really is his sword, isn't it?" asked Efil.

The next barrage of wires sped behind her shield before attacking from behind.

"As long as I keep the wires in, you can't heal."

"DEVOTION SHOT!"

A beam of white energy bore into Devlin's knee, dispelling the armor around it.

Efil rushed forth and sliced Devlin's leg.

The black knight fell backward once the afflicted area aged into dust.

Wires shot out and wrapped around his leg, giving him a quick fix that kept him on his feet.

Devlin dropped Bravery and fired at her with dark bullets from his fingertips.

"DEVOTION ARMOR." Efil's body became coated in a white aura, purifying the bullets before they could hit.

"You have two energies. How is that?" asked Devlin, now firing beams from his palms in addition to the finger assault.

Efil's aura tore out the wires and then filled in the holes. Flowers bloomed on her legs, which released seeds that quickly became trees.

Devlin's Sel beam tore through the trees, but the goddess was hidden.

Lum shots came out from the treetops.

Devlin dodged the first two but was hit by the third.

Part of his helmet dissipated, revealing his golden eyes.

"Your death is just a stepping stone." Devlin's wires shot out, connecting to BoneSaw. "**DEFORESTATION**." The ambitious scientist flung BoneSaw around in every direction, cutting the surrounding trees to pieces. He then released the wires and let the mechanical assassin skyrocket into the exposed goddess.

BoneSaw sawed through her stomach and then rode up the trunk of a nearby tree. It pushed off, rode its floating saw, and zoomed toward the goddess.

A white shot hit the saw, creating vines that gripped the robot.

Efil pressed her hand to her stomach and healed the wound. "What are you after, pawn of Sel?"

"I am not a pawn of Sel. I am at least a knight," said Devlin with a smirk. Wires shot out of his hands and into her back.

Efil severed the wires by rusting them.

A second set of wires gripped the severed set and coiled them around the goddess.

"**DARK EMBODIMENT**." Black energy rode up the wires and entered her body.

Efil fell to the grass, screaming in agony.

"Is that all?" asked Devlin.

Efil limped away as her body was corroded from within.

Devlin picked her up by the hair. "A god cowering before me; I've only dreamed of this power."

Efil tossed a seed at the floor and it instantly became a tree, pushing Devlin away from her.

The tree was sliced in half.

"How pathetic. Once I rule over Sellum, no weakling would ever become a god," said Devlin, glaring into her eyes through the broken bark.

"You will not be able to kill Lum. Sel will fail," said Efil, firing Lum shots while flooding her body with energy to combat the darkness.

"So sure of yourself, are you? Too bad you won't be around to see Lum's death," said Devlin, turning away from her.

Wires shot out from his armor and sliced her to fleshy bits.

Demonica landed in front of her beloved. "Where did the goddess go?"

"I killed her," said Devlin, firing Sel shots at the leftover pieces.

Light energy poured out from the pieces. They expanded and came together, reforming the goddess.

"Don't bother trying to kill her. It's pointless. Her destiny has already been decided upon," said Demonica.

"What?" asked Devlin.

"So says the prophecy, but I have more faith in people than predictions," said Efil, standing tall.

"You doubt Etaf's predictions? Some friend you are," said Demonica.

"I see no reason why she would be the one to strike me down," said Efil, her voice quivering.

"To be killed by her own ally? How tragic, but I can guarantee it won't come to pass." Devlin turned to face Demonica. "We can end this now if we combine our power."

"You really don't get it, do you? Efil was just buying time to let the rest of the visitors escape here. You can't kill her," said Demonica.

"Why not? We are both gods."

"I told you, the prophecy. Etaf's never been wrong. Even Lord Sel knows it's no use to try to kill Efil," said Demonica.

"Then why did Lord Sel send me here to kill her?" asked Devlin.

"Maybe the Dark One is testing you. Or maybe it just wants you to keep her occupied," said Demonica.

"How did Sel's forces bypass the Angel Wall?" asked Efil, holding out blades of both her energies.

"With the help of the Exps," said Demonica.

Efil's eyes widened.

"Think about it. We were never able to enter Lum before," said Demonica with a grin.

"Explain yourself."

"Don't really feel like it."

"No. You're trying to distract me. If Sel sent you here, then…Evol is in danger." Efil created a portal and entered it.

Sel went past Beacon, sneaking up on Evol inside a much smaller dome made out of her pink energy.

"Hello, Evol," said Lord Sel, suddenly appearing behind the god.

"Welcome, Sel," said Evol, compassion ringing through its voice.

"You do know why I am here, don't you?" asked Lord Sel.

"To increase your governance past your own borders. You seek the land of Lum. Time will tell if you are fit to lead."

"I'm here to kill you."

"I don't understand what you mean by 'kill'. Could you perhaps explain?"

"No point. I'd be wasting my time. Just put up a bit of a struggle, would you?" asked Sel with the hint of a smile in its voice.

The ball of light exploded, sending shards in all directions.

They passed through the black cloud.

"I wasn't sure you could fight," said Sel.

"Should you ever find your way here, Lum has ordered me to purify you. By the decree of Lum, you shall reach enlightenment."

Emerging from the shards was what looked like a pink mass of feathers all connected to each other.

"This is your true form? A pillow? How pathetic is that?"

"*Love.*" The wings spread open, sending a pink ray of light at Sel. The light ray was quickly overpowered as the darkness expanded.

Evol was an entity of pure light. Twenty wings spread out from its core and its body radiated white energy.

"You look ridiculous. You can already levitate. Having extra wings doesn't make you more divine," said Sel.

"Your compliments are much appreciated," said Evol, firing a pink beam. The deity rode the path of its beam. The white energy erased bits of the black fog each time it passed by.

"Incredibly nimble...such a nuisance," said Sel, grabbing the deity with a massive hand of dark energy.

Sel suddenly found itself on a current that slammed it to the ground.

The light deity was released.

The Dark One fired rapid shots, each one changing trajectory to converge on the deity.

"*Honeymoon!*" Evol rode its pink energy waves at such speed it looked like it was teleporting.

"Hold still, you accursed beach ball!" yelled Sel, sending out hands of darkness.

The hands converged on a horizontal trail, coming together instead of hitting their intended target.

"Do you feel lighter? Love is a wondrous feeling, is it not?" asked Evol.

"Your love only serves to aggravate me!" Sel fired a beam that merged with the hands, dispersing out from the fingertips as multiple beams.

"*Love Eternal!*" Evol made an infinity sign and rode it, moving so fast it temporarily ceased to exist.

The homing shots lost their course and smashed into the ceiling.

"May you feel the heavenly embrace of love. *Motherly Hug.*"

The shards of Evol's shell collected around the realm god, surrounding it in a sphere.

Sel fired blasts from within but was unable to break through. "You solidified your energy. Well played."

"The same light that gives me power shall purify you. *Love Blossom*."

The shards glowed brightly, strangling the thick black fog around the dark deity.

"You are purified now. May all bear witness to your true form. There is no longer a need for you to find shelter in the shadows. You are perfect and beloved just the way you are. Would you like a hug?" asked Evol, beaming extra brightly.

"All your lovey-dovey nonsense seems like you're taunting me," said Sel, cloaked in pink light.

"I have only compassion for you."

"That sounds a lot like pity to me," said Sel with a darker tone.

"Pity is the precursor to compassion."

"I will kill you with your own prison of idealism." Sel rammed into the deity while still encased in the shell of light.

Evol's wings stiffened, but they were soon overcome by Sel's might. It was slammed back and skidded across the air. The deity became enveloped in its wings before the two spheres clashed.

The Lum auras colliding created gusts of winds and seeds that rode them. The dome soon became filled with a field of flowers and a forest of trees.

The winged sphere was then smashed into the very trees it had co-created. Evol graced the tree with pink energy before zooming toward the realm god.

The Lord of Destruction slid out of the way of the charge. It shot a ray of darkness through the light of its shell that hit the Deity of Love head on.

Evol smashed through the roof of the dome and crashed, creating a flower bed on impact.

Lord Sel was suddenly pulled by the trail of pink energy right up to the goddess. "Using your power only brings you closer to demise."

Evol was rammed by the realm god, making all the land it came in contact with more vibrant and beloved.

After firing a beam to propel the deity off the ground, Lord Sel rammed it, sending it into the skies. The dark god rode the new pink trail, this time running into white fog left by the lovey-dovey deity.

Lord Sel screamed out as the white fog strengthened the encasing. The God of Destruction slammed into the deity, sending it through a series of clouds.

"You shouldn't even be able to harm me! You aren't Lum!" yelled Sel, before ramming into the spherical deity from above.

"Your happiness, where has it gone?"

Sel slammed into the deity from one side and then the other, bouncing it back and forth like a pinball before firing a concentrated beam of energy.

The deity was propelled by the beam into Beacon, creating trees that withered and grew as the opposing energies fluctuated in strength.

"The cleansing is taking longer than expected," said Evol as its wings were devoured by Sel's ravenous energy.

"No amount of light can cloud my soul." Sel dragged the beam onto Evol, speeding up the deity's destruction.

"*Purification*." Evol fired a wave of light that collided with and merged into the casing around Sel.

The shell grew brighter, the light inside it growing.

Sel screamed and crashed to the ground.

Evol continued to fire the ray, concentrating on the casing as Sel continued to erode the deity's life force.

"Strange, my vitality seems to be moving on," said Evol with a ragged set of wings.

"You're dying, you fool!" Sel slid across the grass and rammed into the Deity.

"Dying?" Evol did not budge.

Sel sped around in a circle and then rammed the deity again.

Evol did not budge. "I am one with the realm of Lum and all its people! *Homing Adoration*." Pink and white beams fired out from the tips of its feathers, seeking out the realm god.

"I am Sel itself!" A ray of darkness shot out from the realm god's encasing as it maneuvered through the rainstorm of purity.

The ray pierced Evol, and the deity's body was quickly consumed by it. It then dispersed out, turning the surrounding trees into dust.

Sel slammed into Evol one final time, breaking through the beam and its last defenses.

The darkness tore even the deity's light core to pieces. A pink cloud of energy soared into the sky.

The light that made up the building faded into nothingness.

The encasing around Sel had a small crack. The Dark One turned around as the crack expanded, noticing members of the Remnants of Freedom, Absence, and some of its own pawns.

Chapter 105: Lord Sel

Previously: Napkin frightened Regna out of Beacon once he had gained the upper hand.

Napkin left the knocked out goddess of anger behind and rushed into Beacon's front entrance. The kitty's pace increased once he found Etaf. His friend was drenched in blood and impaled by crimson spikes.

"Don't worry. The chief kamui wouldn't be so kind as to let me die here," said Etaf, forcing a smile.

Napkin mewed until the spikes receded back into the puddles of blood they came from.

A white portal appeared.

Efil grabbed her companion before she could fall. "What happened to you?" she asked, pooling her energy into her injured friend.

"I got caught by surprise. Thanks for healing me, mataki," said Etaf with a smile.

"Evol isn't at its sanctuary. The roof had been blasted open. I fear that Sel has already engaged the deity in combat."

"Then you should find Evol," said Etaf, cringing in pain.

"I will. As soon as you're fully healed," said Efil with a smile.

Napkin looked up at Etaf and mewed.

"Thank you for keeping watch over the Exps," said Efil with a smile.

"Efil will take care of me. Meet up with the Remnants. Stay safe," said Etaf, waving at her little comrade.

Napkin lit up, let out an affirmative meow, and rushed off.

Once Limit's arm was reattached, he created an Absence portal.

"Are you planning on running away?" asked the Baroness.

"I will stay and fight. That portal is for you," said Limit.

"Yes, best to get out of this place while we still can," said the Führer before entering.

"Live to fight another day. I'm heading to the Elysium Asylum," said Limit, pushing the Baroness into the portal before making it vanish.

Kanasta and the other human warriors had effectively evacuated the residents from the building. "It's time you head out."

"What about you?" asked the Rastafarian.

"I need to speak with my brother," said Kanasta before walking off.

His two allies fled through the hole in the side of the structure.

Kanasta dropped to the floor just as a mortar smashed through the roof.

Previously: Deceivant, Ada, and Violet saw something crash into Beacon.

"I only hope Efil evacuated them in time. We need to get as far away from there as possible," said Deceivant, turning away.

"It's best if the two of you run, but I'm not going to. If a Lum god is in danger, then I am obligated to do all I can to protect them," said Violet before rushing off.

"What about our son?" asked Ada.

"Kanasta knows when a situation is beyond his skill level. He's cautious and clever. We can locate him once the carnage dies down," said Deceivant.

"Whoa, did you see that?" asked D.S., pointing to where a mortar had just landed.

"You need to get away before Etah finds you. I must hurry before it is too late," said Occupy before sprinting off with Void in tow.

Kaity and Nina were running side-by-side.

"They were only keeping us distracted. Either way, we know where the prison is now and can lead the others to it," said Nina, speeding up.

"There they are!" Kaity took a sharp turn and sprinted up to Deceivant and Ada.

"Thank goodness you're okay," said Deceivant, beaming at the young girl.

"Where's Kanasta?" asked Kaity.

"He went in the temple. But I'm sure he'll escape and meet with us soon," said Deceivant, patting the girl's head.

"I'm going in," said Kaity.

"Be careful. I'll keep them safe. We'll meet up near the prison," said Nina.

Kaity nodded and rushed off.

"Behold. That power will soon be mine." Devlin wrapped his arm around Demonica as he gazed at Lord Sel firing a continuous beam of darkness into the downed deity.

"Indeed it shall," said Demonica, stroking his back.

Violet fell to her knees in tears.

Occupy's eyes shrank as he watched the Deity of Love fade into nothingness. "The balance has shifted," he said, his voice devoid of warmth.

Kaity rushed up to her papa. "We have to get out of here."

"Devlin is right there," said Kanasta.

"So is Sel!" she exclaimed, tugging at his arm.

182

Riufen rushed in as the building dissipated. "Has the mission been completed, or is there still time for another battle?" His gaze shifted up to the Lord of Destruction.

The pink shell shielding Lord Sel's identity shattered to pieces. The white light emanating around the Lord of Destruction faded away. Everyone in the temple except Demonica watched attentively.

Once the light was vanquished, Lord Sel's white and spherical body came into focus. The god gazed down at the mortals with a single intense blue pupil hovering in the air above them.

"Ehahahahaha! Behold, the true form of the ruler of Sel! The God of Destruction graced you with its presence as the Befriender of Betrayal. You have all been my pawns from the very beginning. Nearly every choice you've made has been tactfully calculated by me. I'm not Deceivant's Exp. The thoughts for my construction were given to him through mental suggestion. And me being Etah's minion, laughable! The truth is I have been waiting to rule over Sellum since before any of you were created! Go, my pawns, wipe out their pathetic resistance!"

Devlin had a look of horror. Riufen's entire body froze up. Demonica was grinning. BoneSaw looked left and right at its allies.

"Wasn't he one of your allies?" asked Occupy.

"No. He was always just using us," said Violet in tears.

"I had feared this was the case," said Kanasta, his arms around his little girl.

"Is he not even an Exp? He was manipulating both sides from the start," said Kaity, trembling in his arms.

"Ah, before I forget, let me revive Karson…again," said Sel with slight annoyance and a nasal tone.

The Atma Blade, an ethereal green and blue weapon of swirling spiritual energy was summoned up. A light blue sphere came out from the tip.

Karson was reconstructed from the soul. He stood in a proud salute. "Oh master, can you please get rid of this accursed button? I would do it myself, but I have no fingers," said the gunman on his knees. He looked around. "Where is Lord Sel?"

"Behold!" exclaimed Sel, emanating an aura of darkness.

"Oh, welcome back, Bob! I knew you weren't dead. It was obvious you were a demon too," said Karson.

"No, you simpleton. I am Lord Sel. It was me who killed you on Earth…the last time, that is. Your soul is bound to my Atma Blade. You of all people should have figured it out."

"I knew you were acting suspicious in Lum," said Karson.

"Indeed. You had me worried for a bit there. Trust is very important to me. If the Freedom Forcers didn't trust me, the reveal of my betrayal wouldn't have the desired effect on them. It wasn't easy winning back their trust, but I did it. And I did it by using you. The doubt you gave them, once disproven, led to an iron bond of trust." The realm god rotated the button 360 degrees with a spectral arm.

The button popped out of its socket.

"Thank you, master! I am invincible now!" exclaimed Karson.

"Go after Deceivant. He is likely fleeing. Oh and don't kill him. I have yet to reveal myself to him," said Sel in a mischievous tone.

Karson saluted and then rushed off.

"Now is everyone ready?" Sel looked down at its teammates, who were still trapped in disbelief. "It's not all that shocking, you know. The difference in power alone should have been a dead giveaway." A fog of darkness poured out from the god, once more shielding his identity. "Bring them all to the Core!"

"It wasn't Etah! You're the one who tore my brother from me!" yelled Kanasta.

"How much of my life has been a lie?" asked Devlin with hollow eyes.

"You were shaping me into your warrior," said Riufen.

"Please, please, we can chronicle my victories at a later time. Now that I've seen the shock and surprise I've been waiting for…you can all die. Go ahead, my pawns, enjoy their final moments," said Sel, his eye red with violent intent.

"That wasn't the deal," said Devlin.

"I know, just a joke is all. I want them all captured. Understood. Hmm, all but one. Kill your brother or I'll destroy Kaity," said Sel with a smile.

"As you command," said Devlin softly.

"Run!" yelled Kanasta, charging toward his corrupted brother.

Kaity chased after Kanasta before leaping out of the way of a projectile saw.

BoneSaw blocked her path, seated on its levitating saw.

Devlin shot a wire at Kanasta, who caught it between his fingers.

The wire coiled around the killer's hand.

Kanasta pulled his brother up to him before unraveling the wire and tossing it aside.

"I don't want to fight you. Let's settle this with a rock tossing competition," said Kanasta, juggling a boulder.

"Kaity's life is on the line. Besides, I've been wanting to fight you for real for some time now. If I played any game with you, I'd be sure to lose. But in a fight, I'm pretty confident I'll win."

Demonica approached Violet with a spark in her eyes. "I've seen the way you look at Devlin. You're competition!"

"I cannot trust you with my creator. You have already led him astray for the sake of your master's ambitions. I will fight to free my god!" Violet's aura came out, poised for battle.

Riufen walked up to the warrior monk and bowed. "You are the most powerful of the guards; it will be an honor to fight you."

"I only channel the Buddha nature within me. My strength is not my own," said Occupy, holding his guru to his chest.

"Then show me that strength," said Riufen.

"Weren't you fighting Crystal?" asked Occupy.

"Indeed. He was far stronger than me. In the end he felled himself," said Riufen with reverence.

Occupy's eyes widened. "Why must such a warrior battle against the balance?"

"My shogun serves Lord Sel. No matter who Sel is, my loyalty to Devlin-sama will remain."

Lord Sel ripped Void out from the devotee's hands. "I am the only one who can kill you. It's best we fight it out."

"Oh great guru, show him your power!" exclaimed Occupy.

Trees collapsed around D.S., blocking his path.

Etah approached the scissor-wielding child. "You ran away like a blessed coward. No one runs from me!"

"Is that because you're a weakling?" asked D.S., sticking out his tongue.

"No one runs from me and lives!"

"I did."

"Die!"

Napkin ran up to Opti, meowing excitedly.

"Looks like the pesky little rodent has been looking for you," said Pesi.

"I thought cats were mammals not rodents," said Opti.

"Rodents are mammals, you stupid idiot," said Pesi.

"Why do you always have to be so mean?" asked Opti.

Nina rushed by and grabbed Napkin.

"Looks like the enemy came right to us," said Pesi.

"I wasn't aware the two of you could split. Opti, come with me. I doubt he will even be able to keep up," said Nina.

"Sorry, Nina. I'm working with Lord Sel now. Uh-huh…yeah…got it. Sel just told me to take you down," said Opti.

"You'll lose," said Nina, one hand on the hilt of her blade, the other with an angry cat dangling from it.

Loyal landed in front of the small creatures.

"Better yet!" Pesi pointed at the mythical reptile. "I shall conquer you and make your power mine!"

"Many have tried. All have failed," said Loyal.

"Then I'm supposed to assume you went to Absence because you died of old age," said Pesi.

"My comrade was killed. I decided to follow him," said Loyal.

"Then I'll be sure to send him to join you once I'm done," said Pesi, sticking out his tongue.

"What makes you think you can beat me?" asked Opti

"You're alone," said Nina, approaching the cheerful traitor.

"No I'm not. Muffins is here with me," said Opti, lifting the chubby brown bunny.

"Well in that case, Napkin is with me. The two of us can surely take you down." Nina grabbed the cat's face. "Opti isn't an ally anymore, understood?"

Napkin hissed and hopped out from the woman's rough grip.

"Muffins, you have to be a team player too. Go on. You can beat that kitty! I believe in you! OPTIMISTIC PAT!" cheered Opti, petting the bunny.

After absorbing his aura, Muffins hopped out of the loving man's arms and confronted Napkin.

Napkin ran off and Muffins followed.

Opti waved his fluffy friend goodbye.

Nina kept her eyes on him, wary as he approached her. "Why do you work for Sel? You're free to do as you want now. We both are."

"Don't try to confuse me. I have been assigned to bring back your old self. So prepare to self-love!"

"I have no mercy for traitors," said Nina, drawing her katana.

"There you are!" yelled Karson, rushing after the lovely couple.

"I'll distract him as long as I can. I'll get back with you as soon as I'm done here," said Deceivant, pushing his wife into the bushes.

"What was that you were muttering about?" asked Karson.

"Just talking out loud, planning out a strategy to beat you," said Deceivant.

"You've got no chance now," said Karson, showing off his button-less back.

"Perhaps we can talk this out," said Deceivant, taking a step back.

Karson fired at the bloke's feet. "Oh no, you can't negotiate your way out of this. You're the arse who put that bloody button on me in the first place! I may not be able to kill you as many times as you have me, but I'll do my best to make it last!"

Ada ran down the hillside. She tripped and fell after something sliced her foot.

"Lord Sel says that no one is allowed to escape. On your feet," said the Captain of Carnage.

"Please. We aren't your enemies. We just want to be left alone," said Ada in tears.

"I have my orders. Don't waste time trying to persuade me. I'm an assassin and I fight for Etah's glory," said the Captain, zooming by and slicing her side.

Limit arrived just outside the wall of light. Evol's death had already weakened the Angel Wall substantially.

Gladius scurried up to Limit, his body healed from the wounds inflicted upon him by the accursed ninja girl. "Come, knight. Let us do battle."

"I spar with Loyal daily. I fight for the glory of Absence. You will not smite me, demon."

Gladius stared at the knight, waiting for his moment to strike.

"Unsheathe your weapon...I mean, let us do battle," said Limit.

Gladius rushed his opponent and lashed his jaws.

Limit shoved the lance into the beast's open mouth.

Gladius slammed his jaws shut, crushing the weapon between his teeth.

Limit punched Gladius' face with his iron gauntlets.

The creature's sharp teeth were sent flying out of his mouth.

"Inhibitor Addition!"

Gladius was overcome with an extreme heaviness.

"Not only are you unable to will your body into motion, even I cannot move you now!" Limit barraged the beast with an onslaught of punches while his power kept his foe in place.

Gladius managed to grumble but could not will his jaws to open.

Limit picked up one of the monster's jagged teeth and jabbed it into its stomach.

Gladius' eyes intensified. "I am in need of assistance," he said telepathically. His head fell off, leaving the bladed tongue exposed.

"What sorcery is this?" asked Limit, ceasing his assault.

"We're in quite a fix, aren't we? No matter." The sheath hopped off the ground and hovered over the knight.

"By Merlin's beard! It must be sorcery!" exclaimed Limit.

"I can pin myself to anything I wish, making it immovable. How ironic it must be to be destroyed by your own ability of immobility," said Gladius' sheath in a whispery voice that echoed.

"Come at me, beast!" exclaimed Limit with clenched fists.

The sheath dropped down and covered the knight.

Limit pummeled the creature from within.

"It's no use. **SHEATH**."

Teeth shot out from within the sheath, piercing the knight within from all angles.

The limitations on the living sword were dispelled.

"Shall I be sheathed?" asked Gladius.

"Yes, we shall," replied the sheath.

"**ASSEMBLE**." Gladius' exposed blade tongue spun around rapidly, slicing Limit as its sheath returned to its usual spot.

"We are Gladius, the epitome of all swords!" exclaimed multiple voices.

Limit placed weights on himself, slamming down on the beast bellow but also slicing himself up in the process.

"Still fighting. I am impressed," said Gladius.

"The battle has already been lost. Know this, demon. If your master seeks entry into the prison, I shall block his advance." The knight stood tall despite his injuries.

"Lord Sel can already access Absence. What the Lord of Destruction seeks is something a bit more complex."

"You aren't even a demon, are you? Why do you serve your master?"

"We follow those with power. We are a collection of parasites living in a mutual symbiotic relationship. We are our own masters," said Gladius.

188

"Indeed. The blade is just the most talkative one," said a wispy feminine voice that echoed.

"Leaving you alive puts stones in my stomach. Even so, I must recover in Absence." Limit left into a clear portal.

Ada kicked the Captain as he approached.

The armor-plated demon lord crawled up her leg, slicing it in the process.

"Why are you being so mean?" Ada knocked him off, only to have his blade pierce her hand.

The Captain spun around her, traveling up and down to slice various parts of her body. He swung out of the way as her fists lunged. "You aren't putting up much of a fight."

"It hurts so much," said Ada in tears.

The Captain pulled his blade back in and then stabbed both blades into the bottom of her foot. He ran up her body, cleaving her leg open. "That should keep you from running about," he said, a blade pressed to her throat.

Karson fired rapidly at Deceivant's feet, causing him to frantically dodge the bullets.

"Dance, you bloke! Dance your way to 'ell. You're the reason I had no choice but to sell my soul to the Devil. I will have to make you die slowly to compensate for all the quick deaths you've made me undergo."

A bullet shot through the inventor's leg, causing him to topple to the floor.

Deceivant jumped to his feet and ran at the gunman, punching him furiously. He then slammed his shotgun against the gunman before firing it off.

Karson swiped the gun from his attacker by having it fuse with his body. "Do you see how weak you really are? It is so great to finally have my revenge." He kicked his enemy with his Uzi foot, shooting rapidly as it made contact.

Deceivant fell to the floor, wallowing in pain.

Karson kicked him furiously.

"Yes, at least I can let you experience the pain of death once," said Karson, smacking the bloomin' bastard across the face with his new shotgun arm.

Deceivant grabbed the gunman's foot only to have it pummel his hand with bullets.

"This isn't enough. I want to see you suffer more! It's so hard to enjoy killing someone when it goes by so fast."

Karson's arms became flamethrowers.

"I know. I'll let you slowly roast." The gunman concentrated the stream, only setting his enemy's hand aflame. "I am Karson the unlimited, an all-powerful being. You are just a scientific pedophile! You could never defeat me! Even if I had that bloody button all over my body, I would still win! Beg for mercy and I might just blow you to smithereens right now."

"Enough of this!" yelled a furious voice.

A figure slammed into Karson, unfazed by the heat of his flamethrowers.

"Who the bloody hell are you?" asked Karson, switching out to shotguns.

"Regna! Now tell me why you're disobeying the boss' orders."

"Who cares if this self-centered piece of trash dies? Get out of my way or I'll take you down too," said Karson, pressing one gun to her chest and the other to her face.

"Lord Sel never should have taken you in!" Regna plunged her hands into the gunman before being blasted off.

Karson got back on his feet and tried to yank out the hands pierced in his body. "Why won't they come out?"

"All that gunpowder is going to make quite the fireworks show," said Regna, lying down with her new hands holding up her chin. "Boom."

Karson exploded, sending shrapnel every which way. His soul was then pulled toward the place where Beacon once stood.

"Oooh, pretty." Regna rolled back to her feet, chased down the limping inventor and pinned him down. "You're coming with me," she said, hoisting him over her shoulders.

"Can I make a bargain to keep Ada safe?" asked Deceivant.

"Good, you know when to quit and you're looking out for your wife. I respect that," said Regna.

"To be complemented by such a beautiful lady is quite the honor," said Deceivant, his usual charming smile smeared by blood.

Regna slammed him to the ground. "Don't you dare mock me! I won't disobey Lord Sel intentionally, but if you piss me off I may just kill you in a fit of rage," she said, picking him up by his throat.

Deceivant pantomimed zipping his mouth with a trembling hand.

Napkin ran until his back was pressed against a patch of thorny bushes. He let out a long guttural meow as Muffins approached. As soon as the intruder was in striking range, the kitty slashed her face.

Muffins retreated and then jumped toward the kitty, only to be clawed at in midair. The bunny skidded across the ground with a gash on her stomach.

Napkin let out an angry snarl and then pounced on the enemy. The two became a ball of cuteness and violence as they rolled across the ground, furiously clawing and biting one another.

The ball reddened with blood and Muffins shot out.

Napkin growled again and leaped toward his chubby opponent.

The bunny hopped to the side, causing the cat's head to slam against the dirt. Muffins then rammed into the enemy from behind.

Napkin skidded across the ground but didn't fall over.

Muffins' body slowly became clear as she went into her Absence form. The bunny hopped furiously as the ground beneath her was erased.

"*Meow!*" Napkin ran in circles, letting out pleading meows as the bunny kept up the pursuit. Exhausted, the cat rolled up into a ball.

Muffins was but inches away from her attacker, ready to hop, when she suddenly fell to the ground unconscious. The Absence bunny went back to her original form, leaving Napkin victorious.

Loyal swooped down on Pesi, gripping him in his talons. Once he reached the clouds, the dragon dropped his prey.

Faster than a whip, Loyal's tail slammed down on the mortal.

Pesi flapped his wings harshly, but not enough to keep him airborne. He slammed into the ground, shattering the bones in his feet. "What was I thinking? I can't beat a dragon! I'm as doomed as the dinosaurs!"

Loyal curled his wings and dive-bombed to his prey once more.

Pesi leaned against a tree and held out his hands. "Nowhere to run. No choice but to fight. I'll use the bleakness of my situation to kill you dead! *PESSIMISTIC IMPULSE.*"

Pesi's aura poured out as a heavy fog.

Loyal dove into the cloud of depression and plummeted to the ground, crashing into trees without any effort to dodge.

"I kept one of these little vermin in case I felt sadistic. But I'll happily waste it on you." Pesi took out one of the bunnies spawned from Needle's body. He flew above Loyal, keeping out of range of his tail. "Mercy is for the weak! *ABSENCE CANNON FODDER.*" He kicked the bunny with all of his might.

Feeling threatened by the attack, the frightened little white bunny went into its Absence form.

The clear-coated mammal shot straight through Loyal, making a bunny-shaped hole through his arm.

"I knew senseless violence had purpose! I will become unstoppable now that I am free of Opti," said Pesi, stomping on the fallen dragon's snout.

"Your power blocks my ability to bring out my own aura. I admittedly underestimated you." Loyal's tail knocked the mortal off his back. "Even so, you

are merely a distraction from the real problem. Something destroyed Beacon."
Loyal grabbed the nuisance in his claws and dragged him against the ground.
"*PESSIMISTIC BULLET STORM VOLLEY BARRAGE!*" yelled the Exp, firing multiple shots at the dragon.

"Enough! I will need maximum willpower to battle the God of Destruction." Loyal smashed Pesi into a tree and tossed his limp body aside. He then took flight toward Sel.

Nina sheathed her katana and tossed eight shurikens at Devlin's simple-minded creation. "I refuse to let her return. I must stay in control. The other Nina can't be trusted."

"Oh, how admirable of you!" exclaimed Opti as he embraced the ninja girl.

"I'm glad you understand. Would you let go of me?" asked Nina, turning away from him.

"Wow, your hair is so soft," said Opti as he stroked her hair.

"You really think so? Do you think Devlin likes—wait! I won't fall for this." Nina kicked her adversary in the crotch.

"I control optimism. I am the giver of self-love," said Opti as he retreated in pain.

"You know what it's like to be taken over by a false personality. Are you really trying to put me through the same suffering? Where is your empathy?" asked Nina, carefully approaching.

"If you join Sel, then you won't get killed. Everybody wins!" cheered Opti, going in for a hug.

"I won't be imprisoned again." Nina tossed an explosive tag at her enemy.

"You can do it, Nina!" cheered Opti after he quickly dodged the tag.

"How did I miss?" Nina rushed up to her enemy and climbed up his body with a flurry of kicks. She wrapped her legs around his head and tossed him to the ground.

"Purple!" Opti looked up to see the pretty lady right on top of him. "That was incredible! You're like a super ninja!"

"I know what I am. Your compliments don't affect me. I live for Devlin's sake; no other reason is needed. You're wasting your energy trying to pander to me," said Nina, relaxing her grip.

"What wise words! *OPTIMISTIC PUNCH!*" Opti punched her chest, sending a burst of optimism through her body.

Nina pushed off of him, stood tall, and pointed her blade at the enemy. "I will defeat you!"

"That's the spirit." Opti ran away and dove into a nearby lake.

Nina gazed into her reflection in the body of water. "I look incredible," she said, pushing up her breasts.

"Now to finish this!" Opti burst out of the lake and grabbed her head. "*OPTIMISM OVERLOAD!*"

Opti's white aura flooded into her mind.

Nina's eyes went blank, and she collapsed to the ground.

"Get your hands off me. I'm too sexy to be handled by you!" Nina knocked his arms off and leaped to her enticing feet.

"I succeeded! That means Sel has to help me now. Ooh, I bet he'll be so happy, he'll make a special room for Muffins!" cheered Opti as he ran off.

Etah ran up to the deceptive coward and hurled the Agony Axe.

D.S. took a step back and jabbed his scissors at the big bad guy.

The axe swooped by D.S.'s face as the scissors pierced Etah's throat.

The god smiled. He reached behind his back and ripped one end of the scissors out the side of his throat and pulled the child in with the other end. By pumping it through his throat repeatedly, he slammed D.S. into him. Etah knocked his head into the foolish mortal, smashing him into the ground. He then ripped out the scissors and shoved them through the arrogant child's chest.

"Stop! Time out! I don't want to play anymore!" cried D.S.

Etah put his foot on the scissors and slowly applied force to them, tearing deeper and deeper into the Exp's body.

"Who's running now?" asked Etah.

"Well, I'm not, you pinned me to the ground," said D.S. as he struggled to lift himself up.

"You test my patience." Etah tore out the scissors and lifted up the nuisance by his throat.

"Why do you work for Sel? You're not the real bad guy. Sure you get angry, but you're not pure evil. You have a fluffy friend. Even when you killed my friends, you said some nice things," said D.S. as he slowly reached into his book bag.

"I joined Lord Sel to attain otherworldly power. Serving the God of Destruction allows me to collect strong souls as payment for my services. With the souls of the greatest warriors at my command, I will become the most powerful being in existence!" yelled Etah, bursting a tree apart with D.S.'s body.

"You would sell your soul for a power up? That's stupid," said D.S.

"You misunderstand. I am gaining power for my soul," said Etah.

"Just do yoga!" D.S. took out his staple gun and fired rapidly at the big jerk.

"Your soul is strong, but it is nothing compared to the bonds I have already obtained," said Etah as the staples just bounced off his body.

"At least I don't take power from others. You're a bully. Bullies aren't strong; they're insecure," said D.S., sticking out his tongue.

"I will do whatever it takes."

The Agony Axe returned to its master, slicing D.S.'s shoulder open in the process.

The big kid fell to the ground, writhing in agony.

"You're lucky Lord Sel wants you alive," said Etah, lifting up his victim with one hand.

Riufen ran up to Occupy and shot out his ribs. Once the ribs hit the warrior monk, they stopped.

"You cannot pierce my body."

"That has yet to be determined," said Riufen as he unsheathed his spine. The samurai jumped up to his opponent and slammed the sword across his face.

Riufen's spine snapped in two, and the peaceful warrior was unharmed.

"We are spiritual disciples, you and I. You are like a brother to me. I don't want to hurt you," said Occupy, outstretching his hand.

"Forgive me," said Riufen softly as he shoved his spinal cord through his own heart.

Occupy's chest was sliced and a metallic clash sound was emanated. "You are forgiven." He put his hand on the swordsman's shoulder.

Riufen's eyes widened the slightest bit. "CERTAIN SEPPUKU." The stoic samurai jabbed his spine rapidly all over his body.

As each slash connected, the monk's body reflected it.

"I can't be sliced. The cells that make up my body obey my every thought. I am indestructible, so just stop already," said Occupy.

"Yet another warrior with full control of his body." Riufen's ribs shot out of his chest, hitting the enlightened warrior before breaking in half. "You're as hard as diamond."

Occupy grabbed one of the rib fragments and tossed it, sending it shooting through the samurai like a bullet.

"How can I still be so weak?" asked Riufen sadly.

Occupy ran up to the misguided warrior and punched him. As an instantaneous result, the samurai's shell exploded.

Riufen's body parts quickly reformed. Once he was brought back to life, he ripped out his spine and tossed it at the superior warrior with all his might.

The spine bounced off.

"May I ask, how many times a day do you meditate?"

"My training is my meditation. I am always training," said Riufen softly as he charged toward his opponent.

"You should be able to harden your skin then," said Occupy before he punched the samurai.

Riufen's body tensed up, fighting against the fist's extreme power. His skin ripped off, but he still pursued. His fist shot forth with great power before shattering against the monk's face.

"You may need a bit more practice." Occupy grabbed the swordsman's back and slammed him to the ground, shattering his structure.

"A warrior learns from his opponents and refines his skill and ethics accordingly. I have never fought Violet and yet I have learned much from her. Such a dishonorable way of gaining knowledge wounds me, but even so, I feel the need to put that knowledge into practice. Have you heard of kundalini energy?" asked Riufen, slowly standing back up.

"Yes, of course."

Riufen closed his eyes and focused his energy. "𝕂𝕌𝕅𝔻𝔸𝕃𝕀𝕅𝕀." The samurai's back glowed from within. "Physical attacks aren't able to breach your defenses." The wise swordsman unsheathed his spine.

The spinal cord was glowing with Riufen's aura, shining the brightest at the tip.

"Impressive. Your skill is welcome in Absence. Perhaps you could become a new guard."

Riufen held out his spine directly in front. "I have already decided on my path." The samurai focused solely on his target.

Occupy rushed in.

Riufen dodged the first punch, noticed the second was a feint, and kicked off the ground to dodge the incoming leg swipe.

The energy on the tip had pierced Occupy's throat.

"A single chance was all I had. You were a great opponent.

𝕂𝕌𝕅𝔻𝔸𝕃𝕀𝕅𝕀 𝔹𝕌ℝ𝕊𝕋," said Riufen before slamming the back of the spine.

The energy traveled up the spinal cord and shot into the iron warrior's throat.

"*CHAKRA SEAL*." Occupy's fingers moved in a single swift motion, pressing multiple pressure points. "Your energy is full of vigor and strength. It was easily overpowered by the void in my energy."

Riufen fell to the ground, completely immobilized.

"You have limitless potential," said Occupy with a smile. The warrior monk created an Absence portal. "I must inform Neutral of what has transpired here. I hope the next time we meet you will be fighting for Sellum's balance, not its ruin."

Violet flung her cross.

Demonica swiped it from the air. She sliced her own hand and licked the blood off sensually.

"*BELIEF CHANGER, SUICIDAL!*" yelled Violet.

"That only works on weak-minded fools," said Demonica before tossing the cross back.

Violet made a lunge for the crucifix, catching it in her open palms just before it hit the dirt.

Blood spikes shot out around the devotee.

"I could have killed you just then. You ought to be more careful," said Demonica.

"I'll have to use all my power to stop you. *ASTRAL INFUSION*." said Violet as she inserted her aura into the cross.

The blades were coated in the aura, doubling their range.

Violet rushed toward the dark temptress.

"Sehuhuhuhuhuhu!"

Violet sliced Demonica to pieces as the death god laughed. She kept cutting until only a puddle of blood remained of her.

"You can't kill me," said Demonica, reassembling instantaneously.

"I must," said Violet, having her energy come out as blades.

"Remember when I grabbed your cross?" asked Demonica.

Bloody tendrils shot out of the cross. After tearing off her clothes, the tentacle's wrapped around Violet's arms and legs.

"Stop!" yelled Violet.

"Naked and screaming. It's a great look for you," said Demonica, sucking on her finger while tweaking her nipples.

The helpless women screamed as the tentacles cracked her bones.

The cross slowly turned around until the blades were facing its wielder.

The tentacles now wrapped around Violet's neck, lifting her off the ground.

Devlin's devotee struggled in pain. The blade from her own cross then shot through her stomach. She spit out a gob of blood, which fell onto the dark goddess' face.

"Don't you see how weak you are?" Demonica ripped the blade out of her victim's chest as she lapped up the blood.

The tentacles went back in the bloodstain on the cross.

Violet fell to her knees in anguish, screaming in pain.

"Would you shut up? You did this to yourself. If you behave, after Devlin and I are married, you can be our pet," said Demonica.

"*ASTRAL PROJECTION!*" Violet's aura burst out from her body.

The God of Death's fingernails shot into the astral body but did no damage.

The projected energy grabbed hold of the dark goddess' head and slammed her to the ground.

Demonica collapsed into blood and sped away from her attacker. "Hmm, I wonder if you can fly."

Blood shot out from the dark goddess' back and hardened into wings. She then took to the skies.

Violet's astral form flew through the air after the demon queen. Its hands cut into her shoulders.

Demonica's arms were sliced off in an instant.

Tendrils took form from the blood gushing out from Demonica's severs. The tendrils stabbed into the astral body from behind but again did no damage.

"Enough playing around," said Demonica.

The blood tendrils combined and elongated till they were pressed to Violet's throat.

"Drop your projection or I'll gouge your throat from the inside," said Demonica.

The astral body dissipated.

Demonica pulled the tendril back in and landed. "As long as the body is well guarded, that astral form is unbeatable. Maybe I should kill her," she said, picking her teeth.

"You'll have to kill me to stop me," said Violet, standing with a powerful aura.

"Such a martyr. Alright, I won't cheat this time. Come at me with your aura."

Violet's aura leaped out of her and fired energy at the goddess.

"Do you have any idea how powerful Sel is?" Demonica fired black energy from her hands.

The energy ate at Violet's astral body until it was nearly gone.

Violet wobbled a bit and then collapsed.

Demonica called the darkness back into her. "Ah, that was a nice feast."

BoneSaw, while riding it's levitating saw, tossed mini saws at the young assassin.

Kaity maneuvered through the saws toward her attacker. "Why are you on Sel's side? Is it just so you can kill people? There has to be some other thought in your mind besides killing. Don't you remember me at all?" she asked as she dodged her friend's swipes.

The assassin prodigy hit BoneSaw before each attack, sending the saws just out of range. "I don't want to hurt you."

BoneSaw launched its levitating saw.

When Kaity swerved to dodge it, BoneSaw sped by along the ground, slicing her leg. After an abrupt turn, the killing machine leaped up with its massive saw. "**KILL**."

"First time I've heard you say something." Her tail smacked BoneSaw away before the little robot could slice open her back. "You must really be trying to kill me."

The moment it hit the ground, BoneSaw burrowed out of sight.

"I can hear your movements," said Kaity, her hand on her sidearm and her eyes on the ground.

BoneSaw leaped out from between her legs.

Kaity tumbled back and unloaded a whole clip of bullets into her attacker.

BoneSaw's back opened up, revealing a giant saw.

"You couldn't beat me when you were on our team, and you won't beat me now," said Kaity, knocking the massive saw aside and stabbing her claws into the robotic assassin.

BoneSaw sliced her leg with a projectile mini saw and sped behind the target.

"It didn't work the first time. Why would it work now?"

Kaity's metallic tail wrapped around the robot. The saws thrashed around in vain before the assassin girl slammed her little friend against the ground.

BoneSaw slid off her tail. Its saws tore apart the earth as it dug underground.

"You're usually not this sloppy." Kaity took out her rifle and rushed up one of the few surviving trees left by Evol.

BoneSaw shot out from beneath his enemy, riding up the tree with increasing speed.

The killing prodigy pushed off the tree. She aimed in midair and fired.

BoneSaw jumped off and ejected its floating saw. It sliced the target three times before being knocked off by rapid bullet fire.

"Why are you doing this?" asked Kaity, loading up another clip.

BoneSaw raised its massive saw and aimed for the target's neck.

"."

Kaity dropped her gun and sliced through the massive saw. "Is that all you say?" Her tail smacked her little buddy to the ground. "I'm sorry." She raised her anti-tank rifle and fired.

BoneSaw skid across the ground with a huge hole through its body. In seconds it had shut down.

Kaity walked up to him, her sidearm ready to fire. Her body was suddenly pulled toward the little robot with extreme force.

The girl's head slammed against the bot's body.

Kaity kicked off and stumbled a bit as she created some distance. "I'm Kanasta's apprentice. I can't lose to you. Sefiwah wanted me to move on and I did. But I've decided to stay by his side till the end. And if I lose him too, then I'll take over the Viper Squad," she said, running on all fours.

BoneSaw sped toward the attacker.

Once her mechanical adversary was in range, Kaity stabbed it with her plasma claws, tearing the robot in half as she flipped over it.

BoneSaw instantly reassembled and lashed its saw at the target.

"Another upgrade?" Kaity leaped back and cleaved the incoming saw apart.

The tiny BoneSaws on her legs exploded.

She tumbled across the ground. "I can still fight," she said, crawling toward the enemy with her claws.

Her arms then burst.

Kaity fell to the floor, sobbing uncontrollably. "I'm not supposed to cry anymore. Happy times from here on out."

Four electric rods came out from BoneSaw's sides and fried the enemy's chest.

Kaity collapsed, a forced smile on her tattered face.

BoneSaw took out his large saw ready to cut her into bite-sized pieces, but once the saw touched her, it stopped abruptly. The robot caressed her hair with the still-bloodied saw.

"Let's make a wager, shall we?" asked Kanasta.

"Sure, why the hell not?" asked Devlin with a grin.

"If I win, you must leave Sel and come back to us," said Kanasta.

"Alright. Then if I win you have to put in a good word for me with Kaity."

"I accept." Kanasta tossed ten cards, but wires shot out from the ground and impaled each of them.

"You can't even touch me as long as I'm in this armor," said Devlin, dissolving his helmet.

Devlin was punched in the face as his opponent ran past him.

The wires quickly connected to the ground, trying to repel the impact.

Devlin lost the power struggle and shot backward, skidding across the ground.

The assassin boss placed a container on his downed brother and then slammed his foot down.

The container cracked, releasing angel feathers.

"I didn't think you could hit me." Devlin held his stomach in pain as the ground burst beneath him.

"It seems Lum energy overpowers Sel energy. That would explain why Bob is being so cautious," said Kanasta, quickly grabbing something from his suitcase.

Devlin fired a fountain of wires and connected to them.

The black knight's wire-coated fist then slammed into Kanasta. More wires shot out from his knuckles, connecting to his attacker's chest and pushing him backward. They then slammed him into a pointed rock below.

Kanasta kicked off the ground, having the jagged edge of the rock just barely pierce his back. He grabbed onto the wires still attached to his chest and tugged them.

Devlin's hand was yanked from its socket.

Wires erupted out from the bleeding stump. They crashed into Kanasta and slammed him against the ground.

With Devlin's attached hand, he plunged Bravery into the floor.

Wires shot out from beneath Kanasta, lifting him to the skies. They then let go and receded instantly.

A single wire, still attached to his back, pulled him all the way back down to the ground.

Kanasta landed on his feet.

A crater formed upon impact.

"The souvenirs I've collected from the afterlife will greatly aid my business," said Kanasta, tugging on a string.

Devlin's body was instantly tangled by small metal strings. "Still thinking about money, I see. When will you realize just how worthless it is? All the money in the world can't stand up to the power of a god," he said as his dark energy ate the strings.

"Is that so?" asked Kanasta, raising the golden chunk he had carved out from the Führer to deflect a Sel shot.

The chunk was devoured in seconds.

"It appears you are correct," said Kanasta.

"What's going on with you? You just wasted a shit ton money," said Devlin, firing beams at his enemy's legs.

"It's the principle behind the job that counts. Taking lives without compensation rids them of all worth. Value must always be attributed, it is not intrinsic," said Kanasta as he maneuvered through the blasts while getting closer to his brother. The assassin boss swiped some feathers from the ground and slammed his fist into Devlin's chest. "I value you far more than that glorious golden chunk of gorgeousness. Come back to us."

"Oh really, then why not throw away Deerg's head while you're at it?" asked Devlin, slashing with Bravery.

"That was a job I took up while working on retainer under you. To abandon it would be an insult to the target, to my client Crystal, and to you." Kanasta slid to dodge the first two swipes and ducked the third. He slammed his hand into Devlin's arm, but the blade would not drop.

"This sword is a part of me now. **_WIRE COFFIN._**" Devlin stabbed Bravery into the ground once more, making wires shoot around Kanasta in a circle. Wires shot out of the wires, connecting to each other until they filled the circle, tearing through the assassin in the process.

The wires then returned to their master's body.

The assassin's head lowered, but he kept his firm stance.

Devlin kicked Kanasta's chest.

The assassin boss lifelessly tumbled to the ground.

"I knew I'd win," said Devlin with a smile.

Lord Sel fired a ray of darkness at Void, but the rock's spiritual energy deflected it. "Thirty rays! All deflected! Argh! I refuse to lose to a rock!" The God of Destruction jammed the Atma Blade into the fortified god.

Void's spiritual energy fought against the realm god's.

The Atma Blade sprung backward and the dark deity along with it.

"That's not possible!" Sel flew up to the overpowered pebble as the Atma Blade swirled with energy. The realm god thrust the blade into the stubborn stone but was pushed away.

"Enough of this!" Sel grabbed Void with a spectral hand and tossed it into the sky. "There. I win."

Loyal swooped by, grabbing the tyrant god in his talons. The dragon god fired a heated blast and then tossed the realm god away from the other combatants.

Lord Sel immediately stopped his momentum. "I have succeeded in killing Evol. There is no need for us to continue our battle."

"You seek entry into the Elysium Asylum, do you not?" asked Loyal, flame gathering in his throat.

"That's none of your concern."

"I will make you reveal your agenda!" Loyal let out a jet of flame.

Lord Sel passed through the firestorm. "What is this?"

Light particles were eating away at his darkness.

"You were an angel before, not a god. How was there Lum energy in that flame?"

"Becoming an Absence god unlocked the potential of the Lum energy I had gathered. Even so, it's only residual. Leave this place at once. I'd rather not waste all of it on you."

"You dare mock me!" yelled Sel, firing a darkness blast.

Loyal's hide became coated in a clear aura, destroying the black energy as soon as it connected.

"I wasn't mocking you. If Evol's energy was not enough to defeat you, then mine will surely fall short as well. It would be a waste to use it on an opponent I cannot beat," said Loyal, swiping his tail and talons at the nimble deity.

"Oh, well, that is indeed true. Evol's energy was stronger than I predicted, but it was still overpowered without too much trouble." Sel slammed into the dragon's side, firing a beam in the same instant.

Loyal reclined in pain and then slammed its tail against the realm god.

The tail passed right through.

"Missed me. Why are you fighting to defend Lum? If my memory is correct, you joined Absence due to your dissatisfaction with Lum," said Sel, chasing the dragon while firing black beams.

"The Lum that rules now is different than the one from back then. Regardless, my loyalties lay with Absence, and allowing you entry into the prison puts my entire realm at risk," said Loyal, creating a shield of Lum energy to weaken the dark god's barrage.

"Demonica and Etah made it into your realm. You know I can go whenever I choose to," said Sel, having his shots maneuver around the shield to hit the beast's belly.

"How is that possible?" asked Loyal, swiping at the shots with Absence-coated claws.

"You're going to die here, so no harm in explaining. Let's just say I have a relic from the first Sellum War."

"From the Destined War? No, you're just trying to confuse me." Loyal turned around and fired a massive Lum beam.

"Guilty. But can you blame me? Seeing that fearsome face all scrunched up and confused is just adorable," said Sel, creating a wall of darkness to absorb the beam.

"You're not the same Sel from that time. When did the previous god fall?" asked Loyal, increasing the strength of the beam.

"You know so little." Lord Sel zoomed out of the way once the beam broke through. The dark deity then slammed into the dragon, firing beams at point-blank range till the mythical beast crashed to the ground.

Loyal pushed off the ground but was weighed down by black chains.

"Funny, right? It's just like your guard's ability. Can't escape without using up a lot of that precious Lum energy," said Sel, pinching the dragon's cheeks with spectral hands.

"If you have the power to enter our realm, then why do you seek entry into Elysium?"

"So many reasons. It's the place where all heroes go. Whoever came up with the name must have had a great sense of humor. The Elysium Asylum. It even rhymes. Well I best get going. You can get devoured by darkness or escape to your safe haven. It's your decision," said Sel with a spectral shrug.

Loyal created an Absence portal and sunk in. "Once I recover, I will return to stop you from entering the prison."

"Then I best hurry!" hollered Sel before flying off.

Lord Sel landed in front of Devlin. "I told the others to bring the defeated here. What are you doing?"

"What do you mean?" asked Devlin.

"Kanasta is bloodied and beaten. I ordered you to kill him. You dare defy me?" asked Lord Sel, glowing with dark energy.

"He put up a decent fight and he cares about me. It would be a waste to kill a potential ally," said Devlin, turning away from Lord Sel's gaze.

The dark god circled around his minion ominously. He then patted the boy's head. "You're thinking long term. Good work." Sel created a portal. "Cast him in."

Devlin kicked Kanasta's beaten body into the vortex.

"One by one I shall break their spirits and turn them into my loyal subjects."

Sel looked around the battle-torn area and then gazed at Devlin suspiciously. "Where is Kaity?"

"She was fighting BoneSaw nearby. Maybe she ran off."

"I'll choose to believe you aren't trying to haphazardly deceive me." Sel entered the spectral realm and scanned for the girl's soul. "Ah, there she is." The dark god returned to the physical plane and knocked aside some rubble. "You can't hide from me," he said, grabbing the girl's limp body with a spectral hand.

"Wait," said Devlin, looking at his bloodied beloved.

"What now?"

"We should heal her," said Devlin with trembling hands.

"I'm a Sel god, remember? Demonica can patch up her wounds by solidifying her blood, but we'll worry about that once we've arrived at the Core."

"Look at her. She may never be able to walk again," said Devlin in tears.

"She's a lot more resilient than you may think," said Sel with a snarl. The realm god tossed her into the portal. "Ah, Riufen, did you succeed?"

"I will grow stronger. This streak of failures is not worthy of Devlin-sama's glory," said the samurai, unable to stand up.

Sel fired a spectral blast into the samurai. "Get up."

Riufen stood up and bowed.

"I had lots of fun," said Demonica, dragging Violet with a crimson chain around her throat.

"Did you...rape her?" asked Devlin, crouching to Violet's side.

"Ooh, does the thought excite you?" asked Demonica before sticking her tongue in Violet's mouth.

"You disgust me," said Devlin with a glare.

"Relax. I only humiliated her. My mission was to defeat her. I can have fun with her later," said Demonica, tossing her spoils in the portal.

"Evol is dead. All the Remnants have been subdued. And I got to show my true form to Riufen. Eheheh. I'd say this operation was an outstanding success!" cheered Sel, bouncing up and down.

"I'll torture them until they either break or join us. Either way, it's going to be tons of fun," said Demonica with a twisted grin.

"Oh, it's so nice to see my little girl smiling like that," said Sel, patting the Goddess of Death like a puppy.

"Why do you fear the Remnants?" asked Devlin.

"It's always good to be extra cautious, especially when there is a single prisoner who can change the tide of this war," said Lord Sel.

"You mean Hope?" asked Demonica.

Sel sank. "You've spoiled the surprise. Ugh, yes her. It doesn't matter anymore, I suppose. They won't be going to the prison and they won't be speaking to Lum," said Sel, watching with glee as its allies tossed their victims into the portal.

Part 13
Elysium Asylum

Chapter 106: Jailed

Kanasta was flung into the Core, bloodied and exhausted.

Tsul and Edirp stood at attention, knowing more prisoners were soon to come.

Kaity was the next to arrive. Her battered and sliced up body brought a smile to Edirp's face.

"Shall we strap them in?" asked Edirp, grabbing the girl by her hair.

"Wait for Lord Sel to arrive. It won't be long now," said Tsul.

Violet fell in, naked and with a collar around her neck.

"Demonica was messing around again. Lord Sel puts far too much faith in her," said Tsul with a grimace.

"This thing is the one who harmed me. Now she is weak and helpless," said Edirp, slamming her heel into Violet's chest.

Demonica entered.

"What do we do with them?" asked Tsul.

"We break their will," she said, creating chains of blood around the arms and legs of the victims.

Devlin entered and immediately rushed to Kaity's side. "Demonica, can you heal her?"

"Of course I can."

Demonica's sex slave came running to her on all fours.

"Disarm them." With a snap of her fingers, the Remnants lost their guns. The weapons appeared in a neat pile in front of Demonica.

"Please, heal her," said Devlin, sewing Kaity's wounds, as best he could.

"I was going to. You're so impatient." Demonica kicked her gimp. "Heal Kaity. Leave the others as is for now."

The gimp nodded and went to the assassin girl's side. The slave placed its hands above her and in an instant all her wounds were gone.

"Incredible," said Devlin, looking at his beloved's flawless skin.

Opti came in, hoisting Ada over his shoulder. "She's hurt pretty bad, can you help her?" he asked, setting her on the ground.

"Sorry, no can do," said Demonica with a shrug.

"Let her go!" yelled Deceivant, squirming out from Demonica's grip and falling to the ground. Once the injured inventor got to his feet, he was immediately gripped from behind.

"Are you going to make this easy or would you rather we harm your loved ones?" asked Demonica, creating spikes around his wife.

"What do you want from me?" he asked, looking for mercy in her cold eyes.

"You're an inventor. Lord Sel wants you to create more Exps," said Tsul.

"Wow!" Opti's eyes widened. "My name is Opti as in optimistic! What is your name, pretty lady?" he asked, eyeing her feathery legs.

"I'm Tsul, the goddess of Lust. I saw you in Sel before if I'm not mistaken."

"That's true, but somehow I didn't notice your pretty legs! Want to be my special someone?"

"Sorry. I'm independent. I fool around sometimes but nothing serious. More often than not, I just satisfy myself."

"Okay. I understand. The search continues," said Opti, walking off with a smile.

Lord Sel entered, followed by the rest of his pawns. "Set the child down." Etah tossed his broken opponent against the ground.

Lord Sel turned away. "Pesi, did you capture Needle? I doubt it will want to help us now that we threaten the balance of Sellum."

"Indeed. Needle brought me to Absence and sent the hero there as well. In return I vowed to never attack its realm," said Etah.

"Well then I guess you'll miss the after-party," said Sel with a grin. "So, where is Needle?"

Pesi took a step back and crossed his arms. "That frolicking numbskull turned Needle into a bunny."

"Is that really the best excuse you could come up with?" asked Sel.

"Opti, tell Lord Sel how you ruined everything!" yelled Pesi.

"How did you two split apart?" asked Devlin, looking at his creations.

"They are two souls in a single body. One of them split off and created himself a new body. All the bodies of the dead Exps aren't real anyway. Unless they cross through the Portal to Earth, of course. Now, Opti, are you going to tell me where our Absence escort is?" asked Lord Sel.

Opti held up the chubby brown bunny.

"This wouldn't be the first time a god has been transformed. But you don't even have your artifact with you. How did you manage to do this?" asked Lord Sel, circling around the fallen god.

"It was the only way I could win. Needle was once prickly, but now it's soft and fluffy!" cheered Opti.

"Of course. By placing your life on the line against Etah you have achieved a strong link with the Influence artifact. That's the only way you could have achieved such a feat," said Lord Sel as Opti pet the bunny.

"Yep. Now me and Muffins are together forever. You're not upset, right?"

"As long as Muffins follows my commands, it makes no real difference. Create an Absence portal, now," said Lord Sel.

Muffins turned to Opti and crinkled her nose.

"No luck. Ugh, this puts a chink in the plan. Oh well, we were planning on going to the Elysium Asylum anyway. This recent development has only changed the importance of a successful abduction."

"When do we attack the prison?" asked Etah.

"We mustn't rush things or we'll get sloppy. Everyone can recuperate for a bit while Demonica and her sisters discipline the prisoners."

"I won't let you torture Kaity," said Devlin, standing over her.

"Considering who we captured, there's only one we need to torture in order to get results. Grab Ada, keep her bound, and don't forget to have fun," said Sel, patting its darling daughter.

"As you command," said Demonica, picking up the crying woman by her hair.

"Don't even think of retreating into your orb or both your husband and your little boy will suffer in your stead," said Demonica before creating a wall of solidified blood.

"Is this really necessary?" asked Devlin, sliding in front of Demonica.

"Absolutely. We need Deceivant to make Exps for us. Having the upper hand is no excuse to be lazy," said Lord Sel.

"I'll do it, okay. Now release Ada," said Deceivant.

"But I can't build a little girl, understood?" asked Deceivant.

"Not something I expected you to say." Lord Sel grabbed Deceivant's notebook from his lab coat. "What do we have here? 'Deceivant's Notes on the "Afterlife".' Still in denial, are we?" asked Sel, flipping through the pages.

"I no longer think Sellum is mere fantasy. I haven't updated the notes since Etah was defeated. I've been too busy just trying to survive," said Deceivant.

"Let's see. Hmm. It appears you are missing some Exps."

"Why mention the dead?"

"Don't act oblivious. I know you plan to collect your dead creations." Deceivant turned away.

"Ooh, I wonder what it says about me." Sel flipped through the pages. "'Vanquished traitors. Bob: Killed by Riufen after being revealed to be Etah's minion. I wouldn't believe it but considering his special minions suddenly vanished, he should be dead.' Is that all you have to say about me? Not a word is said about my charming personality or my supernatural powers. Most of this isn't even true."

"What kind of Exp do you want me to create? I'll need supplies and a capsule," said Deceivant.

"Wonderful, then we'll get right down to the specifics," said Sel, guiding his inventor along with a spectral hand.

"Then who am I supposed to play with?" whined Demonica.

"Violet betrayed us. Use her as an example," said Lord Sel.

"Want to join in?" asked Demonica, hoisting up her latest victim with blood chains.

"You're despicable," said Devlin, turning away.

"By the way, where are the other demon lords you were with?" asked Lord Sel, turning his gaze on the Duke of Deception.

"The Baroness of Blades and the Führer of Fortune fled to Absence," said the Duke with a reverent bow.

"Did they now? I suppose we'll visit them when we bring my army into Absence," said Sel.

"I told the Captain to scout the area for a way into the Elysium Asylum," said Etah.

"Wait a minute. We're missing one. Where's the scary little kitty cat?" asked Regna.

"Napkin must have gotten away." Opti lifted up the bunny. "Muffins was fighting Napkin. When I found her, she was knocked out."

"So that little kitten is still roaming free," said Regna, gritting her teeth.

"It is of no consequence," said Lord Sel, leaving with Deceivant into a dark fog.

"I was thinking we could watch over Kaity together," said Devlin, smiling at Demonica.

"I suppose I can always torture Violet after I've made sure all the Remnants are imprisoned," said Demonica with a shrug.

Kaity awoke in Devlin's lap with a stretch, accidently hitting his face with her tail. "What happened?" she asked, opening her eyes.

"BoneSaw attacked you, but you're all healed up now thanks to Demonica's sex slave. You've been out for a few hours, I think. Hard to tell in this place," said Devlin with a smile, patting her head.

Kaity knocked his arm aside. "Where am I? Where's my rifle?"

"Sel's forces were victorious and your team was disarmed. We put all your allies in a separate prison cell inside the Core—the very center of the Realm of Sel," said Devlin as he stroked her hair.

Kaity's shoulders slumped when she noticed she was trapped in a fortified prison made from hardened blood and coated in Sel energy. "Why are you here? You're on his side!" She wrapped her arm around the traitor's neck.

"I'm here because I want to spend time with you. I told you before, working for Lord Sel is temporary. You really should thank me. I convinced Sel to spare everyone."

"We're trapped."

"You're safe. And once Sel succeeds, I'll kill him. I'm going to rule over Sel and Lum, oh, and Absence too. Taking over the Earth will be easy after that," said Devlin, leaning his chin on his knuckles.

"Is power the only thing you care about?"

"With great power comes the ability to bring about great change. But power isn't all I care about. You know I love you. And with ultimate power I can always keep you safe," said Devlin as he hugged her.

"I won't die. I promise you."

"Sefiwah died fighting. Promises don't make us immortal. If you fight Lord Sel, you will die," said Devlin softly.

"I'm scared and I don't know what to do," said Kaity, her eyes watering up.

"That's perfectly understandable. Please, have faith in me. I'll protect you," said Devlin with a smile.

"We need your help. You're our best chance of getting out of here. You must know some secret exit."

"Doing so would put your life in jeopardy. As long as you're here, you're safe," said Devlin, patting her head.

Kaity grabbed his arm. "I'm an assassin; every day I face danger. The Remnants of Freedom can't stop Sel on our own. We need your help."

"I thought your group was heading to the prison on Deceivant's behalf."

"The only way to win our team back is to defeat Lord Sel. We don't have a choice."

"Maybe this will change your mind. Hey Nina, someone wants to see you!" hollered Devlin.

"Everyone wants to see me," said Nina, strutting up to the prison cell. Her clothes were without any tears, and the cloth once concealing her mouth was buried beneath her scarf.

"Nina, did you join Sel?" asked Kaity.

"She's her egotistic self once more. She didn't want to be imprisoned so she joined us. Why don't you do the same?" asked Devlin.

"I'm not here so you can manipulate Kaity. Sel's orders were for me to keep an eye on both of you," said Nina, practicing new sexy poses combined with hip swaying.

"He trusts you more than me?" asked Devlin.

"Couldn't you keep an eye on us better if you were in the cage with us?" asked Kaity, her ears perking up.

"I'm far too sexy to be confined," said Nina, running her fingers through her hair.

210

"Come on. I promise not to touch without permission," said Kaity, crossing her fingers behind her back.

"Please, Nina. It would mean a lot to her," said Devlin.

"You're a slave to your own love. How pathetic it is to love something other than oneself. It only brings misery. Self-love is the only sure way to be happy," said Nina with a contended smile as she combed her hair.

"It's true that loving Kaity has brought me pain. Knowing that she may never love me is absolute torture. However, just seeing her, hearing her voice, and thinking about her…it fills me with so much joy that the pain subsides. Every time I see that little smile of hers, I am trapped in seemingly eternal bliss."

"What are you going on about?" asked Nina, fiddling with her hair.

"It is greater to love another, even if it is one-way, because you can test your limits. You can see what you would do for someone you wholeheartedly desire! You do everything in your power to make them happy. Loving someone else makes you a better person. That is something you will never understand. Your infatuation with Ada is just a fit of jealousy. You do not know what true love is, so don't judge me," said Devlin.

"Only a fool actively seeks misery," said Nina.

"Better to be a fool than a selfish loner," said Devlin with a shrug.

"I don't need this. I'm going to go watch some other prisoners. Demonica, you can keep an eye on him." Nina strutted out of the area.

A puddle of blood leaked from above and fell onto Devlin's lap.

The blood reassembled into Demonica, hugging her beloved. "Why don't we have some fun?" she asked as she stroked his chest.

"Why don't you understand? I can't love you," said Devlin, turning away.

"You don't understand even though you should! You know what it's like to love someone who doesn't love you back," said Demonica, massaging his chest.

"I have already given my heart to Kaity. I can't wholeheartedly love two people. There is someone special for you. I'll know you'll find them one day," said Devlin, patting her hand.

"I already met my destined man! It's you, Devlin. You just don't know it yet."

"I made a promise to—"

"A promise! Is that really more important than me? Do you think my love can be broken by some baseless vow? You're my special someone! You are my soul mate! I will make you realize this. That is a promise." Demonica walked backward through the bars, staring at her possession with intensity.

"So Kaity, what do you want to do?" asked Devlin, turning to her with a smile.

"Let me have some alone time. I need to think," said Kaity.

"Of course, my beloved, whatever you wish." Devlin stared at her, entranced.

"Devlin, please leave. I need to figure out how to convince Lum to work with us," said Kaity, nibbling her nails.

"Why would she help you!" yelled Devlin, grabbing her wrist.

"Let go of me!" Kaity slapped him across the face.

Devlin wrapped both her arms in wires. "I'm not the boy you so frequently ignore. It's me, Lord Sel!"

"Stop possessing Devlin. If you have something to say to me, then come out and say it!" yelled Kaity, struggling to break free.

"Oh I have plenty to say to you, you dirty little thief!" The wires pulled Kaity's arms behind her back and tied up her legs.

"What are you talking about? Why do you hate me?" asked Kaity.

"Don't you get it? You are the reason why I must kill Lum! Why I must take over all of Sellum! Why I ruined Devlin's life! And why I am left with no choice but to kill you!"

"What? What did I do to you?"

"You have done absolutely nothing! You will have all the glory and power, yet you have done nothing to deserve it!"

"Are you afraid of me?"

"You must be joking. Don't you see; it was all in vain. Your mother went through such great lengths to keep you safe, yet here you are in my prison! All her efforts have been wasted."

"That's quite enough!" yelled Efil, standing outside the cage.

"Impossible. How did you get here?" asked Devlin, still possessed.

"I entered your portal when you were distracted. Lum has requested to speak to the Remnants of Freedom. Release them!"

"She sent her errand girl to intimidate me. I'm insulted."

Devlin teleported outside the prison cell.

Sel's Pawns rushed to the scene.

"Back to your posts. I can handle her." Devlin's fingers shot out wires that connected to the goddess.

"𝕋𝕀𝕄𝔼 𝕃𝔸ℙ𝕊𝔼!"

The wires rusted into dust.

"You are so lucky I'm not in my own body," said Devlin as he shot wires into the ground.

The wires burst out beneath Efil, but she quickly dodged them.

Devlin ran up to her and punched her while she was distracted. His fist shot out wires as it made contact, connecting to her face. The black knight smashed her head into the ground continuously and then reeled the glorified angel right back to his fist to be punched again. "Why doesn't Devlin ever do this?" he asked, reeling her in once more.

Efil grabbed onto the wires and rusted them. She jumped back as ten wires jabbed at her, grazing her leg.

"Better than expected," said Devlin.

Efil swooped down and punched the possessed Exp in his stomach.

Vines shot out of the ground, wrapping around the dark pawn.

"You're just a tool to her!" Devlin's wires sliced the vines to pieces.

"Your clouded mind sees everyone as mere tools. Lum trusts in me and my abilities. My presence here is absolute proof of her faith in my power. TIME LAPSE SHOT."

Her aura came out from her fingers as beams and shot into the prison cells. All the bars of the cages rusted, freeing the Remnants of Freedom.

"Don't just stand there; stop them from escaping!" yelled Devlin.

Efil created a portal to Lum and tossed Kaity her confiscated sniper rifle.

Kaity rubbed up against her beloved gun. "This is really it!"

Violet's astral projection kept Riufen at bay while she led Deceivant and Ada into the portal.

Kanasta slammed into Devlin, knocking him off his feet.

Nina dropped down on Kaity from above.

Kaity shot holes in Nina's legs with her sidearm and then smacked her with the back of her sniper rifle.

Spikes of blood then shot out in front of the portal, blocking their escape.

BoneSaw sped to the scene and blocked Kaity's path.

The assassin prodigy leaped over the projectile saws. She jumped off after landing on BoneSaw, vaulting herself over the blood spikes. Just before she began her descent, she fired six bullets into Demonica.

The bullets passed through.

"Your mortal attacks can't harm me!" yelled Demonica.

The six bullets then shot into Devlin's head.

"Devlin!" yelled Demonica.

The spikes dropped for an instant.

"LIGHT DEVOTION!" Efil fired a light flare into the air, blinding Sel's forces.

The Remnants of Freedom and Efil went through the portal, escaping the Core and returning to Lum.

Chapter 107: The Great Goddess

The Remnants of Freedom were surrounded by a sphere of light. In the center was another sphere of even brighter light.

"This isn't where we wanted to go," said Deceivant.

"I saved you by the order of Lum. Few are allowed an audience at the Observatory. Lum wishes to speak with Kaity and her alone," said Efil.

"If she goes, we all go. How do we know she won't take Kaity hostage?" asked Deceivant.

"Blasphemy! I will have you know that Lum is incapable of such wretched things!" yelled Efil.

"And we're supposed to trust the word of a self-proclaimed god? Absurd. Come on, everyone, let's find a way out of here," said Deceivant.

"There is no way out. We can't pass through the light," said Violet.

"I need to speak with Lum," said Kaity, eyes full of determination.

"Then I'm going with you," said Ada.

"You can't. Only Kaity is permitted entrance. Even I am forbidden to see Lum. The rest of you must wait outside with me. Kaity, tell me what it's like to be in her grace!" said Efil with watery eyes.

"I'll tell you all about it when I get back," said Kaity with a smile.

"You may enter," said Efil with a bow.

A stairway of Arabic letters led Kaity up and into the dome.

Each step was brighter than the last, likening the journey up to that of enlightenment.

At the very top of the staircase was a barrier of light. "I'll be right back," said Kaity as she entered through the filter of light.

Lum lived in an Islamic temple built with polished marble. Arabic calligraphy was inlaid into the stone archway leading to the palace.

As Kaity passed through, she felt a shift in consciousness.

All of a sudden she was in a white garden. The garden was unlike any other. It had miniature forests, jungles, swamps, deserts, and snowy mountains. At the center of the garden was a tree. At the base of the tree was a floating collection of light.

Kaity approached the blinding light, slowly making out its figure.

"Approach no further," said Lum.

"Understood," said Kaity, stopping in place.

"I have brought you here, to the Quwwat al Nur, to ask a simple question: are you willing to fight for this world?"

Kaity's gaze shifted to the miniature remains of Refuge—the temple that was allowed to be destroyed by angels. "I have some questions of my own."

"Very well, speak."

"Why did you allow the Refuge of the People to be destroyed?"

"Only light temples are made without violence. Why should I protect something made without my consent? The humans here think they can barter with angels and then expect us to help them when they are in need. If they are so presumptuous as to think they know better than the Great Goddess herself, then surely they are more than capable of handling their own problems."

"The angels watched as the temple burned. And then Etaf appeared and attacked the rebels. Was that really necessary?" asked Kaity.

"Etaf does not act without reason. Allah's Jannah often recruits humans who have lost their place of idol worship. She was likely taking precautions. You shouldn't let something so insignificant distract you from the bigger picture. Now, are you willing to fight for the safety of this world and its visitors?"

"Did you order Efil to send us to Absence?"

"Efil did that of her own volition."

"Then you didn't want to lock us up in Elysium?"

"If any Exps arrived during my leave, they were to be sent to Elysium. That fortified haven is the second safest place in Lum."

"Did you order the Imam killed, or was that a lie created by Etaf?"

"Etaf is burdened with doubt, but that does not mean she is not loyal. The Imam has set her sights on the Portal to Earth. As Lum it is my duty to keep the knowledge of the afterlife away from the incarnated. But that won't be a concern much longer. Once Sel has fallen, all the humans will be removed from this paradise."

"What do you mean by that?" asked Kaity, pulling away.

"Nearly all the humans here should be spending eternity in Sel, but in order to lessen the influx of demons, I lowered the karmic bar. This allowed for sinners to reach paradise, and made Lum the destination for all animals except humans. In times of war, even universal laws can be bent."

"So once this is all over, you'll order Etaf to kill them all?" asked Kaity.

"I dislike that word. I'm merely going to remove the sinners from the realm," said Lum with a smile.

"I don't understand. I've met many wonderful humans. They were friendly and hospitable. They put their lives on the line to protect us," said Kaity.

"You're mistaking friendly with good. Their own karmas can speak for themselves. Those who leave the planet doing more damage than good are sent to Sel. Humans live a life of entitlement and thus nearly all of them, even those who strive to live morally, have a disproportionate influx of karma. If it weren't for me lowering the karmic bar, you never would have made it to Lum."

215

"That's not true. The Viper Squad kills everyone equally. We accept any job with a fair payment. Each kill we make is without malice and thus we accrue no karma for it," said Kaity, turning away from the presumptuous god.

"I've seen you argue about the injustice of killing kids. You aren't Kanasta, and you shouldn't try to be. In the end, violence is violence no matter the intentions behind it. You can't break yourself free from the effects of your actions simply because you have justified your actions to yourself. But none of that matters anymore. You're safe here," said Lum, reaching out.

"You're not going to let me leave, are you?" asked Kaity softly.

"Don't sound so sad about it."

"You think I'm happy to be held captive just because you're a god? My mother told me to always be skeptical, not to put my faith in gods, and to be wary around those claiming divinity."

"Such a cautious woman. I can relate."

"Why talk to me? Kanasta and Deceivant are the commanders of the Remnants. You should negotiate with them."

"You have what it takes to be a great leader. But the reason I chose you is rather straightforward. I wanted to see you again."

The light emanating from the figure dimmed.

Kaity leaped at the figure, snuggling up against her in a tight embrace. "Sefiwah!" Her eyes shrank. "No. You died. This is an illusion. Is Lum trying to keep me here?" she asked, now scanning the garden for an exit.

"You may leave once we are done talking." Sefiwah leaned down and kissed the girl's lips.

"You feel just like her," said Kaity, running her fingers through her soul mate's hair.

Sefiwah kissed her lover's neck. "That's because I am her."

"I want to believe you. Pr-prove it," said Kaity snuggling against Sefiwah's chest.

Sefiwah's fingers touched Kaity's lips. They went down her chest all the way to just below her belly button. She then tapped her nose. "Proof enough?"

Kaity buried her face in her lover's chest.

"It has been far too long," said Sefiwah, caressing her kitten.

Kaity continued to cry.

"There, there. It's alright now. I'm here." She lifted Kaity up by the chin and ever so lightly kissed her lips.

"I've missed you too," said Kaity, knocking Sefiwah over.

Kaity kissed her passionately as tears continued to flow out.

"I don't think this is the right place for this," said Sefiwah, turning away with the slightest blush.

Kaity took Sefiwah's hands and placed them on her butt. "Is this the right place?"

"Maybe," said Sefiwah, sucking on her kitten's neck.

"Or maybe it's here," said Kaity, her tail brushing up against her lover's flower.

"Oh my." Sefiwah pulled away as the girl lapped at her ear. "I'm sorry, but I can't do this right now."

"Aww, come on. It's been so long since we've…been intimate," said Kaity with a blush.

"I've been through a lot. I'm still in shock I suppose," said Sefiwah, running her fingers up and down her kitten's back.

"That's right! I saw you die," said Kaity, checking her lover's pulse.

"I faked my death. Or rather I reconstructed my body after it was blown to bits."

"Why would you do that? I really thought I had lost you," cried Kaity, clenching her beloved tightly.

"I had to. Evol wasn't properly ruling in my place, allowing many sins to go unpunished. If not for Etaf, I fear that this world would already have been contaminated by humanity's whims."

"I don't understand. What are you talking about?" asked Kaity, pulling away.

Sefiwah tapped her soul mate's nipples through her suit. "I am Lum."

Flowers sprouted from the point of contact.

Kaity stared blankly as the goddess stroked her hair.

Sefiwah pulled a dandelion out of the girl's hair and blew it, spreading the seeds.

"But how are you Lum? How did you become a god?" asked Kaity, touching the familiar snow-like skin.

"I suppose I owe you an explanation. I've put you through so much." Sefiwah emanated light from her hands. "I was Lum before I joined the Viper Squad."

"What? That's not possible," said Kaity, her eyes shrinking.

"I had to keep watch over you. You were an assassin, so I incarnated and became an assassin. But to protect you, I became your lover," said Lum, caressing Kaity's cheek.

"But we're a team. You're an assassin, just like me," said Kaity.

The wraps dropped from the goddess' body. "Killing people is a despicable act. I've lied to you. I'm not a masochist. The damage I have done cannot be undone. The wounds I inflicted upon myself were punishment for my sins. Because of this, I shall never heal them. There is one cut for each life I have

217

sent to Sellum," said Sefiwah, dispelling the light around her and revealing her wounds.

"Ada was telling the truth about you. You really do hate killing. But you smile...when we kill together. That isn't fake, is it?" asked Kaity, a tremor in her voice.

"Only a demon relishes the suffering of others. But in order to become someone you could trust, someone you would love, I had to become a demon. Your friend Sefiwah is just a role I played. All of it was done to keep you safe from Sel."

Sefiwah's hair grew until it touched the floor, radiating pure light.

"Don't go!" whined Kaity.

A dress of white light cloaked Sefiwah, masking her wounds. A radiant light emanated from her bosom. "This is who I really am." The aura sprouted out from her back, taking shape as a dream catcher. The rest of the aura shot up like a minaret, rising through the ceiling of the structure and raining down on the land below.

"No! You are Sefiwah! It doesn't matter if you weren't a killer like me. You still love me, right?" asked Kaity in tears.

"Now and always," said Lum, beaming at her little one.

"I'm sorry. I'm just overwhelmed. I know you love me. You were my first, after all," said Kaity with a blush.

"You've grown so much in my absence," said Lum, kissing her darling's forehead.

Kaity kissed back. "I'd love to stay, but I have to go. My comrades are waiting for me," she said, still holding her lover's hand.

"Stay a bit longer. I'm the one you love more than anyone, aren't I?" asked Lum, her fingers gliding down her kitten's back.

"Can I become a god? I want to do whatever I can to protect you," said Kaity, leaning into her soul mate.

"Your safety takes priority. As long as we stay here, we are in no danger."

"You know who Sel really is. Do you think Bob won't find a way to reach this place?"

"It's thanks to Evol's noble sacrifice that the enemy's true form has been revealed. I had my suspicions before, and now they have been confirmed. Even so, this is a place that can only be entered if I allow it. And it can only be exited with my permission."

"Then I'm stuck here."

"Yes, stuck in paradise," said Lum, making flowers bloom in the air.

"They are counting on me!"

"Don't you want to be with me?" asked Lum, pulling away.

Kaity grabbed her hand. "Of course I do. But I have obligations to them too. What if you come with us?"

"I must remain here. And your allies must not know that I was Sefiwah."

"I understand. I won't tell them, but I have to go."

"I can't allow that."

"Ugh. It seems this whole realm is a glorified prison."

The Great Goddess sat upon her aura. "Lum is neither a paradise nor a prison. It is rehabilitation to prepare souls for their next incarnation. A life-changing pit stop on the journey of life. I took it upon myself to watch over this realm. I was honestly hoping to hire you and your assassins to purify this realm after Sel falls."

"By purify, you mean kill all the humans, don't you?"

"Sel only reached this realm due to human intervention, as did I. Humans and Exps don't belong here. But I'm sure we can negotiate a peaceful removal of your artificial allies."

"Do you have a plan to kill Bob? Can he even be destroyed?"

"That matters not. You aren't safe until that demon ceases to exist. Therefore he must be destroyed. You're going to help me, though you must do so on my terms."

"How can I help if I'm stuck here?"

"As you said, Deceivant and Kanasta are the leaders of the Remnants of Freedom. They both care dearly for you. As long as I hold you here, they must follow my commands."

"Why don't you trust me to fight Sel's forces? I know how to kill, and I know how to survive. I won't stay here as my comrades put their lives on the line. Wait, you win either way, don't you?"

"Both Sel and the Remnants are a threat to Lum."

"How are my friends a threat?"

"Peace is a fragile thing, my dear. If I give Exps unequal treatment, there will be faith lost in Lum's equality. This conflict could lead to a civil war."

"So you're going to just get rid of my friends to keep things simple?"

"They may die, but it's not something I hope for. I'd much prefer Sel be expunged. I'll have Efil relay my orders."

"They are my comrades. I won't let you send them to their death."

"They're already dead. All the visitors in Lum are. You're the only one who was brought here without dying. Regardless, I won't be sending them in alone. Efil will fight alongside your comrades."

"Wait, there's still something I don't understand. If you want me safe above all else, then why did you have your angels turn me over to Etah?"

"I will not permit such a baseless accusation!" exclaimed Lum, standing up from her aura.

"A group of angels tracked me down on Earth. They captured me, took me to Lum, and then bartered me off to Etah. Don't act like you don't know that. You're omniscient," said Kaity.

"I have the ability to see all things occurring in my realm, but that doesn't mean I am all-knowing of every occurrence. Either way, at the time I was incarnated and had absolutely no way of knowing what occurred. I would never put you in danger. I ordered you to be brought to Lum. After Demonica appeared on Earth, it was clear the world of the living was no longer a safe haven. I fear someone must have spoken on my behalf for their own purposes. But what could be gained by putting you in harm's way? I must discuss this with the other goddesses."

"I don't know why, but Sel fears me. Shouldn't you use that against him?"

"You are far too precious to risk losing."

"I won't die."

"It's not up for debate."

The assassin's plasma claws jutted out. "I'll fight you if that's what it takes to meet back with my allies."

"You do realize I'm a realm god, don't you?" asked Lum, her aura rising up like a pillar.

"I've already lost so much. I won't lose them too. If we're doomed to die, then we'll do so as a team."

"You can't persuade me."

"I'll show you firsthand that I can handle myself," said Kaity, rushing at Lum.

The Great Goddess stood her ground.

The plasma claws stopped before they could pierce flesh.

"What's wrong?" asked Lum, taking on the visage of Sefiwah. The goddess swiped Kaity off her feet.

Once the assassin leaped back up, her opponent had vanished.

"Are you sure you want to fight?" asked Lum, creating a whip with her energy.

"I'm sure." Kaity whipped out her sidearm and fired.

Lum maneuvered through each shot before lashing her whip against Kaity's side. The whip shot up and knocked the gun out from the girl's hands.

"I'm a threat at any range," said Kaity, engaging her plasma claws.

"You're fighting with hesitation. Now more than ever I know I must keep you here," she said, deflecting each slash with a white barrier. She wrapped her whip around the girl's legs and toppled her to the ground.

"It wouldn't be like this with Sel. You know I don't want to hurt you," said Kaity, jumping backward, grabbing her pistol and firing a line of bullets into her lover's leg.

"To stop Sel you must abandon your concern for others. His most terrifying trait is his manipulative nature. Sever all bonds! It is the only way you can survive." Lum ran circles around the assassin until she had to reload.

The Great Goddess rushed in, leaped over a leg swipe, and wrapped her legs around the child's head. She flung her to the ground with the might of her legs alone. After her feet were reunited with the ground, she dashed forward and pierced straight through the girl's chest.

Kaity's claws bore into the enemy's arm. The assassin's tail then shot into her opponent's stomach, piercing a hole straight through. "There. I did it. Are you happy now?" she asked, her tears clouding her vision.

Lum tore out her hand, healing Kaity's wound in the process. The metallic tail was pushed out of the goddess' body as the wound healed from within.

"I won't die," said Kaity.

"You're destined to die, but I will do all I can to prevent it."

"Let me go with them. Efil can come along and keep me safe."

"You can't persuade me," said Lum, her aura coating the girl's claws.

Kaity retracted her claws. "My allies aren't stupid. They won't let you use them."

"They don't have a choice. Like you, they are bound by the whims of a goddess," said Lum, kissing her lover's neck as she transformed into Sefiwah. "Lie down, relax, and I'll give you a massage," she said, slowly lowering her partner against the ground.

Efil approached the Remnants of Freedom.

"Where is Kaity?" asked Kanasta.

"She is with the Great Goddess. By the decree of Lum, you have all been appointed as guardians of this realm," said Efil with a bow.

"Does that mean we can enter the Elysium Asylum without repercussions?" asked Deceivant.

"Indeed it does. If you follow me, I'll bring you there," said Efil, creating a portal.

"We'll leave once Kaity returns," said Kanasta.

"She is perfectly safe, I assure you. Lum has taken it upon herself to personally protect your friend."

"She's family and she is more than capable of handling herself in dangerous situations. Assassins don't fear death, only failure," said Kanasta.

"Perhaps it's best if she's safe," said Ada.

"Kaity is safest with us. Bob is already targeting gods. Who's to say he won't find a way here. You don't even know how he and his forces made it into Lum," said Kanasta.

"Um, you mean Sel, not Bob. The mean eyeball is dead," said D.S.

"Of course, you don't know," said Kanasta.

"You must be mistaken, son. I created Bob in a lab, and the only time he even went to Sel was when Devlin teleported him away so he could fight Exp 8 one-on-one. Bob is powerful, but he is not a realm god," said Deceivant.

"Exps are not strong enough to kill gods, and to become a god you must kill one. Either that or convince them that you are more fit for the job than they are," said Efil.

Violet stepped up to Deceivant. "Lord Sel gave you the idea to create it a physical body. Bob is an avatar of Lord Sel, a mere vessel for its infinite power. Exp 8's rebellion was twisted to suit Sel's purposes. The Dark One wanted us in Lum, but most of all it wanted Devlin to serve him."

Deceivant's eyes intensified. "That bastard! Acting like our ally when he's the one who made me kill her."

Ada leaned against her husband to comfort him.

"Bob is a legit G-O-D? Whoa, that explains why he was always bored. The round bully must have been having a difficult time weakening himself so that he could be entertained by us," said D.S. with a frown.

"I never did trust him," said Nina softly.

"If you all know him, then you must know his weaknesses. The Great Goddess has faith that you will be able to vanquish him," said Efil.

"We aren't going anywhere without Kaity," said Kanasta.

"Now, now, calm down. The quicker we go to the prison, the better," said Deceivant, wiping away his remaining tears.

"We only leave as a team."

"Son, she's there…waiting for me to rescue her. I won't lose her a second time!" exclaimed Deceivant, charging up to the portal.

Kanasta grabbed his father by the arm. "You'll get yourself killed if you go alone. Lum needs us to cooperate. That means we have negotiating power."

"If I offer you payment, then will you go?" asked Efil.

"You already owe us. We took down Etah," said Deceivant.

"Yes and that gave the Dark One an opportunity to rise to power. If you cooperate, I'll negotiate for a reward. What do you want?"

"We want safe passage to the Portal to Earth," said Deceivant.

"Where did you hear about that?"

"From a good friend. Now do we have a deal or not?"

"Is that the only way we can reach a consensus?"

"It is."

"Very well. I shall personally escort you and the rest of the Remnants to the Portal to Earth once Sel has been defeated," said Efil.

"Hmm, not good enough for me. Ada, the other non-combatants, and I will be escorted once the prisoners have been freed. Do we have deal?"

"Well, I suppose that makes sense. The rest of you will continue the fight against Sel, correct?"

"We will. All of us," said Kanasta, signaling his fellow fighters to nod.

"I accept the terms," said Efil with a bow.

"Wonderful, we will start the job once I have my whole team," said Kanasta, crossing his arms.

"Oh, I was hoping I could escort you now," said Efil softly.

"Kaity is a part of the team. The deal was that we all rescue the prisoners and then the combatants stay behind to battle Sel, correct?"

"Yes of course. My apologies. I'm not sure Lum will change her mind though. The Great Goddess is very firm in her beliefs," said Efil, her hands folded and her head low.

"If we could only speak to the Great Goddess, then surely she would understand," said Violet.

"I'm not sure we can even trust someone who would take our comrade hostage," said Deceivant, lying on the ground.

"The Great Goddess acts for the benefit of all. Please understand," said Efil.

"Tell her our terms and forward us her response," said Kanasta.

"Lum hears every word spoken here. She is currently busy, but she will give her response shortly," said Efil with a nervous bow.

"Regrettable. No doubt Sel's forces are already on their way to the prison," said Kanasta.

Kaity passed through the wall of light and waved to her allies. "Look who's back," she said, hoisting her specialized sniper rifle.

"Splendid. Shall we get going?" asked Kanasta with a grin.

Efil stood in Kaity's path. "What was she like?" she asked, bouncing in place.

"Like a mother," said Kaity, her hand fondly placed on the cheek Lum kissed.

"Like the mother of all!" exclaimed Efil with shimmering eyes.

"How did you convince her to let you leave?" asked Ada.

"I don't know. Guess she just changed her mind," said Kaity with a shrug.

"Was she beautiful?" asked Efil suddenly.

"She radiated with beauty," said Kaity with a smile.

"Oh, tell me more."

"Her hair is long, like strings of light. Her skin is as pure as snow. Her eyes are calm and loving. She's truly a sight to behold."

"Oh, thank you. It must have been a blessing."

"You've never seen her?"

"Not yet. But once I prove myself worthy, I'm sure she will let me see. Ooh, what was her voice like?"

"It was loving and gentle and…sad," said Kaity softly.

"Oh, she suffers for us all. Lum is so valiant!" exclaimed Efil with overflowing devotion.

"Let's not go to Elysium. I have an enemy in there who wants to kill me. Maybe a couple," said Deceivant nervously.

"What, but it was your idea to go in the first place," said Kaity.

"I don't want to do the bidding of any self-proclaimed God. Why should we have to fight Sel's forces in her stead? If she wants the prisoners released, why not release them herself?" asked Deceivant, crossing his arms behind his head.

"We are going! If you want to stay behind, you can. Sel's forces are on their way," said Kaity.

"Let's not. Bringing in reinforcements just means more casualties. This is a losing battle," said Deceivant.

"Lum is trusting me to stop Sel. I won't let her down," said Kaity.

Deceivant stepped up to the girl. "What did she do to you?"

"She didn't do anything to me," said Kaity, retreating with a blush.

"Then why are you so intent on following her orders?"

"Because she…she is someone very special to me," said Kaity, turning her head away.

"She can change her form. She can look like whoever she wants," said Deceivant.

"What makes you so sure of that?" asked Efil.

"Well, it is true, isn't it?" asked Deceivant.

"Gods are known to shape-shift. It's a great way for them to mingle with mortals," said Violet passively.

"It doesn't matter. Who's coming with me?" asked Kaity.

Kanasta walked to her side. Everyone else stayed put.

"Why don't you guys trust me? Why don't you trust Lum?"

Violet approached Kaity. "We do trust you. And I have absolute faith in Lum. But if we are going to journey somewhere, we must do it together. If you would just tell us who Lum reminded you of, then I'm sure all our doubts would be put to rest."

"I can't say," said Kaity softly, turning away from her allies.

Ada rushed to her little friend's side. "If she believes in Lum, then so do I. We should all put our trust in her."

"Lum chose to speak with her and only her. If the God of Creation put her faith in Kaity, who are we to question her?" asked Violet, walking to Kaity's side.

The other Remnants of Freedom soon followed, leaving only Deceivant.

"Why don't you want to see our children again?" asked Ada.

"I just wanted to find out why Kaity was so intent on going. Oh well, can't force a little lady to spill her secrets," said Deceivant as he joined her side. "Glad we all came to an agreement," he said with a grin.

"If we hurry, we can make it before Sel does. He didn't specify whether or not he intended to kill or recruit the prisoners."

"Let us make haste," said Deceivant.

"I'll escort you," said Efil.

The Remnants of Freedom entered the portal alongside the Goddess of Life.

Chapter 108: Arriving at the Asylum

Outside the asylum, Sel's forces were looking up at a bright wall of light.

Lord Sel, no longer cloaked in darkness, glared at the barrier. "Lum strengthened the barrier around the entire fortress."

"Is that a problem?" asked Devlin.

"Doing so requires a great amount of strength, leaving her weakened. Still, not even Demonica's slave can get us through this. No resident of Sel can pass through. Opti, Muffins, Pesi, Nina, Riufen, all of you go through."

"I'll race you there, weaker half!" hollered Pesi.

"It's time to eradicate Lum's trump card," said Sel.

"I assumed we came here to recruit more followers," said Etah.

"We have plenty. What's most important is making sure Lum doesn't get a hold of them."

"I understand. Lord Sel, I will scope out the area for you."

"Will you now? Are you going to try and breach the barrier? Not even I can assure your safety."

"I ask that you remove my powers from me, if only temporarily."

"Doing so requires more than just your consent; it will use up quite a bit of my energy. I can remove your divinity, but putting it back may take some time," said Sel, circling around its loyal servant.

"Do as you see fit."

"Hmm, are you sure you wouldn't rather negotiate? There's something you want, right?" asked Sel, his pupil gazing into the God of Hate.

"I know you well enough not to barter with you," said Etah, his eyes firmly staring back.

"Eheheh, you've peaked my interest. I suppose I'll play along. Etah, God of Hate, return your powers to me!"

"Yes, my lord." Etah went down on his knees in submission.

The dark red aura left Etah's body and entered Lord Sel.

The fire in Etah's eyes was extinguished. His muscles, though still powerful, softened a bit. His entire demeanor became more relaxed but still embodied strength. "I'll return once I've scoped the perimeter," he said as the lava in his body dissipated.

"We'll await your arrival," said Sel, waving gleefully.

Demonica popped out from behind. "Daddy, after we get what we need from the prison, you'll possess him, right?" she asked with a pouty face.

226

"Yes, yes. A deal's a deal. I'll do it, but I won't enjoy it," said Sel, rolling its eye.

The ex-god pulled back once his rough hands touched the barrier.

"Careful. God or not, you still have some residual energy," said Lord Sel.

"I won't waste it here. Doing so would reveal our position," said the ex-god.

"Yes. Yes. Indeed," said Lord Sel, its pupil widening as its stand-in persevered through the light barrier.

The Remnants of Freedom arrived at the barrier; just beyond was their destination.

"No need for concern. The extra layer around the barrier has already been lowered. Only those with demonic energy will have difficulty passing through. Normally Elysium is all but inaccessible," said Efil.

The Remnants passed through to the other side of the barrier, now able to see the Elysium Asylum.

"So this is where she is," said Deceivant, looking at the prison.

The Elysium Asylum was a heavily fortified fortress, angled like a rhombus. Each wall was made of a sturdy unearthly material and covered by ethereal shields. Four spires outlined the prison and stretched into the cloudy sky. A powerful light aura connected each spire and formed the barrier of light they had just passed through. There were no windows or doors. A moat went around the entire structure, leaving no visible point of entry.

"How old is this place?" asked Kaity, looking up at the castle.

"Long before my time. It was made during the Destined War," said Efil, creating a bridge with her aura.

"Cool! How many wars have there been?" asked D.S., waving at the fishies swimming in the moat.

"Only one I'm aware of. I was a key player in its outcome. You see, it was after the war that the barriers dividing the realms were created. They were supposed to put an end to the conflict between the two realms. The Angel Wall still stands, and yet Sel has found a way to enter our domain," said Efil, visibly shaken up.

"You lost someone dear to you, didn't you?" asked Ada.

"Yes, but I have let go of those attachments. I am wholly devoted to Lum."

"We should get moving," said Kanasta.

Pesi sprung out from the water and stood at the front of the light bridge. "I was waiting for you to show up. I am finally free of that obnoxious nuisance Opti. So, who wants to test my true powerful might?" he asked with a twisted grin.

"I'm so happy for the two of you," said Ada with a beaming smile.

"Yep. Now we can kill you without having to hurt the nice guy," said D.S., raising his scissors.

Nina arrived. "Damn it! I got beat by the pessimistic imbecile. The other Nina would have made it on time, no doubt," she said with a sexy scowl.

"I never should have messed with your programming. Good thing I always have a fail safe," said Deceivant, cleaning the light particles off his glasses.

"You don't have my bomb trigger. That was left behind on Earth. Besides, if you kill me, you'll lose the other Nina too," said Nina with a grin.

"We would never kill you. You should come with us," said Kaity.

"Sorry, I'd rather be on the side that doesn't get me killed," said Nina, combing her hair.

"Efil is going to escort us all to the portal once Sel has been defeated. Then we can all go home," said Ada.

"We were decimated by Etah. How do you expect to beat a realm god?" asked Nina.

"We can't negotiate with her. She's just wasting our time. Ada, commence suicidal illusion," said Deceivant, covering his eyes.

Ada started to bleed from her eyes. All around her body blood poured out. She was then sliced to pieces as she screamed out in horror.

Nina ran to her, hugging her tightly. Her eyes went blank and she fell to the floor.

"End the illusion," said Deceivant, clapping his hands together.

Ada stopped bleeding and came together. "Are you alright?" she asked, lifting her troubled friend off the ground.

Nina looked around curiously. "I'm back. Good work," she said with a nod.

"Oh it was Deceivant who figured out how to bring you back. You should thank him."

Nina stepped up to Devlin's father. "Once you get rid of her completely, then I'll forgive you. Till then I have to be constantly vigilant of her presence," she said, stretching her arms.

"I know that wasn't real, but it was still scary," said D.S., grabbing his mom's hand.

"Hey stop ignoring me! If you want in, you'll have to go through me," said Pesi, flailing his fingernails.

"Very well," said Nina, stepping up.

"Be careful," said Kaity.

"I'll make it quick." Nina tossed a flurry of shurikens at Pesi.

"**FLUFFY MEAT SHIELD.**" Pesi took out an Absence bunny and put it in front of him.

The shurikens touched the bunny before disappearing from existence.

"Hmph, fitting weapon for a coward," said Nina, reaching behind her back.

"Shut up, bleed, suffer, scream, lament, regret, and die!" Pesi tossed the fluffy meat sack.

The disciplined kunoichi sped past the bunny. She leaped over Devlin's violent creation, detached the windmill shuriken from her back, and flung it.

Pesi used another Absence bunny and annihilated the shuriken on contact.

"How long are you going to cower behind that shield of fluff?" asked Nina, turning around as she landed.

"Die. Die. Die. Die. Die!" Pesi rapidly tossed Absence bunnies at the cumbersome female creature.

Nina dodged through the assault.

"Damn it. I ran out of cannon fodder," said Pesi after throwing air in her direction.

"A warrior must have control over their emotions at all times. You let simple insults dictate your actions. You were so busy trying to prove your opponent wrong you became unable to stay focused on the battle. Without balance, a warrior will fail." Nina threw a smoke bomb to the ground, shrouding the area in smoke. She leaped onto the enemy's back and lowered her kunai to his throat.

Pesi smiled and fell backward.

Nina was slammed to the floor and dropped her kunai.

Pesi took out one final Absence bunny and pinned the troublesome wench to the floor.

"You talk of balancing emotions, yet your own egotism is the reason for my victory. Now that I've won, you have to date me," said Pesi, sticking out his tongue.

"You should be aware of your surroundings," said Nina, pointing up.

Pesi was nicked by a giant axe and fell to the floor, screaming in agony.

A huge hand lifted Nina to her feet. The smoke cleared, and the savior was none other than the ex-God of Hate.

"Why did you rescue me?" asked Nina, making some distance between her and the deity who battled Devlin.

"Don't think the new look is fooling anyone. One move and I'll blow your brains out," said Kaity, raising her sniper rifle.

"I no longer serve Sel," said the ex-god, his voice still deep and rough but no longer echoing with the same fearsome intensity.

"Isn't it a little late to be having second thoughts?" asked Deceivant, standing in front of his wifey.

"None of you can stop me. I have no need to explain my reasons for helping you," said the ex-god, un-summoning his axe.

"Go on ahead. I will take care of Etah. How did you even get past the barrier?" asked Efil.

"I'm no longer a god."

"Then now is the time to take you down," said Efil, forming a sword out of her aura.

"Wait a minute. I think I understand. There is someone in the prison he wants to protect. I know who it is too," said Deceivant, still guarding his wifey.

"I don't care what his reasons are. He killed our comrades!" yelled Kaity.

"I understand you harbor malice toward me, but it's best if you put those feelings aside," he said, smiling and inadvertently showing his sharp teeth.

"I won't let you hurt Kaity," said Kanasta, shifting into a battle stance.

"We can trust him for the time being. But as soon as we leave the prison, stay on your guard," said Deceivant.

"You can't trust him. He is an ally to Sel. Those with darkness in their hearts think only of themselves," said Efil, blocking the dark god's path.

"He killed my friends. No way am I letting him tag along," said D.S.

"Would you rather battle Sel's forces without my assistance?" asked the ex-god.

"What happened to your godly powers?" asked Nina, her hand on the hilt of her blade.

"Surrendering them was the only way to make it through the barrier. I am no longer the God of Hate. My name is Atlas. I'm Deceivant's father," he said with a genuine smile.

"I haven't forgotten what you did to Kawai," said Deceivant, eyeing the glowing tattoo on Atlas' arm.

"We don't trust him, and we shouldn't. But right now we need all the help we can get. Atlas, you can come with us. Everyone, keep your distance," said Kaity, lowering her rifle.

"Let's go recruit my Exps," said Atlas.

"Wait, I thought only Deceivant's Exps were in the prison of Lum," said Kaity.

"I really don't think we should let him come along," said Efil.

"Sel's forces are on their way as we speak." Atlas smashed the prison wall to pieces.

Opti rushed in front of the team. "Stop right there!"

"Are you in such a hurry to die?" asked Atlas, picking up the mortal by his head.

"I'm not! I was just, uh, going to announce my resignation from Sel's team. That's right. Since Muffins is here with me, Sel has no way to threaten me. I'm joining your team! Etah, you can put me down now," said Opti with trembling legs.

"I'm not Etah, the God of Hate anymore. You can call me by my true name, Atlas." The ex-god set down his new ally.

"Oh, so you're a different guy. Nice to meet you," said Opti, stepping to his new friend.

"What was your reason for joining Sel?" asked Nina, her blade pressed against the traitor's throat.

"I wanted to protect my friends, of course. Devlin is the same. He convinced Sel not to kill any of you," said Opti with a smile.

"So he was telling the truth," said Kaity to herself.

"What did he say about me?" asked Nina, a little flustered.

"He said something about you being loyal."

"Yeah." Nina perked up.

"Loyal to a fault."

"Oh."

"And that you're his to command. Oh and that only Riufen is more skilled at fighting," said Opti.

"I suppose I'll have to show him otherwise." Nina sheathed her sword. "You can come along. You're not much of a threat anyway."

The Lum barrier around the prison lowered.

"What did you do?" asked Efil, pointing her aura blade at Atlas.

"Only a Lum god could dispel the barrier. This wasn't my doing," said Atlas.

"Are you saying one of the Goddesses did this?" asked Efil.

Lord Sel popped out of the ground in front of the Remnants. The god's pupil darted to its dark servant. "Why are you with them?"

Atlas stood tall. "If you succeed in killing Lum, you will be too powerful to defeat. I must grow strong enough to kill you myself. I am going to be the next ruler of Sel!"

"This is the thanks I get for giving you my power! What, Nina, Opti, you too!"

"I'm not the narcissistic coward who thinks only of herself," said Nina.

"Yeah and my friend NoOne showed me that it's important to protect this place. You weren't able to find his special someone, so there's no longer a reason I should stay with you," said Opti.

"Such insolence. His special someone was a mere dream. She doesn't exist. It's the desperate projection of a lonely man. Still you did use me for your own gain. And you betrayed me at an opportune moment too. I'm proud of you," said Sel, all teary-eyed.

"You were my friend, so I'm glad I didn't upset you," said Opti.

"No, no. Not at all. Now…" Sel turned to face Atlas. "What were you thinking? Why betray me after I absorbed your god powers? I knew you were up to something, but frankly I'm disappointed. This was the worst time to show your true colors," he said, making circles around the warrior he once held in high regard.

"With those divine powers comes your influence. As long as I am a Sel god and you are Sel, I cannot oppose you."

"Hmm. That's a good point. Ah, I shouldn't have been so hard on you. This was a splendid betrayal. Just splendid," said Sel with a warm smile, patting the traitor's bald head. "So, shall we battle now?"

"At a later time. There is something I must do first," said Atlas.

"No rush. Whenever you're ready, I'll consume every soul in your body," said Sel with a grin.

"You won't win," said Kaity, staring defiantly at her enemy.

"So serious. I take it you met with Lum. Not as pure-hearted as she claims to be, is she?" asked Sel.

"You're the one who put that idea in her head, aren't you? You wanted Kaity to meet with Lum," said Deceivant.

"So observant. I am impressed. I firmly believe that if you all knew just how manipulative she was, you wouldn't willingly volunteer to be her cannon-fodder."

"How dare you speak such blasphemy!? And it was I who brought them to Lum, not you," said Efil.

"And I am ever grateful for it," said Sel with a bow.

"Why are you so mean?" asked D.S.

"Oh, I'm just playing around, that's all. Most of you have likely lost faith in Lum, if you even had any to begin with. Why not join my side? This may be your final chance," said Sel, looking over the Remnants.

"They will never join you," said Efil.

Lord Sel looked over the defiant stares of the Remnants of Freedom. "Is all this malice directed at me?"

"Hand over Devlin," said Nina.

"He's chosen to work under me. I'm just so…charismatic," said Sel.

"This may be our only chance to take him down," said Violet.

"You cannot fathom the forces you are opposing. My mercy, tactical mercy, is the only reason any of you are still alive," said Sel.

The rest of Sel's Pawns arrived.

"Hello, my little minions! So does anyone else want to betray me?" asked Sel, turning to its team with a grin.

"We shouldn't waste time. Riufen, lead the way," said Devlin.

The loyal samurai ran across the light barrier.

"BLADE." With a slash by his wielder, Gladius sliced the prison wall open.

"That shouldn't be possible," said Efil.

"I am the blade that can cut through all that has form," said Gladius.

Sel burrowed into the ground, leaving his team alone.

"Just give me a moment and I'll have someone open the front entrance for us," said Efil, already having healed the wall Atlas smashed open.

"No time. Let's hurry in before they kill the prisoners," said Atlas, taking the samurai's shortcut.

The Remnants followed Atlas inside and Efil rushed in.

Once they were inside, the light barrier outlining the prison came back into effect. Another more fortified barrier then overlaid it, like armor over chainmail. The Remnants rushed down many corridors and hallways until they met up with Sel's forces in a circular room.

The room was completely white. Its interior was made out of a hardened aura. The walls glowed with an internal energy. There were two hallways, and each stopped at a dead end.

"Everyone, our brave little warrior has returned. Guess he figured out where we would be," said Nina, trying to pull Napkin off her arm.

"Napkin, stop. You're hurting her," said Kaity, gently pulling her little friend off. "Calm down. You're safe with me," said Kaity, rubbing under the kitty's chin till he retracted his claws.

"Where are all the guards?" asked Sel, popping out from above the goddess of flowers.

"I don't know," said Efil, turning away from his dark gaze.

Etaf teleported into the room. "Lum ordered all guards to evacuate. She doesn't want any unnecessary casualties."

"Sister Etaf, I am so glad to see you!" Efil rushed to her divine compatriot and embraced her.

"It's good to see you too, mataki," said Etaf, patting her friend with a smile.

"Where is the entrance?" asked Kaity, looking down the dead end hallways.

"One is for entering and one for exiting, I presume," said Kanasta.

"Yes, but only a Lum god can enter. If we can get rid of Sel, I'll form a portal and we can proceed to the Hall of Heroes," said Efil.

"Is that where the prisoners are held?" asked Deceivant.

"Yes. Each prisoner is in a separate location. There aren't many prisoners, but each one poses a threat. Elysium was thus named as a warning to visitors that misplaced heroism will result in incarceration," said Etaf.

"Posing a threat doesn't mean they are sinners. There are a number of visitors who were placed here for their own protection. Some even asked to be put in Elysium. Oh it's a rather pretty name, isn't it?" asked Efil, trying to calm her fellow living beings with a smile.

"Let's stay focused. I'm here on Lum's orders," said Etaf.

"Did she send you to stop us?" asked Devlin, raising Bravery.

"You're both here for reinforcements. So let's try to keep the carnage to a minimum," said Etaf.

"Wait, you're letting Sel's team get recruits?" asked Efil.

"But of course. There is no discrimination in Lum, true?" asked Etaf.

"But he's Sel," said Efil, cowering behind her fellow goddess.

"It is meaningless what our affiliation with him is. He is allowed to participate. Besides, he's done nothing wrong," said Etaf with a shrug.

"Nothing wrong! That damned eyeball ruined my whole life! He's done everything wrong!" yelled Devlin.

"According to you maybe, but in truth he is as sinless as a saint," said Etaf.

"You don't give me any recognition," said Sel with a dark glare.

"Right and wrong are merely tools used in warfare. Justice is an illusion."

"Then I will proudly uphold that illusion," said Efil, standing proud.

"I wouldn't have it any other way. My loyalty to Lum is deeply connected to my feelings for you, after all."

"I don't question your loyalty. But we cannot allow Sel to claim even one prisoner."

"We cannot stop Sel as he is now. Our only option is to negotiate with him. This is a rare opportunity. We should take advantage of it."

"Even so...I—"

"We don't have time to quarrel amongst each other. You have yet to fulfill Lum's request, after all."

"You are correct. I will comply, for you, my friend," said Efil with a smile.

"Thank you, mataki. Now, let's get on with this. One Remnant and one of Sel's Pawns will each go into a separate portal. They will be brought into the chamber with the Exp prisoner. What you do when you meet with them is for you

234

to decide. As long as you get them to enter your portal, they will be in your custody. If they do not come peacefully, please subdue them before bringing them in. I will watch Sel's side, and Efil will monitor the Remnants of Freedom. If either side breaks the rules, I will call upon Lum's forces to storm the prison. Only one member from each team is allowed entry each round. Is that clear?" asked Etaf.

"We agree to the rules," said Kaity.

"Sure, we'll play along," said Sel.

"Don't trust the Dark One. It wants to kill the prisoners," said Atlas.

"I only said that to see how you would react. I am not one to needlessly waste potential pawns. I only kill if it is truly necessary, well that and if I'm really bored," said Sel with a wide smile.

"We can handle Lum's forces. Let's storm the prison," said Devlin.

"Patience. We play along, for now," said Lord Sel.

Chapter 109: Wringer & Absorb

Etaf created a see-through barrier of light, dividing the two teams. "Let the competition commence." Energy came out from the Goddess of Fate and formed into a rectangular portal situated above the teams like a television screen. "I'll release the first prisoner." She raised the Destiny Sword toward the screen.

Inside the portal, a cocoon of light dropped from an otherwise desolate ceiling and landed on the hardened ground. Chains shot out of the cocoon and tore it open. The chains then came together as one boulder-sized ball.

"This prisoner is one of Atlas's Exp. He is called Wringer. Choose one teammate to go in and retrieve him," said Etaf, gesturing to the now glowing corridor.

On the Sel's Pawns side were Lord Sel, Riufen, Gladius, Devlin, BoneSaw, Pesi, and Demonica.

On the Remnants of Freedom's side were Kaity, Napkin, Deceivant, Nina, Opti, Muffins, D.S., Atlas, Ada, Kanasta, and Violet.

"Wringer is a self-made vigilante. He has no sight, but is very perceptive to movement. He's also psychotic and violent. I recommend keeping your distance," said Atlas to his team.

"I'll go first," said Kaity.

"Then so shall I," said Devlin, dispelling his helmet.

They walked into their teleporter and arrived at the arena below.

The ball of chains changed into the shape of a human. "March 17th, 2075; market crashes. Shadow banking, housing bubble, deregulations, income inequality, the FED. Cause uncertain. Effect: job layoffs, tax increase, GINI coefficient up to .17, banks bailed out, foreclosures, crime up eight percent." As soon as it assembled, Wringer sent his chains all across the ground.

"Calm down. I'm here to free you. Can you hear me?" asked Kaity.

"April 24th, 2075. Interest rates can't drop below zero, government spending decreases, people save in reaction to crisis, the recession deepens."

"Doesn't seem like it. Sounds like there's a radio in there somewhere," said Devlin.

The chains around Kaity sprung to life. They wrapped around her legs in an instant.

"Looks like this one won't come without a fight." Devlin fired wires at Kaity's attacker.

"Wait, he's just being cautious!" hollered Kaity.

Wringer's whole body revolved like a jet propeller, deflecting the wires. "June 29th, 2075; biggest economic crisis since Great Recession. Riots in the streets, lone-wolf attacks up thirty percent."

The chains holding Kaity tightened as she was being pulled in. "July 4th, 2075, three bodies found."

The assassin prodigy stabbed her claws into the solid ground, but they were unable to penetrate the hardened aura.

Devlin destroyed the chains constricting his beloved with a spray of dark bullets. He then helped her back to her feet. "You're right. He's been trapped in there so long. It's not surprising for him to be wary. I shouldn't have provoked him; but now that I did, I want you to stay back."

Wringer's arms turned into the rails of a chainsaw. They revolved around rapidly as if the interior was present.

"No way am I letting you win this round," said Kaity, cocking her energy rifle.

"Where did you get that?" asked Devlin.

"Secret," said Kaity, locking in on her target.

"Allow me," said Devlin, standing in the way of her shot. Wires crawled up his neck before shooting out at the Wringer.

The scientist suddenly lost his balance and collapsed to the floor. He looked down to see two chains wrapped around his feet.

"Culprit, black, male, five-feet eight inches. Wanted for three counts of armed robbery and two counts of grand theft auto. Fled the scene, police are investigating." Wringer brought the boy right up to him and then assaulted his attacker's neck with the rails, tearing his head right off.

"This guy is really creeping me out," said Kaity, steadying her aim.

"Don't let your guard down," said the disembodied head of Devlin. Wires shot out of the neck, going through the holes in the chains.

"One survivor. Male, Caucasian, thirty-two years old, now receiving therapy." Wringer was pinned to the ground and unable to move in the slightest. "Sept 6th, 2075; therapy ends."

Devlin's headless body leaped up and shoved Bravery into the ground.

Wires came out beneath Wringer, completely surrounding him.

Devlin's head shot out cords and reconnected to its body.

The knight closed his fist and the wires converged on Wringer. "Well it seems that's one point for...."

The chains on the ground came together and formed chainsaw rails. "Michael Phillips, black, male, five-feet eight inches. Wanted for armed robbery on three accounts and two accounts of grand theft auto. Found dead. Police are still investigating."

237

Before Devlin could react, the rails plunged into his stomach and tore it open.

Wringer ripped out the rails, chopping the young man in two. It then turned its sights on the girl. "October 24th, 2075; Walter Jones, possible suspect. Police interrogation. Call back in a week."

Kaity fired her sniper rifle like a machine gun, reloading the instant she fired a shot.

A few chains were shattered, but Wringer kept up the pursuit.

Kaity put away her sniper rifle and engaged her plasma claws.

The chains along the ground all converged on the girl's location. "February 14th, 2076. Charles Davis, black, male, age nineteen, found guilty for the murder of Michael Phillips. Sent to execution. Case closed."

Kaity dodged them as they thrashed about. A rogue chain shot through her arm. She fell to the floor and grasped her wound. The wounded warrior lashed her claws at the chain as she was reeled in from the injury.

The Wringer swayed her back and forth, making her miss repeatedly.

"July 4th, 2076. Henry Bradford, Caucasian, male, forty-seven years old, found strung up on a street lamp, chains around throat. Suspect undetermined. Motive uncertain." A chain wrapped around the attacker's neck before reeling her in.

Devlin came back together and froze his enemy through the intensity of his eyes.

Wringer swung his revved up arms at the attacker. "November 24th, 2076; George Kissinger, strung up, chains around throat. Pattern recognized. Police call the suspect Wringer."

Devlin shoved his hand through the Exp's chest. He took out the capsule, and the chains harming his beloved became lifeless. The loving boy rushed to her side and ripped out the chains suspending her. "Are you okay?"

"Thanks to you I am," said Kaity, leaping into a hug.

"Thank goodness," said Devlin, returning the embrace.

"That was a lot tougher than I expected," said Kaity with a smile.

"I'll always protect you, no matter what happens," said Devlin as she passed through. He then entered his portal along with his bounty.

"That's one for Sel," said Devlin, reeling in the chains from the portal.

"It looked like you were holding back at first," said Lord Sel.

"Why waste my energy on a weak opponent?" asked Devlin.

"Alright, who's up next?" asked Deceivant, turning to his respective goddess.

"I'm not sure," said Efil, closing Kaity's wounds with her energy.

Etaf gestured to the fallen cocoon. "No sign of who is coming out. You'll just have to hope for the best."

"Okay, everyone. Depending on who this is, I may be able to win us a sure victory. Also, if it's not who I'm hoping for, I may die," said Deceivant.

"That's way too risky. Maybe I should go instead," said Ada.

"Riufen, the next one is yours," said Lord Sel.

"As you command," said Riufen with a bow.

"Sorry, Ada, but none of us can beat Riufen anyway. If I can convince the Exp to come along, I can win regardless. I'm the only chance we've got at winning this round." Deceivant walked to the portal.

Ada rushed up and grabbed his hand. "Be careful." She kissed him on the lips.

"I will," said Deceivant before entering the corridor.

Riufen followed Deceivant, and before long they came across the Lum portal.

"After you," said Riufen with a bow.

"Hey uh, if things get dicey, will you keep me alive?" asked Deceivant.

"If you are in need of assistance, then swear loyalty to Devlin-sama and I shall come to your aid," said Riufen.

"I'll keep it in mind." Deceivant entered, followed by the immortal samurai.

The cocoon of light cracked open. A table-sized scarlet sea sponge with orange splotches and glowing golden pores emerged. "I am finally free!"

Deceivant hid behind the samurai's back.

The sponge peeked past the living statue. "Fate must be on my side. It's you! You're the reason I was banished to this damned place. I shall avenge my death and kill you," said Absorb in an echoed voice and an excited, yet vengeful tone.

"There is no need for that. Come with me and I'll get you out of here," said Riufen.

"Trust is what got me into this mess. I don't even know who you are," said Absorb, circling around the strange man.

"I am Riufen. Now may we leave?" He offered his hand and then pulled it back, after realizing his gesture could not be returned.

"Okaaay. I'm still not going with you. I can escape this place without your help. And there are a few things I want to do before leaving," said Absorb, turning to the inventor.

"Then I shall force you to come along. Draw your weapon," said Riufen.

239

"I am a living weapon. Come at me whenever you want. Know I shall not succumb to death again," said Absorb, pushing off the ground by emitting a constant stream of air.

"Deceivant, you are not the one I must battle right now. That said, I will not disrespect you. Though I won't target you directly, I shall not refrain from attacking you," said Riufen, raising his spine.

"By all means please disrespect me. I'm not worthy of the respect of such a great warrior. In fact, I deserve to be ignored completely, the coward that I am," said Deceivant with a nervous smile.

"Nonsense. Your humble nature makes you all the more worthy. I hope you survive so you can bear this wound with pride." Riufen slid by and pierced his spine through his rotund opponent. "BUSHIDA LINK!"

Deceivant fell to the floor, coughing up blood as if he was stabbed.

"Didn't feel a thing!" cheered Absorb.

"I pierced straight through," said Riufen, retreating six steps before drawing another spine.

"You have only made me more powerful! *REPLICATE!*" yelled Absorb.

Bladed spines popped out of all of his pores.

Riufen gripped one of the spinal swords attached to the sponge and tore it out, slicing his adversary from within.

Absorb and Deceivant yelled out in pain.

"Why are you screaming? Your pathetic attempts at feigning empathy won't trick me," said Absorb.

"I have connected you. You now share each other's sensations," said Riufen.

"Ah, so whatever happens to me in turn happens to him." Absorb smashed himself against the ground.

Deceivant wailed miserably.

Absorb shot out one of the swords.

The blade pierced Deceivant's shoulder and knocked him off his feet.

"Let's see if you can handle as much pain as you dish out!" Absorb zoomed across the ground, cutting the hateful man up without harming his spongy hide.

"I shall not interrupt your battle." Riufen sat down cross-legged.

"Battle? This isn't a fight. It's merely revenge." Absorb fired three more blades out like spears and then zoomed toward the object of his hatred.

Deceivant quickly jumped out of the way, only allowing his legs to be sliced by the blades. "I won't die yet, not until I see her again," he said, eyes firm with resolve.

"You can't just stare me down and expect a victory." Absorb shot a sword out from his back.

The blade went into the air before falling on Deceivant's foot.

Absorb floated above his sworn enemy. "Isn't this funny? You're the one who is hopeless now. I wonder if you can die from experiencing too much pain. Ooh, let's find out," he said as the swords receded.

Deceivant yanked the blade out but was unable to stand.

"It's too late for you now."

The inventor put his arms out and lowered his head. "Please, please, Exp 01, don't kill me. I created you. I'm basically your father!"

Absorb slammed into the wretch. "This is the best you've got? I have no father! I'm an Exp, and my name is Absorb. Try your sentimental nonsense on someone who cares." The sponge slowly plunged four blades into his soon-to-be-dead creator's chest.

"This is taking too long. Riufen, strike down the Exp," commanded Lord Sel through telekinesis.

Riufen stood up slowly. He grabbed Absorb from behind and lifted him up.

"What? Here I thought you were just an observer," said Absorb.

Riufen closed his eyes. He then slammed his head into the living weapon. The sponge's body quaked. Absorb then fell to the ground, knocked out.

"Hmm. This technique is quite impressive." Riufen bowed his head to the fallen sponge. "You will get another chance to finish your battle." He heaved Deceivant into his respective portal. He then grabbed Absorb and walked through the portal leading to Devlin-sama's side.

Chapter 110: Renegades

"Another victory. How splendid. Though you could have brought the scientist," said Sel with a glare.

"I believe that would have been against the rules," said Riufen.

"Oh my, I hadn't thought of that. Thank goodness you were so perceptive," said Sel, rolling his pupil.

"Things aren't working out," said Efil, healing Deceivant's injuries with light.

"How many casualties have there been so far?" asked Etaf.

"Well none, but still…."

"That's what matters. Besides, we're still just beginning." Etaf pointed to the portal monitor.

Another cocoon fell. A sticky ball emerged from its prison of light.

"This one's mine!" Opti ran through the portal. Before Pesi could even think of confronting his rival, BoneSaw zoomed into the teleporter.

"Why would Exp 09 be here? Did the angels capture it and bring it to Lum's prison?" asked Deceivant.

"We did it for their safety. Sel's forces would have surely taken the renegade Exps if they were just wandering in Lum," said Efil.

"You mean like you did?" asked Sel with a grin.

Fusion was backed up into a corner.

"Come on, don't you remember me?" asked Opti.

Fusion sped away as it was chased down.

"Uh-uh! No more running!" yelled Opti as thirty bunnies instantly appeared behind him. "I brought a secret weapon with me. Would you please go back into your Absence forms?"

"Isn't that cheating?" asked Lord Sel.

"No. They aren't a part of the team. He just brought them along like weapons," said Etaf.

"Why is that simpleton trying to kill our ally?" asked Deceivant.

The Absence bunnies jumped on Fusion, but instead of destroying the Exp, they stuck to its body. This created a shield of Absence around the sticky ball.

Fusion zoomed toward its attacker.

"UNBRIDLED OPTIMISM!"

Fusion stopped in its tracks, so sure of victory that it need not do anything.

The bunnies defused and ran behind their tall friend.

Opti went down on his knees and patted the bunnies. "I need to be more careful, I almost lost you all."

"*OPTIMISTIC JOURNEY!*"

A guiding spirit of optimism led the bunnies into the portal and out of the arena.

Opti looked down to see one bunny still remained.

Muffins was snuggling his foot.

"If you want to stay, I will not force you to leave," said Opti as he hugged the bunny.

BoneSaw jumped and sliced the enemy's face with its mini saws.

Opti smacked his attacker to the ground.

BoneSaw fired four saws, which zoomed by Opti and intersected at the target's location.

"**FUSE**," said the sticky ball in a squeaky voice.

The saws melded with Fusion, becoming a part of it.

Fusion zoomed toward the killer box, spinning around with razor-sharp saws.

BoneSaw's giant saw shot out from its back. The robot assassin then rushed toward the target.

The mass of saws and the giant saw clashed.

Fusion fused with the giant saw, combining with BoneSaw as a result. The sticky ball charged toward Opti while spinning at an accelerated rate.

"No! Wait! We're on the same side. We don't have to fight at all." Opti took flight to dodge the spinning ball.

Fusion rushed up the wall and used the massive saw to propel itself at the birdman.

"*OPTIMISTIC COMPOSURE!*" Calmed by sunny thoughts and clad in his aura, Opti punched one of the saws protruding from his sticky ally.

The saw shot through Fusion, causing a rainbow of blood to splatter on the floor.

Opti punched rapidly, hitting each saw perfectly, until Fusion was void of all mini-saws.

Fusion plopped to the ground with only the large saw and BoneSaw connected. It propelled itself into the air.

Opti swooped down and punched the giant saw downward, causing Fusion to spin once more. As the saw came up each time, the jolly man whacked it, making Fusion spin faster and faster. He then punched forward with all his might, hitting the saw perfectly.

Fusion was spinning so fast that the saw cut through its whole body.

BoneSaw broke out but was still stuck to a part of Fusion that had merged with the ground.

Opti picked up Muffins. He stabbed a mini-saw into Fusion to pick her up and then he tossed them both through the portal. After this, he yanked BoneSaw off the ground and flung the robot into its portal. He then left the area.

"I knew I would win!" cheered Opti.

"Yeah, but you almost killed Exp 09. You're lucky those saws didn't slice through its capsule. I am mildly impressed though. You thought of using its own attached appendages to harm it, rather like beating someone unconscious using their own arms. To think that I overlooked such an obvious flaw in Exp 09's design," said Deceivant, carefully reassembling Fusion with a special pair of gloves.

Etaf turned to her dear friend. "See? The Remnants won't lose every time."

"Yes. You are right. This is certainly the best way," said Efil.

Inside the monitor portal, a thin cocoon fell. It swayed back and forth like a sheet of paper.

"I will go next," said Nina, speeding into the portal.

Gladius rushed into the portal after her.

Nina unsheathed her katana and held it firmly.

Demo popped out of the cocoon and looked around curiously.

"Come with me. We'll need your help in the fight against Sel," said Nina.

"Negative. X equals zero percent," said Demo in a robotic voice.

"What does that mean?" asked Nina.

Demo slammed into her leg.

"Traitor!" yelled Nina as she raised her blade.

Being as thin as paper, Demo dodged her attacks with ease.

Nina saw an opening and jabbed her sword forward, but it just slid off of the enemy.

Gladius crept up behind the ninja. "There's no rule saying I can't kill you."

His tail impaled the warrior and tossed her aside. The living sword lashed his teeth at Demo, but missed each time.

Nina jumped to her feet and tossed a handful of shurikens at Devlin's father's creation.

The baseball-sized black circle turned sideways and dodged all the projectiles.

Nina put explosive tags on her hands and rushed at the enemy. She lunged her palms at the Exp but could not make contact. After her fifteenth attempt failed, she tossed a smoke bomb to the floor.

In the split second Demo was distracted Nina clasped her palms over it, connecting both explosive tags to the Exps body. She then leaped out of the smoke cloud.

The subsequent explosion created smoke that mixed with the smoke from the bomb.

Nina spun her replacement windmill shuriken around.

Once the smoke had cleared there was an eight-foot cube in place of Demo. The cube raged toward the ninja, sidestepping past the living sword.

Nina jumped up, her shoulder grazed by the cube's corner, and landed on top of it. The kunoichi took out another sword and stabbed it into the cube, piercing its exterior.

The cube raged forward, trying to knock its attacker off, but her grip was too tight. It crashed into the wall just after she jumped off.

The cube transformed into a single dot. Another dot then appeared behind the ninja. "LINE SEGMENT."

A line shot through Nina, instantly connecting the two dots.

Another dot appeared directly above her, connecting to the two points and making a triangle.

Nina was pulled through the perimeter of the triangle, reddening the lines with her blood.

Gladius looked up with a grin. "Help me destroy this nuisance!

DEPART."

The sheath disconnected from his body and expanded until it covered Demo. "SHEATH." It then shot spikes out from within, pinning the triangle inside it.

"MULTIPLY." Thousands of dots appeared outside the sheath and instantly connected to one another.

Demo was now a tower-sized cone that had devoured the sheath.

"Im-impossible," said Gladius.

The cone spun around, rapidly charging toward the living sword.

"Our sheath has been defeated. Help me destroy this abomination," said Gladius.

"No need to ask. We are one. DEPART," said Gladius' tail before separating from the body. The fleshy grip ascended to the top of the cone.

"I am the ultimate grip, the holder of all swords. All blades come unto me! **GRIP**!" yelled the living tail in an echoed wispy voice.

Gladius and Nina's sword were not the only weapons pulled toward the hilt. Riufen's spine, his slanted kirpan, and the Destiny Sword all sped into the portal and to the grip's location. Bravery was pulled in as well but did not detach from Devlin's arm.

The swords hit the top of Demo, causing the cone to topple over. The cone turned back into a dot and a log appeared where Nina was.

"*Bleeding Log Substitution*. And you fell for it," said Nina from the ceiling.

The sheath devoured the dot, and Gladius raged forward to his sheath, revolving his way in.

Demo was devoured in a single bite.

"I failed my mission," said Nina softly.

Gladius ran up the wall and onto the ceiling. "And now you will die!"

Nina stopped the jaws with her daggers. She propelled herself onto the crocodile's back. She locked his head in place with her legs and held his mouth shut with her arms. The kunoichi pushed off with her knees and dive-bombed to the ground with the oni sword headfirst.

By the time Gladius shook himself back to his senses, the nimble nuisance had vanished. He reconnected with his sheath and grip before rushing back into the portal.

Nina kept hold of Riufen's kirpan. "This is all I have to show for my failure."

The Destiny Sword returned to Etaf instantly.

"Riufen has a new sword. Your efforts are wasted," said Devlin.

Nina turned away in tears.

"Jerk! How can you be so cruel to her?" asked Kaity.

"She chose her side. And I've chosen mine," said Devlin.

"I let Demo die. I deserve to be shamed," said Nina.

"I'm just happy you made it out safely," said Kaity, hugging her friend.

"I suppose it wasn't a total failure then," said Nina with a slight smile.

"Stand ready, everyone. The next Exp is about to be freed," said Etaf.

Chapter 111: Image & The Vibrator

Another cocoon fell.

Atlas stepped up to the portal. "Leave this one to me."

"Can we trust him with this?" asked D.S.

"Can you sense who is inside? Is it her? Is it Mom?" asked Deceivant.

"I can feel her energy. I knew I would have to confront her one day. I'll do my best to bring her back," said Atlas.

"You can talk with Image after we've claimed her," said Kanasta.

"Very well then; I leave it you," said Atlas.

Kanasta walked through the portal.

"This is for the best. She would most likely go berserk if she saw me," said Atlas, stepping back.

"I can't let Opti upstage me. Sel, I'm going to bring back the prisoner. But she may have a couple of broken limbs," said Pesi.

"Do what you must, but don't lose. I'm interested in this one," said Lord Sel.

Pesi soared into the portal and landed in front of the cocoon.

Image tore out of the cocoon before stepping out. The slender woman had short pink hair with two tuffs protruding from the sides. Four long woven clumps drooped over her shoulders. A dog collar with the name *Rosette* was placed around her throat, either to aid her in reaching a new way of perception or to examine the mental effects of bondage. Just below the collar was a chained necklace with a Rubik's Cube as a pendant. Stitches lined her forehead, dividing the two hemispheres: one marked L and the other R. Her nerves glowed from within, making the slightest abnormality instantly recognizable. One hand was covered by a black detective glove and the other by a white clinical glove. Around her waist was a band that was filled with a viscous fluid and was wired directly into her nervous system. Attached to the band was a pointer stick, a leash, surveys, her phone, an empty bottle of pills and rectangular glasses. Feathers were grafted on her backside, giving her the full plumage of a peacock. Bright pink bloomers with a white bunny pattern were worn over her black business pants as a visual symbol of sexual deviancy. With her heels cut and bound, they were a perfect fit for her authentic Chinese slippers. Rorschach inkblots formed an eerie smile where the woman's mouth should be.

"That's quite the grin," said Pesi as he slowly walked toward her.

"Keep your distance," said Kanasta.

"I doubt she can hear you!" Pesi punched the woman in the face.

247

Image tumbled onto the ground. "*PRODUCTION*. Her body shivered before a clear barrier appeared around it. "Don't! Please, I beg you!" she yelled, shielding her face with her arms.

"Hmm, I wonder. Do you remember me?" asked Kanasta.

The shield dissipated and her head plopped down. "Of course I do. To forget my own grandson would be, well unthinkable."

"You shouldn't have lowered your shield, pathetic weakling!" Pesi threw another punch.

"*ANALYSIS*. Her head shot up almost instantaneously after she grabbed his fist. "You're too predictable," she said before twisting his arm.

Pesi escaped her grip and leaped back.

"*PRODUCTION*." Image exuded a menacing red light. "Cower."

"Calm down. Please, don't kill me," said Pesi with chattering teeth.

"She's countering based on our mental states," said Kanasta.

Image crouched down to the terrified creature. "Give me his suitcase, and I will let you live."

"I'll do as you command," said Pesi with a grin before taking off toward the assassin.

"Hands off." Kanasta slammed the suitcase into the madman, knocking him out of the air.

Image rushed in and reached out to the suitcase.

"That goes for you as well," said Kanasta, jumping back. "Why do you even want it?"

"I want what you have," she said with a crazed look.

Pesi stood up, clenching his fist. "Let's see if her mental defenses can withstand the powerful psychic might of my mind power! *PESSIMISTIC CORUPTION*."

"I cannot lose!" yelled Image, overpowered with optimism. She punched the street punk vigorously before pinning his arms behind his back.

Kanasta walked up to his grandmother and smacked the back of her head. Image collapsed.

"Well then, I suppose it's just a matter of who takes her in now," said Pesi, rushing at Kanasta and slashing at him with his fingernails.

Kanasta knocked Pesi's arms aside and then rammed him down. The assassin lifted Image over his shoulder and walked back through the portal.

"What just happened?" asked Pesi.

Kanasta arrived and placed Image on the ground. "The family reunion will have to wait."

Atlas lifted her from the floor and into an embrace. "Still just as beautiful as I remembered."

"When you killed her...was it really you?" asked Deceivant.

"I sacrificed her for my own reasons. I have remorse but not regret. I thought you of all people would understand," said Atlas, caressing his beloved's hair.

"I regret what I did, but I won't make excuses. My chance to make amends will be coming any moment."

"Kanasta, open your suitcase," said Atlas.

"You've figured out what she wants?" asked Kanasta, opening his diamond suitcase, courtesy of Crystal.

"Yes. The glasses on her person are missing a lens. No doubt you carry a spare," said Atlas.

"You are correct," said Kanasta, handing the glasses to Atlas.

"Is she always that crazy?" asked Kaity.

"Does she love bunnies too? These bunnies are so cute," said Opti, petting her bloomers.

"Hands off my wife," said Atlas, shattering bone as he gripped the molester's arm.

"Agh!"

"Calm down. Opti's a simpleton. He meant no harm. Efil, can you heal him?" asked Deceivant.

"Yes, of course," said the goddess, eyeing Atlas cautiously.

"Her powers are difficult to control. No doubt being imprisoned hasn't helped her condition," said Kanasta.

"It is time to choose. The next cocoon is about to open," said Etaf.

"I'll have a go," said Demonica.

"It's best if I go next. Demonica is too powerful for any of you," said Atlas.

"You have my blessing," said Violet.

"Is he going to be okay?" asked Opti.

"Course he is! He's super good at fighting. He's even stronger than me," said D.S.

"I have sacrificed much to attain this strength," said Atlas.

"We shouldn't trust him. We don't know what he's planning," said Efil.

"None of us can fight Demonica. And if he says he's going to help us, then he is. He's a straightforward guy. He doesn't keep secrets," said D.S.

"What makes you so sure of that?" asked Deceivant.

"He's bald. He's got nothing to hide. Just like me," said D.S. with a grin.

"I shall return." Atlas entered the portal.

The cocoon shook rapidly.

Atlas picked up the cocoon and tore it open.

"Finally I have been freed! You! What are you doing here! Come to finish the job, have you?" The Exp leaped back. The man had yellow hair that protruded from his head like a radiant halo. A white flaky towel was draped over his shoulders. Just below his neckline was a bowtie and below that was a striped tie depicting Heracles' ascension into the Greek pantheon. The man was wearing a sleeveless bath robe with the tagline "The Vibrator's Beyond Pleasure Spa" on both the front and back, complete with a pocket filled with business cards. After all, a fateful encounter with a wanting customer was as inevitable as Cronos' fall by the hands of his own son. His spa robe was held up by his prized belt, which had a #1 carved into its buckle. The masseur's long slender arms and legs had pistons poking out from his elbows and knees. These were adjustable through the touch-sensitive spherical switches, poking out above his shoulders. His fingers were rimmed at the sides, had pointed knuckles, and were beaded at the ends. Fluffy white spa slippers kept his prehensile toes safe from the eyes of the masses.

"Your soul was partially modified, but another part moved on to the afterworld. I have not come to make my weapon complete. I am here to free you and ask that you fight alongside me against a great evil," said Atlas.

"You know each other?" asked Demonica.

"Who doesn't know me?! I am a living legend. I am The Vibrator!" exclaimed the Exp in a boisterous aristocratic tone, standing proud.

"Sehuhu. What? Is that really your name?" asked Demonica.

"I am a divine tool that gives out pleasure but receives none. No other name could do me justice," said The Vibrator, massaging his temples.

"Etah, did you name him that? Didn't know you had a sense of humor," said Demonica.

"He chose that name. And my name is Atlas!" exclaimed the ex-God of Hate.

"Alright, Vibrator, what say we get you out of here?" Demonica's fingers climbed up his arm.

"Hands off, temptress. Many a woman has tried to lower me to the realm of mortals. All have failed."

"Would you rather stay here?"

"You think I can't escape on my own? Foolish wench, no prison can contain me."

"I am not very good at negotiating. I'll keep it simple. Come with me or you'll be killed again," said Atlas, summoning up the Agony Axe.

"You did kill me. But it was as I planned! I could no longer stay confined to the realm of mortals," said The Vibrator, his hands at his sides.

"He's not altogether there, is he?" asked Demonica.

"He has been diagnosed, by my wife no less. He suffers from delusions of grandeur," said Atlas.

"Why would you make him that way?" asked Demonica.

"I didn't," said Atlas.

"What are you all muttering about?" asked The Vibrator, stepping up to them.

"He was just telling me how delusional you are," said Demonica.

"It makes sense when you really think about it. If an avatar of god came to Earth, then the masses would lock him away in a madhouse for claiming divinity. Only those with proper faith can see the truth." He pressed his fingers against the gooey pads beneath them, releasing natural oils from his fingertips. "Only those who have been touched by my fingers know that I come from the Heavens!" The Vibrator sped up to the non-believer and put his fist to her face. "Behold the touch of the divine! *Divine Vibration!*" His fist shook rapidly and in an instant he had punched the wench hundreds of times, smashing her head to bits. "Me-me-me-me! In death you shall know the truth of my divinity!"

Demonica's neck shot out blood that stiffened and formed her new head. "You were saying?"

"A demoness! A succubus no doubt. They have sent you to take away my tapas! They seek to mortalize me!"

"Maybe we should just leave him here," said Demonica, turning away.

"Sure. I'll take him off your hands," said Atlas.

"Demonica! Hurry up and capture that Exp!" yelled Lord Sel.

"Me-me-me! Time for the master of pleasure to administer some pain." The Vibrator zoomed up to Atlas. His vibrating fists rapidly assaulted the man's chiseled chest.

Atlas didn't budge a centimeter. "Do not forget who gave you power."

The Agony Axe materialized in Atlas's grip.

The Vibrator dodged the weapon as it fell, but was then hit in the chest by the back of the axe on the upswing. He tumbled backward and toppled to the floor. "Is that really the power you gained from trapping a piece of my soul?"

"Why aren't you in agony?" asked Atlas.

"Don't know the meaning of the word." The Vibrator sped away from the madman. "I won't let you kill me again! *Heavenly Quake!*"

The ground shook with tremors.

Atlas kept his balance but was wobbling a bit.

The Vibrator's feet shook rapidly and in an instant, he was up to Atlas. He pressed his finger against the man's chest. "My touch is akin to enlightenment itself! *Celestial Acupuncture*."

His finger drilled a hole through the man's body.

Atlas stood in place. He grabbed The Vibrator's arm. "That hurt."

"It's supposed to hurt," said The Vibrator with a smile.

Demonica had her tentacles coil up The Vibrator's legs while he was distracted. The tentacles receded, bringing the obnoxious man right to her.

The Vibrator's body trembled, breaking free of the tentacles.

"This man is a total nuisance," said Demonica with a grimace.

The Vibrator zoomed up to the demon and stiffened his pointer fingers. "*Celestial Acupuncture, Massage*!" He shoved his fingers through Demonica, making holes through her body.

Blood dripped from the holes and stiffened, healing her almost instantly.

"They sent a goddess after me!" yelled The Vibrator, speeding away.

Atlas jabbed a trident through The Vibrator's back as he sped past him.

The Vibrator shook fiercely, but he only plunged himself deeper into the weapon.

Atlas un-summoned the trident and took out the Bashful Bow.

The Vibrator limped slowly toward Atlas, bleeding all over the floor.

Atlas fired the Appalling Arrow into The Vibrator.

The Vibrator tried to remove the arrow, backing up into the demon.

"*Death Scythe*," said Demonica as she summoned the sickle.

"Don't kill him!" yelled Sel.

"Ugh, fine." Demonica shot a stream of blood from her hands. It solidified around The Vibrator. Before he could break free she tossed him into the portal.

"Good teamwork," said Demonica with a smile, entering her portal.

"Argh, damn you!" yelled Atlas.

The Vibrator looked up at the strange cast of characters. "What do you want with me?"

"You serve me now, understood?" asked Lord Sel.

The Vibrator gazed at the strange creature.

"He doesn't seem all that useful to me," said Demonica.

"Are you Exps or gods?" asked The Vibrator.

"I'm both. I am the God of Destruction, ruler of the Realm of Sel. If you value your soul, you will swear allegiance to me."

"Finally the gods have taken notice. Not sure what took them so damn long. Very well. I'll assist," said The Vibrator.

Chapter 112: Toxic, Crisis, & Hope

"Atlas, I can't bring up the portal to the next prison cell until you come back," said Etaf.

Atlas went through the portal, appearing before the Remnants. His eyes were fixed on the floor.

"Don't worry. It's better if we don't have him on our side," said Deceivant.

"I'm going next," said Ada as soon as the next cocoon fell.

"You are most certainly not!" yelled Deceivant.

"What? But you went. Why not me?" asked Ada.

"It isn't safe. Isn't there anyone else who could go in your stead?" asked Deceivant.

"I'll go, Mom," said D.S.

"I could go as well," said Violet.

"Napkin is afraid to go in. Is it okay if he sits this one out?" asked Kaity, petting his frazzled fur.

"It's fine. I'm going to have to go eventually," said Ada.

"But it isn't safe," said Deceivant.

"We know who the last three are. They won't hurt me," said Ada.

"Okay, but if there are any problems, any danger at all, you run right back into that portal," said Deceivant.

"I will. Promise." Ada coiled her pinky around her husband's. She gave him a kiss and then entered the portal.

"My turn." Sel sped into the portal.

A mechanical snake with red, yellow, and brown razor-sharp scales slithered out of the light cocoon. The snake was five feet long, four inches wide, and segmented in ten different areas. Two pretty pink bows were placed just above her emerald eyes.

"Is this the Exp?" asked Lord Sel, floating above the armored reptile.

"I am Toxic, the corn snake!" said Toxic in a reverberating, mumbling voice, raising her head with pride.

"Be careful Bob, she has poison-tipped scales," said Ada.

"Uh, yeah, thanks for the warning. I think my godly existence shouldn't have too much trouble counteracting the poison," said Sel with a condescending gaze.

"Oh yeah, I guess that makes sense," said Ada with a blush.

"Mommy...is that you?" Toxic turned around. Her full set of bladed teeth were revealed with her wide smile.

"It's really me," said Ada, opening her arms.

"Hmm. Let's see which one of you is weaker." Sel un-summoned the Atma Blade and floated above the battlefield.

"I missed you!" Toxic leaped at Ada, but rather than giving her a joyous embrace, she was dragged across her mother's side violently.

Ada pulled her little one off and held onto her. "Sweetie, please be careful. That hurt."

"I don't know what happened. I'm so sorry," said Toxic, before her tail drilled into her mom's hand.

Ada let go of her little girl and ran toward the portal.

"Are you really going to surrender her to me?" asked Sel, popping out in front of the portal.

"I know it's bad to assume, but are you the one making my sweet little girl attack me?" asked Ada.

"Watch your step," said Sel, just before Toxic whipped herself at her mother's feet.

Ada jumped out of the way. "ILLUSIONARY INSANITY." Twenty identical illusions appeared and then ran around the arena. "Finally my artifact is working."

"What are you doing? Don't you remember me?" asked one of the Ada's before being pierced by the snake.

"Bob, what have you done to my little girl?"

"Oh, just manipulating her to kill you with some telekinesis. That's all."

"I don't want to do this. I can't control my body." Toxic slithered across the arena, attacking the legs of the fake Adas.

The true Ada stepped on Toxic, but the snake leaped up and wrapped around her neck.

"Fight against it! We've come to free you!" yelled Ada.

"Ooooh. Touching. But if she moves, you'll be poisoned," said Sel, floating back down to the ground.

Toxic slithered down Ada's body and onto the floor. "I only release poison if my scales move against an object. Moving alongside it does nothing."

"Fine. Fine. This wasn't quite as much fun as I had hoped," said Sel, appearing right in front of the portal.

"You go in first, Mom. I'll keep him busy," said Toxic, engaging her scales.

"Here I was hoping for some quality drama. Oh well." Sel seized Toxic with a spectral arm. The Dark One whipped the snake against Ada, tearing her skin up violently. "Sometimes you have to make your own entertainment."

Toxic was thrown against the floor. She looked up at her mother in tears. "I'm sorry."

"Oh. This is too sad. I feel bad now. The good news is you won't have to worry about the poison. I won't allow your daughter to kill you," said Sel with a sly grin.

"Thank you. She's a sweet girl, and she's been through so much," said Ada, holding her sides in pain.

The Atma Blade was summoned and spun with energy.

"I'll save you from such a tragic end." Lord Sel shoved the sword through Ada, and she faded away into nothingness.

"Adaaaaaaaaaaa!" Deceivant rushed toward the portal.

Etaf knocked him to the ground. "Do not break the rules."

"Dad, Mom's going to be okay, right? Bob would never...Mommy!" cried D.S.

"Boohoohoo. You should thank me. I got rid of your weakest link," said Sel, gazing through the portal.

"We had a deal, Sel! I put the Button on Karson as promised! Ada is supposed to be safe!" yelled Deceivant.

"She is safe...inside my weapon," said Sel with a malicious glare.

Deceivant dropped to his knees and lowered his head. "Sellum! If you can hear me, then allow me to make a deal!" he yelled, his hands folded.

"Never thought you would be the one to ask for divine help," said Lord Sel.

Deceivant was on his knees, a rush of tears were flowing down his face.

"What just happened? A second ago you had no tears," said Kanasta.

"Wasn't me," said Etaf with a confused look.

Sel floated to his portal with Toxic bludgeoned and unconscious.

Ada's soul exited his blade. She materialized and walked back through the portal as Sel blinked in disbelief.

"I don't know what happened. It was a miracle," said Ada.

"Phenomena intervention!" exclaimed Kanasta.

Deceivant embraced his loving wifey. "It worked. You're safe!"

"Mommy!" cheered D.S., joining in the hug from behind.

"Wait, where's Toxic?" asked Ada.

"Sel took her to his side," said Deceivant.

"Oh no. It's all my fault," said Ada about to cry.

"We will get Exp 02 back. I promise you," said Deceivant, holding onto his beloved.

Sel arrived back with his team, tossing the broken snake to the ground.

"Looks like you attacked an illusion," said Devlin.

"No. It was her. I stole her soul. How did she come back?" asked Lord Sel.

"I'm scared. Where's my mommy?" asked Toxic.

"Do I heal her?" asked Demonica.

"She can't retaliate like this. We'll find a use for her later," said Sel.

"Worry not, sharp one, we will do you no harm," said Riufen.

"Another piece of trash created by my father. What use could she be?" asked Devlin.

"I put those weak demon lords to use. It won't be too difficult to find something she'll be handy for," said Lord Sel.

Only two cocoons remained fastened to the ceiling, and one plummeted to the floor.

"My turn," said D.S., hopping into the portal.

"We don't have anyone else. Can I go again?" asked Devlin.

"One member, one fight. That's the rule," said Etaf.

"You don't expect us to just let them obtain the last two Exps, do you?" asked Lord Sel.

"I shall go in place of one of your allies," said Etaf.

"What? I must have misheard you," said Efil.

"We must keep the peace. And we must follow the rules we uphold." Etaf entered the portal.

A tall, tan man came out of the cocoon. He had brown hair and brown eyes and was wearing a black suit, black pants, red tie, and black loafers. He looked at Etaf and D.S. "Are you here to rescue me?"

"Are you an Exp? You look kinda boring," said D.S.

"I'm an Exp. My name is Crisis," he said in a calm, hopeful voice.

"If you say so. Follow me," said D.S.

"No. Come with me if you want escape this prison," said Etaf.

"I didn't expect anyone to break me out of here, much less the woman who captured me and put me here. Did you have a falling out?" asked Crisis.

"She's the bad guy. And I'm with the good guys. My name is D.S."

"Saying you're a good guy doesn't make me trust you. Both of you are here because you need me. I want to know what you plan for me if I go with you."

"A big party! Lots of balloons! Cake! Um, a pool party! And a big TV. Plus, I'll introduce you to all my friends," said D.S.

"You must think I'm stupid. What about you?" he asked, turning to the goddess.

"I need your help in battle. I want you to join me and put your life on the line. Lum and Sel are warring. We need all the help we can get."

"I want to go back to Earth. Can you do that for me?"

"Yes. But only after one side emerges victorious."

"No. No. I already decided I'm not going to be a soldier. War is always a lose-lose situation. I think I'll take my chances and break out of here on my own."

"Stop being stubborn! Come with me! Don't tell me you don't like cake," said D.S.

"You're working together, aren't you? Too predictable, Etaf. You're trying to make me choose between two intersecting paths. I'm not going to fall for that."

"You're coming with me one way or another," said Etaf.

"Leave, both of you. I'll break out on my own," said Crisis, examining the area for some sort of soft spot.

"Fine, be that way. I'll force you to be my friend!" yelled D.S., whipping out his scissors.

"I control the forces of nature itself. Do you really think you can defeat me?" Crisis put his hand to the ground. "*Natural Construct*"

The ground shook harshly and then split. The tip of a volcano protruded before the entire structure emerged from the floor. The volcano was only twenty feet high.

"Aw, a baby volcano," said D.S.

The volcano spewed out lava that started to engulf the area.

Crisis ran to the back wall of the prison chamber.

D.S. rushed after him, raising his scissors.

"Damn it! They're willing to kill me if I don't comply. Well fine then! I've got nothing to lose," said Crisis softly.

Etaf flew to Crisis and jabbed her sword at him.

Crisis strafed to the side by shooting out wind from his feet. "Too predictable. You can't beat me like you did last time. You'll have to do something different."

Destructus Supplious took out his staple gun and fired at the weather man.

The staples pierced into Crisis' leg, making him tumble to the floor.

D.S. pulled out his scissors and thrust them through Crisis.

"So, how does the party sound now?" asked D.S., slowly opening his scissors.

"What's the occasion?" Crisis propelled himself into the portal D.S. came from.

He arrived on the other side, face-to-face with the Remnants of Freedom.

"Atlas! That guy worked for you! What do you want from me? Was killing me not enough?" asked Crisis before falling over in pain.

Efil rushed to his side and closed up his wound.

"Sel seeks to destroy Lum and take over. We are trying to protect the balance of Sellum," said Atlas.

"I'm just here for a special someone. Good to see you again," said Deceivant.

"We want you to join us," said Kaity.

"Wow, so many Exps uniting for one cause. Okay, I'll fight with you for now. But once it's over, you're taking me back to Earth," said Crisis.

"Sounds great! We'll all go back together!" cheered Kaity.

"I did my best," said Etaf, arriving on the other side.

"I was so worried." Efil rushed into a hug before bumping into the barrier.

"You already know who's going to kill me," said Etaf softly.

"Even if it is true, you shouldn't take unnecessary risks," said Efil.

"Everyone, there is still one more cocoon and I know who is in it!" exclaimed Deceivant excitedly.

"All my Exps have already come up," said Atlas.

"Exactly! It must be Hope," said Deceivant, holding his cheeks.

"I shall personally reunite you with your daughter," said Violet before entering the portal.

"Efil, it's your turn. You need to go in place of Sel's allies," said Etaf.

"What! No way am I helping him!" yelled Efil.

"How unjust not to help him. How discriminatory it would be to treat him unequally. All are equal in the eyes of the Great Goddess, no?"

"Using Lum's sermon's against me? Why are you doing this?"

"Lum wanted me to do my upmost to keep our allies safe. Please, Efil, this is it. Then we can all go home. For the sake of Lum, fight for Sel, just once."

"Okay! Okay! I'll do it. I'll fight with all my strength," said Efil as she walked through the portal.

The cocoon fell and Deceivant leaped with glee.

"Devlin, I now introduce you to the sister you never knew," said Deceivant, gesturing to the portal screen with jazz hands.

"Isn't Toxic my sister too?" asked Devlin confused.

"She doesn't matter. You'll understand once you see Hope!"

"Hope? What's her Exp number?" asked Devlin.

"I would never demean her by attaching a number to her! She's too adorable!" exclaimed Deceivant in glee as his little queen broke out of her prison.

A small girl stepped out of the light cocoon. With the added boost from her high heels, she stood 4'8." A purple corset kept her always standing straight and proud. Mittens were placed over her hands, else she may accidently touch something once handled by a pauper. A royal purple, poufy and frilly Gothic Lolita dress with embedded topaz gems displayed the girl's regality and cuteness all at once. Despite her compact size, her breasts were full, giving her the presence of a queen rather than a mere princess. A pearl necklace with a diamond pendant was fastened just below her bejeweled collar. Two amethyst earrings drooped out just above her shoulders. The crown above her spacious forehead was partly covered by her braided black hair. Thin eyebrows and relaxed topaz eyes surveyed the area. The queen's tiny mouth and powdered puffy cheeks gave her an extra dimension of cuteness seldom found in monarchs. "Why are you all just standing there? Bow!" ordered Hope in a restrained, regal, imposing, yet undeniably cute voice.

Efil immediately bowed, taken off guard by the outburst.

Violet stood up straight. "I only bow to my gods," she said firmly.

"You, whatever your name is, you are safe. However, this one has displeased me," said Hope, glaring at the blue-skinned woman.

"I meant no offense. It's just, well, idol worship is central to some of my beliefs but forbidden by others. I only worship icons as temporary vessels of the divine essence!"

"You are a sudra, aren't you? The lowest of all castes. Your blue skin must be from the poison you ingested to end your miserable existence."

"Devlin created me without caste."

"He created you. Ah, I see. You're an Exp. The new race that will take up the mantle of planetary stewardship."

"Devlin is more than just a creator. He is my god. Well, I worship many gods, but he's special among them," said Violet with a smile.

"How foolish. Divinity is something only a pharaoh or an emperor can possess. The divine right of kings makes rebellion seem all but impossible. Gods are merely tools for kings and queens."

"Lum is no one's tool!" exclaimed Efil.

"Do not speak out of turn," said Hope, her eyes darting toward the plebian.

"The gods are very real. You are misguided, little one. You can feel the power of the divine in relics. Here, hold it." Violet took out her cross.

Hope spit on the archaic relic. "That empire has fallen. Its dogma was overrun by the regime of reason. I don't involve myself with relics of failed empires. I am not so sentimental."

259

"You are lost. It isn't man who gives power to relics. It is all God's doing. It is the divine essence."

"I've heard enough of your drivel. Your false gods cannot dethrone a king, nor can they save a nation. You are so naive. Ohohoho."

"My gods are not false, unlike your self-proclaimed regality," said Violet, crossing her arms.

"Take that back," said Hope, her pupils condensed with intensity.

"I will not. Humans who claim the right to rule others are all abusing God's gifts," said Violet, clenching her fists.

Hope turned to Efil. "Kill her. Chop off her head."

"I'm not going to kill anyone," said Efil, taken aback.

"My once loyal subject has betrayed me. Your beliefs have been twisted by this heretic," said Hope with a click of the tongue.

"You're the heretic!" yelled Violet.

"I serve Lum, not you," said Efil.

"You shall both be punished. I'll begin with you," said Hope, staring at the blue-skinned zealot.

Violet took off the sides of the cross and revealed the blades. "I will fight if I must."

"You raise your hand against me?" Hope pressed her fingertips against the zealot's leg.

Violet fell to her knees.

"It is tyrants like you who taint the will of the prophets and who tarnish the name of God," said Violet.

"**PHYSICAL CRUSH**." Hope gripped the criminal's head. "That's it. Bow. Ah, but involuntary obedience is not what I seek. I will make you prostrate yourself from the sound of my footsteps," said the girl with a smile.

"I refuse!"

"You can't refuse me. **MENTAL CRUSH**. Your belief system is a bloated heap of religious lies, all molded together as a nonsensical contradictory tool of convenience."

Violet started to sob. "Why are you so cruel?"

"You're a weakling who is unable to fulfill her god's whims. And that god isn't even a divinity. You're devoted to a false god; how laughable."

"No! Stop! Shut up! Devlin cares about me! He has his reasons for joining Sel! He hasn't abandoned me!" yelled Violet.

"Isn't Hope just precious?" asked Deceivant with glimmering eyes.

"Even gods bow before her," whispered Devlin to himself.

"Impressive, isn't she?" asked Sel, nudging its knight.

"Face it. Your false god chose power over you. He is a power-hungry fool who stands for everything you're against. Yet you follow him to add some false sense of truth to your crushed beliefs. How pathetic. He used your trust in god to make you do his dirty work for him."

Violet was beyond tears now; she stood there in silent misery.

"Broken already. I guess all those stories about zealots and their religious fortitude was mere fiction," said Hope, pressing her finger against the woman's tilak. "You have no purpose, but to serve my every whim."

"Yes, of course," said Violet softly.

"Did I say you could talk?" Hope slapped her slave across the face.

"Destroy my once loyal subject. And call me Queen," said Hope, licking her bottom lip.

"As you command, my Queen." Violet rushed up to the traitor and lashed the cross at her.

"What has she done to you?" asked Efil, horror in her eyes.

"Ignore her. In fact, don't speak unless I give permission," said Hope.

Violet said nothing as she jabbed her cross through the enemy.

A tree spawned from Efil's chest, smashing Violet into the wall.

Hope approached the flower woman.

"Stay back," said Efil.

"**PₒHYSₒCAₗ CₒRᵤSH**," whispered Hope as she jabbed her hand at Efil.

Vines shot out of the ground, surrounding the child's arm.

Efil then shot a branch out of her hand and put it to the child's throat.

"Come with me. And put Violet back to normal."

"You won't kill me." Hope snapped the branch and walked into the nearest portal.

Chapter 113: Prison Break

Hope came out of the Remnants of Freedom's portal. "Mother, did you rally these warriors to come to my rescue?"

"It wasn't just me," said Ada, holding Deceivant's hands.

Hope's eyes quaked and she looked way.

"My little queen!" exclaimed Deceivant, rushing into a hug.

"Get your hands off of me!" yelled Hope, struggling in his toxic grip.

The doting father released her.

Hope brushed off her dress and stood up straight. "I hereby disown you. You're no longer permitted to speak to me," she said, turning away from the detestable man.

"She is indeed my sister," said Devlin with a smile.

"Why are you so upset? Deceivant is the one who wanted us to come here in the first place. He is the reason you aren't trapped in a cocoon," said Kaity.

"What odd behavior? But it does nothing to quell my feelings of contempt. If he so much as touches me, I will have mother nail him to that wall," said Hope, pointing behind Deceivant. She gestured for Violet to kneel down and then used her as a pedestal. "Everyone, I command you to bring me back to Earth posthaste!" she exclaimed, her voice projected through her regal nature.

"That's the plan," said Kaity.

"Splendid," said Hope.

"Why don't you spit out our little friend?" asked Sel, turning toward the living sword.

Gladius smiled before coughing up Demo.

The little ball looked around curiously.

"This is just dreadful. The Remnants were only able to obtain four of the prisoners," said Efil, tugging on Etaf's wing.

Newly added to the Remnants of Freedom's side was Fusion, Image, Crisis, and Hope.

"If Sel had attacked, then all the prisoners would be his. Considering the vast difference in power, I'd call this a victory," said Etaf.

Newly joining Lord Sel's side was Wringer, Absorb, Demo, The Vibrator, and Toxic.

"We can't just let them leave, can we?" asked Efil.

"Aww, poor angel. We followed the rules and that means we get an easy escape," said Demonica.

"I never said anything of the sort. I said if the rules were broken, then I would call in Lum's forces to storm the base. I never even mentioned what would happen after all the Exp prisoners had been freed." Etaf, pointed the Destiny Sword toward the ceiling.

The roof opened up on the side of Sel's team and a battalion of angels pooled into the area to attack.

"All of this was done to buy time. Your overconfidence has brought you to ruin, Sel. The light barrier was lowered only so that you could be captured. Efil, escort the Remnants out. I will provide Lum's forces with additional support," said Etaf, blocking the exit.

"Hurry, into the portal," said Efil, forming a Lum portal.

Once all the Remnants of Freedom entered, Efil walked into the portal and it vanished.

"I'll get us out of here," said Demonica.

"Don't bother. This is rather unexpected, but it's nothing we can't handle," said Sel, shooting down the first line of defense with dark beams.

Devlin's wires climbed up the walls and covered the roof.

More angels came out from the walls, permeating through them before materializing.

"The goddess who protects Elysium decides who can enter and who cannot. You are trapped," said Etaf.

"She's right. I can't even create a portal," said Demonica, tearing an angel in half with her blood chains.

"The Lum energy is too concentrated within this place. Splendid! We really are trapped!" cheered Sel.

Riufen battled four sword-wielding angels at once, keeping the team's back guarded.

"They must have gotten wind of my presence here! Me-me-me! Come at me, angels!" The Vibrator zoomed up to two angels and drilled through their chests with rapid punches.

Gladius wrestled with a crocodile angel, gaining victory as soon as his bladed tongue burst out his enemy's skull.

BoneSaw was hit with three light arrows before decapitating the angel archer who was attacking from the furthermost corridor.

Pesi was quickly overpowered by an angelic knight and was bleeding on the ground.

"Devlin, revive Wringer so he can assist us," said Lord Sel, staring at the new group of angels that had just broke through Devlin's wire wall.

Devlin fired wires out at the four angels while an extra wire placed Wringer's capsule in the pile of chains.

The chains came to life, and Wringer sprang into action. He layered five chains around the angel knight's neck and sent her flying into the group overhead.

"MULTIPLY." Demo trapped the battalion in a hollow sphere, killing them all as it filled in the gaps.

"Hit the ground!" Lord Sel fired a beam into Absorb.

The beam entered the sponge and erupted out from all his pores, destroying all the surrounding angels.

"Good work." Sel patted his new toy.

"I thought I was going to die," said the trembling sponge.

"I want you to take this whole prison down," said Lord Sel, turning to face The Vibrator.

"The Devil himself needs my aid! Me-me-me! I am a living marvel!" The Vibrator put his hands to the ground. "*Heavenly Quake.*"

Tremors were sent through the entire structure, making the walls shake violently.

"The foundation should break before Helios reigns in the next sunrise. Guard me till the deed is done," said The Vibrator.

"He clearly has a bias toward Lum. Are you sure you want to keep him around?" asked Demonica.

"Why not?" asked Sel with a shrug.

A new wave of angels descended.

"Don't put up a barrier. This batch is mine." Demonica took to the skies and slaughtered the angels with great cruelty.

Sel fired a beam that pierced through ten angels.

The angels were promptly consumed by the corrosive energy.

Etaf emerged from the group, thrusting the Destiny Sword into the Goddess of Death.

"Nice try, but you know I'm immortal," said Demonica, smacking the goddess before her fingernails jutted out and killed seven more angels.

"Don't kill Etaf. She may still be of use. Ignore the angels and rescue the prisoners! Call upon your slave to speed up the process!" exclaimed Lord Sel.

"Can't kill Etaf, can't kill Efil. Who can I kill?" Demonica collapsed into blood and seeped through the cracks in the prison.

"Demo, go with her," said Lord Sel.

Demo went through the crack and rushed down the corridor.

"Once the prisoners are freed my army will have new recruits, both angelic and demonic," said Lord Sel.

Just then a stampede of angelic tigers stormed into the area.

Riufen and Devlin rushed to the front of the corridor to intercept them.

Devlin was knocked backward.

A goddess flew up to the Dark One, pushing its feline allies back with a massive barrier of light.

"Target acquired," said Lord Sel, pouring out energy and pressing against her shield.

The goddess was firmly built and hefty. She wore aura shields like armor and was entirely covered by the overlapping barriers. The goddess' vacant white eyes peered out from her shield-shaped helmet. "I will not let you destroy this place," she said in a firm and stoic voice.

"Another goddess has come to destroy me," said The Vibrator.

"What's your name?" asked Devlin as his wires rushed along the ground.

"I am Tcetorp, Lum's shield. I have been charged with defending this place. My most recent orders are to destroy Sel's forces." She spoke with unwavering power and fortitude. "PUNCBR PRISON!"

Two ethereal barriers pressed against Lord Sel until he was flattened.

Etaf entered the area, quickly crossing swords with Riufen.

The other angels promptly fled.

"Yes, yes. Run! Fear the power of one whom indulges in neither pleasure nor pain!" cheered The Vibrator. "LUMINOUS FORTRESS!"

Barriers appeared around Sel's forces, boxing them all inside.

Devlin slammed against the barrier but was unable to even make it budge.

Efil appeared, equipped with armor made from light and a wooden sword.

Sel energy ate away the barriers surrounding the God of Destruction. Once freed, he fired beams that consumed the barriers trapping his allies. Exerting a great amount of energy, he created a Sel portal. "Retreat!"

Lord Sel's forces rushed into the portal, except for Riufen who was too busy battling Etaf.

The Destiny Sword sliced through Riufen's spine.

Etaf plunged her blade into the samurai and charged into the portal.

"I should go after her," said Efil.

"She won't die. Some of Sel's allies are breaking out the prisoners. Join me," said Tcetorp, grabbing her fellow goddess and rushing down the corridor.

The Sel portal vanished.

Deeper inside the prison, the ceiling of a particularly spacious holding cell collapsed. Hidden above was a cocoon of light the size of an elephant. Imprisoned inside with hundreds of light chains impaled through it was an Exp.

The naked man was about two feet shorter than Atlas but was still built like a powerful warrior. His long blue hair draped past his shoulders. His flaming eyebrows were bushy and extended out from the sides of his face. After the cocoon smashed against the ground, his wizened blue eyes shot open.

"Am I finally free of this prison?" He tore his muscular arms free of the chains. "I must return to my throne." His legs broke free and he tumbled to the floor. "How long have I been trapped?" he asked with a soft-spoken, devout voice.

A final chain was pierced through his back and connected to his capsule.

"Of course. They didn't leave anything to chance," he said, struggling to break the fortified chain."

Demonica's gimp appeared in front of him, holding out a gold nugget.

"How did you get that?" asked the prisoner, picking up the stone and pressing it into his chest.

The gimp vanished.

"I'm not even free and they already sent someone after me. Now, let's see if I can do something about this chain. **compact**."

The chain caved in on itself, becoming a small ball of condensed light.

The man got back to his feet and put out his hands. "The energy here is interfering. Have to get outside." He walked down the corridor but was confronted with a wall of rocks.

Clear energy came out from his hands, completely annihilating the rocks.

Tcetorp came into focus, her eyes widening upon recognizing him.

"Where is the exit?" he asked, leaning against the wall for support.

"You are a prisoner here. You are not allowed to leave," she replied, creating a barrier in front of her.

"Fine, I'll find it myself." He turned around and went down the corridor.

The barrier raged forth and then turned, pinning him against the wall.

Efil appeared in front of Tcetorp. "I found the enemy. I'll need some help taking them down."

"Begin your assault. I will catch up with you shortly," said Tcetorp.

Efil nodded her head and then rushed into a portal she created.

"Let's wrap you up." Tcetorp's body radiated light.

The light crept below the barrier and climbed up the prisoner's leg.

"My people need me," said the prisoner, slamming his fist against the barrier.

"You need to stay here where it is safe. If Sel's forces captured you, your whole realm would be in jeopardy," said Tcetorp, creating a new barrier each time one was shattered.

The light had wrapped around his legs.

The prisoner's hand became coated in clear energy and tore through the barrier without making a sound. He lunged at Tcetorp, his hand just about to reach her neck.

"!"

Two barriers sandwiched him from above and below. His body was crushed, and his arm fell to the ground.

Tcetorp folded her hands. "Forgive me. As the guard of Elysium, I could not permit you to leave. May your soul find peace."

"Already have it." The prisoner grabbed the back of Tcetorp's head from behind her. "**compact**."

Tcetorp was crushed until she was the size of a marble.

The prisoner swiped the ball out of the air and stuck it in one of his wounds. He leaned down over his own remains. "**compact**." The bloody bits of flesh became six balls of the same size.

He continued walking down the corridor.

Efil appeared again. "Tcetorp, I really need your help, Demonica keeps escaping me." She looked around. "Where did she go? Did you kill her?" The goddess readied her wooden sword.

"Out of my way." He knocked the sword out of Efil's hand and slammed his fist into her gut.

Blood seeped through the walls. It materialized into Demonica. Her eyes widened upon seeing the prisoner. "Just the man I was looking for."

"What do you want?" he asked, readying his hand to strike.

"I want you."

Chains of blood emerged from below and wrapped the prisoner's arms.

Efil rushed at Demonica from behind, her blade clashing with a blood blade that formed from Demonica's back.

Vines shot out of the wooden blade and pierced through the dark goddess.

"I'll have to deal with you first." Demonica collapsed into blood and reappeared behind the goddess of flowers with the Death Scythe.

The tip of the blade gleamed as she slashed it at Efil.

A tree came out from Efil's sword and took the attack in her stead. It withered instantly.

"**DEVOTION RAID**." Efil's wings released droplets of light that dispersed and singed Demonica's skin.

"A Lum god's power is reliant on their spiritual well-being. What's wrong, angel? Have you been sinful?" Demonica lashed the Death Scythe at the goddess' neck.

Efil pushed off the ground, dodging the tip of the blade.

Demonica's stomach burst open and tentacles rushed out. They coiled around Efil and slammed her against the ceiling. She turned her head to see that the prisoner had escaped. "I don't have time to waste with you." The dark goddess slammed the Goddess of Life into a blood spike. She then took flight down the corridor. Her target was at the main entrance, encircled by angels.

"If you move. We will shoot," said the main archer, readying her bow of light.

"Go ahead!"

Arrows of light shot into the prisoner's chest.

"Is that his corpse?" asked Demonica with wide eyes.

The prisoner was holding up his crushed upper torso, now pierced with arrows.

Demonica created a circle of blood around the angels. "Be sure to scream for me. **Blood Spike**."

Spikes burst out from the circle, killing all the angels in an instant.

"You can thank me," said Demonica, fastening four crimson chains to the prisoner's back.

"I'm so close to freedom. **compact**." The prisoner's body condensed itself into a ball and rolled down the incline toward the exit.

The ball unfolded into the prisoner, who then sliced through the barrier with an energy-coated hand. He leaped over the moat and successfully exited the prison.

"You aren't going anywhere! **Blood Bondage**." Demonica's chains raced down the incline, over the moat, and connected to the back of his limbs.

The prisoner's limbs became coated in clear energy, and the connecting chains were met with oblivion. "I'm coming home." The prisoner created a clear portal and walked through it.

"The mission is a failure," said Demonica, digging her fingernails into her forehead.

The prisoner reappeared in the realm of Absence.

All of the Absence Guards rushed to meet with him.

Occupy bowed reverently. "I never thought you would return."

The free man lifted Occupy up with a powerful embrace. "Neither did I. But now I'm here. I'm home."

"What happened to you, my Lord?" asked Limit.

"I am no longer your lord. I am just another resident of Absence," said the ex-god with a smile.

"We should host a celebration!" cheered Plagiarism.

"Where is Needle?" asked the ex-god, worry in his voice.

"Needle has not returned. It is still in Lum. We do not know where," said Loyal.

"There is even graver news. The ruler of Sel claims to have the ability to enter our realm," said Limit.

"Yes, he's using a relic from the Destined War," said Loyal.

"Then we must do all we can to prepare for the coming battle," said the free man.

"No! No! No! We've already made ourselves a target by attacking Sel's forces when they went after Evol. We must lay low. It's a shame the Freedom Forcers weren't killed when they fought Etah," said Eil.

"Who are the Freedom Forcers?" asked the free man.

"Why have you returned?" asked Neutral, appearing behind the prisoner.

"To reclaim my throne," said the ex-god, staring at the living outline of a man with hate.

"Leave now and you will be spar-ed. Absence has been stabiliz-ed under my supervis-ion. With you as its king, it would no doubt flourish as before," said Neutral in monotone.

"You have taken my throne, my powers, my comrades, my freedom and my dignity. You will regret not taking my life," said the ex-god as he approached the realm god.

A figure clad in armor appeared directly between the two kings. It raised its arms, each one the size of tree trunk. "I did not expect such conflict in Absence," it said in a deep deity voice.

"My Lord, is it really you? Have you regained the mantle taken from you?" asked the free man.

"As an ex-god, you are permitted to battle. Let us all behold. There may soon be a new god to take the throne," said the armored figure, disappearing and reappearing to a vantage point above them.

"Thank you for this opportunity, my Lord," said the ex-god.

"Our Lord only permits this battle because he knows I will not fail," said Neutral.

"Who do we side with?" asked Limit, his arms trembling.

"We shall be silent observers," said Occupy.

"I will wait for you to strike first. An opportunity you did not grant me," said the ex-god.

"You have been trap-ped in Lum's prison. Kept there only as a potential bargain-ing chip in the com-ing war. I have been hon-ing my powers ever since I struck you down." Neutral rushed up to the ex-god as his hand went into its Absence form.

The ex-god smiled and took out a condensed ball from his mouth. He tossed it into the air and moved his hand like a whip. The hand, laced with clear energy, sliced off Neutral's hand.

"What was that?"

The ex-god jumped up into the air and grabbed the marble. "**Revert**."

The marble de-compacted into a pole, held tightly in its master's grip.

The ex-god of Absence plunged the staff down with rapid jabs.

Neutral dodged each attempt with the slightest of movements. He gripped the pole and planted it into the ground. His hand became coated in Absence energy, ready to chop the pole.

The free man compacted the pole, making Neutral miss. He reverted it once more, piercing it through Neutral's arm.

"You're not as brash as before," said Neutral, looking up at the prisoner.

The pole compacted once more.

The ex-god spun in the air before kicking the compact at Neutral.

The ball reverted as it shot forward, making a huge hole through Neutral's chest.

"*Absence Form*." Neutral vanished from sight.

The free man landed and tensed up. "He can mask his presence completely now. **absence form**." The ex-god's body became coated in a clear aura. He did not turn invisible.

A jab came from behind.

The ex-god's aura reverberated but it did not break. He slammed his elbow into the attacker. "I will not lose!" He leaped after him but ended up attacking the air. "Where are you?" The ex-god was swept off his feet.

A barrage of jabs hit his chest.

The free man grabbed Neutral's arm. "I can feel it in my heart. I will not lose again." His hand climbed up Neutral's shoulder and gripped the back of his head. He slammed his head into Neutral's over and over.

"He who trusts in his heart is a self-ish fool," said Neutral.

A crack appeared, floating in the air.

"Looks like this fool made a dent." The ex-god slammed his elbow into Neutral's face. He then rammed his foot into his opponent's chest, knocking him off his feet.

Rapid jabs bore through Neutral's leg.

"I'll end it now." The ex-god's aura left the rest of his body as it pooled into his arms. "**absence blast**."

The aura burst out, piercing a hole through Neutral's body.

"I have no vitals. I am beyond such things."

Neutral's hands slid through the prisoner's legs. Before the ex-god could react, the hands glided up his body and met at his neck. As they parted, the ex-god's head fell to the floor.

"The more placid soul has gained victory." Neutral diced the rest of the prisoner's body. He then dispelled it with a blast of Absence energy.

The free man's pole suddenly slammed into Neutral's head from above.

"Impossible," said Neutral, looking up at the prisoner.

"I came here prepared to die, multiple times. **absence infusion**." The free man coated the pole in his aura and furiously jabbed it into Neutral's head wound.

Neutral caught the pole between his two palms and endeavored to break through its aura.

"**samsara**."

In an instant, the pole compacted and reverted at a horizontal angle, smashing Neutral's fingers.

"Your mastery of Absence is beyond mine. That's why I've won." The free man grabbed Neutral's hands, held them together, and hammered them into the forehead wound.

The crack expanded before Neutral's aura shattered completely.

"This is in-conceiv-able."

The free man grabbed Neutral's shoulders. "**compact**."

The realm god was crushed into a tiny ball.

"I won't need to revert this one." The free man smashed the compact in his fist.

A cloud of clear energy exited Neutral's body. Neutral's Absence powers shot back into the free man, making him the king of Absence once more.

"You have reclaimed what was stolen. Well done," said the armored figure in a calm voice, while fervently clapping.

"I'm unworthy of your praise, my Lord," said Absence with a reverent bow.

"A new god deserves a proper initiation. I shall move up the coming council meeting," said the figure before vanishing.

The guards gathered around Absence, all bowing as one.

Absence stood upon a platform made from his own energy. "I have returned. Sel's forces were at the prison of Lum, seeking my capture. This realm can no longer remain neutral in the battle between Sel and Lum. I hereby decree that fighting is permitted in Absence. We must all train for the coming battle."

Part 14
Apotheosis

Chapter 114: New Recruits

The golden armored figure sat patiently in a chair made from his own energy.

The planets revolved around the nine-sided room, always under his divine surveillance. Radiating above the God of the Afterlife was the sun, giving him strength all the while reminding him of his limitations. The realm of Sel was to his left, Lum was to his right, and Absence was at his back. All three realms were at arm's length and were subject to his interventions at a moment's notice. Each realm had microscopic lights, representing the souls of the inhabitants present. The souls of angles and demons glowed brighter than visitors and residents, and the spirits of gods were even more radiant. There was a clear cube at the center of each realm. The energy of each realm god was ever-present around its corresponding area but did not flow into it. A single massive collection of light could be seen within each realm, allowing the figure to monitor the movements of the realm gods.

The armored observer raised his hands.

Three birds of energy grew out from his palms and entered the microcosm of each realm.

The observer folded his hands and waited patiently.

The surrounding cubes lit up, signaling the arrival of the three main gods.

The gods could not see each other, being blocked by a clear coating along the perimeter of the cube. However their every feature was visible to the observer, for he was able to see through any substance. His gaze was not ever-present, but it was all pervasive.

"You all have been summoned here because there is a new realm god," said the observer, raising his arms.

"Has Sel been vanquished?" asked Lum.

"What is the origin for such a thought?" asked the observer.

"I am alive and well, thanks for caring," said Sel.

"As am I, much to your dismay," said Lum.

"The new realm God is from Absence. A prisoner from Lum has been freed by the Freedom Forcers and has taken his place on the throne of Absence once more," said the observer.

"Your lordship, if I may correct you, it was my followers who freed the prisoner, not those of whom you gave credit to," said Sel kindly.

"Then my gratitude branches out to you, Lord of Sel. I assure you all that the realm of Absence will benefit from my leadership," said Absence, his adoration beaming out from the walls of his section.

"I humbly accept your thanks."

"You confess to your violent intervention in Elysium?" asked the observer.

"Well, uh, I wouldn't say confess. And it wasn't all that violent until Lum's angels attacked us," said Sel, careful not to grin due to the observer's all pervasive sight.

"You were in our domain. We had every right to attack you," said Lum.

"Yes, and most of the angels who attacked us were humans. You weren't perhaps trying to shed your realm of its potential rebels, were you?"

"How dare you bring slander against me! My actions are for the good of all."

"You imprisoned a realm god of Absence. Do tell the council what purpose this noble action served," said Sel.

"Ex-god, and I owe you no explanation."

"Then would you explain your intent to our newly instated realm god? Doing so may ease some tension," said the observer.

"As you wish. The fallen ruler of Absence was captured by my forces after being banished from his realm. As an ex-god, his excess powers could be used to form a portal to Absence. This could serve as an incentive for Sel's forces to attack our realm. I imprisoned him swiftly and carefully so his realm and mine would be protected from a potential takeover."

"Why was I told none of this? If it was for the safety of my realm, I would have gladly surrendered myself. Eternity in prison would have been my privilege," said Absence.

"Revealing this information to you could lead to unrest in Absence if you ever escaped. If the realm knew of the potential danger of Sel's intrusion, it could trigger a preemptive strike by the protector gods of Absence. I would never have revealed this information if the Lord of Gods had not asked it of me."

"You're cleverer than I expected," said Sel.

"I understand completely. But secrets create confusion and tension themselves. If you had trusted me and explained your reasoning, I would not have resisted capture," said Absence.

"Well, that is if she's telling us everything," said Sel.

"What do you mean?"

"For what reason do you question my integrity?" asked Lum, her fist tightening.

"I can think of plenty of reasons you would keep him locked up. You could use him as a bargaining tool to get Absence on your side. After brainwashing him or striking some sort of deal, you could send him out to kill one of my gods and then feign innocence. Not only that, but you could have kept him there so you would have exclusive travel to the realm of Absence. Your forces could charge in and take over, more than doubling your current army size. But I'm just postulating, take no offense," said Sel with a smile.

"I never thought of that," said Absence, his voice weighted down with dismay.

"I always try to see things from many angles. It allows for greater clarity," said Sel.

"I will keep this in mind," said Absence.

"Don't you see what he's doing? He's trying to turn you to his side," said Lum.

"I'm merely opening his mind to new possibilities," said Sel.

"Your accusations are baseless. I have never bargained with Absence, nor traveled there, and his mind remains his own. Your words are without weight."

"My forces broke him out before you had an opportunity to do such things. Oh well, I guess we'll never know your plans."

"You make a valid point," said Absence.

"All his proposals are baseless. He is the one who invaded my prison!" yelled Lum.

"It's true. I risked breaking my treaty with Lum, but I did not do so out of spite. My informant came across information concerning our current Absence's imprisonment. With this info—"

"Impossible. Only myself and the Lum gods were privy to the knowledge of his capture," said Lum.

"And yet, the information came to me. It's most peculiar," said Sel, feigning surprise.

"Now you condemn the very gods who live for the glory of Lum. Their allegiance is beyond your understanding. You only know deception."

"Regardless of how I got the information, I did receive it. This information is why I sent my forces and even put my own safety in jeopardy to go to Lum's prison and free this special prisoner."

"You broke into Lum's prison for my sake?" asked Absence.

"Not entirely, but your rescue was the sole reason for our struggle in Lum's prison. It would have been much easier to rescue you if Lum's little brigade of Exps hadn't used all their might to stop us."

"They are not my brigade. They are independent actors," said Lum.

"They were accompanied by Efil, a goddess from your realm. I apologize for my mistake. I only assumed that, with your most loyal goddess as their protector, they had some sort of pact with you," said Sel.

"Why would I send them to break out my prisoners?"

"Why indeed?"

"The Freedom Forcers are not my servants. They are not bound to any realm."

"And yet it was one of these Freedom Forcers, as you so respectfully call them, who dethroned the God of Hate."

"You can't manipulate this in your favor. The one who felled your God of Hate is now employed in your service."

"And how do you know that?"

"I know because he destroyed Refuge."

"You mean that base full of rebels who dared to speak out against Luminous? Thank you very much."

"Thank you?"

"You're welcome. Honestly though, Lum knew about my newest god before he went rogue and attacked Refuge."

"Rogue! Demonica and him were both spotted there."

"Indeed. She no longer listens to her master. Shame. So, how did you know about Devlin's ascension into my pantheon?"

"I feel no need to expose my informants to you."

"So you do have an informant. Spying is so tricky. You're so sneaky lately."

"Enough! Explain to us what an Exp is doing as part of your pantheon!"

"After losing the God of Hate, I was shaken up. Getting some of the Freedom Forcers to join me helped me feel a bit more...safe. Did you feel the same way?"

"I won't fall for such an obvious trap. The Freedom Forcers went to the prison to free their comrades. That is all."

"Yet, my forces were overrun by angels, and the Freedom Forcers were escorted out through a Lum portal made by Efil. You see why I'm a tad suspicious, don't you?"

"I have nothing to say to the likes of you."

"A shame. I was hoping you could put my fears to rest," said Sel with a shaky voice.

"There is no need for the two of you to carry on. It was Sel's forces who rescued me. Nothing else is of concern," said Absence.

"Oh yes there is! Let's talk about—"

"Enough. There is yet another concern of mine," said the observer, rising out from his energy chair.

"My Lord, by all means, tell us what bothers you," said Absence.

"Acts of treason have occurred not only in Lum's prison. Evol, Lum's substitute, was slain in combat by Sel. Do you deny this act of treason, or do you take the unbalance of Sellum lightly?" asked the observer, gazing at the cube containing Sel with a quaking fist.

"You can't wiggle your way out of this," said Lum.

"It is just as you said, I killed Evol," said Sel.

"Why did you kill the Goddess of Love? What purpose could that serve?" asked Lum.

"I had to even the playing field. I had lost Etah, Ynnotulg, Htols, and Deerg. I feared invasion from Lum, who still has control over all seven Holy Virtues. I did not attack other angels. Evol was the only casualty. She is the opposite of Etah, after all. I brought Sellum closer to balance."

"You have committed treason. This is intolerable!" exclaimed Lum.

The observer turned to face Lum's cube. "And what about your acts of treason? Do you think that because you are Lum you cannot be seen as treacherous? I know you are manipulating the Freedom Forcers to destroy Sel. I am well aware of the hate that lurks in you. Do you not care for the balance of Sellum? Your desire for goodness to triumph over evil puts us all at risk," said the armored observer with soft intensity, tears flowing out from his helmet.

"Oh, but the peace-loving Lum would never stoop so low," said Sel in a mocking tone.

"Silence. You are the greatest perpetrator of injustice. I may have promised to leave you gods to your realms, but that does not mean your actions elude me. Do you think I am unable to understand these acts of rebellion against me? You have been monitored closely because I cannot trust you. I watched every step you took, every word you spoke. You wish to kill me and rule over Sellum. Was becoming a realm god not enough to sustain your lust for power? You have to be the Omni god. I do not understand the reason for your lack of contentedness. Explain yourself before the council!" exclaimed the observer, his voice suddenly bursting with anger.

"I never said such things. However, I do not think you are fit to be the Lord of Gods," said Sel.

"Then who do you propose would make a better leader?" asked the observer.

"You know the answer! This realm should be mine!" exclaimed Sel.

"I am also at fault for the growing conflict between the realms. Your declaration of treason has been inspired by my inability to control. If you were able to make that declaration at all, how true it must be. Share your mission with me so I may understand," said the observer, regaining his composure.

"I want to expand the land of Sellum, unifying all places into one."

"Then it is as I said: you are discontent. Look at what has happened to Earth due to the discontent of one species. History has a way of repeating itself, when the same acts that inspired it are themselves repeated. Discontent leads to expansion, and expansion leads to war; war leads to death, and death leads to more power to you. Tell me, does this not play a part in your declaration of treason?" asked the observer in tears.

"It does not," said Sel sternly.

"He confessed to killing Evol. We cannot let such an action go unpunished," said Lum.

"I am a mediator, not a judge. If Sel and Lum seek the other's destruction, then there is nothing I can do. The purpose of this meeting was to inform the realm gods of the new Absence. That is all. Meeting adjourned," said the observer.

Previously: the Remnants had escaped the Lum prison. They were in a forest nearby Elysium, waiting for Efil to come and escort them to the Portal to Earth.

Kaity dangled from a branch above Nina, who was seated on a log. "Hey." The playful assassin poked her shoulder.

"What is it? Are we being watched?" asked Nina, slightly turning her head.

"Nope." Kaity rested her head on Nina's lap and looked up. "Do you think I'm pretty?"

"What does it matter what I think? Devlin likes you. He likes you and not me," said Nina, polishing her shurikens.

"Cause I think you're beautiful," said Kaity, leaning her head back and gazing into Nina's eyes.

"Thank you. I'm honored that you feel such powerful emotions for me, but I can't return them," said Nina with flushed cheeks.

"Aww, don't knock it till you try it," said Kaity, poking her breasts.

Nina pulled away. "I'm not the girl you fell in love with," she said as she sharpened her sword.

"Then why are you ignoring me?" asked Kaity with a pouty face.

"I don't know how to deal with affection from others. Nothing I say will satisfy you," said Nina, patting the boyfriend stealer's head.

"You don't have to satisfy me. We can just talk. Oh, but if you want someone to satisfy you, look no further," said Kaity with a salute.

"I'm a warrior. I have no need for such things." Nina shred the surface bark off a nearby tree.

"What are you doing?" asked Kaity, tilting to get a better look.

"I'm correcting a mistake." Nina turned around. She took off her shirt. "My breasts got in the way; I won't let that happen again." She wrapped the shredded bark around her breasts.

"Don't cover them," said Kaity, dropping down from the tree branch.

"They were slowing me down."

"But they're so incredible," said Kaity, rubbing against the comfy hidden lumps.

Nina grabbed her head and pulled her off. "That only adds to the importance of keeping them hidden. Any pride I take in my figure is fuel for the other Nina. Even if she doesn't fully take over, the slightest increase in her power limits my own. I refuse to be limited when I am already outclassed," she said, taking out a kunai.

"What are you doing now?" asked Kaity, grabbing her crush's hand.

"My hair was getting in the way. I'm cutting it short." Nina tossed the kunai to her other hand and started cutting her hair.

Kaity grabbed the kunai. "No, I won't let you cut your beautiful hair."

"The decision is mine." Nina took out another kunai and sliced off all hair below her neck. "There, that should solve that problem," she said, tying her hair with a band made from twigs.

"I will always remember you," said Kaity, holding the locks of unwanted hair in her open palms.

"Why is my back so sore? Ugh, that accursed woman has ruined my posture," said Nina, lying down on the grass.

"I could give you a massage," said Kaity with shimmering eyes, dropping Nina's hair into her pack.

"You don't mind?"

"Not at all," said Kaity, hopping onto her partner's back.

"Much appreciated," said Nina.

Kaity's thumbs dug into her lower back while her fingers massaged the area around.

"Yes. That's precisely the spot. You are quite skilled at this."

"Mhhm. Sefi-chan taught me all about acupuncture. I can't wait to see her again," said Kaity, fondly reminiscing as her shoulders dug into her back.

"You love her, don't you?"

"Yep. Yep! But I love you too," said Kaity, pressing her chin into her back.

"You mean you love the other me," said Nina softly.

"I love both of you."

"Then you love this body."

Kaity leaned over and kissed Nina's cheek. "I love you." She rubbed up against her crush's pretty cheeks.

Nina pulled away. "Impossible. You don't know me."

"Hey, what if all the good things I saw in Nina were your traits? Maybe I do love you. Maybe I've always known who you are," said Kaity, shuffling her feet.

"Do you love her personality or her body?" asked Nina.

"I love both. I love her fiery attitude, her selfish comments, her skill in combat, her smile, her outspokenness, I love everything about her!"

"And what do you love about me?" asked Nina.

"Your cool ninja fighting, the way you blush, your hair, your face, your eyes, your—" said Kaity before being cut off.

"Exactly, all my external features. You don't know who I am yet. I barely know who I am anymore. I don't know if I still want to love Devlin. I was designed to love him, but I feel like my love has deteriorated. Deceivant has made me lose sight of who I am by forcing the selfish program on me. I don't need you trying to love me right now. I don't know what I need," said Nina softly. A tear dropped from her eye.

Kaity kissed her cheek and then hopped into her lap. "You need some lovin', that's all. And you know, it's not just your body I love. You didn't let me finish," she said, poking her crush's cheeks.

"Go ahead then," said Nina softly.

"The way you fight is so majestic. Your personality is so determined and yet you're shy. You may not be as sexy as the other Nina, but you're way cuter." Kaity snuck her hands under her crush's armpits and tickled her.

"You're wasting your time," said Nina.

"You're not ticklish?" asked Kaity, now trying her luck with the woman's feet.

"As part of my daily training regimen I built up my immunities. My body cannot be poisoned, it doesn't succumb to sickness, and it will not react to tickling. But that isn't what I meant. I meant that you're wasting your time loving me," said Nina, turning her gaze away and lying on the grass.

"Why is that?" Kaity's hands massaged Nina's shoulders while her toes got her buttocks.

"I'm already in love…with Devlin," said Nina, her face brightening up.

"I know, but that doesn't mean you can't love someone else. I love you, Sefiwah, and some other girls too."

"What's it like?"

"You mean love? Why ask me? Don't you know?" asked Kaity, massaging her friend's temples.

"I mean loving more than one person. Is it difficult?"

"Nope. I think it's way harder to only love one girl. If I did, then I couldn't fully love you. I'd have to pick one Nina instead of enjoying both." Kaity's hand crawled up to her breasts.

Nina rolled over to face Kaity and grabbed her arms. "I can't return your affections."

"Is it because I'm a girl?" asked Kaity, poking her cheeks.

"I was made to love him and only him. I can't love another, so why bother trying? Now that Devlin no longer loves me, why bother with anything?" Nina covered her eyes before they were overtaken by tears.

Kaity wiped the tears away and licked her fingertips. "Just because he's obsessed with me, doesn't mean he doesn't love you anymore. He's been through so much. He's probably just worried that loving you again will end up leaving him with a broken heart."

"You heard what he said to me. There was no love in his words. I don't know what to do. I need him to love me," said Nina, with trembling hands.

"Devlin was being a jerk because he let power get to his head. You joined us to help Devlin, right? You can't just give up," said Kaity, grasping her partner's hand.

"But who's to say that I'm actually helping Devlin? Maybe what he needs now is for me to stand by his side. If I'm not acting on his behalf, than what am I doing?" asked Nina, tightening her fingers.

"You're doing what you think is best for him. And maybe you're afraid that he doesn't love you anymore. You're avoiding asking him so he won't turn you down."

"Perhaps you're right. I'm so pathetic. I train so hard only to be overpowered by my enemies. My care for my body and feelings of loneliness threaten my existence. And even though I can't stop loving Devlin, I can still hate him. Why am I so dysfunctional? Why can't I be the warrior Devlin needs?" asked Nina in tears.

"You're fighting your hardest. You shouldn't beat yourself up. We're all overwhelmed."

"Do you think he hates me? If so, then my only option is to tear out my own capsule as a testament to my love for him," said Nina with a shaky smile.

"Don't you ever talk like that!" Kaity bopped her friend's head. "You said that Matteria made the wrong decision by leaving Devlin behind. You know better. Suicide doesn't solve anything."

"What else am I supposed to do? If he loves me, I'll return his love. If he hates me, I'll gladly die by his hand. If he's indifferent, I no longer want to live. I need him!" exclaimed Nina, mostly to herself.

"What you need to do is relax and think about something other than Devlin," said Kaity, gripping her stiff shoulders.

"Something other than him?" Nina turned to Kaity with an empty look.

"Yep." Kaity ran her hand up and down Nina's sides.

"I told you; I'm not ticklish. Enough. I can't make you happy, and you can't make me happy."

"Au contraire, every time you talk I'm cheery." Kaity leaned her head on her crush's shoulder.

"My mind is in a jumble, I don't even know who I am. I know you want to believe I'm the Nina you love, but I'm a completely different person," said Nina, looking Devlin's beloved in the eyes.

"I can learn to truly love you. And I can teach you how to love too," said Kaity, grasping Nina's hands.

"Aren't you cheating on Nina if you love me?" asked Nina, slipping her hands out from Kaity's hold.

"Nope. You and her are in the same body," said Kaity, rubbing the back of her head against her friend's squishy bosom.

"You may like me, but I feel nothing for you. The resentment I had toward you was directly associated with Devlin's feelings for you. Now that I know you better, I don't hate you. I have pure indifference to you. My one hope is gone."

Kaity nibbled her ear and rubbed the bottom of her breasts. "Do you feel that?"

"Stop. If I get aroused…if I touch myself, the other Nina gains strength," said Nina, pulling away.

Kaity's tail slid between Nina's legs. "What if someone else touches you?"

"Please stop."

Kaity embraced her. "Sorry. I was just trying to help."

Nina clenched her fist.

"Are you okay?"

"Fine. I'll just have to wait till my arousal goes away," said Nina, covering her flushed cheeks.

"That's no fun! Come on. Friends help each other out," said Kaity, patting her partner's head.

"I don't love you. I can't ask for your help with…something so personal."

"It's your choice. But you don't have to be in love to have some fun."

"So…no strings?"

"None."

"Okay. Maybe it will keep the other Nina suppressed a bit longer," said Nina with a smile.

"Don't think about her. Just relax and let go of some stress," said Kaity, massaging Nina's breasts with her feet.

"You're using your feet?"

"Yep. Just having fun," said Kaity, rubbing her face against her friend's incredible legs.

"I feel a warmth. Not a love kind, but it's nice," said Nina, smiling at her friend through the cloth.

"You know, my cat tail isn't just for show. It's hands-free satisfaction," said Kaity, as her tail slid up and down between Nina's legs.

"Kaity, I…Devlin and I…we mostly cuddled. So, this is rather…."

"Exciting?" asked Kaity, sitting up.

"Embarrassing."

"Oh, should I stop?" asked Kaity, pulling her tail away.

"I feel like I'm being unfaithful," said Nina, hiding her face beneath her hands.

Kaity pulled her hands away. "Come on, this is Devlin we're talking about. I bet you he'd think it's sexy."

"Please, don't tell him about this."

"I won't. Look, if you're uncomfortable we can stop."

"No. I need a clear head. Let's reach the peak, together." Nina hugged her ally.

Kaity grabbed Nina's hands and smiled at her. "One stop trip to Heaven, all aboard. Heehee." After wrapping her tail around her foot, she rubbed it between Nina's legs, all the while suckling on her breasts.

"This is…whoa!"

"Good?" asked Kaity, her tongue making circles around her beloved's nippies.

"Amazing," said Nina, stopping her own hand from playing with her other breast.

"Wow, you're really sensitive," said Kaity, rubbing her hands up and down her friend's back.

"Devlin made me…responsive. Whoa. I…um…I can blot it out, though…by concentrating."

Kaity hugged Nina tightly, playing with her breast while licking it.

"Ah, I feel so free." Nina closed her eyes and pulled her friend in.

"So, had fun?" asked Kaity, leaning against Nina's bosom.

"I can't believe I just did that. I'm sorry. You shouldn't feel obliged to do something so obscene."

"It's not obscene. And I'm more than happy to help anytime."

"I don't even know why I did all that."

"Do you feel better?"

"Yes. I suppose."

"Then what does the reason matter?" asked Kaity, licking her tail.

"I guess you're right."

"Good. Now don't you ever think of killing yourself again. If you're that stressed out, just call for me. I'm here to help and not just with my tail and feet," said Kaity with a big smile.

"You're very kind. I couldn't die anyway; my mission is not yet completed."

"Nina, you have to live for yourself," said Kaity, hugging her friend.

"I can't. Everything I do, I do for Devlin's sake. Even so, I am not strong enough to defeat Sel's forces. Kaity, if I die, I need you to do something for me."

"You're not going to die. You shouldn't talk like that."

"I have no intention of dying. I'm asking this so that I can fight with a clear head. If I do die, please, love Devlin in my place."

"Um. I can't promise that. I mean I like Devlin, but I don't love him. And recently he's been a total jerk."

"Then just give him a kiss on my behalf. You can do that, can't you?" asked Nina.

Kaity smiled. "Sure. It's a promise." She raised her hand in salute. "You should get to know the rest of the team. Just because you can't love, doesn't mean you can't make friends," she said, hugging the shy ninja. She broke the hug and gave her a kiss on the forehead.

"I want to try to move on by finding another man. If Devlin doesn't like me, I at least want to have someone there for me…even if I can't love them back. But I'm horrible at starting a conversation. I wouldn't know what to say," said Nina, pulling her arms in.

"I used to have that problem too. So, when I met with someone I liked I just jumped up and kissed them. If they weren't interested, I'd find out quicker that way. But if they were interested, even a little, I could tell from their reaction."

"Is it really that simple?"

"Yep. Trust me, it's a great icebreaker," said Kaity with a grin.

"That sounds embarrassing." Nina turned away with flushed cheeks.

Kaity hopped into her crush's lap and pressed her lips against the cloth over her crush's lips.

Nina pulled away. "What are you doing?"

"You didn't feel anything?" asked Kaity, tilting her head.

"My heart only beats for Devlin," said Nina, turning away.

"Come on. Just give it a shot. You like guys, so…give the next guy you meet a little peck on the lips. That will get a conversation started for sure."

"Very well then. For the sake of group solidarity, I shall try." Nina stood up.

"That's the spirit."

"Thank you for helping me," said Nina with a little smile.

"What are friends for?" asked Kaity with a big grin.

Nina rushed off and leaped over the bushes. Standing in front of her was Kanasta.

He was tossing pebbles into a river, trying to break his previous record.

Nina steeled herself and then rushed in.

Her lips pressed against Devlin's brother's lips.

Kanasta did not kiss back. He looked at her curiously once she was done kissing him. "That was…unexpected."

"Well yeah. I was just, uh—my name is Nina." Her face was red like the blood of her enemies.

"You are a fine warrior. With your skills you could easily become a master assassin," said Kanasta with a smile.

"My skills aren't nearly honed enough. I am unable to kill that demon sword. And I would be unable to kill you."

"How can you be so certain?"

"My blades would be unable to pierce you. You, on the other hand, could snap my neck with your bare hands. You are far more powerful than I am, even though I'm the one who is an Exp," said Nina, lowering her head.

Kanasta lifted her chin. "Strength is not often the deciding force in a battle to the death. You are faster than me. No point in power, if you can't connect a single attack."

"True. But your defenses are stronger than any of my attacks. The only way I would be able to pierce you is if I got you out of that suit." Nina blushed bright red. "My deepest apologies. I've said something inappropriate. To speak of killing one's own ally is…disrespectful."

"Today's allies may be tomorrow's enemies. You are right to examine my strengths and weaknesses. Though, no matter what side you choose, I could never see you as an enemy."

"Why is that?"

"You fight for the sake of my brother. We both fight for Devlin. I am indebted to you. You took care of Devlin in my absence."

"No. I failed. I let the other Nina take over. She has caused Devlin so much pain."

"That is my father's fault, not yours."

"I should have been strong enough to suppress her."

"Strength can only take you so far."

Nina looked at Kanasta with a smile. "You're right. Even with the suit on, your neck is exposed. I could pierce my katana through your throat and decapitate you," she said, tapping his neck.

"As soon as you got into range, I'd tear out your heart," said Kanasta with a smile.

Ada watched from the bushes. "Aww! They're flirting!"

"Mother, that is the seventeenth time you have become distracted. This is not permissible," said Hope, her bare feet in the incompetent woman's hands.

"I'm sorry, dear. I just can't help it. My boy is finally finding love."

"Ugh. That's enough." Hope stood up and put on her long black socks. "I'm done with you. Your hands are weak, and your mind is easily distracted."

"Why not have Violet massage you, then?"

"What an idiotic question. Violet is my back support. Without her beneath me, my regal head would be lowered to the ground. Such a thing is unthinkable for a queen."

"Of course. I'll go see if anyone has a towel we can borrow."

"No need. Just find me another servant."

"Shall I get your father? He always knows just what you need."

"The only time I want to see him is after his head has been removed from his neck."

"So, do I bring him over then?"

"No! Honestly, you couldn't be more clueless. Go fetch me the little lesbian."

"Now, now, sweetie, it isn't nice to call people that."

"I will not repeat myself," said Hope.

Ada patted her darling little girl's head and then left to find Kaity.

"Does she want to see me?" asked Deceivant, springing up as soon as he saw his wifey.

"She's still in a bad mood, but I'm sure it will pass soon. Have you seen Kaity?" asked Ada.

"Yeah, she was meeting with the new guy, Crisis. She's such a friendly little kitty. I can't claim to be the leader of the team anymore. Kaity has really taken the initiative," said Deceivant.

"Hope has sent me to get her. Oh, but when I get back, can we spend some time together?" asked Ada.

"Of course, my adorable wifey," said Deceivant, pinching her cheeks.

Ada gave him a parting kiss and then left to find Kaity.

Kaity and Crisis were already chatting.

"Yeah, people who think they can't die are just ignorant," said Crisis.

"Those kind of people make easy targets for the Viper Squad," said Kaity, mimicking a gun with her hand.

"You guys are truly living. Day by day, working as a unit, fighting for survival. That's what nature intended. Humans have forgotten to fear nature, and that's why they've forgotten to respect her."

"So then do you create cyclones and stuff just to stir things up?" asked Kaity.

"Whoa. I may be gifted with these powers, but I'm not going to mimic nature. I use my weather abilities for self-defense only. You don't need to stand there. Is there something you want?" asked Crisis.

"I didn't want to interrupt," said Ada.

"We were just chatting. What do you think of Lum?" asked Crisis.

"Me? Well I mean it's beautiful, isn't it? So many creatures living together in peace. So many trees. I only wish Exp 8 was here to share its splendor with us," said Ada.

"I think it's boring and predictable. Before I was captured, I watched a snake for ten minutes. It went by three mice and at least five frogs. All the creatures here are so timid. They don't have survival instincts anymore. They just exist. That's why I have to get back to Earth. The call to nature is strong."

"That's our next stop. I think. We're waiting for Efil to come back. Kaity, I need a favor from you," said Ada.

"Has Nina told you about my skilled fingers?" asked Kaity, squeezing Ada's gravity defying breasts.

"No. It's my daughter actually. She's so lonely. She has been scowling since we rescued her. I think you could cheer her up," said Ada.

"You mean Hope? She destroyed Violet's mind. Our friend is practically a dead body now. I don't want to get anywhere near that little tyrant," said Kaity with a glare.

"She's very defensive about her regality. As long as you don't offend her, I'm sure the two of you will get along just fine."

"If she's going to be a part of the team, I should get to know her. Image is still knocked out. Okay, I'll do it."

"Wonderful!" exclaimed Ada.

"Just wondering. Would pinching her cheeks offend her? Because since the moment I saw her, I've had this urge to pinch her cute little chubby cheeks," said Kaity, bouncing in excitement.

Ada's eyes shrank. "You can't do that. Nothing would upset her more."

287

"What? So you expect me to just talk to her without pinching them? Argh. How am I gonna resist the urge?" asked Kaity in frustration.

"I know it's hard, but find a way. Now I must be off. Deceivant and I are going to have a stroll through the woods!" exclaimed Ada before skipping away.

"What's the point in a journey through the woods if there's no threat of a bear mauling?" Crisis looked in a hole in the ground to see a fox nestling with four bunnies. "This place is boring."

"Try to keep yourself entertained. Maybe you could play with D.S. I'm going to go see Hope…and not pinch her cheeks," said Kaity, lowering her head before leaving.

"Cheer up. At least you found some danger in this haven. The spiders here don't even make webs. Urgh! I hate this place!" yelled Crisis.

"Try to endure it for now," said Kaity, running off. The assassin girl stopped mid-sprint. "Come to think of it, Ada didn't tell me where Hope was." The young assassin saw a hill in her peripheral vision. "That's a good bet." She raced up to the hill and sure enough Hope was at the top.

"You've arrived. Massage my feet. They have had dreadful cramps ever since I was locked up in that prison," said Hope, stretching out her feet.

"Yes, of course, your majesty." Kaity crossed her legs and began the foot rub.

"A peasant who knows the proper way to respond, how refreshing. What is your name?"

"I'm Kaity, and you are Queen Hope, correct?"

"That is precisely right. Kitty, I recall you saying that it was Deceivant who convinced your little brigade to break me out?"

"That is correct, your majesty."

"I still find it hard to believe."

"Why? You're his daughter and he loves you."

"True enough. Oh, he hasn't told you then, has he? Of course not."

"Told me what?"

"That he's the one who killed me."

"I don't see how that's possible."

"Neither do I, but the facts remain."

"What if it wasn't him? A demon impersonated Devlin's brother. Maybe that's what happened."

"No it was him. He was crying as he killed me. Even as his hands took the life away from me, I could still feel their love." Hope's eyes softened.

"What reason would he have to kill you?"

"I don't care. I can't forgive him. No matter what the reason."

Kaity stopped the massage and embraced the lonesome girl.

"Off me, you cur." Hope smacked her servant across the face.

"My apologies. It's just, you were crying," said Kaity, resuming the massage.

Hope snatched a tear off her cheek. "So I was. How pitiful," she said with a forced smile.

"There must be some reason why he would do it. I believe you, but I know there must be more."

"Oh I know why, but it still shouldn't be possible."

"You know? How could he kill you? He loves you more than anything, doesn't he?"

"Apparently not. He must have done it, murdered me that is, in order to find his first love. I was just another sacrifice. You see his love for me and Ada pales in comparison to the feelings he has for that little tart Mika."

"He's never mentioned her before."

"That must mean he's had no luck finding her. Perhaps she's become a void in his heart. I can never let those two come back together. It would ruin me."

"Even if they did meet up, I don't think he could just stop caring about you. Deceivant is a proud pedophile after all," said Kaity with a grin.

"Yes, which brings us to the matter at hand. I refuse to have anything more to do with him. That leaves me without a proper servant. You see, I have trained him to take very good care of me. I'll need you to take his place."

"I can help out here and there, but I can't replace him. When you're ready, listen to what he has to say. You shouldn't just abandon him without knowing the full story."

"I may consider it."

"In the meantime, you should try to make some new friends."

"Enough! You've been staring at my cheeks this entire time. It is quite rude." Hope turned away from Kaity. "And what's all this about friends? I need subjects, not peasants who want to sit around a table and sip tea."

"Sorry, your cheeks are just so—"

"Just so what?" asked Hope with a dark glare.

"They're puffy. And—"

"Cute. Ugh. You should make a decent replacement for him. The little lesbian that you are."

"How did you know that?"

"You act as if it's not obvious. From the way you move, to the way your pitch changes when you talk to girls. Not to mention that look in your eyes. You're a lesbian with an older woman for a love partner. You enjoy killing and like to make friends. I could go on, but why say what we both already know?"

"How do you do that? How do you know so much about me?"

"I wouldn't be true royalty if I couldn't examine my subjects and make use of their abilities, now would I?"

"Is that what you did to Violet?" asked Kaity, her hands frozen.

"What? You want me to fix her? I assumed that everyone would benefit from her being repurposed." Hope jabbed her fingernail into Violet's cheek, drawing blood. "Not a sound. Ah, such an improvement."

"Violet had such religious fortitude. How did you break her?" asked Kaity with watery eyes.

"She is a hypocrite with a shallow and dysfunctional belief system. By combining every religious view, she created an impractical way of life. She only has two choices: either to live wholly as a devotee of the specified religion for a certain period of time, thus abandoning the practices thereof when she chooses to take time for another religion, or to take to heart only what all her religions have in common. The first option leaves her as an unpredictable mess. She may be a Jain follower of ahimsa one day and a Catholic martyr the next, the day after she may be praying to gods that her Catholic self would perceive as idols. Such a way of life leaves her in an ever-changing flux of belief, amounting to partial adherence to any and all rituals and obligations. The latter option is much simpler. Think of a Venn diagram, though this one has more of the appearance of a lotus. She combines all the ideologies of her beliefs and then retains what they all have in common. This would make her religion a bare sliver. Her beliefs would be so vague that they might as well not exist. Take either option and add her devotion to Devlin as a god in the mix and it all crumbles, doesn't it? She was already fragmented. I gave the slightest push, and the whole system collapsed."

"How can you know so much about her?"

"Mere assumptions is all, but I've hardly ever erred. It's like reading a book. Every so often you read a word as something different, but the other ninety-nine percent of the time you have no difficulty."

"What do you believe in?"

"It's not a matter of what for me. I take in the beliefs that support my ascension. Without being applicable, beliefs can fool us into chanting our precious time away or even surrendering our lives for integrity. Religion is a fool's game. I only make use of it to control the fools," said Hope with a smile.

"Will she never speak again?" asked Kaity.

"She'll do whatever I ask her too. Right now I need a headrest, but if I happen to need a stress doll later on, I can allow her to verbally express her agony. Though if I'm not in the proper mood, the noise will be most unpleasant."

Kaity's ears perked up. "Then you can bring her back to the way she was?"

"I can also make her think she's a puppy dog. Now that she's broken, I can mold her mind like putty." Hope dragged her fingers against the slave's forehead.

"So once you've got a new headrest, then you won't need her to be like this. You can have her return to normal?" asked Kaity, her eyes brimming with hope.

"If I so choose."

"Since you can just break anyone, it shouldn't be a problem for you to turn one of our enemies into your slave instead."

"Sadly I cannot break anyone. Only those with a weakness. Etaf, the warrior goddess, is immune to my powers. She has already resigned to her current predicament. She neither regrets nor withholds. If she had any weaknesses, I wouldn't have been captured by her and imprisoned."

"Do you think we can trust her? I mean, she works for Lum, but she's so defiant."

"Nothing more troublesome than a defiant vassal." Hope turned over. "Kitty, massage my back. My feet aren't the only thing in pain."

"Yes, your majesty. Oh, my name is Kaity by the way."

"That's what I said, Kitty. What are you waiting for? Massage me?"

"Sure thing. So, do you and your mom get along?" asked Kaity, using her knuckles on the girl's soft shoulders.

"She's incompetent most of the time, but is wholly devoted to me. Still, Deceivant is a far better slave."

"They're your slaves?" asked Kaity with wide eyes.

"Of course, though I have not mentally crushed them. Their servitude to me is voluntary. I'm starting to wonder why you haven't acted yet," said Hope with squinted eyes.

"Huh? What do you mean?"

"As an energetic cat-girl lesbian, you have the habit of leaping on cute things. You've made no motion of doing so to me."

"I'm not going to risk being mentally ravaged just to glomp you," said Kaity with a nervous grin.

"To 'what' me? I believe the term you are looking for is gropies. You are not going to risk being mentally ravaged just for gropies. I suppose that makes sense. But, do you find me attractive?"

"I feel belittled by your very presence. You have a cute body and adorable cheeks, but the way you carry yourself…it's almost like you're a dominatrix. You're really sexy," said Kaity, moving her legs up and down.

"That's quite the compliment. It's all true, of course. But even so, it's just not enough. I'm not enough for him. No matter what I do, I can't get that Satan-spawn Mika out of Deceivant's thoughts."

"You love him dearly, don't you?"

"I-I do not. I'm merely trying to keep possession of my property. He's mine. Nobody else can have him," said Hope, puffing out her cheeks even more.

A scream was heard in the distance.

"That sounds like Image."

"Don't stop. My shoulders are still sore. And I want a tummy rub when you're done," said Hope.

"Did your papa give you belly rubs?" asked Kaity.

"Yes, tummy rubs and belly blows. While the former is most pleasing, the latter is wretchedly embarrassing," said Hope with flustered cheeks.

"Aw, you're actually really cute," said Kaity with shimmering eyes.

"Alas, I'm not cute enough," said Hope, puffing up her cheeks.

"Aww, yes you are."

"Before you go, I need you to swear loyalty to me," said Hope, turning over.

"Can't I just be your friend?"

"I need someone I can count on."

"Will you fix Violet if I do?"

"I won't even consider fixing her if you don't."

"Okay. Okay. I'll do it. So…uh…how do I swear loyalty?"

Hope held out her pinky. "Do you swear to serve me?"

"Yes." Kaity sealed the pinky promise.

"Splendid. Now go on, you need to find out what that scream was about," said Hope, shooing her servant away.

Previously: In a nearby forest clearing, Image awoke with a wretched scream.

"You killed me!" she yelled, clawing at Atlas' face

Atlas held her in a tight embrace. "I love you!"

"Shut up! I hate you!" yelled Image, her face oozing out a red aura.

"These are for you." Atlas placed the glasses from Kanasta's case over his wife's beautiful face.

Her world slowly came back into focus. Upon recognizing Atlas, she shrieked and crawled backward.

"There's no need for concern, my beloved," said Atlas, offering his hand to her.

"This is a perfectly natural response to have, considering you murdered me," said Image in a contemplative, logical tone with little feeling, scanning the tree for sharp branches.

"Yes, but now that I possess a piece of your soul and have crafted it as a weapon, I have no reason to do you harm," said Atlas, caressing her hand.

"Not true. Perhaps you've come to claim the part left behind," said Image, sticking out her pointer stick.

"It was my hesitancy that fragmented your soul. I wasn't willing to absorb you completely. And I have yet to use the weapon I carved a fragment of your soul into. I came to rescue you. I want to make amends for what I did."

"You can't make amends so easily. And don't expect me to be happy to see you," said Image, pulling her hand away from him.

"You still resent me? I can't blame you. Would you like me to leave?"

"I want you to get me back to Earth. I will forgive you after you've truly made amends. How soon can we leave?" asked Image, standing up.

"I understand how you feel, but I can't just abandon this world. If Sel succeeds, then Sellum will fall out of balance. I will return you to Earth, but right now I have obligations here."

"This place complicates things. Normally those who claim to have seen Heaven are suffering from minor delusions, but here it's different. How long before I can return to my old life?"

"After Sel is suppressed, I will force our way to the portal of Earth if need be," said Atlas, clenching his fist.

"Then I suppose I'll stick by you till then." Image stood on her tip toes and gave her husband a kiss. "I missed you," she said gently.

"As did I." Atlas lifted her up into a passionate kiss.

Kaity came out and waited for them to break the kiss. "Looks like you two made up."

"Not quite. I can't deny my own feelings though. I love him without condition," said Image, pressing her hand against her chest.

"This is Kaity, the leader of our team," said Atlas.

"When did I become the leader?" asked Kaity.

"As soon as Lum chose to speak to you and only you."

"How do you know that?"

"Sel has ways of finding out things he shouldn't be able to."

"I'm still not sure I'm ready to lead."

"You rallied your allies to fight after I killed Exp 8. I can never atone for what I have done, but I heartily accept you as my new leader."

"Then you're staying with us? You aren't going to join Sel?" asked Kaity, poised to run.

"Sel must be stopped. Though I still lack the power to do so, I will offer my aid in any way I can," said Atlas.

"I can help you come to grips with past failures and help the team form a positive self-image for the future," said Image.

"We're fortunate to have you. Now come with me. Efil just arrived. We're all meeting up to head out to the Portal to Earth," said Kaity.

"Are we leaving before stopping Sel?" asked Atlas.

"Well the non-combatants are. Come on, follow me," said Kaity.

"Then that means Hope will leave, correct?" asked Atlas.

"Yeah. And I was just getting to know her too," said Kaity with a frown.

"Hope is dangerous. Even as the God of Hate, I was unable to mold Violet's soul. Hope defeated an enemy I could not and did so with mere words. I am greatly relieved that she will be leaving the team," said Atlas.

"I don't know how I feel," said Kaity softly.

"I'll be happy to listen to whatever is bothering you," said Image.

"Thank you so much. But right now, we really should get moving. We've fought hard to make it this far."

Chapter 115: The Deal

The Lord of Gods was on a rocky cliffside on Earth, looking intently at the sun.

"How selfless you are. Bringing life to all yet asking nothing in return. I hope to reach your benevolence one day," said the observer, shrouded in joy.

"Am I late?" asked a woman dressed for mourning.

"Casey, I didn't think you would come," said the observer, still gazing at the sun.

"What's bothering you?" asked Casey in a solemn tone that lacked compassion.

"The conflict between Sel and Lum will only escalate. I fear Absence will inevitability be drawn into it. Yet I cannot intervene. Look, over there," said the observer, pointing beyond the hill to a city a few miles down.

"I'm not sure what it is you're trying to tell me."

"Look at how discontent has affected this planet. Those who stray away from the natural order, or even worse try to bend nature to their whims, will only bring death to the land. If only they could understand the beauty of the lives they are destroying," said the observer with burning conviction.

"Yes. A life spent in a prison is no way to live."

"Precisely. They've become enslaved by their own mental constructs. Intrinsic good and intrinsic evil are mere guises for the truth: they have lost their way and refuse to ask for help."

"I've come for your help."

"Sel and Lum are at the brink of war, and the God of Destruction seeks my death. What am I to do?"

"Please, only you can help him."

"I won't," said the observer, turning to her.

"Then why did you call me here?" asked Casey, tightening her fingers.

"Sel seeks my death. I'm distraught. I suppose I want to speak with someone who will listen," said the observer reflexively, tears pouring down his helmet.

"Then I will free him without your help," said Casey before rushing off.

"You will try," said the observer, appearing before the troubled soul.

"I won't let you stop me."

"I won't get in your way, but someone else might."

"Who? Where are you keeping him?" She stared him down, not moving an inch.

"Why should I help you if you won't help me?"

"Use the Freedom Forcers. Make them into your warriors. Have them stop the coming war."

"Bringing them in will only create more conflict. Their presence in Sellum has already changed so much," said the observer, eyes alight with vigor.

"What is your plan?"

"Not everything has been unfortunate of late. The Absence bunnies, self-aware fragments of the First Guard of Absence, are now safe. I sent them all to the Earth replica I created. I gave them a home free of conflict. Why can't all problems be solved with compassion and charity?" asked the observer, raising his arms to the heavens.

"Why indeed?"

"I did what I had to," said observer sternly.

"You asked my advice. Please, tell me where he is," said Casey in tears.

"I can't. Goodbye," said the observer before teleporting away.

Previously: Devlin and Demonica watched the Remnants of Freedom in the sky above the forest.

"Hope has her guard down. Should we capture her?" asked Demonica, looking down at Devlin.

"Who cares about her? I'm watching Kaity," said Devlin.

"You are so simpleminded." Demonica descended and dropped her beloved off by a cave.

"Is this where the portal is?" asked Devlin, peeking inside.

"We are close by, but it's not in here." Demonica entered the cave.

"Then what are we doing here?"

Demonica created blood bats that screeched throughout the cave.

Bears, bats, bunnies, and foxes all rushed out, fearing for their lives.

A tentacle came out from Demonica's belly, wrapped around Devlin's arm, and pulled him in. "Nobody can hear us in here," she said, whispering seductively in his ear.

Devlin shrugged her arm off. "Look, I'm really not in the mood for this, Kaity's been ignoring me recently," he said with a solemn look.

"Why must it always be about Kaity?" asked Demonica as she caressed his leg with her fingertips.

Devlin pulled his leg away. "I said quit it!"

"Do you remember when we first met?" asked Demonica, gripping him by the back of the head.

"Yeah, you tied me up!" exclaimed Devlin.

"Oh, tell the truth; bondage turns you on," said Demonica as she gracefully moved her fingers across his crotch.

Devlin fiercely grabbed the dangerous woman's hand. "It freaks me out. Why can't you just leave me alone?"

"Why must you play these games with my heart? Look into my eyes and tell me you love me," said Demonica, digging her fingers into her shoulders.

Devlin looked intently into her purple eyes. "I don't love you. And I never will." He turned away from her gaze. "You should give up on me."

Every word he said sent shivers throuhout Demonica's body. Her eyes were flooded with despair. "Nononononono...."

"I should get going. Are you coming along?" asked Devlin, knocking on her head.

Demonica's eyes moved beyond despair and now shimmered. "You will love me. We are going to make a child now." She forced herself on top of Devlin and tore at his armor.

Devlin pushed her off. "I can't love you. Stop making this harder than it has to be."

"You know how I feel. Once you've found your special someone, you can't give up. They become your everything," said Demonica, crying in her hands.

"I'm not your soul mate. But I know that you'll find that special someone one day," said Devlin, patting her head.

Demonica gripped his wrist. "I will never give you up. Unlike you, I will take action. I'm doing this for the good of our love. Sel, I need your help!"

Sel emerged from the earth below Devlin. "I suppose this can't be postponed any longer. Ugh."

"How is Sel going to change my feelings for you? He can't brainwash me to forget about Kaity," said Devlin, standing up.

Demonica pulled her man in into her embrace. "We will make a baby, whether you are willing or not."

"*Soul Submission*," said Sel as his pupil swirled.

Devlin turned away from the hypnotic gaze. "I won't let you control me again."

"Hmm, much more resistance this time. No matter," said Sel, releasing dark energy into Devlin's armor.

The energy rode up the armor and flowed into the helmet.

"What are you doing to me? Why can't I take it off?" asked Devlin, struggling in Demonica's grip as he grabbed his helmet.

"Breaking your composure, that's all. A frightened host is much easier to manipulate. Though I prefer soul absorption than possession, this is a special case." Sel collapsed, his eye hollow.

Devlin removed his dark armor and turned to his cherished comrade with a smile. "Success. Now, uh, let's get this over with," he said with a blush.

"Oh Devlin, hold me and be mine," cried Demonica, embracing him tightly.

"Of course, my beloved." Devlin held his platonic minion in a loving embrace until her tears stopped flowing.

"I knew we were destined for each other," she said, rubbing cheeks with him.

"No barrier can break us apart. Not Sel, not Lum, not even death." Devlin placed kisses up her neck until he reached her lips. "You are my one and only." He pressed his lips against her's, channeling the passion of his current role.

The kiss became more potent as Demonica's passion took over. She leaned toward her dark prince, and the two fell to the floor.

"Devlin, tell me you love me," said Demonica, bouncing in his arms.

"I love you and I always will," said Devlin as he hugged her tightly.

Demonica grabbed the back of his head and snuggled his face to her breasts. "I've been longing to hear that for so long," she said as tears flowed from her eyes. The lovesick demon queen grabbed her beloved's hand and put his finger in her mouth, slowly caressing it with her tongue.

"That feels kind of strange," said Devlin, looking up from between her breasts.

She pulled his finger out and licked the tip. "You don't like it?"

"It's not a bad strange," he said with a smile.

Demonica shoved his whole hand down her throat. She then pulled it out and licked his fingers.

Devlin caressed her hair with his free hand. "You are so beautiful, the most beautiful girl in all the realms."

"And you're so sexy!" Demonica leaned into her dark prince, knocking them down to the rocky cave floor. She sliced at his blood-red undershirt until it was in tatters.

"You're uh, rather excited, aren't you?" asked Devlin, putting his hands over his chest.

"Oh yes! You excite me to no end!" Demonica pinned her man's arms to the ground and rubbed up against him.

"Careful," said Devlin, pulling back as her nipple-spikes pierced into his chest.

"It's not sex without blood," said Demonica, digging her fingernails into his arms.

"I'm not so sure I feel comfortable with this," said Devlin as he tried to wiggle out of her grip.

"I didn't expect you to be. Hmm…maybe these are a bit too sharp," said Demonica, fiddling with her nipple-spikes.

"Yes, let's tone down the violence a bit," said Devlin with a nervous smile.

Demonica pulled out the spikes and made circles around his nipples with them, never pushing hard enough to draw blood.

"That feels really good," said Devlin with heavy breaths.

"That's just the start. Soon your whole body will be convulsing with pleasure." Demonica's serpent tongue licked the edges of his ear and blew puffs of air into his ear-hole.

Devlin squirmed around in delight.

"Hmm…still not enough. I know." Demonica's tongue licked his cheek, kissed his lips and then dragged itself along his eyeball.

"That feels so strange but yet so wonderful." Devlin grabbed her butt and squeezed it. "Wow, I had no idea this was so squishy."

Demonica's tongue licked his eyeball.

Devlin squirmed around and giggled.

"Aww, look who finally got up," said Demonica, wiggling his hardened shaft.

"Yes, I uhh…suppose I've broken past fear and have entered arousal," he said, caressing her back.

Demonica gripped his rod and pressed her thumb against its tip. "It's just the right fit for my hand," she said, biting her lip.

"Wow, that's quite the sensation," said Devlin with heavy breaths.

"You are so cute. I haven't even removed your pants yet," she said, bouncing his joystick between her fingers.

"Well, then let's get naked!" exclaimed Devlin.

Wires came out from his arms and slipped under Demonica's clothes. They pulled her whole outfit off at once, leaving her in the nude.

"So skillfully done. Have you been thinking about how to undress me for a while now?" she asked, rubbing her bare breasts against his chest.

"I just had the thought and his…my wires did the rest. They're rather handy," said Devlin, unknowingly gripping her breasts with his wires.

"Ah yes, that's it! Incredible!"

The wires rubbed Demonica's breasts up and down Devlin's chest all the while fiddling with her nipples.

"I've never felt something so amazing," said Devlin, with hazy eyes and a bit of drool.

"Let's add a little lubrication to make it even better," said Demonica, pressing into her eternal beloved. She grabbed her breasts and squeezed them, spraying his chest with warm blood.

"You're really a one-of-a-kind woman," said Devlin with an awkward smile.

"Before I became the Goddess of Death, all they could do was squirt milk," she said, pressing her mouth to her nipple and squeezing her breasts. She pulled away with a blood-smeared smile.

"So, do you want me to strip, or do you want to take off my pants?" asked Devlin as he fondled her breasts.

Demonica sat up in his lap. "I'll do it." She rose back to her feet, using his chest for solid footing.

Tentacles came out from her belly, wrapped Devlin's arms together, and lifted him off the ground.

Two of the tentacles pulled Devlin's pants off while the other six kept him suspended in the air.

"Mmm, I could just you eat you up," said Demonica, tapping his juicy manhood through his underwear. She bit onto his underwear and pulled it down with her teeth.

"Do you need any help?" Devlin's superfluous protrusion slipped out and bopped the corner of her eye.

"Sehu. Nope. I've got it covered," she said, caressing his legs.

"I can't really do much with my hands tied," said Devlin as his wires pinched his nipples.

"Sure you can." Demonica put his legs over her shoulders and dived down on his pulsating pillar.

"Whoa! That feels very…unique! That really tickles," said Devlin as he squirmed around.

Demonica's fingers dug into her partner's squishy butt cheeks, drawing blood.

"Oww, that hurts a lot! Stop!" yelled Devlin.

Demonica pulled away, but her serpent tongue continued to orally pleasure him. "I want to taste you," she said as her tongue constricted his marvelous member.

Two of the tentacles smacked Devlin's butt cheeks while three more plunged into his anus.

"I don't think this is how you make a baby," said Devlin with wide eyes.

"All things in good time, my beloved," she said before pressing her lips around his tasty shaft.

Devlin moaned in delight. Words escaped him. His body convulsed as he reached climax.

Demonica pulled away for the last wave of spunk, letting it drip down her breasts. "Have a taste," she said in a muffled tone. Her serpent tongue popped out of her mouth and kissed her one true love, spitting out a wad of sperm once it was deep in his throat.

Devlin pulled away and spit out as much as he could. "Blech! You actually like this stuff?"

"I absolutely love it!" she said before gargling it in her mouth and swallowing.

"It's gone limp. This makes things rather difficult," said Devlin, poking his odd protrusion with his wires.

"Not really. We just need to get you up again."

Demonica's tentacles caressed his chest and sucked on his nipples.

"I feel so helpless," said Devlin, squirming around.

"I can make you hard as many times as I want." Demonica gripped his rod and pulled his blood into it, resulting in an instant erection.

"I'm a fool for ignoring you all this time," said Devlin with a smile.

"I want you inside me," she said, pulling open her stomach wider.

Tentacles rushed out and wrapped around Devlin. They pulled him into her and then receded.

Demonica wrapped her arms around him and fell to the ground. She rolled around as she rubbed up against him. The horny demon wiggled her hips and gripped his shoulders. "Are you ready?"

"I am a bit hesitant, but don't let that stop you," he said with flustered cheeks.

"I won't. Aww, you are so cute." With a single thrust Demonica plunged her beloved into her. She collapsed in his arms, savoring the moment.

"Why are you bleeding? There's no way you're a virgin. If you hurt yourself, it wasn't my fault," said Devlin.

"I solidified a wall of blood I made. I can regrow my hymen as many times as I want. And that means you can pop me as much as you like." She leaned down and kissed his lips.

"It's so squishy and wet. Is this normal?" asked Devlin, slowly pushing in and out.

"Virgins are just too adorable. I want to see you squirm." Demonica tightened her gateway, nearly crushing his rod.

"Are you trying to break it off!" yelled Devlin, struggling to push her off.

"Ooh, now it's even harder! How about a massage?"

The inside of her moist cave vibrated and spun around.

Devlin gripped her tightly and held her to his chest as he came inside her.

"Aww, don't you want to spill some on my body?" she asked, rubbing against him affectionately.

"No, my beloved, I want to have children with you. I want to leave a legacy behind."

Demonica broke down into tears.

"Did I say something hurtful?" asked Devlin, cleaning the tears off her face.

"I just can't believe this is really happening. Be sure to fill me up," she said, dragging her finger across his lips.

"You've already gotten hold of me. I couldn't escape if I wanted to," said Devlin with a shrug and a dazed smile.

Demonica pulled Devlin out of her. She gave his pleasure rod a long kiss, making the blood rush up it instantly. She then pressed herself against it.

"Ready for the final round?" asked Devlin, his head wobbling from side to side.

Demonica rolled around till he was on top and pressed against her. "I am now," she said, stretching her opening with her fingers.

"Sorry, my beloved. I can't hold it back anymore." Devlin plunged into the skilled succubus, slamming into her innermost chamber and breaking her wall all at once. He pulled out before plunging into her again, leaving her just enough time to reconstruct her inner wall.

"Ah yes! That's incredible!" Demonica wrapped her legs around his back.

Wires burst out from Devlin and sliced away his skin. They formed into a tail and wrapped around Demonica's throat.

Lord Sel awoke, blinking a few times. "Ugh, I feel so dizzy." He bumped into the cave wall and turned around to see Demonica being ravaged by Devlin's Exp form. "Didn't expect to lose control there. Oh well, I think he can take it from here."

Devlin stood up from the ground without breaking the connection. His wires wrapped around his attacker, lifting her up before slamming her down.

The puddle of blood became wider and wider as their rampant sex continued.

Demonica's eyes intensified. "This is how it should be! Sex is a battle!"

Tentacles came out from her belly and wrestled with Devlin's wires.

"Today sure is an odd day," said Sel, rolling on the cave floor.

Devlin plunged into Demonica with full force.

Wires burst out from her skin and sliced her.

He filled up Demonica till his essence gushed out from her opening.

Devlin's wires created a cocoon around Demonica as soon as they overpowered her tentacles.

"That's that then. If Exps and demons can procreate, then she's sure to get pregnant. I don't think I'll possess anyone again anytime soon. I'll leave you two to it," said Sel, watching the bizarre spectacle.

Chapter 116: Non-Combatants

Meanwhile: in a realm where passion fades away, Absence was training with the second guard.

Occupy was punching at him furiously.

Absence reverted into a ball. After rolling behind his attacker, he reverted back into a grapple stance.

Occupy was slammed against the ground but diverted most of the impact by flipping back to his feet. He jumped in the air and rapidly kicked his leader's face.

The God of Nothingness knocked Occupy's foot aside and slammed his hands into his chest.

Occupy took the full brunt of the attack and wrapped his legs around Absence's neck. He tossed his god with his legs before he rushed up into an uppercut.

Absence compacted himself, slid down Occupy's arm, and reverted back. His punches were blocked by the warrior monk's palms. "I suppose I'm still rusty."

"You aren't just rusty; it's as if your power has diminished." Occupy knocked the fists aside and slammed his palms into Absence's chest. "There's no need to hold back on me."

Absence skid backward before toppling over, he compacted into a ball to weaken the impact. After bouncing into the air, he reverted back and coated his fist in Absence.

Occupy rushed up and slid past the fist. He grabbed Absence's arm and flipped him onto the ground.

"You win again. I suppose my battle with Neutral tired me out more than expected." Absence got back to his feet. He created a chair from his clear energy and sat in it. "You'll have to spar with someone else in the meantime."

"Get some rest, my Lord," said Occupy with a bow.

"I'm a bit tired myself." Limit collapsed to the ground and transformed back into Plagiarism. "I may copy bodies, but I can't copy your willpower."

"Another glorious victory!" cheered Limit.

"Indeed," said Loyal, holding Crystal against the ground.

"Eil, would you like to battle me?" asked Limit.

"I'm really not much of a fighter. Needle used to protect me, but it has yet to return from Lum. Htols doesn't even have the energy to hold me up. Things just aren't going my way as of late," said Eil.

Absence looked down at Eil. "You shouldn't let despair set in. You and Plagiarism both look so expired."

"Well, we are rather old," said Eil.

Absence hopped off his throne and picked up Eil. "Nonsense. You are the newest guardian. You weren't even around back when I was a god. You should join us in our training."

"I can't move, so I can't fight. I'm just stuck like this. It's so dull," said Eil.

"There is no need for you to sulk. I have Tcetorp with me. I am quite certain she can make you a body with her powers." Absence took out a ball from one of his many pockets. "ᴿᴇᴠᴇᴿᴛ."

The ball de-compacted.

The goddess stood up, completely unharmed. "Didn't I die?" asked Tcetorp, touching her face.

"My artifact allows me to revert the object to what it was before it was compacted. By reverting the object, I manipulate time to bring it back to its former shape."

"That's quite the fancy ability. It must be great for heavy lifting, grocery shopping, and traveling. Why it makes just about everything portable," said Eil, gaining back some of his energy.

"You are very clever. Yes, it is rather handy," said Absence, scratching his head.

Tcetorp looked around curiously. "Where am I? I feel dizzy," she said, almost falling to the ground.

"You are in the realm of Absence. You are alive and well," said Absence, wrapping his arm around her.

Tcetorp jumped back. "You're the one who killed me!"

"I compacted you into a tiny sphere. As you can see, you are unharmed," said Absence with a smile.

"I need to bring you back to the prison. Rrrugh! Why can't I make a Lum portal?"

"The atmosphere here is different than what you're used to. You're the prisoner now. With you in my possession, Lum cannot attack this realm."

"What nonsense. Lum has no interest in Absence, neither as an enemy nor an ally. Why can't I get out of here?"

"I control what is allowed here. I've forbidden you to escape. Now, if you cooperate, I'll be more than happy to allow you to return to Lum."

"I don't have a choice, do I? What do you need from me?" asked Tcetorp with a scowl.

"I need you to help my comrade here feel young again. Could you perhaps coat Eil in skin?" asked Absence.

"If I do, you'll let me leave?" she asked, with a suspicious glare.

"Three favors and then off you go," said Absence with a smile.

"Very well, I'll assist you. But know I do so for the glory of Lum," said Tcetorp, folding her hands.

Absence picked the skull off the ground.

"This is greatly appreciated and so very kind of you. But to be quite frank, I rather enjoy being a skull," said Eil.

"Isn't it a burden to be immobile?" asked Absence.

"Not really. There's not much reason to roam around in a void anyway," said Eil.

"Nonsense, space is a beautiful thing. It is infinitesimal and boundless," said Absence.

"I can see its splendor from here. I like not being able to feel. It gets me into the vibe of Neutral," said Eil.

"You mean Absence?"

"Yes, yes. I mean this body is quite splendid once you get used to it. I feel so hollow in this form. It is an absolute joy," said Eil.

"I will not hear a word of it. You don't remember the perks of a body, that's all. Tcetorp, I leave it to you," said Absence with a slight bow.

"I've never tried anything like this before, but I'll give it a shot. You shall have a body once again. Ⓥ︎Ⓘ︎Ⓣ︎Ⓐ︎Ⓛ︎ Ⓒ︎Ⓞ︎Ⓝ︎Ⓢ︎Ⓣ︎Ⓡ︎Ⓤ︎Ⓒ︎Ⓣ︎."

"No! Stop, you imbecile!"

Cells formed around Eil, creating body tissue, which differentiated into organs and linked functions to develop organ systems. Muscles formed and finally his skin grew.

Absence had a glint of surprise in his eyes. "It's you," said Absence softly, blinking several times.

"I suppose you recogn-ize me," said the naked young man in a toneless voice.

"You're Neutral. I crushed you in my hands. How are you alive?" asked Absence.

"Explain-ing does not change the situation," said Neutral.

"You shall not steal this throne from me a second time. Explain now, or all of my gods shall attack at once," said Absence, crossing his arms.

Neutral looked around to see the gods who once served him. "After I defeat-ed you and be-came the new god of Absence, I banish-ed you to Lum. I am here now to correct my mistake."

"That doesn't explain how you're alive, standing before me now."

"What you kill-ed was a projection. It was a collect-ion of my Absence energy. My soul manifest-ed it-self as a skull that act-ed as a guard-ian of Absence."

"Was this part of some devious plan?" asked Plagiarism.

"The plan fail-ed. I sent Needle to aid Etah in exchange for peace between our realms."

"You love this realm, don't you?" asked Absence.

"I became attach-ed, but now I feel apathy toward this place. I order-ed the Exps to be pacif-ied, but they are too will-ful to be neutral-ized. The Exps will only bring conflict to Sel-lum, your-self includ-ed."

"I still don't get why you would fake your death," said Absence.

"As the realm god of Absence, I felt it made sense to rule with-out a presence. And once I was defeat-ed, I surrender-ed my energy to you to fool you into believ-ing I died. Make sense?" asked Eil, covering his naked body with Absence energy.

"You stole the throne from me like a coward. No surprise you ruled this realm while staying in hiding."

"I had hope-d to ambush you when you were at your weak-est. No matter. You're exhaust-ed from fight-ing my aura and from your train-ing. I will now take back my throne," said Eil completely monotone.

"I have the powers of a realm god; what makes you think you can kill me?" asked Absence with a clenched fist.

"God of Absence or not, I will win. I will end you with my Absence power reserves," said Neutral.

"**compact**!" Absence punched Neutral's arm.

The arm was ripped off from the pull of being compacted. Blood exploded out of the arm as it was crushed into a single ball.

Eil flicked blood droplets, coated in his energy, from his shoulder wound at Absence. The droplets created a crevice in the realm god's chest.

Absence kicked Eil's jaw, causing him to lose his balance and fall to the floor.

"You are train-ing for a los-ing battle. Absence must not go to war. The integrity of neutral-ity is at stake."

"Then you ask that we bow our heads as they take over our home?"

"Yes. Absence must remain neutral to the very end."

"This place is worth defending. I will fight and die to keep Absence a place of refuge." Absence moved his hand like a blade past Neutral's throat.

The ex-god's head slid off and fell to the ground.

"Farewell," said Absence, piercing Neutral's chest with his Absence-coated fingertips.

"You underestimate the power of a hollow shell. *Soul Separation*!"

The ground rumbled violently beneath Absence before splitting open.

Hundreds of skulls emerged and swarmed Absence, biting ferociously.

"I buri-ed every-one who ever di-ed in this place. If fear took over this realm, Absence would not be sustain-ed. Their hollow remains are a suit-able vessel for my energy."

Absence thrashed his body around, knocking the skulls off of him. "**COMPACT**." He vanished from sight.

The skulls looked down to see a small ball and leaped to bite it.

Absence reverted, smashing a few of the skulls. He kicked one of the skulls up. "**COMPACT**," he said, condensing the skull. The realm god punched the ball downward through the ground of Absence.

The ball hit a teleporter almost instantly, shooting through four of the skulls as it came full circle.

Absence compacted their pieces into a single ball and punched it through the ground. Once they popped out of the teleporter, he reverted them back into pieces.

The skulls were smashed to bits by their fellow skull fragments until only one remained.

"I told you mobility is necessary," said Absence.

"Even with-out the gods, I am not alone. Absence energy has been stor-ed in all my molecules," said Neutral, firing clear blasts.

Absence leaped around but was unable to close the distance. He projected his energy out as a barrier, but it shattered upon contact. The shards sliced his skin, taking it with them into oblivion.

"I took you down as a realm god before. Now will be no differ-ent," said Neutral, clawing at the space in front of him to bring his opponent closer.

"You don't speak the same way. You've spent so much time as Eil, you've forgotten who Neutral is."

"Eil, Neutral, neither are real. There is no ego and no self. We are part of a single conscious-ness that has divid-ed it-self with trivial concepts. A soul is a mere fragment-ation of the absolute."

"Whether the ego is a construct or not is irrelevant. It directs us on our path, brings us karma, and builds our soul memory. Our ego ultimately shapes the absolute within us. Neutral, your true self has withered away beneath your false persona. All the while I've been locked up in Lum, spending my time in absolute peace." Absence closed his eyes. His aura cloaked his body, deflecting the clear blasts.

"Then I will pour what remains of my nothing-ness into you." Neutral jumped up at Absence, biting into his aura with Absence-coated teeth.

The realm god's aura pulsed, shattering the skull's teeth.

"I will defend this realm, whether its enemy be from Sel, Lum, or Absence." Absence flicked a clear-coated ball with his thumb.

As soon as the ball was in Neutral's mouth, Absence reverted it.

The ball expanded, bursting Eil to pieces.

Absence picked up the pieces and compacted them. "You will not come back." The realm god popped the compact into his mouth and swallowed. "Once he is dissolved, I will absorb the rest of the power he withheld from me. Only then will I truly be the God of Absence."

"I never expected Neutral to be capable of such incredible theatrics," said Plagiarism.

"What theatrics? Neutral was merely playing the role of king because of his addiction to power," said Limit.

"That is incorrect. He believed in Absence. As do I. Though he sees Absence as nothing, I see it as no thing. It is beyond description, beyond presence, but is infinitely valuable. Our battle was due to a difference in thinking, but our devotion made us kin," said Absence, bowing to his greatest teacher.

"With Eil gone, Htols is without a guardian to protect. What shall we do?" asked Loyal.

"Htols is relieved of her post. A new first guardian will be chosen alongside their guard. After all, it is the bond between a guard and guardian that gives them the power to protect this world," said Absence.

"Such wisdom. We are truly fortunate to have you return to command," said Limit.

"And I am blessed to have such dutiful gods to guide me."

Tcetorp approached the god. "I did as you asked, though it did not turn out in your favor. What else must I do?"

"I want you to create armor for anyone willing to fight."

"No. I will not help a potential enemy." She turned away from him.

"If Lum does not seek to control this realm, then you have nothing to fear. I will stand and defend Absence from invaders, but I will not leave it to mount an attack."

"Lum has no interest here."

"Exactly. There is a prisoner held here that Sel must not get hold of. By helping this realm, you are serving your Great Goddess."

"All I do is for the glory of Lum. I shall offer my aid in any way I can."

"Wonderful, the last condition will be revealed upon completion of this task."

"I only hope that this is Lum's will," said Tcetorp, folding her hands.

Previously: After breaking free from Lord Sel's possession, Devlin clashed with Demonica.

After an intense battle, Devlin was on the ground.

Devlin's arms, legs, and head had been separated from his torso and were strewn along the floor of the cave. His bare body was covered in dents, gashes, bite marks, and scratches. Blood, sweat, demonic juices and seminal fluids, both from him and his attacker, coated his front and formed a puddle beneath him.

"One more time?" asked Demonica, poking his cheek. "Aw, I think I may have broken him." She turned to Lord Sel with excitement. "Maybe you could possess him for one final round?" she asked, rubbing her palms together.

"No! I told you I won't enjoy it, yet you insist on doing it again and again and again! I already took over him multiple times after he passed out! I'm done, okay! Sheesh, how many children do you want anyway?" Sel poked her bloated belly.

A glob of Devlin's love popped out from between her legs.

"What are you doing? I can't waste a single drop." Demonica bent down and sucked up the fluids with her gateway to Sel.

"Disgusting." Sel passed through the ground.

Demonica bit her finger, sprayed the blood on her crotch, and then solidified it into an iron clad plug. "I feel so full," she said, lying down.

"You can't hide your presence from a ninja. Did you really think I wouldn't notice you hovering above my team? It took me awhile to track you down, but I found you. Turn over Devlin to me!" Nina rolled into the cave with an explosive tag between each finger. "What is that thing?" asked the ninja, looking at the metallic remains.

"That thing is Devlin," said Demonica.

"Lies. Where are you hiding him?"

"You mean you don't know. You dedicate your entire life to him and yet you don't know that he's an Exp. How pathetic?"

"Where is he!?"

"Come on, you know Deceivant isn't man enough to knock up Ada. Which means the only way they could have a child is to make it from scratch. Don't those beautiful golden eyes look familiar?"

Nina's eyes shrank. The loyal warrior rushed to the severed head. Her eyes popped. "Dead?"

"You know that feeling when all your hard work pays off. Ah, it's incredible," said Demonica with a smile.

The devout warrior turned her blade on Demonica. "What have you done?"

"He's alive. We just had some fun together, He poured his passion into me and I plunged my hopes into–," said Demonica before her head was sliced off and her heart was pierced.

Devlin started choking. He spit out a globule of spunk and drowsily looked up. "Nina, is that you?"

She picked up her beloved's head, wiping away the toxic liquids. "I should have been there for you."

"I need some rest," said Devlin, closing his eyes.

Demonica collapsed into a puddle and fled the cave.

"You will not escape me!" Nina set Devlin's head down and rushed after the enemy.

Nina flung shurikens and kunais, her aim gradually being diluted by her tears.

The puddle traveled up a cliff and the ninja pursued, stabbing into the rock with her katana with great fury.

The puddle split into eight smaller puddles, each one going a different direction.

Nina raced all the way up the cliffside, losing track of the blood puddles when rushing through the bushes. "Damn it all!" She stabbed a nearby tree repeatedly, her tears pouring out along with her rage. "Devlin is my lover! He's mine! He made me to be his. And that woman, that demon! Argh! She took him from me!"

The tree collapsed.

The skilled warrior didn't even bother to dodge it, allowing it to press her against the ground. "I need to keep it together." She smacked her tear-stained cheeks. Nina then closed her eyes and took a deep breath. "It's over. Any chance I had with Devlin…it's gone now. I need to move on. If I don't abandon these feelings, they will no doubt destroy me." She pushed aside the tree and stood up with resolve as tears flowed out of her eyes like a waterfall. "I will find her and make her pay."

Lord Sel reentered the cave and attached Devlin's head to his neck. "Get up."

The naked Exp didn't budge.

Lord Sel summoned up the Atma Blade and fired a soul blast into Devlin.

The exhausted Exp suddenly rose up, its eyes filled with newfound energy.

"Good, you're awake," said Lord Sel, waving at the Exp with its own arm.

Devlin looked down at his bloody, beaten, defiled, and limbless body. "What the hell happened to me?" His gaze shifter upward to the dark deity above him. A layer of fear tinted his eyes. "Did you do this?"

"Eww, why would you even...ugh! No. I didn't do anything to you. Demonica forced herself on you. It was...something to behold," said Sel with a wide pupil.

Devlin's torso shot out wires that connected to his limbs.

"Should have left before things got gruesome," said Lord Sel, looking at the special blends on the cave floor.

"You were watching. Why didn't you stop her? What the hell did she do to me?" Devlin tried to wipe the fluids off his body.

"Once she gets started, not even I can stop her. Moving along, I need your help," said Sel.

"I'm the one who needs help. My ass in so much pain! What did she do to me? I'm bleeding, everywhere! Who the hell thinks this is sex?!" yelled Devlin, struggling to stand.

"She is rather rough, isn't she?"

"My arms and legs are scarred, and were separated from my body! She is insane!"

"Yes, yes, as I was saying. I need you to clean up–seriously you're disgusting–and get ready for battle."

"What? Battle? Do I look like I'm ready to fight?! I was raped, goddamn it! She's a crazed violent rapist!"

"I know, it must be traumatizing for you, but I need you to just get over it and suit up for battle."

"All you do is abuse others. You wouldn't know what this feels like."

"I bet it feels like betrayal. She takes after me in so many ways," said Sel with a spin.

"I feel so defiled," said Devlin, starting to cry.

"There's a waterfall just outside the cave."

"I don't care! I just. I want to be left alone," said Devlin, cuddling himself in a ball.

"Well, we don't have time for this. It's almost time to storm Samsara. I'll need you in tip-top shape. We move as soon as the Remnants make their move. They're meeting with Efil soon, so it shouldn't take too long."

"Where's the waterfall?" asked Devlin, standing up.

"Follow me," said Sel with a smile, the dark armor in tow.

Previously: The Remnants of Freedom gathered at the hillside where Efil was waiting.

"No time to waste. Bring us to the portal," said Deceivant.

"Of course. Right this way," said Efil, creating a portal.

"Hey, where's Nina?" asked Kaity.

"That's odd. Where did she run off to?" asked Deceivant.

Nina approached from the shadows.

"Are you okay?" asked Kaity.

"I left him alone and now he's gone," said Nina to herself.

"Who is?" asked Ada.

"Devlin."

"What happened to my son?"

"Nothing. I just…lost track of him."

"Are you sure?"

"Yeah. So, Efil's here. Time for me to fulfill the mission Devlin entrusted to me," said Nina, smiling at Ada.

"Wait! Before we split up, I'd like to welcome the new members to the team," said Kaity.

"Such a pointless ritual. I'd much rather return home as soon as possible," said Hope, seated on her living chair.

"Bonding is very important, and it shouldn't take long," said Image.

"It won't. I promise. Violet, do you have the extra bracelets?" asked Kaity.

"She won't respond unless I ask her a question. I believe you are referring to these," said Hope, dropping the bracelets into Kitty's open palms.

"Yep, that's them," said Kaity, slipping one onto the little queen's wrist.

"For being the team's symbol, they appear rather dull."

"Here's one for you and one for your husband," said Kaity to Image.

"These are from the Sikh tradition, aren't they?" asked Image.

"That's correct," said Ada.

"So after we put the bracelet on, that's it?" asked Crisis.

"Here you go, sorry we lost sight of you," said Kaity, dropping the bracelet onto Fusion.

"Now it's time for my favorite part," said Ada with a smile.

"Not yet." Kaity walked up to Efil. "I want to thank you for all you've done for us. Consider yourself an honorary Freedom Forcer," she said, slipping the bracelet onto the goddess.

"I am honored," said Efil with a bow.

"Alright, everyone. Group hug!" cheered Kaity, putting her arm around Nina.

"Yay!" exclaimed Ada, lifting her darling little Hope off the ground.

"I don't think I have any right to join in," said Atlas.

"Why not? You're our friend," said Opti, grabbing the big man's hand.

Kaity grabbed Hope's hand, completing the circle. "Despite being chased by Etaf and Sel, despite some of us being locked away, we've all managed to come together. I don't know what will happen later on. And I know that some of you will be heading back to Earth before the rest of us. There's a chance that those of us who stay to fight Sel won't see you again, but we're together right now. And no matter what happens, we're all Freedom Forcers. Exp 8 formed the Freedom Forcers to fight for the freedom of his people. Now we're joining together to fight for Lum and the safety of its people. We had lost hope and given up on fighting, but now that we've decided to take a stand, we are no longer mere Remnants. We are a force of freedom that will take down Sel!"

"Not a bad speech. You continue to impress me, Kitty," said Hope.

"You've grown into a fine warrior. I'll gladly fight by your side," said Kanasta.

"As will I, along with the souls of our comrades," said Atlas with a nod.

"A battle against a god; doesn't get much more unpredictable than this," said Crisis.

"Well then, shall we proceed?" asked Efil.

"Please do," said Deceivant, holding his wifey's hand.

"As per our agreement: Lum permits the following non-combatants to be escorted back to Earth…." A scroll of light appeared in Efil's grip.

"It won't be much longer now," said Deceivant to his little queen.

Hope turned away.

"Deceivant," said Efil.

"Naturally," he said with a grin.

"Ada."

"I can fight. Just not very well," said Ada sadly.

"Image."

"I will join you once Sel has been dethroned. That is, if you will still have me," said Atlas.

"Napkin."

"Meow!" cheered Napkin.

"Muffins."

"Even if we get picked, we don't have to leave. Isn't that right?" asked Opti.

"Would you like to stay? You're next on the list."

"Yeah. I'm staying to protect this place," said Opti.

"And Fusion." The scroll dissipated into light. "Now if the aforementioned will—"

"Efil, you made a mistake. Please read it again carefully," said Deceivant.

The scroll rematerialized.

"Let's see…nope. I mentioned everyone. Is there a problem?"

"Yes. Why isn't—?"

"Why am I not on the list?" asked Hope, refusing to let Deceivant speak on her behalf.

"Lum made no mistake. If you look at Violet's current condition, you will see quite clearly that Hope is a combatant. A particularly strong one, I might add," said Efil.

"Uh-uh, no deal. Tell Lum that Hope is going with us to Earth. I'll even surrender my spot for her," said Deceivant.

"I'm sorry, but Hope alone could change the tide of this war. It's even possible her powers would work on Sel himself," said Efil.

"That's your problem, not hers. She's just a little girl. She shouldn't have to fight in a war she has nothing to do with," said Deceivant, breaking down into tears.

"Go on ahead with Ada. I'll keep her safe. After all, she is Devlin's little sister," said Nina.

"My very own ninja to command, most splendid indeed," said Hope to herself.

"That's not good enough. You can't guarantee her safety. Look, either she goes back to Earth or none of us are fighting for Lum. Got it?" asked Deceivant.

A portal appeared and Etaf emerged. "Efil, Lum wishes to speak with you. I'll handle things from here."

"Yes. Understood," said Efil before vanishing.

"You know what's going on. Make Lum change her mind or I guarantee the Freedom Forcers won't be defending Lum," said Deceivant to Etaf.

"Such a shame, and after Efil went through so much trouble to convince the Great Goddess not to have you eliminated. I've been ordered to kill those who won't fight for Lum," said Etaf.

"Calm down," said Kaity.

"We are all friends here. There is no reason for us to fight. Let's just agree that unless Hope comes with us, we will stay. Sound good?" asked Ada.

"No. You have to go, regardless of what happens. It isn't safe here. Sel already tried to trap your soul," said Deceivant, grabbing his beloved's hand.

"Well I don't want to leave. Even if Hope came along, so many of our cherished children wouldn't. Toxic, Absorb, Demo, D.S., and even Devlin would be left behind. What kind of mother would I be if I just abandon them when they need me most?" asked Ada, hugging her husband tightly.

"It appears that none of you wish to return to Earth, at least at this time," said Etaf.

314

"I am staying with my husband. And don't try to convince me otherwise," said Image, smiling at Atlas.

"Then it's settled," said Etaf, closing the portal.

"You don't like Lum anyway, isn't there some way you can distract her long enough for Hope and Ada to get through the portal?" asked Deceivant.

"You misunderstand. I may not have sworn allegiance to this Lum, but I will do all I can to keep this place safe," said Etaf, her hand to her chest.

"It was your angels who captured me after Devlin teleported me away. I was sent to Etah by your orders, wasn't I?" asked Kaity.

"You've figured me out. It was on Lum's behalf. She never did tell me why. I have some theories, but they are all blasphemous."

"You're lying. I spoke with her directly. She never ordered me to be captured. What do you have to gain? Do you want to overthrow her, is that it?" asked Kaity, stepping up to the goddess.

"Are you sure I'm the one who's lying?"

"They are both speaking the truth. There's just some sort of misunderstanding, I'm sure of it," said Ada.

"Kaity, why do you have so much faith in Lum?" asked Deceivant.

"What, you trust Etaf more? She's tried to kill us, multiple times!" yelled Kaity.

"If I had wanted you dead, you'd be dead," said Etaf.

"How many of the Sikhs did you slaughter?" asked Deceivant.

"My apologies, I wasn't counting," said Etaf.

"You truly are a terrifying woman," said Hope, fixing her mittens.

"I propose a new plan," said Kaity, standing atop a large rock to garner their attention.

"Go ahead," said Deceivant, glaring at Etaf.

"I think we should all fight for Lum and then, once Sel is defeated, we will head back to Earth together," said Kaity.

"I must first complete the job assigned to me. I'll be damned if the Viper Squad name is tarnished," said Kanasta.

"I agree with Kaity," said Ada.

"Well, I don't," said Deceivant.

"Neither do I. War is for fools. Diplomacy and compromise are the proper way to expand a kingdom. War should only be used as a means of self-defense," said Hope.

"But, sweetie, Lum is being attacked by Sel. It's self-defense," said Ada.

"You think I don't understand that? This place does not fall under my domain, and my kingdom is not allied with Lum. Why should I send my forces into a battle that I have nothing to gain from?" asked Hope.

"Umm, do we work for her now? Did I miss something?" asked Opti.

"Yeah, I'm confused too," said D.S.

Crisis turned away. "Sorry but if we aren't really united in our mission, well then we're all going to die. I'd rather not go through that again. Maybe we'll run into each other again."

"Wait! We have to stick together!" exclaimed Kaity.

"What guarantee do we have that Lum won't kill us once she's done with us?" asked Deceivant.

"Yeah, it's like cousin Pharma said, 'the ones claiming to be good aren't always the good guys.' I know it's confusing, but it has to do with white power and other bad things. He'd be able to explain it better, but he's not here," said D.S. with a frown.

"I have faith in Lum. Why can't you?" asked Kaity.

"She's using you, Kaity. Did she appear as your mother or someone else?" asked Deceivant.

"Perhaps a lover?" asked Hope.

Kaity turned away. "You wouldn't believe me."

"Anyone who doesn't want to die fighting against Sel, come with me. I'll try to find us a temple nearby we can stay at," said Deceivant, pulling out the temple map he found on Violet.

"I'm staying with Kitty," said Hope with a sly grin.

"You can't be serious," said Deceivant.

"Go on. This won't be the first time you've abandoned me for your own happiness," said Hope with a scowl.

"I'll come along," said Crisis.

"My dear, if I stay with Kaity, will you stay with Deceivant?" asked Atlas.

"I can defend myself. I'm not leaving your side. So stop asking," said Image.

"I apologize, Kaity. I must keep Image safe. When do we head out?" asked Atlas, walking to his son's side.

"Wait. Due to the recent development, Lum has reconsidered something," said Etaf.

"Fickle as ever," said Deceivant, rolling his eyes.

"She has ordered me to convince all of you that Lum is worth fighting for...worth dying for."

"Easy for her to say."

"I won't bother trying to appeal to your ethics or emotions—or even your logic. Let me complete the rest of my story. After that, you are free to decide what you will do next," said Etaf.

"So she thinks the hands-off approach will work? What's stopping me from leaving now?" asked Deceivant.

"If you listen to the rest of my story and decide not to fight, then I will personally escort Hope, along with any others who wish to leave, to the Portal to Earth. Are you interested now?" asked Etaf.

"What don't you understand? He doesn't trust you. There's no guarantee you'll live up to your word," said Hope.

"I accept. Hope's right, of course, but there's nothing to lose. I'll listen to the rest of your story. We all will," said Deceivant.

"We agree to the terms," said Kaity, shaking Etaf's hand.

"Splendid. To summarize the story thus far—"

Hope stares into Etaf. "A young, hopeful girl wanted to be something her society did not permit. She practiced in secret, got caught, banished, found a new home, and was then called back when a calamity struck her hometown. Feeling herself indirectly responsible for the calamity, she returns and performs the duties asked of her. Being the paranoid child she is, the girl foresees future calamities and in trying to stop them from happening, she gives them enough mental focus that they come into being. Broken and tired, she settles—"

"Stop. You'll ruin the rest. Let's continue from there. After my brother died," said Etaf, devoid of emotion.

"How did you know all that?" asked D.S., wide eyed.

"Look at her. She is someone who has given up on freewill. She is an empty husk, following the will of a god she has no faith in. What else could have led to that? It was obviously a result of a past life experience. Though I'm not certain of the details. The more information we have about this place, the better. I rather like it here. One day, this place will be mine," said Hope with certainty.

"Alright, everyone. Sit down, relax, and hear the rest of my story," said Etaf.

"And then we can go home," said Deceivant, grabbing his wifey's hand.

"If you so choose." Etaf unsheathed her sword and carved a frame into the air. She then projected her aura into the frame, forming an image that gradually came into focus.

Chapter 117: Fear & Duty

There I was, looking up at the stars, the merciless upper echelon *kamui* did nothing to comfort me. The *kamui* were all worthless. No amount of prayer or *inao* could do anything to amend the situation.

Brother.

His warm hand was still in my grip, but it was an empty warmth…soon to fade like everything else.

I had misinterpreted the prophecy. It appeared like I would be the one to kill him, making him invincible to all others. The vision was showing me removing a spear, not plunging it in.

Of course it was. Why didn't I realize it in time?

My tears were still flowing despite all my efforts to stay *okira*.

May my brother find my father in the next world.

The sadness sapped at my resolve. I didn't want to do anything. Despite the urgent information that only I could pass to the chief, despite my brother entrusting me to do so…I couldn't move. It wasn't that I wanted to die or stay there…holding his hand. All motivation was gone. I merely existed and nothing more.

When I was shaken to my senses, the stars were still in the sky so it couldn't have been too long. My eyes put forth the effort to focus on the object before me.

Isepo? Come to finish the—Eoha!

Still unable to speak, I flung myself on top of him with a sudden burst of energy. Even if I was only hallucinating, I would savor every moment before I would wake up. He had blood on him.

That's right. He was possessed. He killed them…his own people…to keep me safe.

I noticed his smile and smiled back. His hand went over mine and slowly tore me away from my brother.

Goodbye, dear brother.

He applied salve on my wound, a slash at my right side just under the ribcage. It wasn't as bad as I had originally thought.

If it had been fatal, this would all be over. I could see brother again.

"*Ai-oh!*"

The heat from the soot he set aflame closed the wound.

Next thing I know, Eoha has me hoisted over his shoulder. He carried me all the way back to the cave, changing directions each time there was rustling in the bushes.

"I'm sorry." He used his *amip* to wipe away my tears. "We'll stay here for the night. I'll keep watch."

My hand gripped his wrist on instinct. "Stay."

He sat down next to me. "Okay."

"How many?" I asked, after sitting in silence till it hurt.

"Possibly three groups, maybe six men each. I can't be sure. I heard them, but I didn't see them."

I shook my head. "How many did you kill?"

Eoha looked down. "I'm…not sure."

"They are dead, right? You didn't just wound them? You made sure they were dead, right?"

Brother wanted them all dead. I do too.

"Ebui." He held me tightly.

"Horekeu. Isepo. What's the difference?"

His grip tightened.

"They killed him. They killed my…."

Eoha pressed his forehead against mine. "*Chishirikirap.*"

We sobbed in each other's arms.

As long as he's here, I can bear it. But how long before he is taken by fate?

"My…." My lips froze.

I can't say it. Why can't I say it?

I cleared my throat. "He left me with a mission."

"It isn't safe to go out right now. The Isepo chief is dead."

"Good."

That's all I could think to say about it. I once looked up to the man. There was even a time when I hoped the Shitumbe would follow his example of peace. I was so wrong.

"You shouldn't be moving around with that wound," he said, breaking apart from me to make some soup.

"Aren't the Isepo your friends?"

"Some of them are," he said before wiping his eyes.

That's right. That one Isepo warrior said he knew Eoha. He was banished…why was that again?

"This isn't the first time I've killed a friend." Eoha stirred the soup.

"I'm sorry. I…."

Why did I even ask? It was so cruel of me.

"I have no allegiance to the Isepo, you know that. Still, I need to know the mission you were left with."

"It's something I need to tell the chief."

Eoha sat next to me and held the soup bowl to my mouth. "Just take it slow, okay? What do you need to tell him? Can it wait till morning?"

I pulled away. "It was my brother's dying wish!"

The soup spilled on Eoha. I didn't even realize I knocked it out from his hands.

Eoha pressed his forehead to mine. He held me till I stopped shaking, and then got up to make more soup.

Was he really dead? Was my brother not coming back?

It felt like him and father had just gone away on a trip. Any moment they could arrive.

But they don't know where this cave is! I have to get home so they can find me!

"Ebui!"

I came back to my senses. I was standing at the cave exit. If there were Isepo or Horekeu nearby, they would no doubt have spotted me.

Eoha grabbed my hand. "You should get some rest."

"My mother. She doesn't know. She's waiting there all alone, not knowing where I am, where he is…when we'll come back…."

Eoha put his fingers over my lips. He seized my head and caressed my hair.

Each stroke took away a layer of worry. He tried to get me to sit down, but I didn't budge. "What if it's infected and I die before I can give the message?"

"Our best chance of survival is here. The wound is not infected. I made sure of it. Will you tell me what the message is?"

I looked into his amber eyes, so pure and well-intentioned.

So alive.

"The *tusu-guru* before me was poisoned by the Horokeu. It was at the bear ceremony of the Isepo clan. They sought to cripple my people by leaving them without a shaman. I'm their next target."

"The Horokeu didn't kill you so that they could use you as a bargaining chip to get the Isepo chief back, right? That means that the Isepo and the Horokeu have a strong alliance."

He figured all that out. Now for sure he won't let me leave.

"Ebui, this information will be just as useful tomorrow morning as it would be tonight. They are after you, you said so yourself. We should stay here."

"We need to prepare for war."

And kill every last one of them.

Eoha grabbed my hand. "Pan'ambe and Pen'ambe, the two foxes. One became rich. The other was impatient and is now poor."

Those are just stories. This is different.

"They want war. And we have no idea when they will attack," I said, my hand tightening into a fist and escaping his hold.

"The information is yours to pass on, and you will choose when to speak it. This is my advice; do with it what you will. There is distrust and panic in the air already. Telling the chief tonight or even tomorrow will only create more panic. Let us send off the dead. Once the village has calmed down, then I think you should tell the chief your message."

"You lied to me."

Eoha turned to me, his expression like a wounded dog.

"You said you have no allegiance to the Isepo. You don't want them to die, do you? You don't want my brother to rest in peace!"

"If the Shitumbe wage war against the Horokeu and the Isepo together, they will surely lose! I won't lose you," he said as firm as a mountain.

"You don't get it, do you?" I pushed him away. "My village will burn no matter what I do! I saw the broom star and then the vision came. All my visions have come true! Every, single, one!" I screamed out, not caring who heard me.

"What if…what if you only had that vision after seeing the *rikop* because you were scared? We don't know the future, Ebui. Every decision we make can change it."

"I hear teacher die and she died. I saw my brother die and he died! I thought becoming a *tusu-guru* would make sense of it all. I thought it would give me some control. But it hasn't! It's just made me realize how powerless I am!" I sobbed.

Eoha pushed me to the ground. He grabbed a spear by the side of the cave and ran off.

This was my chance.

I left, even though I knew it was wrong, and I knew he was in danger and that I was putting myself in harm's way. I don't know if it's because I was upset with him or scared he might convince me otherwise. Whether or not it had to do with the mission brother left me or my loyalty to my people–something I thought I had let go of.

Maybe brother's loyalty was passed down to me. Maybe his spirit is with me right now.

All I knew was that I had to return. Any doubt I had was buried and burned once I pictured the worry on mother's face.

It's okay, Mom. I'm coming home.

I arrived at my *chisei* without being spotted by anyone. Once I made it to the door I froze up.

How am I going to tell her?

I wasn't prepared. I hadn't rehearsed what to say. I hadn't figured out how to break the news. I was drawn there as a little girl seeking her mother's warmth. It was too soon after father's death. News of brother's death could make her ill.

I have a mission.

I turned away from the door.

Facing the chief and telling him the news didn't seem all that daunting in comparison. I had to fulfill my brother's wishes. This was more important than seeing my mother. I was the only *tusu-guru* my people had. I needed to take up teacher's mantle with pride.

Not sure whether I was really feeling that strong of a determination or if I was just too afraid to see Mom, I made my way to the chief's *chisei*.

I didn't even realize I was running.

If I get chastised for this, I'll end up crying again.

The noise woke up the chief. He sat up from his mat. "You've returned." He smiled.

"The bamboo-tipped arrows in my vision. It's true."

The chief's face went pale. "You're sure?" he asked, holding onto just a sliver of hope that maybe I had overlooked something.

"There were Isepo warriors working alongside the Horokeu. My brother uncovered their alliance after he captured a Horokeu spy in our village. Eikashu's death was not from the plague. He was poisoned at the Isepo bear ceremony."

The chief looked at me intensely and stood up. "Thank you for this information, Ebuike."

"That isn't all. My brother...."

"I shall inform the others in the morning. You are dismissed," said the chief.

"The morning? Look, the Isepo still have two sub-chiefs. If we form a night attack squad, we can find and kill the other chiefs. That will put their clan in disarray. Then when the Horokeu come to assist—"

The chief raised his hand. "I need my rest. You are dismissed."

Why isn't he more serious about this!?

I bowed and left walking backward, careful not to show any more offense than I already had.

I wiped my eyes.

Tears. He must have noticed. That's why he silenced me. Despite all I've done, he still treats me like a kid.

For some reason, I found myself smiling.

There was only one place left to go: home.

Once I arrived, I opened the door. She was standing just beyond the door. Before I knew it, her arms were holding me in a tight embrace.

"You shouldn't have run off without telling me. You worried me," she said, fixing my hair and dusting my *amip*. She noticed the cut. "What happened?"

I sat down on my mat. "I was attacked. Brother rescued me. Mom…." I wiped my tears. "He won't be coming home."

Her face contorted as she did her best not to cry. When she finally broke down, it came out as gurgled sobs.

It was my turn to comfort her.

I held her tightly and caressed her hair. I couldn't hold back my tears, but I stifled any sound that came out.

She was the babe now.

I found myself thinking back to my little bear cub, Noyuk.

Is that when it all went wrong?

I can't remember when I passed out, but I hope it was before mother did. I awoke the next morning.

I looked outside the window and saw some men gathered together.

They were the ones who were with brother!

With a sudden burst of energy I left my *chisei* and approached them. They were all alive, hardly wounded.

Why did they get to live and not him?

One of the men noticed me and signaled the others.

"What are you talking about, Isonash?" I asked, squeezing my way into their circle.

One of the men turned away. "We were so full of fury. We forgot our obligations to you. All of us ran off to kill the Isepo chief. At least two of us should have stayed behind. You were wounded and we left you."

"I needed to be alone. You did what had to be done," I said with newfound strength.

"It will not happen again. Two men at each side of your *chisei*, day and night. If you go out, we will escort you. And if—"

"Have you seen Eoha?"

"I do not know who that is." Isonash turned to the other men. They were equally confused.

"Of course you don't. My apologies. He is an outcast from the Isepo tribe. We met at Moyuk, the village of outcasts. He was the one who bandaged me up," I said, pointing to my wound.

"Ebuike, we have not seen him."

I froze up.

He couldn't be dead, could he?

"We have not informed the chief of the enemy alliance yet, but we will do so once he awakens. I recommend your friend stays away from this village. There is already suspicion toward the Isepo, and that will soon explode into hate once news of the alliance reaches our people. Right now we should all be care...." Isonash stopped mid-sentence.

Some men were rushing to the outskirts of the village. They were carrying spears.

The group of men I was talking to rushed ahead and I followed along.

At the foot of the hill we came to the source of the disturbance.

Eoha!

He was alive and well! He was also carrying something in an Isepo garment.

"Everyone, I am an outcast from the Isepo clan. I wish to join your tribe. May I speak with your chief?" asked Eoha, taking a step back once the spearmen approached.

"I am here," said the chief, coming up from behind me.

Eoha bowed. "Great *paunguru*. My name is Eoha. I offer up my allegiance to your tribe."

"Is he crazy?" "I don't trust him." "Could be a spy." Voices of ignorant men whispered gossip of suspicion.

The spearmen took another step toward Eoha.

I rushed in front of them, willing to get stabbed to keep him safe. "He is my friend. He saved my *ishu*."

The spearmen did not lower their weapons.

"What proof do you have that you are no longer a part of the Isepo?" asked the chief, having the spearmen step back once he approached.

Eoha opened up the garment and showed what was inside to the chief.

The chief's eyes widened.

I peeked over, getting an uncomfortably close look at the head of the youngest Isepo warrior.

The chief told Eoha to cover it up. He nodded to the spearmen. "We will welcome you into our tribe once the funeral ceremony is over. Come back tonight."

"My parents are still at the village. May they come too?"

"I will consider it," said the chief.

Eoha bowed, smiled at me, and then went into the forest.

"So you realize your people are the enemy now?" I asked.

"This head belonged to my friend. I found him fiercely wounded, but still alive. It was a mercy kill. Even in death he has helped me out. I thank him for helping me become welcomed into your village."

"He died attacking my brother. For all I know it was his spear that...."

My tears silenced me.

"Ebuike. You must lead the ceremony. Get some rest. We will start at sunset," said the chief before walking off.

Sunset came sooner than expected. I had gathered all of brother's *korobe* and placed them in a large box. I made sure everything, from the food to the placement of the hearth, was properly prepared for him.

I hope you're watching, brother.

As the people gathered, I placed some convolvulus roots near the fire to increase the heat.

Warmth is supposed to keep us from the coldness of death. But it couldn't do anything for him now. Nothing could.

The men came and brought his body—all dressed up in white—and placed it on the right side of the hearth.

Brother's flint, hunting knife, utensils, and cherished bow and arrow were placed at his side. A cup of boiled rice and some sake were placed near him so that he could take in their essence.

Brother was never much of a drinker.

I placed the *inao* around my brother's lifeless body. Even though it was time for me to speak, I froze up.

The chief noticed my hesitancy and spoke in my stead. "Atnep has left us. We gather here now to honor him and to bring his soul to the next world."

"We must burn away all his possessions so that he can move on, unattached," I said, unfolding his mat before tossing it in the fire.

After this is over, I won't be allowed to mention him. This is my last chance to share his story.

"Atnep was a rather difficult brother. He used to resent me because I was more attached to our second mom than our first. It's more than that...he blamed me for mother's death. I still loved him and I always admired his strength. But I thought he didn't love me. After I was banished, I think he realized how much he missed me. He had faith in me when I didn't, and he realized that I had nothing to do with mother's death. He came to bring me back home from banishment and on the way we finally connected. We were catching up on so many missed opportunities. He fought bravely till the very end. Atnep was one of the greatest warriors the Shitumbe have ever had. He was a great friend to so many. And even though I didn't realize it for many years, he was always a loving brother to me."

I kept my composure despite all the emotions swirling around inside me. "I beseech the goddess of fire to guide this spirit to the *kotan kara kamui*." I then began chanting.

Each trinket I tossed into the fire made me feel like I was losing another piece of him. I never thought his dirty bowl, his cup, and his other utensils would be so important to me. My hand shook as I tossed them in.

Brother's lifeless face was looking less familiar and more foreign by the second.

As I chanted, the ceremonial wine cup was passed around. Each person took a sip before offering three drops to my brother. Once the cup reached my lips, I could hardly see through my tears.

I closed my eyes, took a sip, gave him three drops, and offered the remainder of the wine to the *Abe Kamui*.

When the prayer and offerings were complete, two men wrapped my brother in a *toma* and attached his body to a pole. The men hoisted him up and began their journey to the spot where he was found.

The mourners, all women, followed in a single-file line, each bearing a small trinket to be buried along with him. The men, with spears raised, chanted *wool, wool, wool* all the way to the place he was killed.

When we arrived, the men smacked the surrounding area with their spears, chanting *wool, wool,* to scare off ill-intentioned spirits.

Brother was placed in the hole, still wrapped in the mat. The women broke the trinkets they brought with them and set them in the hole. The men then covered the hole with a slab of wood.

I turned away as my brother was buried under the dirt.

Despite all that happened, a part of me expected him to push off the mat and emerge from the pit.

Once the spear-like post was placed at the grave, with his headdress at the top, I had to accept it.

He was gone.

Not only was he gone, but I wouldn't even be permitted to visit this spot. Everyone would avoid it, avoid him. After all he's done for them, this tribe, and all he's done for me.

It isn't fair!

We returned to the village for *wen iku, wen ube*. After a funeral, the men would drink away their sorrows while the women wailed. Some of the mourners were faking, but some were genuinely shaken up by his loss. A few of brother's close friends gathered around to share tales of his bravery and of his *ishu* in general. Apparently he talked about me all the time and he looked up to me.

If I only I knew sooner. I can never gain back the lost time between us.

When the scent of sake became too strong for me, I prepared to leave. *Also, I didn't want to hear about brother killing a mother bear.*

Noticing I was sneaking away, the chief called everyone to attention. "I have important news to share." After he made sure everyone's eyes were fixed on him, he cleared his throat. "The Isepo have allied with the Horokeu, and the Isepo chief was killed by one of our own. We must stay vigilant at all times."

"Great chief, what is our plan of action?" I asked.

"We must be wary of our actions. The Horokeu are strong on their own, and the Isepo are clever. We cannot win a fight against both of them."

"Then I will lead a party to kill the Isepo's sub-chiefs. That will throw them in disarray."

"We cannot solve this problem with violence. If we fight, we will lose. We must try to negotiate with the Horokeu."

"They killed my brother!" I yelled. Noticing my outburst, I took a step back and lowered my head. "They poisoned our shaman."

Gasps and exclamations of horror erupted from the crowd.

"Ebuike, I have a responsibility to our people. I'd rather bow to the enemy than be annihilated by them."

"Please, chief, allow me and a small group to attack," said brother's closest friend.

"Absolutely not. We will not engage in combat unless we are attacked. The sub-chiefs and I have decided upon the proper course of action to take. I will leave in the morning to negotiate a treaty between us."

I couldn't listen anymore. I ran off, else I would have surely lost my composure.

The chief wants to befriend our enemies. Brother wanted every Isepo dead. I won't give up on his wish.

The next morning, Eoha was welcomed to our village—though not without some difficulty. Many of the men and women didn't trust him because he was once Isepo, but after showing them the head of an Isepo warrior, both him and his parents were welcomed in. The chief made sure each of them had a place before he left with a small group for negotiations. After wishing him a safe journey and making several offerings for his sake, I waved farewell to the chief and rushed to Eoha.

I was rather nervous when Eoha introduced me to his parents. They were very kind and rather fond of me. There were no doubts that Eoha already spoke with them about his plans to marry. At dinner the mother mentioned that my cooking skills would make me a great wife someday, and the father said he hopes his son will find a girl so beautiful.

After dinner, Eoha and I led them to their *chisei*—an elderly couple said that they were welcome to stay with them. Eoha and I went back to my home.

Finally, I had a chance to speak with him one-on-one.

I found myself in his arms before I realized it. "I missed you," I said, clenching him tightly.

"I am here now." He kissed my forehead.

"That Isepo warrior, did you kill him? What I mean is…were you possessed?"

"He had located us. I didn't have a choice. I don't regret it. Came out rather handy in the end."

"Did you know him?"

I immediately regretted asking the question once it left my lips.

Eoha broke the embrace and placed his hands on my shoulders. "I will do whatever I need to do in order to be with you."

I leaned in and kissed his lips.

"Have you thought about my proposal?" he asked, kissing my neck.

"Yes," I said, pulling back a bit while caressing his sides.

"And?" His warm hands touched my cheek.

"I need more time to think."

"Of course. You've been through so much," he said, holding me in his arms.

"Eoha, if there is a war, I want to fight. Will you fight with me?"

"The chief will do all he can to prevent a war."

"But there's no point! It's going to happen and likely in just a few years."

"Then we must prepare. I'll ask one of the men to train us."

"Good."

"Ebui, can I sleep with you tonight?"

"Please do," I said, grasping his hand.

How long before I lose him too?

Chapter 118: Union & Separation

The chief never came back. To make recompense for the killing of the Isepo chief, he gave up his life. The peace between our tribes was further maintained by giving up a portion of our harvest—fifteen percent to the Isepo and twenty-five percent to the Horokeu. We were no longer proud foxes. We had been reduced to beggars. My brother sought the Isepo's annihilation, and I wouldn't let anything get in the way of his wishes. Eoha and I trained to be great warriors. The peace treaty between the tribes went on for two long years, but the trees were growing. My prophecy was looming closer each day.

"Nice catch," said one of the men, referring to the way I had thrust my spear through a particularly large trout.

My mind flashed to the time I shot the squirrel with my brother, like it often did.

The old me was afraid of killing. That child didn't have the fortitude to do what had to be done for my people. With nearly half our harvest handed over as a peace offering, we did more gathering and, of course, more hunting as well. I was a woman now and a blooming warrior. I wasn't the only woman learning to hunt either. More and more were realizing that the treaty would not last.

I had become skilled at killing in such a short time. Each time I released an arrow or thrust my spear, I pictured the face of one of the men who killed my brother. It was a surefire way to remove any hesitation.

I looked into the pain in the fish's eyes. He flapped around, hoping by a miracle to escape the spear. But even if he did somehow escape the iron tip, he would surely die from blood loss.

I never did grow out of my paranoia. After any kill I would always remove the eyes of the victim, that way their spirit wouldn't recognize me.

"Are you sure you don't want any?" asked one of the men, scaling his most recent catch.

"The *moshiri ikkew kepp* is a trout on which every island resides. I don't want to anger him by eating his offspring," I said.

"If you don't want to kill them, you don't have to. We can reach our quota on our own," said one of the men.

"I must prepare each and every day for what is to come," I said, removing my catch's eyes before tossing him to one of the men.

"A storm will be coming soon. We should dock and wait it out," said Eoha, standing at the bow of our boat.

"A storm, after all the offerings you gave them?" asked one of the men.

"Perhaps I should offer more," said Eoha, starting to carve more *inao*.

329

"Why not? Though it seems *Shi-Acha* has been overtaking *Mo-Acha* this season," said one of the men.

"I don't think that's it. They're playing with us, the both of them. One wants to be revered and the other feared. The eldest *kamui* is no more evil than his younger brother," I said, glaring at the sky.

"*Mo-Acha* stops storms and makes sure we arrive safely. How is he as bad as the storm bringer? You should be careful what you say," said the man.

"I think *Mo-Acha* is the crueler of the two brothers. He gives us hope and then has his elder brother dash it to pieces. Besides, who's to say *Shi-Acha* isn't just trying to protect the *chep* from us?" I asked before obtaining another kill.

"That's right. To the Ainu, *Mo-Acha* is a guardian, but to the trout, *Shi-Acha* is a guardian. This world is a series of islands surrounded by one interconnected body of *aka*. Each island holds its own viewpoint. As do the fish, the bears, the Shitumbe, and the other tribes. Good and evil is just a matter of perspective," said Eoha, putting his arm around me.

He's wrong. The Isepo and the Horokeu are both evil. And they will both be dealt with.

We docked at the beach, near the forest surrounding our village.

"We're going to collect some berries. Carry on without us once the storm is done," said Eoha, grabbing my hand.

"Be careful and don't get near the border. We've lost four women to the Horokeu this season," said the man.

"We will stay vigilant." Eoha turned to me. "There isn't a storm coming, is there?"

"Maybe not," I said, connecting my fingers behind my back.

"You miss him, don't you?"

"I nodded."

Hand in hand we made it to brother's burial spot.

It was *hatto-an* to visit a burial site, but I wasn't afraid. Not because I had thought brother's spirit had already moved on. On the contrary, I felt safe because I could always feel his presence there.

"Hello brother. Sorry I haven't visited in a while. It's been difficult to break apart from the group. But now that I am here, I have good news. The men are getting restless. I doubt the peace treaty will last the rest of the season."

"Is that really what you want?" asked Eoha, looking at me with worry.

"It's what you want, isn't that right, brother? As you know, Eoha and I have been training a lot. I've heard killing a man is different than killing an animal, but in the end it's all about tearing through flesh and bone. And most *chikoikip* are cleverer than the Horokeu, so I'm not too worried. Of course, I'll be careful. But I'm getting a bit restless myself. Hopefully the chief will end the treaty soon. I promise, when the time comes, their blood will be spilt. The forest will be washed in it, and then the Shitumbe can be free. Sorry I can't stay for long, but the others are already a bit suspicious. I know it's been so long, but soon you'll be able to rest."

"I will keep your sister safe. I will fulfill my promise to you," said Eoha with a bow.

"Farewell for now, brother." I grabbed Eoha's hand and rushed down to the lake.

He was so handsome.

Eoha had grown in the last two years but still had a rounded childish face. His arms were muscular, though not like brother's were. Black hair went over the left side of his face like a quarter moon, giving him a mysterious charm. Most importantly, his amber eyes gazed at me with love and respect. They didn't mirror his carefree spirit like they used to.

We stripped down and washed each other in the cool water. "You don't really think we're contaminated by his spirit, do you?"

Eoha smiled. "I don't, but it's always good to be careful. Spirits have powerful energy."

I turned around and kissed him. "Is that the only reason?"

"I'd be a fool to miss an opportunity to wash you," said Eoha.

We got out of the bath, and he beat my back with *inao* to dispel any negative energy still clinging to me. Once finished, he handed me the *inao* and turned around.

He has such a cute butt.

Once we were sure the other was clean, we dressed each other.

"As beautiful as ever, *chiri-po*," he said, his arm over my shoulder.

I looked into the lake and gazed at my reflection.

I was still shorter than him, though the difference was almost negligible now. I proudly wore the dress my mother made, which displayed my devotion to my tribe with an embroidered Shitumbe pattern. My long brown *attush*, made from the inner bark of elm trees, was held together with shells–one of which was given to me by my beloved. My hair came out from beneath my headdress. It was long and flowing, defiantly branching out in multiple directions. The sooty, dark blue tattoo mark around my lips was accentuated by my rosy cheeks. My blue eyes sparkled like the stars in the night sky. The beaded necklace my mother made me kept me from ever feeling lonely. The special charm, attached to a second necklace, was given to me by Eoha for my protection and as part of a promise two years ago.

"Only a few more cycles now," he said, jiggling my charm and caressing my hair.

"Yeah, it's getting hard to hold back," I said, leaning into him.

Eoha blushed and nodded.

So cute.

"You sure made it difficult," he said with a smirk.

He was right. I did.

About half a year after the chief left to negotiate, Eoha finally got me to accept. It was on the day of the bear sacrifice, no less. He proposed to me once the bear cub had been taken out to be killed. I was shocked at the time, but with such a large crowd I couldn't say no. I don't even know why it took me so long to agree. Anyways, after proposing, he told Noyuk's story. After hearing about my love for the little bear and to celebrate our future union, the bear cub was set free. Many of the girls and some of the women even protested against the cruelty of such a ceremony, though the men weren't as understanding. I had never been so moved by Eoha before. Sometimes I wonder if he's too good for me.

We returned to the village.

A man came up to us. He informed us of the situation and led us to the *chisei*.

Eoha's father was pale in the face.

"Father, when did you start feeling ill?" asked Eoha.

"A few days ago. I didn't think anything of it at the time," said the patient, his face a bit pale.

"He has been cursed," I said softly.

A few months ago, Eoha's father was cursed. We couldn't locate the culprit, but it was likely one of the men who still refuses to accept him. What's strange is there were quite a few cases of others trying to curse me, yet I haven't been plagued by illness since I returned from the village of outcasts. The *kamui* have other plans for me, it seems.

Eoha and I worked together to drive away the curse and within only a few days the father had recovered. Working along with our close friends, we tracked down the perpetrator.

We placed some wine at the East end of the *chisei* for our ancestors and headed out.

Four men were each holding a string attached to a fox skull. When there are multiple culprits, the *shitumbe marapto* or ceremony of the fox, is the preferred way of determining the perpetrator. Each man pulled a string. The one responsible, made apparent by the skull's jaw falling facedown, was promptly tied up.

I was surprised it was Isonash. I thought when he warned me not to bring Eoha here, he was concerned for his safety. Then again, he was even more open about killing the Isepo than I was. He was a close friend to my brother and blames the Isepo for his death. After his wife vanished near the border, he has been doing all he could to rally the others to break the treaty. He had already been beaten with a club for his first offense: being caught near Eoha's parents' home after dark.

Such a shame. He could have been useful.

His arm was placed in boiling water. I never heard a man scream so loud.

"Let's go," said Eoha, grabbing my arm.

"He caused harm to your father. Don't you want to watch him receive judgment?"

"I do not. Why do you, Ebui? Us watching won't change his sentence. Father is safe," said Eoha.

"He'll curse your father again unless he learns his lesson. I want to make sure he has a change of heart."

The man screamed as the heated stone was placed in his hands. If his hands were burnt, that would prove his guilt. Then he would have to confess. If he is lucky he won't get banished, but considering this is his second offense, I'm pretty sure we won't be seeing him again.

"I'm going to see how the harvest is doing," said Eoha, walking away.

I chased after him. "Did I upset you?"

Eoha cleared his throat. "That man is a Shitumbe; he isn't our enemy."

"Anyone who threatens my family is my enemy. How can you be so forgiving?"

Eoha's father and I had gotten rather close. He was like a second father to me. Our mothers got along too.

"You've changed so much. I don't think your brother would want to see how vengeful you've become."

"He is still here because I haven't fulfilled my promise to him. My brother won't move on until all of them are dead."

"He's watching over you. That's why he is staying."

"You don't know him like I do."

"The Isepo will be coming in a few weeks. If you wear your hatred of them on you, they will notice. Our marriage can mend the tension between the two clans. We must be careful of our thoughts just as much as our actions," said Eoha, placing his arm around me.

"I don't want peace."

"I know. But let's make it last as long as it can," he said, kissing my forehead.

I turned away from him, unable to agree.

Two weeks came and went. After much preparation and anticipation, the day of our wedding had arrived. It was three days after I turned sixteen. I already felt like a woman, but the marriage added a new layer of purpose to my growth. My mother prepared me a special soup in the morning. After breakfast, Eoha's mom and my mother dressed me up.

On the way to the ceremony, I saw a young boy scaring away a crow. "Go away, it's my bread," he said with a grimace.

I bent down to the child. "You should not complain about any living being. They all have a purpose."

"What purpose? All they do is steal from us."

"The crows take what they have earned. It was a crow that flew into the Nitne Kamui's mouth to save the sun."

"Yeah, yeah, but what about mosquitoes? They're a total nuisance," said the boy.

"Be wary of what you say. Mosquitoes only take a little bit of blood. Hobgoblins take blood, flesh, and bone. You should not complain about such small problems."

The boy crossed his arms. "Okay."

"The evil one spoke of the bramble bush being superfluous, and then his tongue was eaten by a rat. We must be respectful."

The boy nodded with some hesitancy. "You're right."

"I'm sure you'll make a great mother," said the boy's mom.

"Thank you," I said, with a blush.

I love children, but I could never be a mother. What if my child was taken from me? Or what if they were born with the same burden of dark premonitions?

"You look *shiretok*." I turned around to see Eoha all dressed up for the ceremony. Just like me, he had a new garment specifically embroidered for this occasion.

Mother joined me and together we distributed the millet and rice cakes we had made the other day. Eoha and his father gave out the rice wine. We then joined in the center and held hands.

"My son has found his other half. His bride is so beautiful and intelligent. As his father, I couldn't be happier. The two of them will surely bring about great change." Eoha's father stepped up to his son. "I present the groom with the family *aumshup*, passed down for eight generations." He handed him an antique bow, complete with a quiver full of bamboo-tipped arrows.

Eoha bowed to his father.

Shitumbe and Isepo both cheered.

The Isepo men seemed so calm and good natured. No. I know what they have done and what they will do to my people.

I noticed a small Isepo girl hoisted on her mother's shoulder.

They have a family. Should I really wipe them out?

My mother touched my shoulder, bringing me back to my senses. She placed grandmother's earrings in my hands.

Orange and shaped like a curled up fox. They were so cute.

It was usually the shaman's job to make the *inao*, but since we were the ones being married, the men of the Shitumbe and Isepo prepared them beforehand.

Eoha and I offered the *inao* to many deities, asking for their permission.

Would the gods allow for the ceremony to complete? Would they really let me find happiness? If so, how long before it would be taken from me?

Once the offerings were completed, we came back to the center.

"Ebui, I first noticed you when I saw your face. But I fell in love when I saw how much you cared for that little bear. You're the light of my *ishu*. You saved me when I was banished, you gave me a home, and most importantly, you returned my love. This is the most memorable moment of my life. You are my bride forevermore."

"Eoha, you fought to save Noyuk, my little boy. I may have nursed you back to health, but you've freed me from my curse. This is a prophecy we made together, and I hope that it is only the start of many more miracles. You are now my husband. I'll never leave your side."

I placed my head against his chest and he held me dearly.

Songs, dancing, wine, and revelry filled the rest of the night. After finishing my meal with my new family, I grabbed my husband's hand. The main ceremony was completed, so Eoha and I got up, bowed to the chiefs and left.

Once inside the cabin we became locked in a passionate kiss. I stripped him down as he stripped me, rejoining to kiss the moment our garments were removed.

My hands moved up his sides.

He grabbed me and laid me on the mat. His kisses traveled up my thighs all the way to my neck.

The gentle kisses sent surges of passion through my body.

He rubbed my thighs as our noses pressed together. "We did it, *chiri-po*. We created our own future." A loving *chopchose* was placed on my forehead.

"I've figured it out." My hands went up his sides and caressed his chest. "This is the promise you made him. If he was going to entrust me to you, he needed you to marry me. Brother wanted to make sure you were serious about your feelings for me. That's why you were so pushy, wasn't it?" I asked, fiddling around with his ear.

Eoha smiled and lowered himself so he was lying at my side. "That isn't it, Ebui. I promised that I would convince you to bear a child." His placed his hand just below my belly.

Of course! I should have figured it out sooner!

"It would be irresponsible of me to have a child," I said, turning away.

"I would never force you to do something you were uncomfortable with. Your brother knew how much you love children, and he wanted to prove you aren't cursed. I didn't even bother to bring it up because we hadn't married yet. This marriage was a prophecy we created. Now that it has come to fruition, we can start a new prophecy," he said, caressing my hair.

I do want a child. I've looked forward to being a mother for so long.

"What if something bad happens?" I asked softly.

"You don't have to be afraid. If you want a child, then you should have one. You deserve it, Ebui. The *kamui* won't deny you lasting happiness. Our marriage proves this, does it not?"

I turned to him, tears welling up in my eyes. "Don't you see? They want to give me hope before taking it all away. They only permitted our union so they could break us apart. If by some miracle I become pregnant, then it will bring about either my own end or the demise of our child."

Eoha held me tightly. "There's always a chance of that happening, but wouldn't you rather take the chance than regret not doing so your whole life? I want to raise a family with you. I want to prove that we can both be happy."

"It will end as a tragedy. I just know it."

"When was the last time you had a grim prophecy?"

"Two years ago," I said softly.

"Exactly. The stars have shifted. We are free to forge our own path."

"We are not. The village will soon burn. Nothing can stop it."

Eoha grabbed my hand. "We will deal with that if and when it comes up. When we dwell on negative things we give them power. Why not think positive thoughts instead."

"Whenever I hope for a future, that's when things fall apart."

"Our marriage was a success," he said, kissing my hand.

"Yeah."

"I've told you my feelings. But I can't change yours. This is something we must both agree on. Would you like to get some rest?"

He's so sweet.

"I want to be with you," I said with a smile.

He kissed me deeply.

I love him so much.

"We don't need children to be happy. Perhaps you should become a teacher. After all, you don't need to birth a child in order to be a mother. We can take in one of the orphans. Perhaps that is best," he said, rubbing his nose against my cheek.

"Yes, that sounds wonderful."

"You are so very beautiful."

I gripped his sides. "But I want two kids." I peeked up at him with a reluctant smile.

"We can adopt two."

I pressed up against him. "I want one child to come from our union."

Eoha blushed bright red. "Are you sure?"

Despite all my worries, I nodded.

Side by side we joined together. We moved as one.

"Wait. It hurts a bit," I said, slightly pulling out.

It didn't hurt at all. It felt amazing. I'm still a bit worried, that's all.

"Whenever you are ready," he said, combing a lock of hair away from my eyes.

I took a deep breath. "Okay. I'm ready."

Eoha gripped my sides and turned us so that I was on top of him. "Take it at your own pace."

I kissed his cheek.

Was it too late to quit? Maybe I should tell him to stop.

"Creation is an act that takes two. If only the woman or man made children, they would be no different than that parent. It is the melding of two bodies, two minds that becomes something wholly unique. Without uniqueness, it is not creation. If you are worried, then we can stop. If we do make a child, I want that moment to be full of love and passion, and free of doubt."

"I love you," I said softly, gazing into his eyes.

"I love you too," he said with a blissful smile.

I moved my body up and down. The two of us squirmed around until his hopes burst inside me. We lay in each other's arms, kissing until we fell asleep.

That night we made a new prophecy for a better future. I went to sleep hoping that the *kamui* wouldn't interfere with our happiness.

Chapter 119: Loss & Emptiness

We decided to wait on adopting until we had our first child. That way we could have both a boy and a girl. Four months passed and I fell ill, despite having a protective *chikappo*.

All the charms in the world couldn't keep me safe.

My husband found an effigy of me placed upside-down in a hole by the east end of the village. Someone wanted me gone. Even after the effigy was removed, I didn't recover.

There were quite a number of men who opposed Eoha's union with me, so it took some time before the suspect was found. It was four days into my illness, after my husband and I took a bath in the lake near my brother's grave post, when my *amip* were stolen. My husband tracked down the perpetrator, retrieved my clothes—which thankfully hadn't been cut—and brought him in for judgment and punishment.

My illness worsened despite the source of it being uprooted. Two weeks later, my water broke.

My husband rushed to my side. Considering how soon it was, we both knew the baby wouldn't make it. My husband held my hand and sang to me.

"The bunny was lost in the rain. Lost in the rain…."

After singing me the song I once sang to him, my husband informed me of the recent developments. The other tribes increased the amount they usually confiscated from our harvest. Eoha told me this with a concerned look. As for me, well, I couldn't hide my smile. This was what was necessary to push the Shitumbe to fight back. My only hope was that I would be in good health before war was declared. I looked forward to the day I would be back on my feet and cutting down Horokeu and Isepo alike.

Four days later, the illness had passed.

My husband sat by my side at dinner-time. "Ebui, I can't express my regret over what happened."

It was strange. I know he meant what he said, but he was so relieved I had recovered that he was smiling at the time.

I grabbed his hand. "It was our decision."

"Either way, our child is lost…and I almost lost you," he embraced me and cried against my shoulder.

"Just promise you'll trust me next time. If we try again, it will just end up the same."

"Miscarriages happen. This has nothing to do with a curse."

"You have no way of knowing that," I said with a firm tone.

"Did you have a vision?" he asked softly.

I turned away. "No. I didn't."

No doubt if I had tried to see the future, I would have known my child would die.

My eyes shrank.

Even without trying to see my future, prophesized events still occur. I cannot escape this curse.

"If you didn't, then they are unrelated," said Eoha.

"Are you certain?" I asked, my gaze intensifying.

"It matters not. Both of us agree that trying again would put you at risk. Take it easy, and perhaps in a few days we can pick out a child from the orphans."

"No. After what happened, I cannot. I will not tie anyone else to my fate."

"Bearing a child was supposed to break you free from paranoia," cried Eoha.

"Instead I hope it brings you to accept reality. There is no way for me to escape misfortune. I'm not allowed to be happy," I said.

"Get some rest, *chiri-po*. I must attend the meeting to discuss our village's next course of action."

That night I dreamt of a *kunne* cave, screams, and blood.

In three days I had fully recovered from my illness. Things between the Shitumbe and the two tribes had reached the tipping point. Young men were being trained for battle. In the dark of night, the men would gather. The chief seemed unaware, or perhaps he knew there was nothing he could do to stop it. One night I came into the room full of men.

The men stood at attention. "Great shaman. What are you doing here?" they asked, one of them casually putting away the war plans.

"I am here on behalf of the *paunguru*. Your actions could bring about a war," I said, walking to one of the men and seizing the plans.

"The elder does not know what is best for the village. His fixation with peace will bring about our destruction," said the shortest of the men.

"You best watch your tongue and show *uainu* to your elders. After all, they may be the great Okikurumi in disguise," I said, overlooking the plans.

None of it made sense to me. I wasn't sure what tribe was which symbol. I assumed the pointed shapes were archers, but even that was just a guess.

"Perhaps that's the problem. Okikurumi founded all the tribes, not just our own," said one of the men under his breath.

"He no longer sees things as we do. His ascension has left him blinded by our plight. Despite him having the best intentions, he has led us down a path of ruin," I said.

"We are in agreement. What is the problem then?" asked the leader.

"I want in on these meetings, and I want to be trained in the art of warfare."

"Absolutely not. You are our *tusu-guru*; you are far too important to be risked in battle."

"If we don't win, then we'll all be killed. War makes everyone into equals," I said, picking up a spear that was leaned against the wall.

"I know you've been hunting with us, but this is different," said the tall man.

"Let me prove myself," I said, gripping the spear with both hands.

"You are not your brother," said the leader.

"Three men. All I ask for is three men to accompany me to the caves. I will slay a bear. That will prove I am capable of fighting our enemies," I said.

"And if you fail, we will be left with only one shaman," said the leader.

"I've seen past that moment. In my vision, I stood alongside the men, cutting down a treacherous Isepo spearman."

I hadn't really had that vision, but they didn't need to know that.

"Even so—"

"If I die, then my premonition was incorrect and I would have been worthless to my people as a shaman. I will not fail," I said, staring into the leader's eyes with my brother's strength.

"I'll go. Who else will come along?" asked the leader.

My hunting captain stepped up, as did one of his subordinates.

"Tell the chief it is time to prepare for another bear ceremony," said the leader.

"How wonderful. All the tribes will come to attend." I handed the leader the plans. "It will certainly be an unforgettable day."

He smiled at me. "We leave first thing in the morning. Get some rest, men," said the leader.

I nodded and went back to my *chisei*, cuddled up to Eoha, and fell asleep.

When the sun rose I snuck out, careful not to wake my husband.

Even when sleeping he is so handsome. I hope he doesn't worry too much when he can't find me.

The men were just outside the western entrance to the village. They were playing *ukara*.

The leader's back was hit sixteen times with a club. He raised his hand, signaling the man to stop. Once he noticed me, I saw a slight smile form on his face. "Come, join us."

"Isn't that a game for men?" I asked.

"It's for warriors," he said, hitting his chest with a firm fist.

Most of the men snickered and whispered as I stepped up.

The leader raised his club to my back and struck it seven times. I knew he was holding back, and I was impressed at how he hit so softly while appearing to hit hard. Even so, it hurt a lot. As he pulled back for the eighth, I raised my hand.

"Seven hits. Not bad," he said, slugging my arm.

One of the men, likely with a lower score, stepped up. "You weren't hitting at full force."

"Is that so? Come up and see for yourself," he said, raising the club.

The man smiled awkwardly and stepped back.

I approached the leader. "Why are there six? I said I only needed three."

"As long as you're the one who makes the kill, you've proven yourself. The more men there are, the less likely any of us will die. Follow me."

With me staying behind, the hunters received the chief's *inunuke*. After they met up with me, we asked protection from the gods: for the mountains to lead us and for the river to carry us safely, as well as for the spring to nourish us, and the fire to keep us warm. We then ventured into the forest. The trek to the mountain took three days and another to scale it. At each rest spot we paid tribute to the local deities. When it was my shift for night watch, the leader would always join me. He was so fascinated by my stories. I had assumed men like him were only interested in bragging about their exploits. His calm but powerful demeanor kept me at ease. And hearing about the times he took down a bear helped prepare me for what was to come. Despite this, I froze up when we arrived at the bear's den.

"Stay focused," he said, bringing me back with a touch to my shoulder.

I pressed my feet deep into the snow, trying to find some firm footing.

The leader signaled two men to get on each side of the cave and prod it with their spears. Since the bear did not come out, the leader smoked it out with a torch.

Big bear.

It was even bigger when it stood up on its hind legs.

Here I am, doing something I know is wrong and dangerous. But I'll do what I have to.

One of the men jabbed his spear at the bear. With a single whack, the spear snapped. Another whack and the man was on the ground with blood spilling out from his garments.

I raised my bow and fired the poisoned-tipped arrow into the bear's neck.

I know it was typical for bear hunts, but, using poison made me feel awful. My father was poisoned by the Horokeu, and I always saw it as a tool for cowards.

One of the men rushed behind the bear, grabbed the spear he left on the ground and pierced the bear's back.

The spear bore fairly deep before the man holding it lost his grip and fell down.

The leader rushed at the bear with a small knife, howling at it to give it even the slightest intimidation.

I fired an arrow at its side before his dagger pierced its chest. He ripped the dagger out and leaped back, just barely dodging a swipe aimed at his head. One of the men who plunged his spear into its belly was not so lucky. A single strike to the head snapped the man's neck. His face contorted into a gruesome display of pain.

This was what war was like. Alive one moment, dead the next. Crucial decisions and moments of instinctual insight. It could end right here. Then I wouldn't have to see the village burn. But it would still burn, and my brother's spirit would linger.

I raised my bow and fired another shot, and another, and another. I had gotten the bear's attention.

The leader sliced the bear's side, causing blood to gush out.

I dropped my bow.

A swipe to the head, my neck twisted, and I fall dead.

I never expected to have a premonition like this, in a moment of life and death.

I ducked the inevitable swipe and plunged my dagger into the bear's throat.

The leader, along with the other men, pierced it from behind.

The bear wailed in pain, crying like a child before falling over dead.

There was no cheering. The men rushed to their fallen comrades. One was gravely injured and the other clearly dead. It took me a moment to recognize him. It was the one who taught Eoha and I how to *emoni*. Of course he would be the one to die.

Seems my curse is still alive.

It didn't bother me. I didn't feel much of anything. I wasn't sad or angry. It wasn't even that I expected him to die. I guess after losing so many, he had just become another. Besides he was a hunter, killing was his *ishu*. It seemed unfair to feel sorry for him.

The leader and the men turned the bear over, said their prayers, and began carving. Once the bear was skinned, I offered *inao* to the gods.

What gods were protecting the bear from us? Do bears give praise when they successfully defend their homes from invaders?

Many questions bounced in my head as I paid tribute.

"You've earned this," said the leader, handing me the bear's head.

"I don't want that. I want to be trained as a soldier, that's all."

"You've proven yourself worthy. The one who deals the final blow receives the head and—"

"We all made the kill. Are there cubs inside?" I asked, walking past the eating men.

Four small bears came out from the cave. They went to their downed mother and solemnly licked her wounds.

I wiped my tears and took a deep breath. "We should take the oldest one," I said, my voice cracking.

The leader and three men tied up the largest of the cubs, and we began our journey home.

That night, the leader and I kept watch. I was hoping for a confrontation. Poison arrows were best used against the Horokeu, anyway.

"I knew those men very well," he said in a gentle voice I wasn't aware he was capable of making.

"*Chishirikisap.*"

"You knew Raiochi as well."

"Yeah, I did," I said, trying to sound sad.

"Yet you are unfazed by his loss."

"I've grown accustomed to it."

He placed his hand on mine. "You are unlike any woman. You have power, skill, intelligence, and beauty."

I pulled my hand away. "And I have a loving husband."

Is this why he agreed to my terms? To swoon me?

"Haha. It is common for a man to have many wives. But it is unheard of for a shaman to be a woman. You broke a tradition. Perhaps we can break another." His hand climbed up my side.

I grabbed his arm and glared at him. "I'm not interested."

"A shame. The women in our village are too timid for me. Either too timid or too talkative. Are you sure?"

"Last night I had a vision of a man who was too pushy. He grabbed a woman in the dark and was poisoned by an arrow."

"Okay. I understand. Oh well, I suppose I'll have to keep searching."

That night I realized just how much I missed Eoha. There isn't a single man I'd rather be around.

But the more I love him, the more likely he is to die.

We made it back to the village and shared the meat in silence.

When one of our own dies, there is no retelling of the adventure, the feast is done in mourning. Supposedly the *ibehe* loses its flavor, but it tasted the same to me.

Eoha saw me and met me with a warm embrace.

"I missed you too," I said, kissing his cheek.

"What were you thinking?"

"I wanted to be a warrior."

"You could have been killed."

I lifted my shirt and turned around. "No injuries, see?"

"What are you planning to do at the bear ceremony?"

How did he figure me out?

"I'm not sure I follow."

"The Horokeu and the Isepo will be there. What are you planning to do?"

"Nothing," I said with a shrug.

It was true. I didn't quite have a plan of action yet. I wanted to discuss things with the other men. Judging by the size of the cub, the ceremony would take place in a month. It was more than enough time to figure out how to deal with my enemies.

My village will burn and many will die. I'll just have to make sure more of them die than us.

Chapter 120: Fire & War

I went through intensive training for several months. I became a full-fledged warrior, though still a fresh one. Before I knew it, the day of the bear ceremony had arrived. I had discussed my plans with my allies in advance. I also made sure to mix the poisons properly. Getting the balance right so it would kill, but not immediately, was very tricky.

The ceremony started out as usual. It pained me to watch it. But I would only have a chance to deliver the poisoned drinks after the bear cub was killed. Even more than the abuse of the bear cub, it was the anticipation of seeing the enemy chiefs dying that made me restless.

The little bear cried out for its mother as it died.

Shut up! Just go away already!

I hated the wretched sounds it made.

I passed out the wine and watched, though not in a suspicious manner, as the chiefs of both the Horokeu and the Isepo emptied the cups.

After the food was finished, one of the chiefs stood up. He said he was tired and wanted to rest here for the night. Our chief gladly agreed.

As the Horokeu chief walked to his temporary abode, he collapsed.

It wasn't supposed to happen this soon.

A Horokeu shaman went to his fallen chief's side. The color in his face died out.

Before he could say 'poison' we attacked.

Grabbing our hidden spears we rushed at the enemy.

I rammed my spear into a Horokeu and kept pushing till it pierced through an Isepo.

This is for my brother!

Twelve men and I took out thirty-three enemies in a rush of adrenaline.

"Ebui, stop!" yelled Eoha.

The tip of my spear was resting in the chest of an Isepo woman.

I saw the fear in my victim's eye and froze up. She was indeed Horokeu, but all I saw was a terrified woman.

One of the men finished what I had started. "We cannot let them flee!" After finishing off one of the women, he rushed into a group of four that were sprinting to the trees for safety.

They were all killed in a matter of seconds.

I turned and wretched.

Every one of them must die. Why am I feeling this way?

"Tie up the shaman. We can use him to bargain back our freedom," said the leader.

Eoha picked me up and took me back to our cabin. "Why did you do this?"

"The fire will happen. Our people will be killed and our village will burn. I can't stop my premonitions from happening, but I can make sure they happen on my terms."

"They will retaliate and soon. Pack up tonight. I won't lose you to this war. We leave in the morning."

"You want me to abandon my people?"

"By inciting war, you've already abandoned your people! The Shitumbe will be wiped out. We must go to Moyuk. We'll be safe there."

"I'm not afraid of death."

"How would your brother feel if you died?"

"How would he feel if I fled? I will stay and fight."

"You will be killed."

"Then I die a warrior."

Eoha embraced me. "Please, Ebui…."

"You should go. This was my premonition and my plan. I'll handle the consequences."

"I'm staying." Eoha kissed my cheek.

"Okay."

With our chief having fled, the new chief decided everyone must be trained to fight. Every able-bodied man, woman, and child found a weapon they could handle and learned to wield it. When they attacked, we would be ready.

One, then two, then four weeks passed, and no word from our enemy. We stayed focused.

The day they would come to collect our harvest was in three days. That night, I heard a horrible noise.

"Wool! Wool!" chanted a man.

The smell of smoke filled the air.

I looked outside my window.

I saw Eoha fighting an Isepo spearman before the battle went beyond my field of vision.

I rushed out of my *chisei*, not even thinking of grabbing a weapon. As I came to help, I caught a glimpse of Eoha's eyes. They were cold and vacant. He sliced through three enemies and sped into another group.

I was caught up in a night raid. Fire, bodies pierced with bamboo-tipped arrows—the prophesized catastrophe had arrived. Bows, sticks, stones, clubs, men fighting men, women fighting women, even children picking up what they could find to attack other children—it was all-out war.

This would not end until one side was completely wiped out.

Just as I picked up a spear, I heard children. They were screaming. The little ones had been trapped inside a burning building. The homes would burn in very little time. I had to hurry.

I am their shaman.

I rushed into my home, which was already starting to catch fire and grabbed my staff as well as a raccoon skull.

Teacher, guide me.

There was only one way to put the flames to rest. I had to call the rain, and with Eoha possessed, I had to perform the *shiriwen hokki marapto* ceremony alone. I prayed to the goddess of fire, the *kamui* of the river and springs. While praying to a raccoon skull, I thought of Moyuk village.

I never should have left.

I prayed more as I offered libations to the skull and dripped water over myself. Despite all my efforts it did not rain.

Was the great kamui taking the sides of our attackers? No. Impossible. The dreaded Nitne Kamui must have deceived the kamui into going against the chief kamui himself. The Dark One is winning the heavenly war.

"Take this!" The leader of the bear hunt tossed me a spear. I grabbed it and pierced it through a woman who was coming at me with a sharpened stick.

She was dead. I killed her.

I had to keep killing to survive. The women came after me, one of them firing an arrow into my side.

Eoha came into view, spears and arrows in his back.

It didn't seem real.

He moved as if he wasn't injured. The wounds were deep. I had to help him.

I rushed to him, almost getting speared by him once I got too close. "It's me, your little flower bud." I was breaking down into tears.

He charged into more enemies.

Three men came at me at once. I parried the first strike, but the second pierced my arm. My spear was pulled from my grip, and I was pinned down before I could grab any arrows.

Whack!

My head exploded with pain and I fell unconscious.

I awoke, breathing intensely.

Was it all a dream?

The *chisei* I was in…it didn't feel like home.

A figure entered.

Horokeu.

I pushed my back against the wall and looked for some kind of weapon.

"The battle is over." He smiled at me.

"Eoha. Where is he?" I asked, my body trembling.

"Your people brought this on themselves, you know. The Isepo came to us, seeking to unite all the tribes. We despised your people, but the Isepo were very convincing. We set up peace negotiations to be held after the bear feast."

"And that's when you poisoned our shaman."

"Wrong. It was one of your own who did it. They didn't want peace between the tribes. They wanted war."

Brother wouldn't do that. Not ever.

"You have no proof. He had no motive."

"You know him well. He would not accept peace. I didn't want it either. Besides, with the shaman dead, your village would have to welcome you back. His hatred of us and love of you brought him to kill one of his own. And it ended up with your people destroyed."

It all makes sense. Why does it make sense?

"You used poison. You must have."

"The Horokeu are proud warriors. Our two tribes have fought for many generations. We never once used poison against your people."

"That's a lie! Father was killed by a poison arrow."

"Your father was killed by an arrow, but it wasn't poisoned."

"How would you know?"

"I was the one who fought him."

I rushed at the man, digging my nails into his throat before he pressed me to the ground. "Be careful. If you act out, the captive people of your tribe will be put to rest."

I stared at him defiantly. "Your people enslaved us. That was the outcome you wanted, isn't it?"

"After the Isepo chief was murdered, we tried to convince the Isepo to wipe you out. They refused. Instead they decided that we each take a portion of your crops. If we kept you suppressed, there would be no need for your annihilation. But your people spit at our offer and killed both of our chiefs."

Is this how the world is. One is seen as evil and the other as good. Eoha was right. There is no good and no evil. Eoha! He has to be alive.

"Tell me! Where is he?" I broke down into tears.

The man had the audacity to place his hand on my shoulder. "The women and children who survived are working in our gardens." His honeyed voice twisted my stomach. "The men of your village have all gone away."

Gone.

I didn't cry. I couldn't. Emptiness took over me. I could not will myself to move.

"You should be grateful. I won't make you slave away in the fields. You can't be a shaman anymore, but you will be my wife." He leaned down and grabbed my face.

Nothing feels real anymore.

Days went by, all meaningless. With Eoha gone, I decided to go into mourning. When my captor was away on a journey, I shaved my head with a sharpened shell.

The pain was welcoming. It was my punishment for cursing my people.

The Shitumbe were no more. All my fault.

When my captor returned, he found me in a widow's bonnet and dressed in black.

He sat down and cleaned the cuts on my head.

I hope my curse takes his life.

I sat in silence.

After three days of silence, he brought me teacher's staff.

I tossed it into the hearth and watched it burn.

Never again will I speak to the gods. Even the goddess of fire had betrayed me.

My captor took me out for a celebration feast once the memorial rituals were over.

I zoned in and out of consciousness periodically.

A young woman tried to speak to me, but I heard nothing.

Time lost its hold over me.

My captor dressed me up for the coming bear festival. There were Horokeu and Isepo attendees, as well as *ainu* whose garments I was unfamiliar with. I turned away once the bear cub was brought out.

I can't watch him die.

In a daze I stood up and placed my body over the bear cub.

Please, let me just save one life.

My captor lifted me up and pulled me aside.

"If you stop it, if you save him, I'll do anything for you," I said in tears.

He approached the chief and spoke on my behalf.

It was all for naught.

The little bear screamed as he died.

In the end I was unable to change anything. It was all meaningless.

That night my captor took me out to the lake. His words did not reach me. *Nothing did.*

He cooked and we ate together. He complimented me and slowly undressed me. His fingers felt cold as they touched me.

Eoha, I miss you.

I pulled back and cried.

I slept alone that night.

One day there was great panic. The sun had been swallowed up by the moon.

Men and women both were screaming "The luminary is dying!" "The sun is dying!"

This was it, a total eclipse. The end of all life.

My dreams of complete darkness may have been premonitions after all.

At this point, I welcomed the darkness to come. I wanted it to swallow up the whole world.

Men tossed *aka* in the air, pleading "*Kamui atemka.*" "*Kamui atemka.*"

They were powerless in reviving the sun god.

I will end it myself. The longer I postpone my destiny, the greater the pain it will bring.

I walked out of the village and ventured into the forest. I found a cliff and dropped down.

The kamui can no longer control me. I'm free.

The entire world was consumed in darkness.

Chapter 121: The Mirror World

The flashback ended. The Freedom Forcers slowly associated back into reality.

Etaf stared at them, unfazed by her own strife. "If you don't have any questions, we can proceed."

Napkin rubbed against her leg, trying to comfort his dear friend.

"You poor thing!" Ada rushed up and hugged the troubled woman.

"Losing someone you love. It hurts so much," said Kaity, wiping away a few tears.

"You fought bravely to fulfill a promise to your brother. I have nothing but respect for you," said Kanasta with a salute.

"I should have figured out he was behind the poisoning. I was so foolish back then," said Etaf.

"The harsh events you went through robbed you of your childhood. You were so cute before," said Deceivant with a frown.

"It must feel good to share your pain with us," said Image.

"That's not why I'm doing this," said Etaf bluntly.

"I think we should help Lum. Etaf will be lonely if we don't. Don't worry, we can all be your friends," said Opti.

"Yeah, I think so too," said D.S.

"We shouldn't be so hasty," said Nina.

"Indeed," said Atlas.

"That story was very entertaining. I want to hear what happens next. I'm sure there are even more surprises to come," said Crisis.

"Agreed. I'm genuinely curious. How did someone as dark as you become a Lum goddess?" asked Hope.

"I'll show you," said Etaf, raising her sword and re-initiating her flashback.

Total darkness. I awoke in a daze.

Am I alive?

In front of me was a tunnel. I went into it, not sure what lay beyond.

I soon realized where I was. This place was the *Pokna Moshiri*, the intermediary zone where spirits can mingle. I noticed some familiar spirits as I journeyed deeper.

No point in staying. They will just be taken from me once again.

I walked past friends, family, and even Eoha, following the light until arriving at a three-way fork in the path.

One road led to the *Kamui Moshiri*, one led to the underworld, and the other would bring me back home to *Kannaa Moshiri*.

Eyes glowed in the dark.

If I tried to take the wrong path, they would surely catch me.

I didn't feel like going anywhere. I didn't want another chance at life. Only misery would await me. I wasn't worthy of going to *Kamui Moshiri*, but I didn't desire punishment either. Maybe just staying in this intermediary zone would be best. Here I could fade away, along with all my misfortune.

Broken and forgotten, just like my people.

Flames erupted and took the form of the fire goddess. Her glory was beyond comprehension, just as she shifted into something recognizable, she turned into something else.

"Do you deny the violence you committed? If you do, I will conjure up your entire life, every violent word and action."

But not my thoughts. Not even the gods can see into our minds.

"I let my desire for revenge and my sense of hopelessness erode my morals. I killed man and animal unnecessarily. I am fully aware of what I have done. I ask for no mercy. Do as you see fit," I said, lowering my head.

"For your transgressions, you belong in *Teinei-Pokna-Shiri*. However, your honesty is worth considering, and you yourself were deceived. Go to *Kamui Moshiri*. Leave now before I change my mind."

I followed the path, guided by guardian *kamui*, until the light got brighter and brighter.

At one point I must have lost consciousness.

I awoke in a white grass bed.

Is this it?

It was different than I expected. The grass was white, or maybe I just perceived it as white.

I wandered around the area for what felt like days before discovering a small community.

They were all Ainu. I recognized some of the people from my own village, others were Isepo, and the dreaded Horokeu were there as well, along with some other tribes.

What happened? Did they give up on their tribal rivalry once they died? After what happened to the Shitumbe, how could any of them live alongside Horokeu?

I have to find out what's going on.

I went into one of the huts.

"Who are you?" asked a young girl.

"How long have you lived here?" I asked.

"I don't know. The sun never goes down," she said.

"Do you know someone called Eoha?"

The girl shook her head.

"You died, right?"

She nodded.

Everyone here is a spirit. I made it to the mirror world. That means I have to find Eoha. Then we can remarry and live together for the rest of eternity.

I walked around and asked if anyone had seen Eoha. They had not, and they didn't know where other villages were.

What if he didn't make it? What if he went to the wet underground world? I'm to blame for all his misfortune.

I didn't stay in the village. The sight of all the tribes getting along twisted my stomach. I ventured onward to look for other villages.

Before I could find the next one, a bright pink ball of energy appeared before me.

"Welcome to Lum. I am Evol, the Deity of Love. It is a pleasure to be reacquainted with you," said the floating ball of energy.

I didn't know who or what this was, but I lowered my head in respect. "My name is Ebui. Are you aware of the eclipse? Has all life come to an end in the world of the living?"

"The eclipse has passed. Life is progressing all across the living world. All is well," said Evol.

Then it really wasn't the end of times. Though I suppose it makes no difference. Everyone I cared for is already gone. Wait, they're dead!

"Evol, I'm looking for a young man called Eoha. Is there any way you could locate him for me?"

"You must let such attachments free. As long as you hold memories and desires, your next incarnation will be out of reach."

Another incarnation. Another life of misery and misfortune. I'd be a fool to want that.

"I want to stay here. Eoha is my first spouse; we're supposed to get remarried here. If you don't know where he is, can you lead me to someone who would know?"

"Would you like to know how to reincarnate?" asked Evol.

"I want to leave that world behind. I don't want to be a human again."

"There are many potential incarnations. You could return as a wide variety of animals."

What? That wasn't what I was told.

"I need to speak with your leader. Can you grant me an audience with the *kotan kara kumui*?"

"Lum is beyond us all. I can take you to see another deity."

"That will be fine."

"I'll lead the way."

I followed the chipper *kamui* up to a river.

"Is it going to meet us here?" I asked, staring into the *aka*.

"Surely you understand. The river is the Deity of Fate," said Evol.

Fate.

"This body of water goes across every region of Lum. It shifts the tides of events both in this world and the world of the incarnated."

This kamui was responsible for my misfortune. It brought about the annihilation of my people. Yet I'm powerless to do anything against it.

"Fate says that it has located Eoha. Follow me."

"No."

As long as this god exists, misfortune will cling to me. Joining back with my husband will only bring him strife.

"Leave me be."

"I'm very proud of your decision. When your soul is ready for your next incarnation, I'll send an angel your way," said Evol before vanishing into a door of light.

I was alone and powerless. All I could do was wait until all my memories faded and with them, my identity.

I rested by the river bank, though I found myself unable to sleep.

It was something about the air in this place. It made it difficult to relax.

That night, I heard a voice. It came from the river. "You were destined to go to Sel, but I saw potential in you. The possibility of you going to Lum became a reality."

I leaned over and stared into the body of water. "What do you want from me? Haven't I gone through enough already?"

"You are one who understands destiny. Both Sel and Lum seek to change the balance and shift destiny in their favor. You can save both realms. Speak with the Lum gods on my behalf. But before that, you must become an angel."

"I will decide what I do," I said, staring defiantly at the *kamui*.

"Your destiny is not yet writ. Will you incarnate again?"

"I refuse!"

"Or will you become a mawali and shape the system?"

"What is a mawali?" I asked.

"Mawalis are visitors who have bathed in the Good One's light. They are like angels only they were not born from the union of two angels."

This was my chance. If I joined the gods, I could change the way the entire system works. I might even be able to break man's reliance on the gods.

"What do you stand to gain?" I asked.

"Peace of mind."

I was thrown off. I never expected a god to say something like that. I always believed they sought entertainment, not peace.

I stood up from the ground. "I'm going to help you."

"Together we can save Sellum."

I will change this place and my own world along with it.

Chapter 122: Mawali

As soon as I sought out Evol, the *kamui* appeared.

"Can you read my thoughts?" I asked.

"I felt your desire to see me," said the *kamui*.

"I've decided. Make me into an angel," I said, channeling a strength I thought had abandoned me long ago.

"You will make a wondrous addition to the sustainers of Lum," said Evol with a twirl.

This is merely the starting point.

The *kamui* led me to a massive tree. "This is the World Tree. From here the Good One's grace is filtered into this world. Hop on." Evol sprouted wings and had me mount.

The *kamui* rose up the tree.

This tree is taller than any mountain I had ever seen. This world is so different than the stories I was told.

Once we were out of the foliage, I could see the very top.

A waterfall of light was pouring down from a dome partly concealed beyond the clouds. The waterfall broke at the top of the tree and dripped down the sides, revitalizing it with the essence of the gods.

"What will happen to me?" I asked as I was brought closer to the light stream.

"You will be purified and become divine."

And then I will hold sway over the system that traps me and my people. I will change the system that binds all of creation.

I entered the light stream.

No going back now.

Thoughts and memories were buried under an overpowering radiant devotion. But the feeling of my cursed existence and the unjust way of the world was too complex to be taken over.

The light coated my body and erupted out my back as white wings.

I had become a lesser *kamui*.

"Purification successful. You will be assigned a region to overlook by the deity of life."

I jumped off the deity. My wings spread and carried me through the skies.

Freedom.

The wind felt so welcoming. It was as if I could go anywhere. I wanted to keep flying around, but I was focused on my goal.

I landed at the entrance to the World Tree.

Evol appeared and led me inside. "The Deity of Life is responsible for assigning the angels their posts and overseeing their actions."

Even angels are at the whims of the true kamui.

The Deity of Life was something entirely unrecognizable. It was small and clearly not human. The creature's voice echoed in my head. "You will govern the village of humans you first came across. Report to me if they break any commandments."

Just as I was about to ask what the commandments were, I stopped. Somehow I already had knowledge of them.

Evol created a light doorway leading to the village. We entered and arrived.

Here I am, a guardian kamui over my own tribe and the tribes of my enemies. Is this just another game orchestrated by the chief kamui?

Evol talked to the six chiefs and told them that I would be surveying them. The chiefs reluctantly agreed.

Time was immeasurable here. Still, it felt like a few cycles passed without any problems. Then came the day I found a young man and woman wrapped together. It brought flashes of some experience I had but with whom I had no idea. The couple noticed me and froze up.

They had broken Lum's commandment.

I grabbed the man and separated the two.

"Please, we love each other dearly. Perhaps we can offer you something," said the young woman, folding her hands.

She was of Horokeu and he was Shitumbe.

The two clans should never merge.

I can't explain what came over me, but in a fit of fear and rage I attacked the woman.

The man grabbed onto me, pleading me to stop.

A part of me felt I should report the crime to Efil.

No. I can handle this on my own. Without showing my independence, I will never ascend.

"If I find you two making contact, even if it is merely holding hands, I will dispense justice on you myself."

The moral fabric of this realm was fragile. Firm decisions were needed to keep Lum pure.

I left the *chisei*.

It wasn't too long before I found them again.

They looked so happy together.

357

I disposed of the threat swiftly. One hand pierced through both of their throats. They were dead before they even knew I was there.

Death wasn't supposed to exist in the afterworld. Wait. Of course it does. Why would I think anything to the contrary?

I took the empty husks and tossed them into a gathering of people. "These two were caught trying to usurp the Good One's power. Creation belongs to the gods and the gods alone. The next visitor who defies the Good One will face a more painful end."

My words felt foreign to me. Had I really become so cold?

I felt a sudden calling to return to the World Tree and immediately took flight.

Efil greeted me upon arrival. "Why did you not report the disturbance to me?"

"I was more than capable. I gave a warning. They did not listen."

"Mawali, you cannot allow your own ego to compromise the stability of this realm."

"All I do is for the Good One."

"There is something you should know. Recently, the Good One has sent angels past the realm's border. They have killed demons from the other side. This has caused demons to attack Lum periodically. Balance can only be maintained as long as both sides of Sellum are in harmony. Compromise is our only option."

"I have my duty, but I will choose how I carry it out."

Even when fated, we can always choose how to confront that fate.

"The Good One has asked me to send you past the border. You will be grouped with a squad of angels and mawali."

I bowed.

I'm moving further up the ranks already.

Four mawali—myself and three humanoids—two fox angels as sub-commanders, and a wolf as commander made up the attack squad.

There is something about the commander that irks me.

Our mission was to cross the border into the other side of Sellum and covertly kill off a charismatic demon lord.

The mawalis, myself included, were suited up in armor, though not the fortified armor that the true angels were clad in.

Fear overcame me once we reached the border.

The other side of Sellum, the dark side, was charred and foreboding. Rather than trees, there were metal sculptures popping out of the land. The surface of the ground was made of animals, all human. They were still alive.

What kind of world is this?

The despair in their eyes pierced through my armor. I looked away.

We stood just at the border, letting the soot cling to our armor till it no longer shined.

"Conceal your wings. Follow me," said the wolf angel, rushing ahead.

"Is this your first time crossing? It's mine," said a male human mawali.

"It is," I said, hesitation clinging to my voice like the soot around me.

Our squad, Purity's Warriors, successfully infiltrated a village of demons.

Such hideous creatures. No wonder the Good One wants them removed.

The demon lord, our target, was speaking to a crowd. He was keeping them all focused on him and not on us.

"We must retreat," said the wolf.

One of the demons had spotted our fox angel and was coming to investigate.

The wolf angel emitted a blast of light. Together we rushed out of the village and to the other side of the border.

"We cannot complete the mission as we are now," said the wolf commander.

"We can try again later," I said.

"The peace we have with the other side is fragile. I shall discuss with the other commanders to form a new strategy." The commander left us.

I returned to my post at the tribal village. After following one of the men as he discretely left the village, I saw him grab a weapon beneath the grass. He may have noticed me because it took him some time before putting his plan into action.

He invited one of the men to go hunting with him. The two of them set off when I turned the corner, not knowing I would immediately turn around.

They entered the woods and came across a bear.

As one man raised his bow at the bear, the other raised it at the other man.

I have to act quickly.

I dropped down from the trees, shot in place of the bear. The other arrow pierced my attacker. As the bear hunter bled out, the human hunter fled.

I took flight and dive-bombed into him, causing us both to tumble down the hillside.

The man's face lit up upon seeing me. He embraced me. "*Mataki.*"

I pushed him off.

Why does he feel so familiar?

"Why were you hunting?" I asked.

"That man was Horokeu; they may live with our people in this place, but they cannot be trusted. They killed you too, didn't they?"

How did I die?

"My past life is not your concern. Why should I not kill you?"

"Sister, what happened to you? How did you die?"

"I don't know who you are. And it doesn't matter how I died. I live for the Good One."

"Has becoming an angel made you forget who you are? I am Akno, and you are Ebuike. We are Shitumbe at heart." The young man lifted his shirt, revealing a fox carving on his chest.

This was not mere trickery. This human knew me. And that symbol means something to me. He looked so familiar.

He was older than me and taller too. With his muscular build, hunting bow and war club, he looked rather capable in battle. His messy hair separated him from some of the more well-groomed humans. Whenever they looked at me, his eyes would sparkle. He was both foreign and familiar all at once.

"If I catch you hunting again, you will join the others who defy the Good One."

"I invite the Horokeu men to hunt with me and then I kill them. If they were willing to break the commandments of Lum by killing a fellow visitor, do they not deserve death?"

"You are not an angel. Such action is not permitted. Only those worthy of upholding Lum's commandments have the authority to punish those who defy them."

"I understand. I shall never fire another arrow. But if I can get them to agree to go hunting…if I lead them out here, will you kill them?"

The hope in his eyes made me feel warm.

"Why not become an angel? You feel very strongly about Lum's commandments," I said, grabbing his hand.

"There are things I refuse to forget. So, shall we work together?"

"Those who would succumb to temptation are just as guilty as those who sin without provocation. We shall purify this village of all those who defy the Good One."

"I shall signal you when I find another sinner," said Akno.

Images from my previous life would flash for an instant before being buried under devotion. I was once a mother, a warrior, and even a lover. It all seemed to be from the same life, but I had no way of knowing for sure. It wasn't too long before the wolf commander approached me.

It was time to try again.

"Come with me." The wolf led us into a cave.

"Why are we hiding?" asked the male human mawali.

"Only humanoid angels can infiltrate the other side. But you will need a disguise first." The wolf suddenly jumped the human man.

Before I could react, one of the foxes was on top of me, clawing and biting at my flesh.

I didn't struggle like the others. It was obvious that this was done so that we would look like demons.

The foxes sewed up our wounds with metal string.

An already injured human mawali entered the cave with a torch.

The others struggled and tried to flee. I stepped up to go first.

With our flesh charred, our skin sewed up and our bodies beaten, we were ready to fulfill the Good One's task.

With each successful mission I will gain credibility. That credibility shall bring about my ascension all the way to the top.

Chapter 123: Ascension

We successfully infiltrated the demon lord's rally.

"They should really treat us better. Without humans in Lum, this operation would be impossible," said the male mawali.

"You don't think they allow humans to become angels just because we look like demons, do you?" asked the woman human mawali.

"Destiny has brought us here. Now, let's complete our mission and get out of here," I said, gradually moving closer to the stage.

Our target was a demon lord from the envy region. He had grafted angel wings onto his back and was dressed in white.

Strange behavior for a demon.

"Did you hear what he said?" asked the male human mawali.

"Balance can only be maintained through compromise. We cannot allow hate to tempt us into war with the angels. Lum and Sel are two sides of the same realm. Though different, they are not antithetical. Both serve a purpose."

The demon lord spoke of peace, not war with the angels.

None of this makes sense.

"Are you sure this is the right one?" asked the male human mawali.

"Absolutely," replied our human commander.

"Shouldn't we be going after the warmongers?"

"We have a mission to uphold."

"I don't understand," said the human female mawali.

"Peace is not an option. Demons by their very existence threaten the stability of Lum. As mawali, it is our duty to fulfill Lum's mission," said the commander.

"I understand," I said softly.

Good and evil were fighting for supremacy. It all felt so familiar. But why would the good desire war?

"We move in all at once," said the commander, forming a light spear.

I nodded.

All four of us rushed the stage.

We fired beams of light to blind both the crowd and the guards on stage.

By the time the demon lord's body hit the floor, we were already at the exit.

Panic caused the demons to disperse, masking our escape all the way to the edge of the village.

"We should be working with demons like that, not fighting them," said the male human mawali before a spear pierced his throat.

I took a step back, watching our commander to decipher his next attack.

"Why did you kill him!?" screamed the female human mawali.

"Fresh mawalis were chosen for this job specifically because it was controversial. The Good One left me in charge of keeping things under wraps. She doesn't trust mawali," he said, tearing out the spear and turning his sights on the woman.

I stepped up to him. "What kind of god lives in fear?" I gripped the spear, tore it from his grip, and beheaded him. I dropped the weapon and approached my fellow mawali. "We should report back. The captain died during the mission, agreed?"

She nodded, still fear-stricken.

"Are you coming?" I asked.

"If we go back, they'll kill us. We're already in disguise. We should stay in Sel, where humans are welcome."

"If that's where you feel you belong, then go," I said before walking off.

When I met up with the angels in the cave, I reported that the mission was completed, but I was the only one left. To fill the void in the chain of command, and because of my skills, I was promoted to the rank of captain. I did some reconnaissance missions with a new group of mawali who looked up to me and put their faith in my leadership. When I wasn't doing recon, I was killing sinners alongside my human ally. Eventually I was assigned to negotiate with Absence: the realm between realms. On my own, I went to the rendezvous point and met a rather peculiar character.

"Ah, you must be the one I've been looking for," he said, staring into me.

The emissary of Absence was a crystalline man wrapped in a clear robe.

"Have you been waiting long?" I asked, bowing in apology.

"We are kindred spirits. We both seek change beyond our abilities," he said, stepping up to me.

How does he know so much about me?

"Are you going to take me to Absence?"

"In a moment, yes. Tell me, what is it you seek?"

"All I do is for the glory of the Good One."

"Ah, yes, of course." He created a portal and walked in with me.

We arrived in a land of nothingness. There was no earth or sky.

"The Good One has proven to be a useful ally."

"What is it you seek?" I asked before suddenly dreading the possible answer he may give.

"Freedom, just like you. There are obstacles in our way. Etaf is determined to keep things as they are. I would prefer you as the Deity of Fate."

How did he know what I sought? Had someone told him? No. I'm the only one who knows that. He's dangerous.

"You needn't be afraid. The system of Sellum has grown stale. Even when flooded by Lum's light, you can see that. But if you were to become a goddess, I could dispel that light from you," he said, touching my wings.

"What do you want in return?" I asked, looking at him with all the strength I could muster.

"We both want the same thing. You owe me nothing. Now, shall we get on with this charade?" he asked, leading me into another portal.

After the peace meeting, which proceeded smoothly, I was escorted back to Lum.

"How can I become Etaf?" I asked.

"I'll put in a good word for you. The Good One favors me and my advice."

Things proceeded as normal, with peace meetings in Absence, sabotage in Sel, and cleansing in Lum. After killing three sinners at once with my human ally, the emissary of Absence appeared.

"Who is he?" asked Akno, standing in front of me in a protective stance.

"I am Crystal, guard and emissary of Absence. How did someone like you make it to Lum?" he asked, peering beyond Akno's flesh.

"What is that supposed to mean?"

"Of course. Vengeful, violent and war hungry—you were chosen for your vices not your virtues. The Good One should be more particular about who she lets in."

I approached the emissary. "Why have you come to this village?"

"I came to forward the Good One's message. By reasons beyond my understanding, Etaf is no more. The river exists and still flows all across Lum, but it's as if the deity's individuality was fragmented and could not be sustained. Naturally the deity's powers have returned to the Good One."

"Absurd, *kamui* can't die," said Akno.

"Death isn't what I would call it. Either way, you must meet with the Good One. She has chosen you to be the next Etaf. You will represent more than the Good One, you will represent all mawali and every human in Lum. Whether she chose you for political reasons or due to your qualifications, your actions have enough weight to bring either peace or war."

Every word he spoke felt like it had a hidden meaning. Nothing he said could be trusted. Even so, I couldn't have gotten this far without his help.

Akno put his arms around me. "You've broken age-old traditions once more. I couldn't be more proud of my little sister," he said, beaming at me.

"Thanks." I hugged him back.

He felt so warm and welcoming. It was like I was home again.

"Come with me," said Crystal, bringing me into the forest to meet with Evol.

The Deity of Love congratulated me and created a portal.

I went inside and arrived in a place hidden behind the clouds. It was a castle of light.

"Your loyalty has not gone unnoticed. Neither have your appointments with that human," said the Good One, her voice emanating from the floor, walls, and ceiling all at once.

"His actions only serve to uphold the peace and stability of your realm," I said.

"You care for him deeply, don't you?" asked the voice, each word echoing in my mind.

"He knows the me that I've forgotten."

"Some things are best forgotten. You are soon to be a goddess. I don't want you meeting with him anymore. Is that understood?"

"As you command," I said with a bow.

"You will obey my every whim. My words are that of the realm itself," said the Good One.

"You are absolute," I said, bowing with reverence.

"If you betray me, human, you will be disposed of. This is the only chance your kind will ever get. You are now the Goddess of Fate," said the Good One.

Light energy came out from the walls and pooled into me. It wasn't like the concentrated light from the waterfall; it was far more powerful. It revitalized my body without affecting my mind.

"The merge was successful. Return to me once you've had a vision. I must know what the future holds for my realm. Evol shall be by your side as an interpreter. I'm not foolish enough to trust your word. Now, be off," said the Good One.

I formed a portal and arrived just outside the village I was once charged with monitoring.

Crystal rose out from the lake that was once a deity. "Ah, rather refreshing, isn't it? I see you've been promoted. Many congratulations," he said, clapping his hands slowly.

"What happens next?"

"There's been rumor of a promiscuous mawali who has transcended the species boundary. I am rather interested—"

"I mean with me," I said, gazing at him in hopes of uncovering his plan.

"You're right where you need to be. Once I've returned your memories, we needn't meet again."

"I don't want that. I've grown stronger without my memories."

"Then I wish you luck in all your future endeavors." He walked off into the forest.

I doubt that's the last I'll see of him.

My duty as the Goddess of Fate was enjoyable. Evol would interpret the overall vibe of my erratic dancing, but the deity was unable to fathom negative concepts so I always had to re-decipher its interpretation. There were prophecies as simple as the ascension of a new mawali, but there were also visions that led to the discovery of rebel spies in the angelic infantry. One particularly peculiar prophecy was about the ascension of a deity. The Good One at first interpreted this as a potential threat to her throne. I felt my interpretation, that the alleged "ascension" would be more accurately understood as "death," made more sense. Each subsequent premonition led to another piece of information, until it was readily apparent that the Deity of Life, who had existed in Lum even before the Good One herself, was to die by my hand. Finding this prophecy problematic, Lum sent me to Sel on a mission to retrieve a god who was assumed either captured or dead. If I returned without the god, the Good One threatened to purge the village I once kept watch over.

At the edge of the realm, I found myself face-to-face with the emissary from Absence yet again.

"It's a bit worrisome that the Good One is sending you without informing the other gods."

I channeled my aura into a sword and raised it. "Was it you who put that vision in my head?"

"Pardon?" he asked so authentically it was suspicious.

"My power is to create crystals, nothing more, nothing less," he said.

"Then how were you going to bring back my memories?"

"I was going to propose you allow the River of Fate to cleanse you of Lum's light, but you decided not to. Have I ever given you a reason to doubt my intentions?" asked the emissary.

"I have a mission to fulfill," I said, walking past the border and into Sel.

"Ah, but if you truly wanted to follow the Good One's wishes, you would not complete it. Having a mawali, and a human at that, go traitor would fit her agenda nicely."

"Is that what you're after as well?"

"That has yet to be determined. If you do return, things will no doubt change."

"I will return, and I will bring glory to the Good One."

"Your loyalty is superficial; you wear it as armor. Before I go, here's something for you to ponder. Once the war is over, what will happen to the humans? And what use are mawali in times of peace?" asked Crystal before vanishing.

More tricks and deception. I will not give his paranoia the attention he desires.

I entered Sel, but with my divine aura it was impossible to blend in. Not that I needed to. No mere demon could stand against me or the Destiny Sword. I must have killed hundreds of them. The longer I spent in this place, the less devotion I held toward the Good One. It was as if my faith was being sapped by the energy of the realm and slowly filled in with doubt.

What if the Good One sent me here to kill demons? Perhaps she doesn't want to paint me as a traitor after all. It seems even more likely she is using me to inspire mawali and humans to seek war with the demons. I'm a scapegoat for her war propaganda, and since she banished me, the Good One need not take responsibility for my actions.

Unable to vanquish me, the Dark One sent an emissary to bargain with me. The emissary was clad in golden armor formed by his shimmering aura. He was clearly no demon.

"I am Egaruoc. Were you banished, or did you come here of your own volition?" he asked.

"I am Etaf. I was sent on a mission to retrieve you. I didn't expect you to come to me. Tell me, have you allied with these demons?" I asked, ready to draw out my sword at a moment's notice.

"It takes bravery to go into battle against a powerful enemy. But it takes true courage to see things from your enemy's perspective, reevaluate your position, and fight for an end to the hostility. I ask that you join me in my quest to unify Sellum once more."

"Once more? You think Sel and Lum were once at peace?"

"They were indeed. Before the second wave of realm gods took over, the realms had no conflict. The concept of good and evil is what has brought about the turmoil between them. And it is that very concept that I have sworn to oppose."

Good and evil are universal truths. They can't be mere constructs…can they?

"Come with me."

The God of Courage led me to the demon graveyard. It was several acres long and had small tombstones that paid tribute to the demons killed by Lum's forces.

"I'm partly responsible," I said, turning away as I noticed a loved one praying to their dearly departed.

Egaruoc placed his hand on my shoulder. "As am I. We are gods, Etaf. We have the power to make a difference for angels and demons."

I drew my sword. "There is someone I wish to see again. If I don't bring you back, I cannot return. My loyalties lie with Lum above all else."

"Giving away your freewill won't protect you from sorrow. Letting someone else command you does not rid you of the responsibilities you have for your actions. This is your chance to join with me to bring back the balance."

His words remind me of Crystal's. Has he been compromised by that dubious emissary?

"Good and evil may be mere concepts, and I may be acting selfishly, but I will bring you back. Draw your weapon," I said, summoning up the Destiny Sword.

"If either side is annihilated, then both sides lose. There is no victory in war."

I thrust my sword at him.

"*COURAGE*."

Golden chains wrapped around my blade.

"I was the commander of Lum's forces before I was captured. You will not defeat me."

"My destiny is to return. No amount of skill or cunning can change that." I jumped back and cut the air.

"*VALOR*."

A shield of golden light appeared in front of Egaruoc, but my slice passed right through it.

"All things collapse when faced with their destiny. SPATIAL SLICE."

Another cut and I had him on his knees.

"Enough. I concede. I'll come along with you. Please, allow me to say goodbye to my beloved. I do not know if she and I will ever meet again."

"Love is something that must be abandoned if we seek equality."

"Love is the fuel to my rebellious spirit," he said, standing up.

His wounds had already healed.

I raised my sword.

"Make the portal. I'll come along," he said, raising his hand.

I formed the portal and made sure he went through first.

"I have returned, along with the Lum god. My mission is completed. Have I proven my loyalty?"

A portal appeared and the Deity of Life emerged.

"Is the Good One pleased with me?" I asked.

"Egaruoc has been in Sel far too long. He has been compromised. Kill him and the Good One will welcome you back."

"I seek peace, not war," said Egaruoc.

"I am a mere servant to the Good One. I do not judge your actions. That said, I cannot defy the Good One's wishes," said Efil.

"What you can't defy is fate. I will not kill him, but if you attack, I will kill you," I said with firm intensity.

"You cannot sway me," said Efil.

"You will die, Efil. And it will be by my blade. It has already been predetermined. Are you certain you wish to bring that destiny into the present moment?"

"You cannot kill life itself, but all it takes to kill courage is the certainty of death." Efil released its aura, transforming the landscape into a jungle instantaneously.

"I cannot die yet. My union with my beloved shall bring both the realms back together! BRAVERY!" exclaimed Egaruoc, layering strands of his aura into a sword. "With Bravery in hand, I will fight!"

"I have never once been in battle," said Efil, swerving out of the way of each slash.

"Defend yourself, Egaruoc. I must be the one to strike down the deity!" I exclaimed before slashing the air.

"LIFE." Efil aged a tree next to me, causing it to topple over.

As I took a step forward to slash once more, the ground beneath me crumbled.

My slashes passed through Efil.

How is that possible?

"I control the aging process. Your aura can only target the living."

"Wait? He died to dodge your attack? We cannot win the battle. We must run," said Egaruoc.

"You can't run," said Efil, condensing its aura.

Egaruoc dodged and his sword fired chains at the deity.

"One day even time will cease to exist," said Efil.

The jungle around us died and regenerated. Efil used the reanimated trees as cover and fired its aura out as a beam at us.

Egaruoc pushed me aside and created a shield with his aura.

The shield dissolved.

"Stop hiding! Fight me face to face!" yelled Egaruoc, dodging the incoming blasts.

The ground beneath us fell apart.

Egaruoc solidified his aura beneath him and grabbed hold of me.

"I am every creature that will ever take form. *ADAPTATION*." Efil's aura burst out, forming muscles, scales, and feathers around it.

The once tiny deity had become larger than a bear.

"You need not kill the deity. We need to make it back to Sel, that's all," said Egaruoc, forming a portal.

"*LIFE*."

Energy burst out from the ground, aging the portal into oblivion.

Scales fired off from Efil and pierced into me. The deity then slammed into me, gripped me in its talons, and took flight.

"*COURAGE!*" Egaruoc fired his strands of energy at the deity, piercing its wings. "My will can surpass any obstacle!" he yelled, running up his own energy strands toward the deity.

The deity shed its feathers. The feathers turned into a torrent of birds that sped into Egaruoc.

The God of Courage stacked multiple shields with his golden aura as he rushed to the Deity. Once close enough, he fired out chains of courage.

Glyphs of energy formed around the deity. Its skin then emitted seeds which grew into airborne trees that deflected the chains. The deity's aura then erupted out from the tip of the trees and crashed into Egaruoc.

This time fate is mine to command.

I closed my eyes, focused my aura into the Destiny Sword, and plunged it into Efil. "*DOOM*."

My aura flooded the deity from within. The deity burst, its flesh decaying before touching the ground.

"Blind loyalty brings only sorrow," said Egaruoc, grabbing me in midair.

"How did you survive that?" I asked.

"A brave spirit keeps you young I've been told." Egaruoc flew toward land and set me on the ground by a lake. "It seems even gods can age."

My body was no longer that of a teenage girl. Efil's aura must have hit me when the deity burst. I had developed into a woman in an instant.

"Let us return to Sel…where we can work toward peace. There is no negotiating with one who believes she is all that is good," said Egaruoc.

"Go on without me." I wiped away my tears.

"Were you close?"

"No. It's not that."

Even as a god, I cannot escape destiny. After becoming fate itself, I thought things would change.

"Leave. I will not be returning to Sel," I said.

"Etaf, you have more power than you realize," said Egaruoc, before leaving.

The Good One sent angels to attack my village. Rather than fight against them in futility, I joined them in the purging. I made sure their deaths were swift and decisive. Akno had a look of confusion as my spear pierced his heart.

Flashes of another life suddenly came up.

Had I killed him before?

The Good One was impressed with my performance and decided to put me in charge of punishing those who tried to procreate. It was strange, I felt a bit of satisfaction when ending the lives of the pregnant women.

Why should they be entitled to happiness?

Surrendering my will gave me a sense of freedom. Rather than fighting destiny, I moved along with it. Perhaps that was what my duty as Etaf truly was. The more premonitions I had, the more I realized that war was coming. I was given my own battalion to train. I raised the angelic warriors with my philosophy: there is no good or evil. This allowed them to kill without hesitation. Soon they became the most feared angels in Lum.

One day, I had a vision. When Evol spoke the meaning of my divination, I was at a loss for words. "Etaf will either kill Efil or die by her hands."

There wasn't a new God of Life appointed yet, so the prophecy made no sense. Had I misinterpreted before? Was this new Efil the one I was destined to kill and not the old one? The strangest thing about this prophecy was that it gave me a choice: to either kill or die. Egaruoc's words gained new meaning. I did have the power to choose, but yet, not even as the Goddess of Fate could I determine where that choice would lead. Even so, being able to choose empowered me. I was determined to work alongside the new Efil and make her either a worthy enemy to kill or a worthy friend to be killed by.

Chapter 124: Fate & Choice

The image faded and the screen dissipated.

"How could you kill your own brother?" asked Kanasta.

"His death was inevitable. I gave him a swift end," said Etaf.

"It is inexcusable. He loved you dearly," said Kanasta.

"No use hiding it. I killed him for my own reasons. He made me feel something. I'm not sure if it could be called hope, but it was something warm. With him out of the way, I was finally free of all attachments. Now the only one I hold bonds with is Efil," said Etaf.

"Are you really planning on killing her?" asked Ada softly.

"I do not plan. When the time comes, I will fight her. It is destiny that will decide the outcome," said Etaf.

"That wasn't the same Lum, was it?" asked Kaity.

"Seemed the same to me," said Deceivant.

"I'm unsure myself. After the Destined War, which came about soon after the events I showed you, Lum's personality shifted. This change could be the result of the end of the war or from someone taking over in her place."

"Why serve her if she isn't even the same person?" asked Atlas.

"I follow Lum. Who Lum is or becomes is irrelevant to my loyalties," said Etaf.

"Lum banished you, burned the village you protected, and used you to bring about war. How can you serve someone like that?" asked Atlas.

"I'm a Lum goddess, it's that simple. If I had gone to Sel, I would be devoted to the Dark One. Perhaps the previous Etaf knew this, and that is why I was brought to Lum despite my actions."

"I understand. As a ruler, I fought to defend my kingdom despite its many flaws," said Atlas.

"Any other questions?" asked Etaf, looking over the crowd.

"Crystal looked the same, but he acted differently," said Kanasta.

"Yes. I think being in Absence eroded his ambition. He is bereft of desire now," said Etaf.

"I do not believe they are the same person," said Riufen.

"Um, how did you get your memories back?" asked D.S.

"Once I became Etaf, I gained access to the soul memory of those I can exert my willpower over. As such, despite the Lum energy still in me, I am able to see my own memories. It's strange though, I feel so detached from the events. It's almost like I am seeing someone else's life rather than my own."

"And the narration?" asked Opti.

"I hoped to convey my thoughts at the time as authentically as possible. And to save time, I used narration to cover prolonged events. Now, I have a question for you. Having seen my past, you should now understand why I fight and live for this realm. It's decision time. Will you join Lum's forces to fight against Sel?"

"Lum and her forces seek the destruction of Sel. Why should we aid them in their violent ambitions?" asked Deceivant.

"And we all saw that only a god can kill a god. Our efforts would be wasted. We're going to the portal," said Crisis.

"And the rest of you?" asked Etaf.

"I still don't trust you," said D.S., crossing his arms.

"We can all do something to help Lum. Isn't that reason enough to stand up and assist?" asked Ada.

"It's a losing battle. You'll only be killed," said Deceivant.

"Perhaps Lum is seeking to shift the balance in her favor. Let's act upon what we know. We know Sel wants to kill Lum. Shouldn't we focus on stopping him before worrying about Lum's intentions?" asked Kaity.

"I'm a scientist, damn it. The whole afterlife can fall apart for all I care. This isn't our war," said Deceivant.

"I will stay and fight, for Devlin's sake. But I will do so after Devlin's parents, and his sister, have arrived safely back on Earth," said Nina, standing resolute.

"You know, I was all for helping out Lum before, but now I'm not so sure. What if Lum kills us once we're no longer helpful?" asked Opti.

"She wouldn't do that!" exclaimed Kaity.

"Meow!" exclaimed Napkin with a nod.

"We can't know for sure. Best to get everyone back to Earth," said Deceivant.

"Lum is after control, not power. I came to this place to stop those with grand ambitions from taking over. Sel is my opponent, not Lum," said Atlas.

"Let's all stop arguing. We should focus on the matter at hand," said Image.

"That is what we are doing, mother," said Deceivant.

Image approached the troubled woman. "You've been through so much. Don't you feel better now that you've shared with us?"

"I already explained my reasons for sharing my past," said Etaf.

"So you say, but if that were the case, you would have only shown us the portion that took place after you died. Sharing with us the life you led before is a cry for help. I'm here to assist in whatever way I can," said Image with a soothing voice.

"I'm beyond help. I no longer live; I simply exist. I showed you my pre-life so that you could see that good and evil are mere constructs. What matters are the choices we make, not what side we are on," said Etaf.

"I'm so confused. You really are loyal to Lum, aren't you?" asked Opti.

"Absolutely," said Etaf, her eyes without emotion.

"Everyone coming to Earth, stand here with me. Etaf promised a personal escort if we listened to her story," said Deceivant.

"I'm just not sure what to do," said Opti.

"That's not the point. There's no reason not to work with Lum. This is a golden opportunity. Whoever wants to leave can go." Kaity approached Hope. "We could really use your help, but I won't force you."

"Don't you dare try to seduce my Hope with those puppy dog eyes!" yelled Decievant.

"They're kitty cat, not puppy dog," retorted Kaity.

"Enough squabbling, all of you. As the only one present with regal blood, I shall take on the burden of deciding this matter," said Hope.

"It's your choice if you want to go home. But we aren't all obligated to go just because you want to," said Kaity.

"Do not speak out of turn," said Hope.

"Wait. It's only fair I warn you. If you chose to head to the portal, I've been told to kill all non-combatants."

"What!?"

"Well then there isn't much to lose now, is there?" asked Hope, glaring at Deceivant.

"That wasn't the agreement!" yelled Kaity.

"I said what I needed to say to get you to listen. You're naïve if you believe Lum will allow someone as powerful as Hope to return to Earth," said Etaf.

"I am sick of Lum's games," said Deceivant, clenching his teeth.

"It's not Lum's fault! Etaf has been lying the whole time! She's been speaking for Lum in her absence. You've been turning us against her from the start," said Kaity, her hand on her sidearm.

"I don't care who is pulling the strings! I am bringing my daughter home!" yelled Deceivant.

"Do not speak on my behalf. As for you...." Hope turned to Etaf. "You shouldn't make promises you can't keep. You and your leader should be more careful."

"You've seen how futile it is to oppose Lum. If even gods cannot do it, what makes you think you can?" asked Etaf.

"Hold on! We aren't just going to go along with whatever Hope says," said Kaity.

"Bite your tongue. I'm doing all of you a favor. The goddess' story showed us that Lum cannot be trusted. Her words bend according to her agenda. Honestly, such a fickle being is unfit to rule. As a representative of my people, I speak on behalf of all the Exps in the audience today. I will not bow to the wishes of your tyrant queen. My kingdom and its people cannot be threatened. Since we are unwilling to reach compromise..." Hope steps up to the Goddess of Fate "I declare here and now that if you get in our way, you will be destroyed. Move along, everyone. We set off toward the portal at once," she said, turning away and holding her head up high.

"Wait, hold on. She doesn't really speak for all of us. We never voted for her to lead us. I sure didn't," said D.S. waving his hands nervously.

"You're wasting my time. Hope, I accept your declaration. Step forward and fight me. I won't hold back," said Etaf.

"Okay, so our options are either work with Lum and fight Sel's forces—a surefire way to die—, or go against Lum's wishes and head to the portal, likely leading to death at the hands of her forces. Other than the way we die, it's pretty clear how this is going to turn out," said Crisis.

"Come on, Lum will send us all home once Sel is gone. She has no reason not to," said Kaity, tugging at Nina's arm.

"Hope is Devlin's sister. I will have failed Devlin if I cannot protect her," said Nina, drawing her sword.

"I'll help Lum, okay? I'm not sure what I can do, but I'll help!" exclaimed Ada.

Etaf sliced the air.

Atlas stepped in the way of the slice, protecting Ada. "Run, now! We'll hold her off for as long as we can." He turned to Deceivant. "Nina will protect Hope. I need you to take my wife with you and run as fast as you can."

"You've made Lum into your enemy. There is nowhere you can run."

Twelve angels came out from the trees: a bear, a snake, a wolf, a tiger, a shark, a hawk, a fox, a gorilla, a crocodile, a killer whale, a rhino, and a hippo. They were decked in Lum armor, had their wings engaged, and had no feeling in their eyes.

"These are the Sassanians. Remember those dead humans you found after leaving Absence? They were all wiped out by these twelve angels. My battalion has survived one war already. They can surely handle you," said Etaf, rubbing under the bear angel's chin.

"You aren't as cold as you think you are. You're so lovingly touching that bear," said Image.

Etaf's hand pulled away from the bear angel. "D-D-Don't think you understand me."

"Please, Etaf, there is no need for us to fight," said Image.

"I disagree." The Goddess of Fate turned to her warriors. "Kill them."

Hope stepped off her living platform. "I order you to fight."

Violet stood up and rushed at the enemies, splitting apart from her astral body in mid-sprint.

Atlas fired appalling arrows in a circle around the non-combatants. "Stay there for now. They won't be able to touch you," he said, holding back the angel shark by prying open its mouth. Blasters from the side of the shark pelted him with shrapnel.

"I won't do it. I won't fight against Lum," said Kaity.

"Our lives are being threatened. We are merely defending ourselves," said Kanasta before slamming into the gorilla.

The gorilla angel swiped his fist at the enemy.

The assassin boss dodged before slicing off the gorilla's arm with a metal string.

The gorilla picked up his arm and beat the enemy with it, his eyes never losing sight of its target.

"You attack without malice and with great strength. You would make a great addition to the Viper Squad," said Kanasta before slamming his leg into the gorilla.

Nina leaped from tree to tree, dodging slices destined to hit her.

D.S. rushed at Etaf before being slammed by a rampaging rhino. "Bring it!" he yelled after getting back to his feet. The childlike Exp slid under the rhino as it charged and plunged his scissors into its belly. "I won't let you kill me!" he yelled, being dragged along as he snipped frantically.

The hawk dive-bombed toward the non-combatants, but swerved out of the way when getting too close to the appalling arrows.

"We really are safe," said Deceivant.

"I don't belong here. I can fight," said Image, biting her lip.

Fusion zoomed by the fox angel, connected to it, and then attached to the wolf angel. After gaining momentum, it slammed into the bear angel, tearing it up using its fellow angels.

"Squeak." Muffins fired needles at the snake.

The reptilian angel swerved to dodge the needle barrage. It tore a thistle from the ground with its tail and stabbed it into the bunny.

Muffins squeaked in pain before the snake sunk its teeth into her hide.

Napkin was running around, scaring any angels that came close to Kaity.

Having been sliced by the Destiny Sword, Nina tumbled down a tree. "I really can't win this," she said, slapping explosive tags on her palms. "**OPTIMISTIC SHOT!**" A bullet of morale burst into Nina.

The ninja stood up, despite her sliced leg, and rushed at Etaf. After ducking two slices, she slammed her katana against Etaf's.

The Destiny Sword slipped out from the goddess' grip.

"Emotions have their place on the battlefield," said Nina before diagonally slicing the goddess.

"Watch out!" yelled Kaity.

The Destiny Sword floated behind Nina and was about to slash when it was knocked aside by a sniper bullet.

"I'll take care of the goddess," said Crisis, just having felled the hawk by slamming it against the ground with an angled tornado.

Nina tossed explosive tags on the ground and leaped out of the way of subsequent destiny slashes.

"It's rather difficult to summon a weapon like this," said Atlas, holding back the flying shark with one hand and the killer whale with the other. He closed his eyes. "**CHAOS CHAIN.**" The glowing chain tattoo, which connected each tattoo together, lost its shine. The chain shot out from his arms and wrapped around the two angels.

"Splendid work, sire," said the Captain of Carnage while maneuvering around the crocodile angel.

"It is good to see you are well, my friend. As you can see I am no longer a god. You need not serve me any longer," said Atlas before he kicked the crocodile aside.

"God, king, peasant. It makes no difference to me. You are a proud warrior. My blade is yours to command," said the Captain with a bow.

"And if my orders are to go against Lord Sel?" asked Atlas, punching the crocodile as it came back for more.

"Then treason will be my privilege," said the Captain, blasting the crocodile with the mounted gun on his back.

Violet's astral form sliced the hippo angel before being knocked off its feet. While airborne, the energy body fired at the angel.

The hippo took flight, dodging the shots before biting into the enemy.

"**Earthly Exhale!**" Crisis lifted Etaf off her feet with a gust of wind. "**Terra's Tears!**" He barraged her with a hail storm. "I know what it's like to feel out of control and helpless. That's how things are. Nature has no sympathy; it also has no malice. Living beings aren't strong enough to change nature. We're fools if we think we can."

"**DIVERGENCE**." Etaf sent the hail back at Crisis with a blast of her aura. "I agree entirely." She turned to see that her sword had yet to kill the ninja. The goddess took flight.

Crisis rode a geyser up to Etaf and coated his fist in lava before slamming it into her. "If you agree, then why do you want us to fight Sel? Exps aren't gods. We can't change the tide of the battle."

"Lum wills it. That's reason enough. I will do whatever I must to fulfill her wishes. Win or lose, it makes no difference to me," said Etaf, pushing off the lava with her aura.

Kaity opened fire at the sword each time it tried to slice the air.

"Conserve your ammo. I can dodge most of it," said Nina, running in circles.

"No need. This baby fires energy. The capsule inside refuels after a cool down," said Kaity before firing with her sidearm.

"I will not fail Lum. **DOOM**." Etaf fired her aura into Crisis' arm, causing it to burst open.

The goddess slammed into him, sending him flying, and then flew toward Nina.

A tree popped out beneath her, disrupting her flight pattern.

"What are you doing?" asked Efil, standing atop the tree.

"Following orders. Come to help?" asked Etaf.

"There are more pressing matters to deal with. Sel's forces are attacking another temple. If we both fight, we can surely stop the assault."

"No distractions this time. The Exps refuse to serve Lum. They must be killed before they become a problem," said Etaf, calling her sword back to her.

"The Exps are living beings. We can't force them to fight for us. It's their choice," said Efil.

"They were brought to Lum for this purpose. Most of them would be in Sel if not for Lum lowering the karmic bar. Exps are just like the humans. They are here out of convenience, not made worthy by their virtues."

"We are the same. And yet we both were welcomed into Lum. They are here now, whether they deserve to be or not does not matter. Withdraw your forces."

"If I do not stop them here, they will force their way into Samsara and go through the Portal to Earth."

"If they chose that path, then we will strike them down together. Now, come with me. It isn't too late to stop the demon's assault," said Efil, creating a portal.

"Sassanians, stand down!" Etaf jumped off the tree and approached the non-combatants. "You win this battle, Hope. But if you step foot in Samsara, then you will have declared war on Lum," said the Goddess of Fate, pointing her sword.

"So loyal. It's a shame I can't break you, but you have already surrendered your will. To gain power through submission…you are rather interesting," said Hope.

Etaf approached Efil, who was healing injuries on both sides of the battlefield. "Let's get going."

"Let me just finish healing his arm," said Efil, pooling her energy into Crisis.

"You're too kind," said Etaf with the slightest bit of sweetness.

"Okay. I'm ready." Efil created a portal and left with her divine companion.

"Is everyone alive?" asked Kaity.

"Yes. And we have gained a new ally," said Atlas, gesturing to his loyal friend.

"The Captain of Carnage at your service," he said with a bow.

"Yay! Now nothing will hold back our friendship," cheered Ada, lifting up the demon lord.

"You serve your lord dutifully. Welcome to the team," said Nina with a bow.

"Is that cloth from the flag of the Hero's Militia?" asked the Captain.

"It is. The hero was made by the same man who made me," said Nina softly.

"Let's stay focused. Why didn't Etaf kill any of us? Any theories?" asked Hope, looking out at her people.

"Nina and I kept her at bay," said Kaity, hopping on her partner's shoulders.

"The Sassanians were no match for us. Clearly she knew this, and she only targeted those who were the least likely to die from her attacks. A single cut could have bypassed the barrier Atlas created and killed all the non-combatants. Her behavior is most peculiar," said Hope.

"Maybe she secretly wants to be friends," said Opti.

"We got lucky, that's all," said Deceivant.

"I don't think that's what happened," said Kaity.

"Then you agree with me?" asked Hope.

"No. I think Etaf wasn't following Lum's orders. I think she wants us to distrust Lum."

"That is possible. It's more likely that, as we saw in her past, Lum is using Etaf as a scapegoat for actions she would rather not take responsibility for," said Hope.

"That's not the same Lum. Her voice was different, it was cold. The current Lum is loving," said Kaity with a little smile.

"Thank you. As you can all see, Kaity has been compromised and is unfit to lead. I will take over. No objections, I presume?" asked Hope, looking at Deceivant with disinterest.

"None at all," said Deceivant.

"I will follow what the majority decide," said Atlas.

"Good," said Hope, smiling to calm her Freedom Forcers.

"Then I guess we're heading to Samsara, aren't we?" asked Kaity with a frown.

"Absolutely not. We lack sufficient military power to breach a base guarded by goddesses and angels," said Hope.

"Then what is the plan, sweetie?" asked Ada.

"Queen. Call me queen. I was hoping to get some suggestions. This is an open forum; you won't be killed for speaking," said Hope with a snicker.

"There are already rebels who are planning on storming the portal. I declined their offer at the time because my priority was rescuing my daughter. I motion that we meet up with Allah's Jannah and see if we can work with them," said Deceivant.

"Agreed. Lead the way," said Hope.

"I don't know where they are stationed," said Deceivant.

"And just like that you've outlived your usefulness," said Hope with a belittling stare.

"Violet knows, but she's not all there right now," said D.S.

"Nina went! Oh, but it was the other Nina," said Ada softly.

"Hope, we need you to put Violet back to normal. Otherwise we won't be able to find the base," said Kaity.

"It isn't that simple. Crushing is easy, but putting the broken pieces back together is a tedious, uncomfortable, and cumbersome process," said Hope with a shrug.

"I understand. Everyone, you must compliment me. Exaggerate as necessary. We need to bring her back," said Nina.

"I approve. Do what you must," said Hope.

Kaity grabbed her friend's trembling hand. "We'll bring you back as soon as we arrive at the base."

"Thanks," said Nina with a smile.

Part 15
The Portal to Earth

Chapter 125: Preparation

"Well everyone, lay it on me," said Nina, closing her eyes.

"You have beautiful hair!" cheered Opti.

"And an amazing body," said Kaity.

"Intelligent, tactful, and deadly in a fight. You are a great warrior," said Kanasta.

"You can be incredibly cute, especially when you blush," said Deceivant.

"Enough! There must be some other way of changing her," said Hope, crossing her arms.

"What are we doing exactly?" asked Crisis with a tilt of the head.

"Nina, you've done a fantastic job of protecting us. You've made Devlin so proud!" cheered Ada.

Nina smiled and then collapsed. She rolled into a cat crawl. "And so the goddess of sexiness returns," she said, licking her lips.

"Welcome back!" cheered Kaity, jumping on her back.

"Some allies you are, only bringing me out when you need me. I'm not sure I should even help you," said Nina with a stretch, tossing the girl off her back.

"Please, Nina, you're the only one who knows where Lotus is," said Ada.

"I'm not sure. I've been buried for so long. My memory is all hazy. Ugh, did she really have to tie down my breasts?" Nina took off her shirt. "Stop staring," she snarled. The egotist unwrapped her breasts and put her shirt back on. "What did she do to my hair?" asked the narcissist in tears, tugging at what remained of her once long flowing hair.

"I tried to stop her," said Kaity softly.

"Stop your sniveling and get moving," said Hope.

"Who's the brat?" asked Nina with a grimace.

"How dare you? I am Queen Hope. Without my approval, you wouldn't be here right now. Hmph," she said, sticking her nose in the air and crossing her arms.

"I will only help on several conditions," said Nina.

"Very well, name your price," said Hope.

"One: none of you will try to bring the other Nina back. None of you," she said, glaring at her treacherous fan.

"But I promised her," said Kaity.

"Who do you love more, her or me?"

"I love you both."

"We accept the first condition. Anything else?" asked Hope.

Nina turned to Kanasta. "You will not kill the Imam."

"I cannot agree to this," said Kanasta.

"Then no deal," said Nina.

"Are you kidding me? Son, we need to get Ada and Hope home. That should be our priority. Killing the Imam was all a set up to get us banished anyway. There's no need to follow that order," said Deceivant.

"It's a job. And I will complete it," said Kanasta.

"How about this, don't kill the Imam until after I've made it through. Got it?" asked Nina.

"Very well. I accept."

"Third: I'm the first one through the portal. Fair enough?" asked Nina.

"I suppose so," said Hope.

"Good. Follow me. I was blindfolded at the time, but I recognize the terrain."

Nina led the team through the forest all the way to Lotus. "Girls, come with me. Okay, I've been meaning to ask: what happened to Violet?"

"I broke her and turned her into my transportation. Does it bother you?" asked Hope.

"Come on, my little queen. I'll carry you. Violet will be very helpful with negotiations. Please bring her back," said Deceivant.

"I don't want your lecherous hands anywhere near me. And I will have no difficulty handling negotiations," said Hope.

"Yay, something I can help with!" cheered Ada.

"Yes, I suppose you can come along. Image, Kitty, Muffins, follow me," said Hope.

"What about Fusion?" asked Ada.

"It's neither male nor female," said Hope.

"Exp 8 said she was his sister. That makes her everyone's sister!" exclaimed Ada, beckoning her little girl to come along.

"So what should us boys do?" asked D.S.

"We should head to Samsara and scope it out. Though I'm not sure where it is," said Kanasta.

"Of course! Violet has a map!" cheered Ada, grabbing the map from her dazed friend's robe.

"How did we forget that? If only we had remembered sooner," said Deceivant, his eyes darting toward Nina.

"Oh I remembered. I can't be the only one who missed her," said Ada, hugging her elegant friend.

"Stop. You're making me like you," said Nina, turning away from her one true friend.

"Aww, you do blush!" cheered Kaity.

"Shut up! Let's stay focused," said Nina.

"Kanasta, I leave the map with you," said Hope, seizing it from her mother before handing it over.

"Bye, everyone. Stay safe," said Opti, waving at the girls.

"Can I have a hug goodbye?" asked Deceivant.

Hope glared at him. "Get down. On your knees."

"Yes. Like this?" asked Deceivant, lowering himself.

"You may kiss my foot," she said, sticking it up.

"Thank you, my queen," said Deceivant, placing his love on the top of her stilettos.

Hope kicked his face. "Now get out of my sight."

Deceivant bowed and rushed to catch up with the guys.

"And so I'm back," said Nina, gazing at Lotus.

"Wow, it's huge," said Kaity.

The mosque was entirely white, blending in with the rest of its surroundings. The garden was well-kept and provided ample cover should there be an assault. The one-way windows, which went completely around the structure, offered multiple vantage points and were made with thick glass to defend against projectiles. There were four pillars, one for each corner of the building. The pillars served as watchtowers, with several diligent snipers on the alert. The center of the fortress had a protrusion at the top of the main pillar, though this was merely decorative and served no tactical purpose.

"Are you going to keep gawking or are you going to move?" asked Nina, shoving Kaity aside.

"Don't bully my servant. Make yourself useful and knock on the door," said Hope, shooing the rude woman onward.

"It's me, Nina. Open up," she said, knocking repeatedly.

The door opened. Heaven's Thunder stood in the pathway.

"Oh, it's you. Look, I haven't spoken to anyone about what I saw in the prison. And I won't snoop around again, okay?" asked Nina.

"The Imam has forgiven you. Ah, you've brought your comrades with you. Where are the men?"

"Scoping out Samsara. I am the elected representative for the Exps. You will address me as Queen Hope," said the pampered child, standing tall.

"I am Heaven's Thunder," said the warrior with a bow.

"Oh cool! Do we all get code names?" asked Kaity.

"If you want," said Thunder with a shrug.

"Is your leader here?" asked Hope.

"She is."

384

"I would like to speak with her. Lead the way," said Hope, smacking Violet's behind to get her to crawl inside. Once the doors closed, the little queen hopped off. "Since we're on elevated ground, I suppose I can walk. But everyone must stay behind me."

"Shouldn't we check them for weapons?" asked one of the teachers.

"Exps are living weapons. They are deadly armed or unarmed. There is no need for concern. I believe they seek the same thing. Follow me," said Thunder, clearing the way for the Imam's newest allies.

The female Freedom Forcers were brought to the meeting room.

It was a simple room with mats instead of chairs and geometric pictures painted on the walls.

The Imam stood upon noticing Nina. "You've returned."

"She has and I have as well," said Hope with a smile.

"It has been some time," said the Imam, scooting forward.

"How do you know her?" asked Nina.

"I told you before. There have been Exps in Lum before your group arrived. Hope was under our protection. She was captured when we were deliberating with Efil. On behalf of Allah's Jannah, I apologize for any harm that has come to you," said the Imam, bowing slightly.

"Apologies are only meaningful as a political ploy. We want access to the Portal to Earth," said Hope.

"As long as your forces help us breach Samsara, I have no objections to any of you passing through. Exps are part of Allah's plan as well. I have no qualms working with non-humans," said the Imam.

"Splendid. When do we leave?" asked Hope.

"Wait. I have a question. You said there were other Exps in Lum. What are their names?" asked Kaity.

"Hope is the only one we had direct contact with. We have heard stories of others who predate the time of her arrival," said the Imam.

"Are there any others who will be joining us?" asked Hope.

"I do not know. Messengers were sent out after Elysium was breached. If the angels catch wind of our plans, they will be unable to react in time. We will find out who has accepted once we arrive."

"You say we, but you aren't going, are you?" asked Hope.

"My place is here. If we attack Samsara, the angels will retaliate. We must defend ourselves."

"Wait. Maybe we shouldn't do this. We don't really want to upset anyone," said Ada.

"Lum has taken over Heaven and has turned god's children into outcasts. We must retaliate."

"Perhaps there is some other way."

"Our memories belong to us. If we wish to reincarnate with them, that must be our choice. Our choice has been stripped from us. We cannot even decide what we will reincarnate as. Is that fair?" asked the Imam.

"Well no, but—"

"Silence, Mother. Not all things can be solved diplomatically. There are times when rulers must side with rebels in order to achieve their goal. I don't like it myself, but without an official army, I must make exceptions," said Hope with a frown.

"I am moved by your mother's virtue. Sadly, things aren't so simple here. Some of the women here are pregnant, others have already given birth. It's only a matter of time before the angels find out. And when they do, their babies will be torn from them. Reaching the portal is a matter of survival for them and their children," said the Imam, grabbing Ada's hand.

"I understand. I'll do whatever I can to help," said Ada with a sniffle.

"Do you have more niqabs? Mine was lost," said Nina.

"Yes. And you should all dress up. Not knowing there are Exps in our ranks will give us an advantage," said the Imam.

"Which brings us to the matter at hand: when are we leaving?" asked Hope.

"Allah's warriors are taking a cleansing bath before the battle. Go with Thunder. She will tell you what you need to do," said the Imam.

"Then let's all take a bath," said Hope.

"Not yet. Nina, my offer still stands," said the Imam.

"What offer is she talking about?" asked Kaity.

"Not a clue. Let's get going," said Nina, swinging open the door.

Thunder led her fellow females to the communal bath. "We have more members since the recent temple attacks. Girls only, of course. I hope that when graced with the Imam's benevolence, they take up the religion of Islam as their faith."

"This is as far as I go," said Nina.

"Agreed. Communal baths are for commoners," said Hope.

"Oh come on, it's just us girls," said Kaity.

Nina glared at her.

"What did I do?" asked Kaity.

"Are you really going to ask that?"

"Is this because I made that promise with Nina? She was scared. I'm her friend; I'm supposed to help her," said Kaity.

"You violated me!" yelled Nina, her voice quaking.

"What!? When did I do that?"

"You did it while I was asleep," said Nina, turning away from the molester.

"Let's all keep calm. Kaity, are you sure you don't know what she's talking about?" asked Image.

"I don't. Nina doesn't sleep," said Kaity with a worried shrug.

"How dare you! You took advantage of my body after seducing the other me! Don't you dare deny it!" yelled Nina.

"Oh." Kaity's eyes popped. "I didn't think about it that way. I swear. I'm so sorry."

"Do you really think an apology will make me forgive you? Trust isn't something I give easily. I'll never trust you again," said Nina with a glare.

"I didn't use my hands. I touched with my feet and tail only. That's got to count for something," said Kaity in a frenzy.

"Not to mention your mouth! Don't try to sugarcoat what you did. Any violation of my body is reprehensible!"

"She's just so different than you. It's like I'm with another person."

"Yeah, another person with my body. Devlin had enough respect for you to not violate you after Demonica turned you into his obedient doll. You said you loved me. I actually thought you meant it. You were just after my body and you're willing to seduce my sworn enemy to get to it."

"I don't think of you two as enemies. You're both my friends!"

"Not anymore. As far as I'm concerned, you chose her over me. Other than Ada, you were the only one who cared about me. The others don't see me as a person. I'm just a means to an end for them. I never should have trusted you."

"I saved your hair," said Kaity taking it out from her pack.

"I don't want it. It's been polluted by your touch."

"There's nothing I can say that will make up for what I did," said Kaity, stepping back.

"Thunder, where are the weapons? Let's get suited up," said Nina, stealthily wiping away her tears as she stormed off.

"Wait up! She didn't mean to hurt your feelings," said Ada.

"Stop!" Kaity grabbed Ada's arm. "I caused this. I'll deal with the consequences."

"Giving Nina distance is the best thing to do right now," said Image, calming Ada down.

"Worry not, Kitty. We won't keep that Nina around for much longer," said Hope.

"We can't just get rid of her. She's my friend."

"You really prefer her over her more skilled, sociable and cuter form?" asked Hope.

"It's not a matter of preference. I love them both."

"You're quite fickle, aren't you? No matter, let's get going," said Hope, walking alongside the commander.

"Let's get suited up first. Maybe after they've cooled down, they can enter the bath," said Thunder, leading the way.

They arrived at the armory, which was located behind a bookshelf in the library.

It was a dusty room, with crossbows, spears, bows, arrows, and other weapons leaned against the wall.

"Someone should go after Nina. It's best for her to be equipped as well," said Thunder.

"I'll meet up with her later," said an angelic human woman, leaning against the back wall with a cross bow in her grip.

"Don't be alarmed. This is Light Fury. She has been helping Allah's Jannah since the group's inception. Etaf took away something dear to her. She despises Lum more than most," said Thunder.

Light Fury approached the Exps and looked them over. "In Lum, living beings don't age, and they don't need to sleep or eat. Exps are beyond such things whether they're on Earth or here, right? What I want to know is: how did all of you manage to die when you existed in a heavenly state of being on Earth?"

"It's an unsettling subject," said Hope softly.

"My apologies. Alright, let's get you suited up. First things first, let's get you all some armor, nothing too heavy though," said Light's Fury.

"I'll take care of that. You get them weapons," said Heaven's Thunder, walking to the corner with the armor.

"Do all of you know how to use crossbows?"

"You point at someone you don't like and shoot. It's horrible. Is there something less violent I can use?" asked Ada.

"Give me a spear," said Nina, entering the room.

"Sure thing." Light skipped over to the spear section. "Let's see…here you go." She tossed the Exp her weapon. "You should be able to keep it hidden."

Nina spun it around and practiced her thrusts, all the while staring at Kaity. "It's good enough."

"Catch," said Light.

Ada jumped up and grabbed the object. "Is this a gun?"

"It's a stun gun," said Fury. "You're going to need to fire a few shots to take down an angel though. I prefer something like this," she said, hoisting up a shotgun.

"How did you manage to obtain guns in Lum?" asked Hope.

"We've been preparing for this day for quite some time now. After the prison breach, we knew that the time had come."

"This crossbow works fine. I'll take it," said Image, picking out her favorite from the bunch.

"What about her?" asked Fury, pointing to the dazed woman.

"She has her own weapons already," said Hope.

"And you?"

"Fufufu. Weapons are beneath me," said Hope.

Thunder approached the team with a crate full of armor. "Suit up. Once we're done here, we're heading off to battle."

Chapter 126: Storming Samsara

The male Freedom Forcers looked up the snowy mountainside to see the structure that harbored the Portal to Earth.

Samsara was a metallic fortress where no life was permitted to enter. The stronghold was guarded by angels of various species. They were stationed on the mountainside, in the moat and in the sky both above the building as well as the surrounding area. There were eight different entrances where lines of light blue souls awaited their turn to be reincarnated. To make matters worse, human angels, each armed with crossbows, watched from the balconies on the second floor.

"A sneak attack seems impossible," said Kanasta, gazing up at the open field leading up to the mission zone.

"We have no choice but to charge in. Stay behind me. I won't go down easy," said Atlas, cracking his knuckles.

"Shouldn't we wait for the others to show up?" asked Crisis.

"My wife and daughter are with the others. If we can clear a path to the portal now, they can enter safely when they arrive," said Deceivant.

"Yeah, but how are we going to do that? The place is guarded from every angle. We don't even know what it's like inside. We storm this base, we die," said Crisis.

"When assassinating someone on the battlefield you must allow the conflict to begin before sneaking through," said Kanasta.

"So we let someone else die while we slip in? That sounds like something a bad guy would do," said D.S.

"I have obligations as a father and a husband. We stopped by a number of temples. No doubt someone will attack and soon," said Deceivant.

"Um, guys, the angels are dispersing," said Opti, pointing at the eagles coming their way.

The eagles soared right past them.

"Efil did mention a temple being attacked. Does Bob know that we're planning on going back to Earth?" asked Deceivant.

"It is possible. Either way, this gives us an advantage. We should move now," said Kanasta.

"Wait up. Why would Bob want us to go through the portal? Could he be planning something that we're overlooking?" asked Deceivant.

"I think it's just a coincidence," said D.S.

"Hey you, why are you all gathered here?" asked a human angel, landing in front of the group.

"We heard about this cool place where souls go to be alive again. We just wanted to take a look, that's all," said D.S.

"This is Complex. You belong in Masculino," said the angel.

"Good Sir, we only came to visit. Could you perhaps give us a quick tour? Once it's done, we'll be on our way," said Deceivant.

"Etaf warned us that some Exps would likely try to break in. You realize it's impossible. Vacate the area and we can both be on our way," said the angel.

"Lum hired me to dethrone the Imam. You must let me through or I cannot complete my mission," said Kanasta.

"Nice try, but the Imam isn't here. And Lum doesn't need you anymore. Etaf has sent a battalion to Lotus in order to finish off the Imam and her forces," said the angel.

"Then this is where we part ways," said Kanasta, turning away from his team.

"You can't be serious! We have a mission to fulfill. Don't you care if Hope arrives safely?" asked Deceivant.

"I will provide assistance as soon as I return," said Kanasta, rushing off.

"You don't even know how to get there," said Deceivant.

"I do not." Kanasta grabbed the angel and put a dagger to his throat. "Lead the way."

"No need to threaten me. If you want to help kill Lum's enemy, I'll gladly escort you," said the angel, leaving with the assassin.

"Great, we lost one of the best fighters on the team," said Deceivant, pacing in a circle.

"They know we are coming. That makes things tricky," said the Captain of Carnage.

"We aren't the only ones," said Atlas, pointing to a battalion of Christian warriors rushing up the mountain side.

"This is our chance. Okay, everyone. Stay focused on survival first and foremost. There will likely be more troops joining in the assault, so making it inside is secondary to staying alive. Now, let's show those angels what the Freedom Forcers are capable of!" cheered Deceivant, rushing up the snowy mountain.

Atlas launched Appalling Arrows to disperse the incoming bird angels. "Stay behind me!"

The Captain of Carnage fired his blunderbuss at a human angel who broke out of formation.

"Hey, why are all the ground angels humans?" asked D.S. before splitting one with his scissors.

"I was wondering the same thing!" hollered Opti, flying in a diagonal direction to further divide the enemy forces.

Atlas was about to engage a wall of human angels with spears, situated at the quarter point of the mountain, when Napkin rushed ahead and roared ferociously with closed eyes. "*Mew. Mew. Mew. Mew. Mew. Mew.*"

Some angels froze in fear, others bolted away in a crazed panic.

"Splendid work," said the Captain, before ziplining off a wounded human angel, slicing up a flock of bird angels along the way.

Deceivant stood near D.S., only firing off his shotgun when the enemy went in his line of fire. "Humans are seen as expendable. Makes sense to put them on the front line."

"So are they good guys or bad guys?" asked D.S., before cutting the fleshy part that kept the head on the body.

"They are soldiers, fighting for a cause they believe in. We're in a battle, son. Morality must be placed to the side if we hope to make it out of this," said Deceivant, raising his shotgun and then freezing up. "It's a child."

Noticing the distraction, the teenage human raised her crossbow and fired at the enemy leader.

D.S. shoved his father aside, getting shot in the process.

"Don't you dare kill her!" yelled a woman before kicking D.S.'s scissors aside.

"Hi, Nina! Wait; are you the mean Nina or the nice one? Whoops, they were both kind of mean. Okay, are you the—"

"Shut up!" yelled Nina, draped in a niqab.

"Is Ada with you? What about Hope?" asked Deceivant.

"They'll be coming with the third wave. The first wave is only for trained combatants," said Nina, before whipping out a machine gun and firing at an incoming swordsman.

"Thanks. And thanks for stopping D.S. I can't believe my own son would attack a little girl," said Deceivant.

"But she was trying to kill you. You said things are different in battle. Ugh, typical adult, says one thing and then does another," said D.S. with a big frowny face.

"Do you know who that girl is?" asked Atlas.

"I'm not sure. It happened so fast. Looks like she went inside though," said Nina, taking off her gloves and detonating them once they landed in the enemy squad behind them.

"I thought you only cared about yourself," said D.S. with a suspicious look.

"I look out for number one, of course. But I'm not just going to let a little girl die. I need my fans—I like having fans, that is," said Nina, combing her hair with her fingers.

"Damn!" Deceivant was gripping his bloody shoulder. An arrow had made his flesh into its new home.

"Are you alright?" asked Atlas before dividing an enemy with his heated sword.

"It's the archers on the balcony. They have better aim than I expected," said Deceivant, standing behind D.S. for cover.

"Not to worry, friend. I'll keep them busy," said Opti, zooming by with a salute.

"Dad needs help. I'll bring him to the girl team. Where are they?" asked D.S.

"Forget about it." Nina hoisted Deceivant over her shoulder. "I'll take him."

"Wow, you're really nice now," said D.S.

"Useful. The word is useful. Don't forget it," said Nina, taking a detour to avoid the incoming swordsmen.

"Another army engaging the enemy to the West," said Atlas, tearing arrows out of his shoulders before flinging them into incoming enemies.

Naked men with spears and painted faces ran up the snow-topped mountainside with a thunderous battle cry.

"You cannot change the way of the world. You can only fight to protect it," said Atlas, whipping enemies coming from both sides.

"Truer words have never been spoken," said Crisis, finally stepping out of formation. "*Earthly Exhale*." With a wave of his hand he sent a gust that knocked a squad of angels off their feet. Noticing enemies above, he fired hail from his free hand until they dispersed. "I'll take out the archers. Cover me.

Planetary Purging." Molten lava poured out from his shoulders, setting his clothes aflame before shooting off as a superheated mortar.

Seven aerial angels pooled their aura together, creating a wall of Lum energy that blocked the mortar.

"Two can play that game. *Earthy Exhale, Barrier*," said Crisis, waving his hands to create a current of air that hovered above him and his allies. "I have to keep it maintained, but the arrows shouldn't be able to hit us anymore," he said, staying in the middle for maximum efficiency.

"We've almost reached the midway point," said Atlas, slamming the Agony Axe down on a bear angel, before kicking the writhing enemy into an incoming squad.

"It's not just humans anymore," said D.S., surrounded by spear-wielding howler monkeys.

"Nothing a few bullets can't take care of," said Kaity, firing at the monkey angels.

"Thanks for the help," said D.S., rushing ahead to catch up with the other guys.

"No problemo. Hey, where's Kanasta?" asked Kaity.

"He's going after the Imam, but once she has Xs over her eyes, he'll be right back to help out," said D.S.

"Can you handle things here?"

"Yeah, but he'll be fine. You don't need to help him out. He's crazy strong," said D.S., jabbing his scissors to keep the wolf and fox angels at bay.

Kaity ran on all fours, navigating through several different groups already engaged in battle.

The female Freedom Forcers watched the second wave of Allah's Jannah's troops head up the snowy mountain.

"Okay, everyone. We're going to be joining them in just a few moments," said Heaven's Thunder, standing firm and tall.

"So, what's the name of the mountain?" asked Ada.

"Mainaka Mountain," said Thunder.

"Like in the Ramayana?" asked Violet, her eyes alight.

"Silence, slave," said Hope with a glare.

"Stand ready. Today we will leave this false paradise with our identities and our memories intact. We will return back to our homes, our families, and our congregations. Once we arrive, having with us the knowledge of the afterlife, we will have the attention of all the people of the world. We will tell our global society that paradise has been hijacked by a self-proclaimed god and is being run by an armada of false angels. When those from the next generation of our people die, they will come prepared to battle the injustice in Lum. Once we make it through, we turn the tide of the revolution!" cheered Thunder.

The women cheered, all raising their weapons.

"That was such a motivational speech. I feel fired up!" cheered Ada.

"I am merely a mouthpiece for the Imam's message," said Thunder, smiling through her cloth.

"Is there a medic here?" asked Nina, setting Deceivant on the snowy floor.

Ada rushed to her husband's side and grabbed his hand.

"I'm fine. The cold weather is freezing the blood," he said, covering the wound with his hand.

Hope got off her living throne and approached the foolish man. She kicked his arm aside, revealing the bloody wound. "You haven't even removed the arrow." The girl crouched down, pulled the arrowhead out from her father's shoulder and smiled when he let out a high-pitched scream. "You've made my gloves an awful mess," said the little queen, putting her mitts in a patch of wet snow.

"Let me. I trained to be a nurse before I found my true path," said Image, tearing off a piece of her niqab and cleaning the wound.

"Maybe we should postpone the attack," said Ada, looking over at her injured hubby.

"We can't. Give him some support. The second wave has engaged the enemy. We move in now. Make it look like we're joining up with the second wave, and then make a bee line to the adjacent entrance. Let's scale this mountain!" cheered Thunder, beckoning the troops ahead.

Chapter 127: Scaling the Mountain

The female Freedom Forcers and Deceivant, hadn't even reached the quarter-point of the snowy mountain when another group of warriors joined them.

"You survived," said Deceivant, looking at the Sikh leader.

"Where are the rest of your allies?" asked Rambir.

"They're further up the mountain. Rambir, I'm sorry about the lives that were lost."

"We are warriors. We died protecting, rather than just fading away like Lum intended. Why do you seek the portal, my friend?" asked Rambir before cutting down a human angel with minimum effort.

"I have to get my family back home. What about you?" asked Deceivant, leaning on Ada as they traveled up the mountain.

"With our gurudwar destroyed and our friends lost in battle, most of the survivors decided that they will either force their way back home or die trying."

"You don't feel the same?"

"It doesn't matter how I feel. I am their leader. If the portal is what they seek, then I will do all I can to bring them to it."

A stray arrow hit Hope's dress, ripping the hem of her skirt. "Who dares attack me?" asked the little queen, her eyes scanning the archers.

Nina rushed in, wrapped her scarf around four archers, and triggered it to burst. "They're all dead now. Hey, you know, there are quite a few attractive angels here. Seems a lot of pretty women gave up their independence. It's just as I said, not even angels compare to my beauty," she said, leaping out of the way of a volley of arrows before opening fire on her attackers.

"Who here knows how to stitch?" asked Hope, looking out at her soldiers.

"We're fighting right now. I'll fix your dress later," said Image, firing arrows into the attackers with minimal success.

"One moment." Nina detonated her thigh-highs, destroying the line of enemies blocking their path. She rushed up to Hope, crouched down, and sewed her dress with an acupuncture needle.

"You're rather handy to have around," said Hope with a small smile.

"Kindness is a beauty in and of itself, is it not?" asked Nina, waving her hair side to side.

"I suppose so," said Hope with a shrug.

Fusion rolled over the latest collection of weapons and opened fire at the winged warriors descending upon its allies.

"Squeek!" Muffins created needles from beneath her fur. The chubby bunny shot them out once a group of swordsmen got too close.

The quills pierced into their necks, knocking them out while causing minimum injury.

"Aw, Muffins is so sweet. She's helping out without hurting anyone," said Ada with a smile.

"Hmm. This isn't quite working out. Mother, carry me," said Hope.

"Sorry, sweetie pie, Mommy is helping your father right now," said Ada, shooting four stun bullets into a spear-wielder before it fell over.

"Go away!" Hope tossed a snowball in the face of an incoming spearman. "Thank goodness I'm always wearing mittens. This place is so cold," she said, holding her sides.

Nina cut the spearman down and crouched in front of the spoiled brat. "Get on," she said, rolling her eyes.

"You continue to impress me," said Hope, putting her legs over the woman's shoulders.

"Keep your head down," said Nina.

"I'll be wary." Hope looked back. "Slave, you aren't carrying me anymore. Go on ahead and break through the incoming enemy line."

Violet nodded and rushed ahead.

"Om bhur bhuvah svah

tat savitur varenyam

bhargo Devasya dhimahi

dhiyo yo nah pracodayat," she chanted.

The power of her mantra stopped the angels in their tracks. The path was cleared. There was no longer an inclination toward violence from the angels.

"Impressive. I thought I was the only Exp capable of mentally disarming my opponent," said Hope.

"Violet can do anything!" cheered Ada, waving at the friendly angels.

"We'll catch up to the others in no time," said Nina.

The male Freedom Forcers were confronted by a stampede of angels.

"Hold your ground!" yelled Atlas, grabbing a rhino before tossing it aside.

"I'm trying to!" yelled D.S., whacking a rampaging bull with his scissors.

"Opti, distract the archers," said Crisis.

"Will do," said Opti before flying off.

"I'll take care of the stampede." Crisis released the protective gust of wind, freeing his hands. "No living being on the planet can withstand the full wrath of nature! *Gaia's Gust*" Crisis fired out a twister before enlarging it with smaller gusts of wind.

The stampede was derailed and sent flying every which way.

"We must evacuate. Wayward souls, follow me," said an angel commander, guiding the line of souls toward the southern end of the mountain.

"We've almost made it," said Atlas, readying his bow.

Elephant soldiers left their post at the door and charged at the enemy, wielding massive swords with their trunks.

"Crisis, buddy, a little help here," said D.S., brought to his knees after defending against an elephant's sword swipe.

"If I don't control the twister, we may get caught up in it too," he said, redirecting it toward one of the elephants.

"These warriors are strong, but their souls are subservient to Lum. I will not dilute my arsenal with their weakness," said Atlas, firing multiple arrows into an elephant while deflecting its attacks.

The elephant battling D.S. suddenly collapsed. "Wow, I did it!" he cheered, raising his scissors.

"Not quite," said a shifty character, appearing from behind the elephant.

"Don't move! I can't remember if you were a good guy or a bad guy," said D.S., pointing his scissors at the fancy demon.

"I'm here for the portal. Same as you. Where are all the lovely ladies who were with you?" asked the Prince of Pleasure, his fingers oozing poison.

"Where is the rest of your band of treacherous demon lords?" asked the Captain of Carnage, after rushing up to the Prince.

"No idea. I'm alone at the moment. Well, mostly alone." The Prince clapped his hands.

Lust demons rose out from the snow and instantly engaged the surrounding angels in battle.

"Why do you seek the portal?" asked the Captain, pacing around the traitor.

"I'm an outcast in Sel. Where else can I go?" asked the Prince with a shrug.

"Stand down, Captain. We'll accept your help for the time being," said Atlas, dual-wielding to keep up with the two elephants he was battling.

"There you are," said Thunder, approaching her unlikely ally.

"I buried my forces near the entrance. Seemed like the obvious thing to do," said the Prince.

"Hi, friends," said Opti, waving to the girl team.

"Hey, there seems to be a problem," said D.S., being pushed back by the light wall blocking the entrance.

"What? I thought that was made to keep out demons. Can only angels pass through?" asked Thunder, before slamming into the barrier. "Look for another entrance. I'm staying with the Exps," she said, signaling her troops.

"There's no way in. And more and more angels keep coming. Should we retreat?" asked Deceivant.

"Hey, I bet Muffins can get us in," said Opti, picking up his bunny pal. "Go on, enter your Absence form."

Muffins twitched her nose and turned away.

"Why don't you want to help us?" asked Opti.

"This bunny, was it not once Needle, the Absence guard?" asked Atlas.

"Uh-huh," said Opti.

"Needle seeks balance between the worlds. As an emissary of Sel, Needle understands things beyond the scope of its own realm. Breaching Samsara goes directly against its beliefs," said Atlas.

"Wow, you know Muffins so well," said Opti, rubbing the bunny's ears.

"Yes, perhaps I can reason with Muffins," said Atlas.

"Oh, look. More of your friends showed up," said Ada to the Prince, pointing to a portal that appeared about a third of the way down the mountain.

Lord Sel exited the portal, followed by Riufen, Gladius, the Duke, Wringer, The Vibrator, and Absorb.

"Seems we're a bit late. No matter. Riufen, lead the troops to the entrance. I'm going to take a slight detour." Sel zoomed into a line of souls, dodging incoming attacks while devouring the tasty blue orbs.

"What have you done?" asked an angel, trembling while holding out a spear.

"Created a makeshift army. *Spirit Infusion*," said Sel, spawning Jiva in a line while heading toward the next grouping of souls.

The oftentimes invisible minions of Lord Sel manifested in a straight line. Though their bodies were visible, they were clear, meaning they were souls without bodies. The bodies they had were wispy and green. They broke formation and started stealing soul essence like a vacuum cleaner collects dust.

The Vibrator sped up the mountainside in record time, arriving in front of the inventor. "You're the team leader, right?"

"He is not. I am, obviously," said Hope, hoisted on Nina's shoulders.

"What is your master after?" asked Deceivant, standing in the enemy's path.

"Sel isn't my master. I don't have a clue what that thing wants. Either way, my mission is to capture you. The Dark One seems to think quite highly of you," said The Vibrator.

"Set me down," said Hope, patting her servant's head.

Nina crouched down and Hope stepped off. "I thought you didn't want your feet to touch the floor."

"Do not let that man capture Deceivant. Go on, protect him," said Hope, shooing her servant onward.

"Me-me-me! You think you can stop me? I'm a being who has felt neither pleasure nor pain, you cannot breach my transcendence," said The Vibrator.

"If you've never felt pain, then you cannot understand the drive to survive. You have no fathom of its power. Come at me," said Nina, poised for battle.

The Vibrator zoomed by, swiping the boastful woman off her feet. He kicked off the ground before being knocked aside by the woman's spear. "A hidden weapon. Well played."

"Bob was expecting us to go for the portal. There's nowhere for us to go," said Deceivant while he reloaded his shotgun.

"Indeed. You should surrender," said Riufen, hoisting up Gladius after dispatching three angel bears.

"Aw man, I have to fight him, don't I?" asked D.S., sulking over to the samurai.

"Is something wrong?" asked Riufen.

"You're, like, waaaay too strong, but whatever. I have to protect my dad," said D.S., pointing his scissors.

"Aha, there you are," said the Duke, pointing its lady fingers at the renegade demon lord.

"You were tasked with killing me, weren't you?" asked the Prince.

"Lord Sel, in its awe-inspiring omniscience, predicted that other demon lords would be here," said the Duke, stretching its strings.

"Did your master predict my presence?" asked the Captain, zooming by and slicing the string as it shot toward the Prince.

"Of course he did," said the Duke, flinging its strings at the renegades.

"Hey, everyone! Muffins did it!" cheered Opti, gesturing to the entrance with jazz hands.

"Hurry inside. I'll hold back Sel's forces," said Atlas, standing guard at the entrance while fighting back a horde of Jiva.

"Watch out!" yelled Ada, leaping in front of her husband.

A volley of arrows reigned down, all aimed at Deceivant.

The arrows were pulled into a floating figure above.

"Why must it be my job to protect you?" asked Absorb, floating down to the man who killed him.

"Thank you so much!" cheered Ada, hugging her big boy.

"Where are Devlin and the Sinful Sorority?" asked Deceivant.

"As if I'd tell you anything," said Absorb, circling around the detestable man.

"Will you tell us?" asked D.S., parrying Gladius' lunge with a well-placed jab.

"Each missing member of Lord Sel's armada is attacking a separate temple. This is done so that the angels must divide their forces. I outright refused to attack the temples. Devlin-sama and Demonica are likely attacking Lotus as we speak," said Riufen, following D.S. into the structure.

"Not another step," said Atlas, summoning up the Searing Sword.

"You are no longer a god. You cannot defeat me," said Gladius with a toothy grin.

Atlas slashed the demonic beast and cut down the remaining Jiva. "These souls are too weak."

"My body! Why is it burning!" yelled Gladius, rolling around to put out the invisible flames.

"Those are the fires of my fallen comrades. They are strong, but they will not stop me. Devlin-sama tasked me with making sure nobody makes it through the portal. I will not fail him," said Riufen, unsheathing his sword and coating it.

"I see only one way to solve this then. **AGONY AXE**," said Atlas, standing firm.

Riufen ducked under the sudden swipe. After seeing an opening, he leaped up, slicing Atlas' arm with his sharpened spine.

CHAOS CHAIN!"

Chains came into being and fired off Atlas' arms, catching the samurai in midair.

"My blade cannot cut through. I must grow stronger!" Riufen sliced off his legs and crawled backward on his hands into the building.

The rest of the Freedom Forcers made it inside.

"I'm never late for an appointment. Now will be no different." The Vibrator sped past the building's guard.

"No! I will not let another pass through!" yelled Atlas, wielding two weapons in each hand.

Lord Sel popped out of the ground. "You look exhausted." The realm god tapped Atlas, and the warrior collapsed, unconscious. "Good work, my Jiva. Hurry on in, everyone."

Lord Sel's forces pooled into Samsara while the Jiva armada feasted on the essence of angels still on the mountainside.

Chapter 128: Obligations & Ambitions

Kaity followed Kanasta's trail all the way to Lotus, the rebel base in Femina. "Knowing the Boss, he's already inside," she said, squinting to see further. The young assassin, draped in her niqab, approached the base.

"Not another step," said an armed rebel once the girl approached the steps.

"Sorry. Don't have time to argue." Kaity kicked the guard aside and rushed in. "Now where could he be hiding?" she asked, scanning the rebels who were all seated and eating light fruit.

"Do you need help with something?" asked Miriam, looking up at the new girl with her calm blue eyes.

"Where is the Imam?" asked Kaity.

"We are waiting for the angels to retaliate. The Imam is in hiding," said Miriam.

"Her life is in danger. I need to find her," said Kaity.

"I know where she is," said Illiana, walking up to the new member.

"Can you lead me to her?" asked Kaity.

"How do I know you aren't here to kill her?" asked Illiana, crossing her arms.

Kaity grabbed the girl's hand. "I came here to save someone."

Illiana stared and examined her eyes for the slightest hint of deception. "Follow me," she said, leading the girl out of the dining hall.

"My name is Kaity. What's your name?" she asked as they traveled up the stairs.

"I'm Illiana. You're one of Matteria's friends, aren't you?"

"Yep, that's right," said Kaity with a smile.

"Is he with your other friends?"

"Matteria's trapped right now. We're working on a way to free him," said Kaity softly.

"Don't give up! He means so much to so many people," said Illiana, leading her down the hallway.

"I won't. Promise," said Kaity with a salute.

"See those two guards there? The wall behind them is a secret door. Fatima told us about it before she disappeared."

"Last we saw her, Efil was tending to her wounds. Why hasn't she come back yet?"

"I hope she's okay."

Kaity waved the girl farewell and approached the guards. "Hiya."

"Stay with the other children. You may need to be evacuated if there is an attack," said one of the guards.

Kaity grabbed their necks and hit a pressure point.

They collapsed.

She slid the wall to reveal the hidden passageway. Her eyes scanned the darkness as the assassin made her way down the steps.

Once at the bottom of the steps, she stealthily crept down the hallway.

A man turned the corner and nearly bumped into her.

"There you are," said Kaity, stripping out of her niqab.

"Ah, come to help me finish the job?" asked Kanasta, patting his protégé.

Kaity looked up at him. "You have to stop this."

Kanasta looked down at her curiously.

"You're so obsessed with completing this job that you abandoned your allies."

"The Sassanians were sent to kill the Imam. If I don't act fast then—"

"Then the Imam still dies."

"Then the mission is a failure and the Viper Squad loses credibility."

"Who cares?"

"What?"

"We are in the afterlife. We aren't assassins anymore. There is no Viper Squad."

"As long as I draw breath, the Viper Squad lives on."

"If we don't focus on survival, we are going to die."

Kanasta turned away. "Then we will die completing our mission."

The assassin girl hopped in front of him. "What are you afraid of?"

"It isn't a matter of fear. It's a matter of integrity."

"Your integrity got everyone banished to Absence."

"We're wasting time. This place is a labyrinth. If you are determined to argue against your boss, do so as we walk," said Kanasta, moving onward.

Kaity speedily walked alongside him. "I'm worried about you."

"I am an assassin. I am well prepared to fight against death and willing to accept it should it ambush me," said Kanasta, his eyes straining to see beyond the darkness ahead.

Kaity grabbed onto her papa's arm. "Well I'm not ready to lose you."

"You won't. We've had more difficult jobs," said Kanasta, taking a right turn.

"Why do you have to do this?"

"I refuse to fail a job."

"Why?"

"I don't want the Viper Squad to lose credibility."

"It's not like anyone would find out. We're assassins. Only a small portion of the populace even knows we exist. Why bother?"

"It's my duty as an assassin."

"Why?"

"I won't let my father down."

"Why?"

"He believes in me. I owe it to him! I will not give up on any mission until I am dead!" yelled Kanasta, breathing harshly.

"Deceivant doesn't care about that. Your father wants your help reaching the Portal to Earth."

"I wasn't talking about Deceivant."

"Wait, you have another father? Why didn't you tell me?"

"Keeping secrets is part of the job."

"You don't have to be an assassin. I'll still love you if you aren't. Everyone will."

"An artist must put pen to paper. A musician must write songs. I must kill. It's what I'm good at. It's what I have to offer the world. It's who I am."

"Uh-uh. You're a lot more than that," said Kaity, hugging him from the side.

"And so we arrive," said Kanasta, looking at the target beyond a line of fifty-seven soldiers.

"I expected you would return. You are fixed in your ways," said the Imam, looking at the killer.

"As are you," said Kanasta.

"What do you have to gain from killing me?" asked the Imam.

"That's what I've been asking!" exclaimed Kaity.

Kanasta took a step toward the target. "The life of an assassin isn't about gains or profit. It's about upholding the ideals of equality. Everyone is equal when seen through the lens of a sniper scope."

"Hand the girl over to me," said the Imam.

"She's her own person. I can't make her do anything," said Kanasta.

"I've done him no wrong. And I will do you no harm. Come to me, child."

"I'm staying with papa. If he makes a bad decision, I'll be there to back him up," said Kaity, stripping out of her niqab.

"Come with me or die," said the Imam, a quiver in her voice.

"I'm not going anywhere," said Kaity, her hand on her sidearm.

"A shame." The Imam turned away.

Just as Kanasta sprinted into action, gates rose up around them. The assassins were boxed in.

"Stay close to me," said Kanasta, slowly approaching the gate.

The bars on the sides of the corridor slowly lowered. Pained moans slipped out of the darkness alongside wet footsteps.

Meanwhile: Devlin and Demonica arrived just outside Lotus.

"Are you ready to have some fun?" asked Demonica, gripping his hand.

Devlin abruptly pulled his hand away. "The two of us for one temple—seems a bit overkill, no?" he asked, smiling from beneath his black helmet.

"We're both here because we're on a date," said Demonica, kissing the top of his helmet.

"We're not," said Devlin, shivering.

"You're still shaken up about what happened, aren't you?"

"I could have done this alone," said Devlin, turning away from the woman who violated him.

"We work well together. Devlin, what I did, I did out of love," she said, caressing his armored shoulders.

"Stop. Don't talk about it."

"Fine, we'll talk more after we've returned from our date," said Demonica with a smile.

"Looks like we're not the only ones on a mission," said Devlin, pointing to a group of men heading up the stairs.

A man approached the dark figures. "Hey you two! Are you demons?"

"More like gods," said Devlin, creating dark energy from his hands.

"You're after the bounty too, aren't you?" asked the man, hoisting up a spiked club.

"You mean for the Imam?" asked Devlin.

"Well yeah, she's the main prize. But each one we kill, whether an old lady or a little girl, grants us bliss aplenty," said the man with a grin.

"Is that so?"

"It sure is. Angels offered this job to bounty hunters all across Lum. Guess we'll be competing once we're inside," said the man before turning his back.

A single wire shot into the man's back, coiled around his spine, and tore it out. "No we won't."

"So quick. I was hoping we could play around for a bit," said Demonica.

"There are plenty more," said Devlin, setting his sights on a group approaching the rebel base.

Demonica shot out chains of blood that pulled the sinners up to her and her date. "How did any of you make it to Lum?"

"I remember my sins, and I ask for forgiveness. God forgives those who repent."

"You need a penitent mind to truly regret. And regrets don't do anything for anyone. One must make amends for what they have done through their actions," said Devlin, calmly lashing his wires against the lowlifes.

Demonica looked at him longingly.

"What is it?" asked Devlin, turning to her as his wires strangled one of the men.

Demonica offered her hand. "May I have this dance?" she asked, batting her eyelashes.

"Heheh-ahahahaha! Sure, why not?" Devlin's helmet dissolved as he grabbed her hand.

Demonica spun him around as she fired blood bullets from her fingers. Their fingers parted only to rejoin by tearing through a man's chest. Her blood shot out like daggers alongside his serrated wires, creating fireworks of violence as they leaped through the air together.

"This is what I've always wanted," she said, holding her beloved to her blood-drenched bosom.

"Let's continue this dance by the stairs. It's up to us to clean up after Lum's mess," said Devlin, slicing off the head of one of the whimpering cowards.

"Lead the way," said Demonica, her eyes linked to his.

Meanwhile: inside the underground labyrinth beneath Lotus, Kanasta, and Kaity were fighting off tortured humans from all sides.

"Ugh. More of them? Why are there even demons here?" asked Kaity.

"Such things are not our concern. You have your side covered?" asked Kanasta, slicing the demons in front of him with a razor-sharp string.

"I do, but they just keep coming. I'm running low on ammo. I guess I should have stopped by the armory," said Kaity, piercing her claws into a demon's throat.

The roof exploded. Rubble came crashing down on the assassins.

Kanasta busted out from beneath the pile and immediately started digging for his daughter. "Kaity, are you alright?" he asked, trying to ignore the demons biting at his legs.

Kaity stood up, holding her head. "I'm a bit dizzy," she said, steadying her aim before getting a headshot on an approaching demon.

"This place is caving in, and there are likely more traps ahead. Head back up the stairs. I'll meet with you once the job is complete," said Kanasta.

"Just come with me," said Kaity, tugging his arm with one hand while shooting incoming demons with the other.

"Not an option." Kanasta tore the demons off him and tossed them aside. He then hoisted his apprentice onto his shoulders. "We'll go together."

Tormented screams echoed from behind them.

A small boxy robot zoomed by, partly melted from the acidic blood on its body.

"BoneSaw!" cheered Kaity.

The mechanical assassin waved at his fellow killer while speeding past them.

"The gang's all here," said Kanasta, slamming through the gate and sprinting down the hallway.

On the steps of Lotus, blood, gore, and flesh dyed the pearly steps and the once white grass beneath them.

"That was incredible!" gasped Demonica, grinding against her dark prince.

"They never belonged here. And now they can't pollute the world by reincarnating," said Devlin, wiping a filthy red spot off his cheek.

"Shall we head inside? There should be plenty more little toys for us to break," said Demonica, her eyes gleaming with excitement.

"Lum wants the rebels dead. Why should we do her dirty work? Our target is the Imam. Let's find out where she is and end it," said Devlin, his wires spreading out from his back to finish off any injured bounty hunters.

Meanwhile: Kanasta and Kaity were rushing through the labyrinth.

"BoneSaw has cleared the way yet again!" cheered Kaity, dangling upside down while her legs kept her hoisted on her papa's back.

"BoneSaw's run into some obvious triggers. It's unbecoming of a skilled killer," said Kanasta.

"My little sibling is just looking out for us. Little guy's taken a bullet for me more than a few times," said Kaity.

An explosion was heard up ahead.

Kanasta rushed onward to find his child buried under some rubble.

"Is BoneSaw okay?" asked Kaity, hoping off Kanasta's back.

The little robot rolled onto its treads and gave a salute.

"Good work," said Kanasta, saluting back.

Kaity picked up her robot pal. "That's enough. You could get seriously hurt. Let's all stick together from here on out, okay?" she asked, rubbing the robot's surface.

BoneSaw nodded.

When they reached the fork, the little bot pointed right.

"Already scouted ahead. I'm impressed," said Kanasta, making haste down the hallway.

They soon reached a dead end.

"Another one?" Kanasta rolled his eyes.

Kaity leaned against the wall. I hear sounds from the other side.

"Well then." Kanasta punched the wall, making it crumble.

The Imam and her troops were just beyond, in a circular well-lit area.

"Wait, this is oil? I thought it was just grimy water," said Kaity.

"This is your last chance. Turn back now or burn here," said the Imam.

Kanasta took a step forward.

The archers loaded their flame arrows.

"I do not make empty threats. Another step and death awaits."

"Kaity, can you make the shot?" asked Kanasta, plopping her on his shoulders.

"Do we really have to do this?"

"She's Lum's enemy. Don't you want her dead?"

"I guess so," said Kaity with a shrug. Her rifle unfolded. She raised it.

"Fire!" yelled the Imam, turning away.

The archers fired their flaming arrows into an oil canister partially buried in the oil stream.

Kanasta kicked BoneSaw and jumped up in the same movement. The explosion sent him smashing into the ceiling.

He dug his fingers into the wet rock.

"They live...how?" asked the Imam, stepping back.

"The suits my dad made are flame resistant," said Kaity, lining up the shot.

The Imam's warriors stood in front of her.

"Kaity's plasma bullets can shoot through a line of tanks. Go for it. Take the shot," said Kanasta, looking up at his little girl with pride.

Kaity lowered her gun. "We only have one target. Can't have people saying the Viper Squad is sloppy. Plus, I think the little guy's earned it," she said, sticking out her tongue.

A projectile saw sped past the Imam. Blood spurted out from her side before she collapsed.

"Another day, another job," said Kanasta, dropping from the ceiling.

Chapter 129: Guardians of the Portal

Previously: The Freedom Forcers gained entry into Samsara.

The inside of Samsara was cold and the air was thin. The walls were made up of swirling energy and the floor was entirely metallic. Angels were lined up on the balcony, with light arrows prepped for firing. Two goddesses stood in front of the portal: Efil and Etaf. The Portal to Earth was too small for anything but a soul to enter.

"We're almost there," said Deceivant, flashing his darling little queen a smile.

"Obviously," said Hope.

"Turn back. If you leave now, I won't have to kill any of you. This isn't how it was supposed to turn out," said Efil, wiping her eyes before forming two swords.

"We're done being pulled along by Lum's will. We are heading home," said Deceivant, raising his gun.

"You take them. I'll handle Sel's forces," said Etaf, raising the Destiny Sword.

"Oh, there appears to be a misunderstanding. We're here to help safeguard the portal," said Sel with a bow.

Atlas entered the room, using a staff as a walking stick. "My wife is going through that portal. Not even you will stop that," he said, glaring at his ex-boss.

"Let me fight Sel's forces," said Efil.

"Weren't you listening? I'm on your side," said Sel.

"No, Efil. You chose to side with the Exps. It's your job to end them now," said Etaf.

"You'll die if you fight Sel," said Efil.

"I can only die by your hand," said Etaf with a smile.

"Are you so sure? I mean, the prophecy said one of you will die in a battle to the death. It doesn't say whether you are fighting each other or an enemy," said Lord Sel.

"Silence. It's my prophecy. I know what it means," said Etaf, approaching the enemy.

"Fine. If you want to fight us, then we will breach the portal. Who wants to return to Earth?" asked Sel, turning to its pawns.

"The people need me," said The Vibrator.

"Home. Home. Home," repeated the Wringer through its tape recorder.

"I'm only going if Deceivant goes. Then I'll kill him and once he arrives in Sel, he'll be all yours," said Absorb.

"Well then, that's that. Strike her down. Fighting a Lum god is forbidden, so my hands are tied," said Lord Sel, seeping into the ground.

Etaf tossed her sword. After teleporting up to it, she sliced the enemy at her side.

The Wringer was cut in two.

Gladius lunged at the goddess only to have his eye pierced by the sword. "Insolence!" he yelled, slamming his tail into the armored goddess.

Etaf kicked the tail aside and parried the hardened spine of her next attacker. She teleported once more before grabbing her sword from overhead and slicing the warrior in two.

"Shame that it came to this. I expected as much from Nina, she only cares about herself. But for the rest of you to betray Lum…I'm beyond mercy now," said Efil, the compassion in her voice replaced with disgust.

"If Hope was just allowed to go through the portal, we wouldn't be here. You brought this upon yourself," said Deceivant.

"Another step and I will kill you," said Efil, staring at the treacherous inventor.

"Fatima, is that you?" asked Thunder, peering at the angel behind the goddess.

Fatima's body was cloaked in Lum energy, wearing it like a skin-tight suit. Above the thin aura were plates of solidified light armor. The girl's eyes were white, like pearls. She looked up at the rebels without emotion.

"What did you do to her?" asked Nina.

"That's the girl we trusted with you!" yelled Deceivant.

"Lum decided it would be best to make her into a mawali," said Efil, looking at the ground.

"She forced this transformation upon her. My child would never give into Lum willingly," said Thunder, raising her spear.

"Fatima is your daughter? How did you both end up together in Lum?" asked Nina.

"She was killed before me, a victim of violence and hate. I swore to avenge her and set out to kill every member of the local anti-Muslim groups. Once they were all dead…I couldn't leave her alone. If it weren't for the Imam, no doubt I would never have met my daughter in the afterlife," said Thunder, smiling beneath her cloth.

"Here I thought you were just a muscle-brained blind follower. I'm pleasantly surprised," said Nina with a smile.

"Thunder, I'll do all I can to help your daughter," said Deceivant.

"To think you would be the one who understands me most," said Thunder, smiling at him.

"If you all leave now, there won't be any casualties," said Efil, staring at the rebels with extra conviction.

"Move aside, evil lady," said D.S., pointing his scissors.

"You murdered angels just so you can force your way into the Portal to Earth. You are breaking the ancient laws of Lum for your own selfish reasons," said Efil, stepping toward Lum's enemies.

"Hey, uh, she's kind of got a point. When did we become bad guys?" asked D.S.

"Stop her, slave," commanded Hope.

Violet rushed in and slashed Efil with her aura blades.

The goddess healed upon injury and kicked the entranced enemy aside.

"Good or evil, I'm protecting my family and my friends!" yelled D.S., running in.

Efil's blades passed through his scissors, rusting them and making them break in two.

"Snippy! How could you?" D.S. grabbed the broken sharp parts and lunged them at the mean lady.

Thunder came around the back, thrusting her spear at the goddess.

Fatima fired arrows in a line up the rebel's side.

"You don't recognize me at all, do you?" asked Thunder, tearing out the arrows as she dodged the next volley.

"*Earthly Exhale*."

Efil was suddenly flung into the air by a powerful gust.

"Your ancient laws aren't real. They're an artificial construct. If nature deemed us unfit to return to Earth, then we wouldn't be able to go through the portal," said Crisis, riding his own gust. "*Terra's Tears*." The weatherman buried the goddess under seven feet of snow. "Go through now!"

"I don't think so!" Lord Sel popped out from below and fired a laser at Deceivant.

Ada rammed into her husband to propel him to safety, but not before his chest was pierced.

"Alright, what gives? You said my job was to keep him alive but then you shoot him!" yelled Absorb.

"Yes, you didn't do a very good job," said Sel, turning side to side.

"Does that mean I can kill him? I really want to," said Absorb, floating around his creator.

"No, but you know what it does mean: we're the only ones who can save him now that Efil is an enemy. He has to come with me or he'll die," said Sel with an intense gaze.

"I don't get this at all. You were our friend!" yelled D.S., running to help his daddy.

"You cannot permit him to die," said Hope, grabbing her warrior's arm.

"What do you expect me to do? It's a fatal wound," said Nina.

"No excuses! Save him!" yelled Hope.

Nina rushed off and kicked Fatima into the air. "A mother shouldn't have to fight her own daughter. I'll keep her busy."

"No. I must take responsibility for what happened. I should have been there for her," said Thunder, pinning her daughter down.

"Stand ready. She's back," said Crisis, firing a hailstorm at the goddess. "CHRONO BARRIER." Efil created a wall with her aura, causing the hail to become air once it passed through.

Crisis leaped out of the way when the barrier was fired out.

Efil teleported up to Deceivant. "TIME LAPSE." Her aura shot into his wound.

The injury wasn't healed; it was as if it had never happened.

"Why are you helping your enemy?" asked Sel, popping out behind Lum's pet.

"You are Lum's greatest enemy. I will not hand him over to you," said Efil.

"As if you could stop me," said Lord Sel with a smile.

"Kaity and Kanasta, where are they?" asked Efil, turning to face the Freedom Forcers.

"Forget about them. You're dealing with us," said Atlas, limping up to the goddess.

"They left for Lotus to kill the Imam," said Hope.

"It's as I thought. Etaf, I must finish the mission Lum gave me. I leave defending the portal in your hands." Efil created a portal.

"Wait, you said that mission was a lie," said D.S.

Etaf turned to Efil as she fought off her enemies.

"I was lying to you. I didn't want you to think of Lum as cruel," said Efil with a shaky voice.

"Protect your leader. I'll make sure your daughter comes back alive," said Nina.

"Thank you. May Allah watch over you always." Thunder fired at the goddess before rushing inside the portal to Lotus.

"Hurry up and go. The Sassanians are waiting just outside Lotus, meet with them and make a portal underground," said Etaf, leaping to dodge various attacks.

"What about you?" asked Efil.

"I can handle all of them," said Etaf, teleporting around the regenerating samurai after each slash.

Efil nodded. "Come along, angel." The goddess created a new portal and entered it.

Fatima fired arrows at Nina as she rushed into the portal.

"Damn it, she got away!" yelled Nina, rushing in before the portal vanished. "You know what, forget her. She doesn't recognize me anyway. I'll just find someone else to worship me."

"Now's our chance," said Deceivant.

"Our chance for what? The portal is too small for us to fit," said Hope.

"Won't know until we try." Nina ran toward the portal before being swiped off her feet by a badly dressed man.

"You of all people are not getting through!" yelled The Vibrator, pummeling her with punches all the way to the back wall.

"Neither are you!" Absorb slammed into Deceivant, pushing him out of the structure.

"We don't need him," said Hope, grabbing her mother's hand and walking toward home.

Etaf flung her blade, kicked Gladius and then teleported in front of the portal, holding out the Destiny Sword. "This is as far as you go. Fire!"

The angels on the balcony aimed at the goddess and fired.

The arrows pierced into Etaf, sending Lum energy flowing into her.

"KAMUI'S WRATH!" The goddess sliced the air, cutting everything in front of her with her honed aura.

A black wall of energy erupted, devouring the unseen slash.

"There's no need to kill them. Some of them could be rather useful to me," said Lord Sel.

"You've interfered for the last time." Etaf slashed the air as the dark god spun around.

Lord Sel entered his phase form, making the slashes swirl around him. "You are rather impressive," said the Dark One before passing through the ground, causing the slashes to hit the floor instead.

"Now to end you." Etaf froze in place. Her eyes shrank as they met Napkin's.

The little kitten was sitting up, looking right at her.

"You dare defy fate?" she asked, her hands trembling.

413

"Tata, mortals!" cheered The Vibrator, placing his hand on the portal. He then vanished without a trace.

"Ah, so it's a teleporter, not a portal," said the Prince of Pleasure, placing his hand on it.

"I will not permit him to wreak havoc on my lord's homeland!" yelled the Captain, rushing after the Prince.

"Home," said Wringer, touching the teleporter.

"There, can you fight now?" asked Hope, looking up at the large man.

"Yes. I feel completely revitalized. Thank you, Violet," said Atlas with a bow.

"Your gratitude should fall upon me. I'm the one who ordered her to heal you."

"Thank you, Queen Hope," said Atlas with a nod.

"Well, that's more like it," said Hope with a smile.

Atlas fired Appalling Arrows at Sel's forces, stopping their intrusion.

"Son, get her home. Mommy is going to stay with Daddy, okay?" asked Ada, touching her big boy's cheeks.

"Uh-huh. I'll make sure she makes it!" D.S. grabbed his older sister and brought her to the teleporter.

"You've done well. Slave, stay and protect my mother and that dreadful man," said Hope before vanishing.

Violet nodded and approached Ada.

"I'm going in. Are you coming?" asked Opti, looking at his fluffy comrade.

Muffins hopped out of his arms.

"I understand," said Opti, flying to the teleporter.

Atlas picked up his wife. "Let's go."

Riufen blocked his path. "I have my orders."

"And I have obligations to get my wife home," said Atlas, summoning the Searing Sword and then wrapping the Wailing Whip around it. "Family bonds are not to be underestimated." He jabbed the sword at the samurai.

Riufen ducked only to be sliced by the spikes of the whip. He clenched his teeth, fighting the need to cry out, and sliced Atlas' side with his spine.

"Stand aside. He's trying to help his wife!" yelled Crisis, knocking Riufen off his feet with a gust of wind.

"Thanks for the help," said Image.

"You helped me too." Crisis turned to Atlas. "I'll keep her safe from people like you, okay?"

"You're coming along, right?" asked Image, looking at her husband.

"I was created to defend Zenero. But living as a god in Sel made me realize that the balance of Sellum is worth protecting as well. I may not return, but my love for you cannot be vanquished."

Image smiled at him and kissed his lips. "If you survive, we'll go on a nice long vacation, okay?"

"I look forward to it," said Atlas, before his wife went back home.

"You know what, I think I'll stay. Things are a bit more interesting here. *Earthly Exhale*," said Crisis, sending mini tornadoes at the approaching enemies.

"Suit yourself. I'm out of here," said Nina before vanishing.

Napkin looked out at his allies.

"Go on, the rest of us are staying," said Atlas.

"*Mew!*" Napkin stayed his ground, making sure Etaf could not move.

"Move aside!" yelled Gladius, glaring at the muscle-bound ex-god.

Lord Sel popped out from between them. "What, you want to go to Earth too?"

"If I don't go after them, they will only inconvenience you in the future," said Gladius.

"Not really. You see, what they touched isn't the actual teleporter," said Sel.

"To Sel it isn't," said Gladius, touching the portal before vanishing.

"What are you saying?" asked Atlas.

"It did teleport them, but not to Earth," said Sel, circling around the special object.

"Then where are they?" asked Atlas, turning to grab the teleporter.

Sel fired a beam of darkness that ate up the device. "Who knows?"

"You allowed your allies to go through, knowing they would be in danger," said Atlas.

"Is it the uncertainty that bothers you? I mean, you did murder your comrades. Honestly the ones who went through were, well, expendable. They weren't truly loyal to me, and their abilities aren't all that special. Maybe they won't die; maybe they will. Perhaps we'll find out one day…or not," said Sel with a shrug.

"Expendable? Gladius was my sword. There must be a way to retrieve him," said Riufen, approaching the dark realm god.

"I gave him fair warning."

A bright light poured into the room.

"What is that?" asked Lord Sel, cowering under a fog of darkness.

"Your army of Jiva have been neutralized," said the voice.

"How?" asked Lord Sel, spreading out darkness as it was being destroyed.

"They lacked a will of their own. That allowed you to turn them into your slaves. I simply purified them of your influence." The light focused into a beam and barraged the Dark One's barrier.

"So I finally got you to come out," said Lord Sel, swerving to dodge the beam while closing in on his target.

"I've already put up a barrier. You cannot run. I will finish you here and now. RAMAH AN-NUR." Light poured out of Lum, forming into a spear.

"You've blocked off my escape, you have hordes of angels here to command, and you can channel energy from everything around you. Wonderful! This should be fun! *Eyeball Ram!*" exclaimed Sel before slamming into the goddess.

The Great Goddess was pushed out of the structure.

With his dark sword pressed against her light spear, Lord Sel looked up at the barrier around the mountain.

"Oh, it's that time already?" Lum's energy erupted from her throne room, creating a pillar of light signaling all to prayer. "The dark king will perish before the visitors complete their sanctioned prayers to me."

Chapter 130: The Job, Portal, & the Throne

Previously: Devlin and Demonica entered Lotus, seeking out the Imam.

The guards inside Lotus were fighting off the bounty hunters who had breached the building.

"It's the Black Knight!" screamed one of the guards.

"And his lover!" exclaimed Demonica, putting her arms over his shoulders.

Devlin's wires pulled her arms off.

"Are you afraid of me?" she asked.

"Where is the Imam?" asked Devlin, his wires coiling around a guard who approached them.

"I'll die before I tell you anything," she said, glaring at him with raw faith.

"Very well then." Devlin's wires seeped back into Bravery and he moved out of the dining hall, pushing aside anyone who got in his way.

"Auuuh. That was boring. Come on, can't we just kill a few of them? Ooh, ooh, the guards are by the staircase. They're fighting the bounty hunters. We can kill them all at once," said Demonica, grabbing onto his arm.

"Might as well." Devlin turned around and fired black energy out from his fingertips.

The scum fighting the rebel guards fell one by one.

"Lord Sel has tasked us with keeping the Imam safe. You all know Lum wants her dead. Where is she?" asked Devlin, looking over the crowd of shocked eyes.

"I'll take you there," said Heaven's Thunder, approaching the demon gods.

Demonica smiled at Devlin. "Your cruelty gets my juices flowing. But it's your kindness, your love, that makes my heart tremble. Your drive for equality made me fall in love with you," she said, barraging his cheek with kisses from her serpent tongue. "Not that it doesn't turn me on as well. It gets me so hot," she said, licking his ear.

"You're one of a kind. Come on, let's move. There may already be some assassins who have found her," said Devlin, following their guide up the steps.

Previously: in a moment of confusion, the Imam was mortally wounded by BoneSaw.

The Imam's blood dripped on the wet earth.

417

The rebel soldiers gathered around their fallen leader.

"It's no use. BoneSaw is a skilled killer. There's no need for you to fear for your lives; the Imam was my only target," said Kanasta.

"Watch out!" Kaity turned around and fired at the approaching figure.

A blood spike shot past her and bore into the assassin boss' shoulder.

"Watch it, you almost hit Kaity," said Devlin, glaring at the demon queen.

Thunder leaped up, grabbed Kaity, and slammed her to the ground. "Surrender now."

"Okay, whatever. The job is done anyway," said Kaity, letting go of her sniper.

"No." Thunder froze, giving the young assassin an opening to knock her off.

"It's true," said Kanasta, stepping on top of the rebel warrior.

"She seems fine to me," said Demonica with a grin, patting her handy little gimp.

"When did he get here?" asked Devlin.

The Imam stood up. Not only had the wound healed, even the slice in her niqab was fixed. "You almost arrived too late," she said, walking past her guards.

"But I didn't," said Demonica, creating blood chains to pin down the assassins.

"Wait, I'm confused, aren't we here to kill her?" asked Devlin.

"Not at all. I just like messing with you," said Demonica with a sly smile.

"This goddess is an ally to Allah's Jannah. She has supplied us with warriors from her realm and asks nothing in return," said the Imam, bowing to her dark ally.

"I find that hard to believe," said Devlin, staring at the tricky goddess inquisitively.

"Is it really? The Imam's forces have openly declared Lum an enemy. Why shouldn't I offer a helping hand when we have so much in common?" asked Demonica, layering extra chains over the struggling assassins.

"Should we run?" asked Kaity.

"An angel said that the Sassanians were on their way. We must break free and kill her before it is too late," said Kanasta, pushing off the ground.

"And here she is," said Demonica, looking at the Lum portal with wide eyes.

Efil emerged from the portal of light, followed by the Sassanians and lastly a human angel.

"Let my daughter go!" yelled Thunder, rushing at Efil.

The human angel fired an arrow into the attacker.

Thunder tore out the arrow before being tossed aside by the gorilla angel.

"Alright, I'll make this really easy. Come with me and I won't kill all the angels here," said Demonica, summoning up the Death Scythe and pointing it at Efil.

"Lum has tasked me with a mission. If you intrude, you will regret it." said Efil, forming dual aura blades.

"You were the one who hired these assassins, weren't you?" asked the Imam, taking shelter behind the demon goddess.

"I know not who hired them. All I know is that Lum needs you to leave," said Efil, slashing through two guards and aging their bodies to dust.

One of the guards went on all fours and leaped at the light goddess.

The winged shark caught the enemy in midair, spraying acidic blood on its body.

"Taking demons in as your protectors, is there nothing you won't do to achieve your goals?" asked Efil, slicing down an approaching guard with minimal effort.

"Which one of us defends the Imam?" asked Devlin, raising Bravery.

"Who cares about her? I came here for Efil. Subdue her and bring her in," said Demonica.

"Understood. **RUIN**," said Devlin, firing a dark ray at the goddess.

Efil emitted a blast of white energy from her hand, dispelling the darkness.

"**Crimson Shower**," Demonica fired out blood droplets that collected in the air.

Efil swerved to dodge a Sel shot. "**CHRONO BARRIER**!" The goddess projected an age shield, aging the incoming blood bullets into oblivion.

Thunder slammed her spear into Fatima's crossbow, shattering it to pieces.

The angel girl sprouted wings and slammed into her enemy, bringing her into the nearby oil stream.

Kanasta looked up at the Imam. "What do you value more, your life or your title?"

"Why should I answer you?" asked the Imam, glaring at the killer.

"Depending on your answer, I may protect your life rather than take it," said Kanasta with the slightest smile.

"My life. If things go according to plan, I may not even need my title as the leader of Allah's Jannah," said the Imam.

"Then renounce your title here and now in return for my assistance!" yelled Kanasta.

The Goddess of Death stepped up once the Goddess of Life was within range. "ᴅᴇᴠᴏᴛᴉᴏɴ ᴇssᴇɴᴄᴇ." Efil stacked her auras and projected them out from her blades, aging blood projectiles and purifying darkness beams.

"Keep her busy. I'm going to kill all her little minions," said Demonica, walking past Devlin.

"Wait! There is no longer a reason to fight!" yelled the Imam.

"My orders are to end the Imam. I will not fail Lum," said Efil, signaling all the Sassanians to attack the radical leader.

"I renounce my title as the leader of Allah's Jannah. I am no longer the Imam! I am Aisha now. Just another soul in Lum."

Efil teleported in front of the terrified woman and raised her hand, stopping the Sassanians in their tracks. "Then does that make Thunder the leader?" asked the goddess, scanning the oil river for movement.

"No! Allah's Jannah is officially disbanded!" exclaimed the ex-Imam.

"And so I dethroned the Imam, just as my client asked," said Kanasta.

"You just saved her," said Kaity with wide eyes.

"Indeed. A true assassin is just as ready to grant life as to take it," said Kanasta, breaking free of the blood chains.

Kaity extended her claws and tore up the bindings around her.

Thunder came flying out of the lake while being strangled by her daughter.

"Stand down, angel. Our orders have changed," said Efil.

Thunder rushed up to Demonica. "Please, save my daughter. She has been corrupted by the light."

"As a future mother, I am empathetic to your plight. Go on, slave!" yelled Demonica, stabbing her heel into the gimps back.

Gimpy raised its hands. "ᴅᴀʀᴋɴᴇss." Demonica's slave poured darkness into Lum's puppet.

The angel girl screamed as the darkness ate away at her.

"You're killing her!" yelled Thunder, rushing to her daughter's side.

"This is the only way to save her from Lum's influence. You'll thank me later," said Demonica.

"Okay, so what do we do now?" asked Devlin, pooling Sel energy into his hand.

"Our mission is the same: capture Efil," said Demonica, flying toward her opposite.

Efil blinded everyone in the area by emitting beams of light from her body.

When she could finally see, Demonica found herself sliced in two and gradually being purified.

The gimp teleported up to Mistress and poured its energy into her, stopping the light from consuming her completely.

"If the mission was to kill her, she would be dead already. Devlin, I leave the rest to you," said Demonica, grinding her teeth.

"You can't leave just yet. Please, send me to the Observatory," said the ex-Imam.

"Sure, why not? Slave, take her there. And bring Thunder along too," said Demonica.

Gimpy bowed.

Demonica, the ex-Imam, and Thunder all vanished in an instant.

The Vibrator was the first to touch the teleporter to Earth. He did not arrive where he expected.

The room was spherical and rotating. Sections of the floor were colored green; others were more of a sandy color. Most of it was blue, though there were some red splotches next to the dead bodies.

"Well, well, looks like we weren't the first to arrive," said the Prince of Pleasure, looking at the broken bodies of humans of all creeds. "Mmm, they smell fresh."

"I won't allow you to bring this place to—where are we?" asked the Captain of Carnage, looking at what appeared to be miniature landmasses.

Wringer was the next to arrive. It immediately left the group and explored the area.

"I'm not sure where we are. What do you say we call a truce until we both arrive safely on Earth?" asked the Prince, outstretching his hand.

"I only came here to stop you. We are beings of Sel; we cannot return to Earth." The Captain sped by, slicing the Prince's arm.

"Nasty little critter," said the Prince, shooting out poison from his wound at his nimble enemy.

"Ah, now it makes sense," said Hope, looking out at the dome.

"You know where we are?" asked The Vibrator.

"But of course. There cannot be a single portal to Earth. If that were the case, then each and every new life would have to spawn in the exact same location. This place has multiple portals from which their locations can be adjusted via the knobs at the sides," said Hope, spinning the knob and cycling through the wombs of many animals in the New Zealand region.

"So then our intrusion will no doubt lead to stillbirths worldwide," said Image, noticing that the portals were all closed off.

"Indeed. We've fostered an event that will be etched in history," said Hope with a slight smile.

"Um, this isn't Earth," said Nina, looking around.

"You there, find a way to open up the portals. There's some kind of shield blocking them," said Hope, pressing her heel against the coating.

"I only took orders from you so that you wouldn't let my team throw me away. Now that I'm heading home, I don't need you anymore," said Nina, triggering her shirt to burst.

The explosion did not break the barrier.

"You say that, and yet you're doing my bidding," said Hope, walking past the warrior to a nearby portal.

"Aright! Come out!" yelled Gladius.

"Foolish reptile, we are the only ones here," said The Vibrator.

"You're the fool. Do you not see the dead bodies?" Hope pointed to a sixteen-foot statue, partially covered in fresh blood. "No doubt that thing is more than a decoration."

"Well then, what are you waiting for? Come at us!" hollered Nina to the statue.

No response.

Napkin appeared, looked around curiously, and then lowered his head.

"I order you to intimidate that statue into dropping the barriers," said Hope, rubbing under the cat's chin.

Napkin nodded. He looked up at the statue and then turned around.

"That was an order." Hope turned around to face the two demon lords. "And stop fighting, you two. We may need you to take down the portal guardian. We all want to go back home. For the time being, we must cooperate."

"She's got a point," said the Prince, leaping out of the way of the Captain's blunderbuss blast.

"My mission is to stop you. If we all die, then so be it!" yelled the Captain, quickening his pursuit.

"Little one, stop him," commanded Hope, nudging the cat with her foot.

Napkin went up to the Captain and roared. "*Mew*."

The armored demon lord was frozen in place. "I'm a proud warrior. Why do I feel fear?" asked the Captain, grinding his teeth in frustration.

"Good. Nina, destroy the statue," said Hope with a commanding finger.

"Already on it. *Super Sexy Slow Mo Strip*," said Nina, taking her time removing her trappings.

"What are you stalling for?" asked Hope, tapping her foot.

"You wouldn't understand," said Nina, rolling her eyes as she slipped out of her garments. "*Dynamite Body, Explosive Clothes!*" The sexy survivalist tossed her clothes on the statue's joints and triggered them to burst.

The explosion did no damage.

"Such immodesty." The arm of the statue reached out and grabbed the survivalist.

"So, you've finally decided to speak. I am Queen Hope, ambassador and ruler of the Exps," said Hope, straightening her dress.

"I am Ytitsahc of the Seven Holy Virtues. You have entered a place you do not belong. As the Virtue of Chastity, I shall strike you down," it said in a deep reverberating voice, walking toward the tiny mortal.

"I thought the Virtues were looking for a peaceful solution to solve the war between Sel and Lum," said Gladius.

"Indeed we are," said a proud, brisk voice from behind the statue. She leaped out and landed in front of the ambassador. "I am Ecnedurp, leader of the Seven Holy Virtues. Your presence here, at the Dome of Decision, has caused a disruption in our peace meetings. Once you have all arrived, you will be dealt with swiftly."

"Would it be proper for me to address you as the Queen of the Virtues?" asked Hope.

"Hey, tell it to let me go," said Nina, struggling in the living statue's grip.

"That title seems appropriate enough, Ambassador Hope," said Ecnedurp with a salute.

"I'm a bit confused. Are Sel and Lum officially at war?" asked the Prince.

"They are not, but because she is a forward thinker, Ecnedurp decided to form strategies to end the war should it occur. It's really none of your concern though. She'll be done with the both of you in less than a minute," said Gladius with a toothy grin.

"Your people have caused a disruption in the influx of souls. As the only one fit for the task, I am charged with determining the proper incarnation for the visitors based on their soul memory. Going against the laws of Lum is one thing, but you have put me behind schedule," said Ecnedurp.

"Enough talking. Hey lady, if I beat you, then you'll open up the portals. Sound good?" asked The Vibrator.

Ecnedurp turned to her challenger. "I accept the terms you have proposed."

The Vibrator zoomed up and slammed his fist into the lady. His arm shattered.

Ecnedurp moved both her and Hope out of the way before the blood could spray on them. "What say you in defense?"

"Ecnedurp, she's going to slip out of my grip. Is it okay if I crush her? I don't think the others are coming," said Ytitsahc.

Ecnedurp turned to Hope.

"I represent all Exps, but that one has been rather defiant lately. Do as you please," said Hope, smiling at the living statue.

"Enemy of Lum, I'll permit you a moment to repent for your crimes against chastity," said Ytitsahc, bringing the heathen up to its face.

"I'm a virgin! And I'm determined to stay that way forever," said Nina.

"Wonderful. You shall die a virgin," said Ytitsahc.

"Wait up! Would an enemy of Lum carry Allah's Nur with her?" "The sacred scripture? You have it?"

"That's right. But I can only show you if you release me."

Ytitsahc nodded and released her grip.

"Just for the record, I'm not lying about the virgin thing." Nina turned around and ran as fast as she could.

"Show me the scripture or die now!" yelled Ytitsahc, chasing after the heathen.

"I really did have it, well the other me did. She handed it over to Ada for safekeeping. Speaking of which..." Nina knocked her knuckles against her head. "Hey, are you listening? I surrender control over to you! I know you won't go through the portal, but I don't care about that right now! You better not get us killed!"

Nina's eyes closed for a second before she leaped over the deity's fist. "I will bring Devlin's family back home." She ran up the massive arm, all the while slicing it with her katana.

"Shall we continue?" asked Hope, turning back to face her fellow queen.

"We shall."

"I have nothing to say in defense of the transgressions of my people and their disruption of your work schedule. However, given that you value your time more than the laws of your leader, I have a proposal. Rather than spend time deliberating or killing us, open the portals and let us through. That way we won't bother you any longer and the influx of souls can resume uninterrupted."

Ecnedurp stared at the ambassador in silence.

"Take as much time as you need thinking it over. I'm in no rush," said Hope with a smile.

"Who exactly are you asking me to grant passage to?" asked Ecnedurp, crouching down to examine the queen's reaction.

"Napkin and Image. I had planned on going through, but I was expecting someone to come along with me. Given that they aren't here, I'd rather return to Lum with my devoted ally Nina and the brave demon lord. I believe he called himself the Captain of Carnage."

"And what of the others?"

"They are not my responsibility."

"Ytitsahc, where are the others?" asked Ecnedurp, looking around the dome.

"They're…gone? You were distracting me so they could escape, weren't you?" asked the armored virtue, slamming its foot down on the heathen.

"You only have yourself to blame," said Nina, scanning for an open portal as she ran up her opponent's back.

"Well then, do we have a deal?" asked Hope, outstretching her royal arm.

Thunder and Aisha arrived inside Lum's throne room.

"This is really it. We've reached it," said Aisha, raising her hands.

"To think I once spoke out against making deals with demons. Demonica ended up far more trustworthy than Efil. I pray she really is healing my daughter," said Thunder, shaken up.

"Look at the mountains and the forests. All of Lum is before us!" exclaimed Aisha, smiling extra wide through her cloth when noticing Lotus.

"Now that we are here, what are your orders?" asked Thunder.

Aisha turned to the ex-commander. "You have no orders. I am no longer the Imam. That makes the two of us friends. No more, no less."

"I swore my life in service to you, not merely as thanks for saving my daughter but because of the compassion, love, and fortitude you ruled with. Imam or not, I am your loyal subject," said Thunder, folding her hands and bowing.

"Fine then, my loyal friend. We must search the area for Allah's Nur. That bastardized Quran shall soon be no more!"

"Understood!" Thunder rushed off to find the blasphemous mockery of her scripture.

Aisha traveled past the jungle gardens and found a seat made of light. She hoisted herself onto the seat and gazed out at the land. "It's just as I thought. There is no Great Goddess. Lum is whoever is sitting in the chair. All the angels are without a commander. Finally this land has been reclaimed for Allah!"

Chapter 131: Sel vs Lum

Previously: Thunder, Aisha, and Gimpy vanished from the underground passage.

"Now to prove my usefulness. Kaity, watch in awe as I take down a goddess," said Devlin, sending out strands from Bravery.

The golden strands passed through Efil's protective auras and pressed her against the back wall.

"I don't want you to! Efil is my friend," said Kaity, firing energy bullets at the golden strands.

"Stand down, brother," said Kanasta.

"I have to do this. Don't get in my way." Devlin willed his wires out, pinning down his former allies.

"You've been corrupted beyond redemption," said Efil, firing Lum blasts.

Devlin didn't need to dodge. The blasts landed at his feet, causing bushes to grow around him. "Pathetic." He sliced them with a hand coated in darkness.

A concentrated beam of Lum energy slammed into him.

Wires came out from the gaps in his armor and bore into the ground, keeping him in place. Bravery sent out strands at the goddess.

"How dare you wield a Lum weapon against me," said Efil, aging the roof to collapse above her and provide some cover.

"Is it now? I wasn't aware," said Devlin, pooling dark energy into the beam until it was extinguished.

The Sassanians saw their opportunity and rushed at Devlin all at once.

"You've been brainwashed by Lum's gospel. I hope you find salvation in death," he said, firing dark bullets from his pointer finger.

The light armor around the angels deflected the shots. The Sassanians piled on top of the Dark One's warrior.

"Get off me!" Devlin's wires shot out and pressed all the angels against the wall. "Killing you is merciful. **DARK EMBODIMENT**," he said, sending his black aura down the wires.

"**TIME LAPSE**."

Devlin's chest armor cracked open as a tiny tree emerged from it.

"That Lum blast weakened my armor and transported a seed. Well played," he said, trying to hold his armor together.

Efil leaped out from behind cover and sent her aging aura out as slashes.

The aura sliced the wires that were pinning down the Sassanians.

"Wait! Don't kill him!" yelled Kaity as the goddess approached.

"Worry not, my beloved," said Devlin, raising Bravery.

Efil rode a self-made vine to dodge the golden strands, all the while firing light-coated seeds into Devlin's armor.

"𝕋𝕚𝕞𝕖 𝕃𝕒𝕡𝕤𝕖!"

The armor burst to pieces before being devoured by the light.

"It matters not! I'm still the God of Ruin!" Devlin raised his palms.

Efil dropped her aura and approached. "You've been fooled," she said with a smile.

"What did you do with my powers? How did you sever my link?" he asked, capturing the goddess with golden strands.

"You were never a god. Your dark lord tricked you. That armor was condensed Sel energy. Don't you see? The power you once controlled came solely from that armor."

"You freed him! Great job!" cheered Kaity.

"Brother, welcome back," said Kanasta.

"Yes, and now that I have purified him as Lum asked, it is time to absolve him of his sins," said Efil, aging away into dust.

"Where did she go?"

Efil appeared behind Devlin and pierced his chest with an aging blade. "Repent as your body collapses. 𝕮𝖍𝖗𝖔𝖓𝖔 𝕻𝖚𝖑𝖘𝖊."

The Goddess of Life left the blade inside. Each second the time blade shot a pulse of energy inside the Exp's body.

Devlin tried to grab the blade, but his hands ended up fading into dust.

Gimpy teleported up to Devlin. The blade was suddenly in its chest. Demonica's slave then vanished.

"The residual energy will continue to spread. Hurry and repent while you still have time," said Efil, her gaze bearing down on her foe.

"Kaity, I'm sorry for all the pain I've caused you," cried Devlin, reaching out to her with his stubs.

The strands of Bravery retreated back into the sword.

Kaity rushed up to Devlin and embraced him.

"I love you," he said with a peaceful smile.

Kaity held him close. "You're free now, okay? Find your way to Samsara. You can reincarnate there."

Kanasta stood by his brother. "I won't let you die!" He tore open Devlin's chest and removed the capsule.

"Efil, this isn't you. You're one of us," said Kaity in tears.

"You and your allies have broken Lum's trust. I was wrong to put my faith in you," said Efil, the bracelet on her wrist aging into oblivion.

Devlin's eyes became lifeless.

"It's all in vain," said Efil, looking away.

"Why did you kill him!" yelled Kaity, staring daggers at the goddess.

"Lum's orders. But there's still one more who has to die," said Efil, pointing her sword at Kanasta.

"Take his capsule. We will bring him back," said Kanasta, placing his brother's heart in his daughter's hands.

Previously: Lord Sel rammed the Great Goddess outside Samsara.

"Should we be praying?" asked Ada, looking at the aerial pillar of light.

Violet went down on her knees and bowed.

"Hey, so where did the other rebels go anyway?" asked Crisis.

"They likely assumed that the Goddesses would go after the Exps and thus they let us enter here on our own. Thunder presumably stayed with us so that she could confront the Goddesses," said Atlas.

"Do we attack them, or is our job done?" asked the Duke of Deception, turning to the samurai.

"Our leader is occupied. We should stay put for now," said Riufen.

"Hey, team, we should find Dad and get out of here," said D.S., standing by the entrance.

"I will keep Etaf from following you. Leave while you can," said Atlas.

"Thanks for all the help. I'm sure we'll meet again!" hollered Ada, leaving with her allies.

Atlas looked up at the realm gods battling outside the structure. "I am not so certain."

Lord Sel's rapid beam assault was deflected by waves of light. "Is defending all you're capable of?"

"LUMINOUS MOLTING." Lum's feathery aura shed from her body and zoomed toward the Dark One.

"You can't touch me!" Sel swerved past the energy missiles and powered up a laser. After slamming into a barrier of light, he released the beam. The dark energy pressed against the shield, sending the realm goddess down toward the ground.

"You do realize where we are, don't you?" asked the Great Goddess once her feet touched the sacred land.

"Looks like a warzone to me," said Lord Sel, looking down at rebels being killed on their knees as they prayed.

"We are in my domain." Light erupted from the ground as radiant beacons of energy.

Lord Sel zoomed through the beacons as he closed in on the Omni Goddess. "I'm well aware. I don't fear you or your pathetic world."

"Lum is one who controls the light." Lum directed the beacons at the embodiment of evil.

Lord Sel poured out more black fog to mask his presence. Whether or not the beacons pierced him was uncertain.

"Lum is one who wields the light!" The Great Goddess gripped the beacons with arms of light and sliced at the black fog.

Sel shots reigned out from the cloud and clashed against the swords. A misfired shot bore into the ground below the realm goddess.

Lum blasted the dark energy as it suddenly sprouted and turned into a tendril. "Your deception is predictable." The Goddess of Creation coated her hands in energy and formed four light glyphs. "Lum is one who directs the light. INEVITABLE-SALVATION!" Energy poured out from the glyphs as a powerful torrent, automatically seeking out the darkness.

Having occupied her sworn enemy, the realm goddess teleported to a nearby angel commander. "Guide the souls into Samsara. We mustn't allow anything to interrupt the influx of souls."

The commander bowed.

Lum teleported behind the black cloud and clasped her hands. "PURIFYING RAY!"

Light erupted from the heavens above, decimating the fog concealing the cowardly realm god.

"I didn't see you there, well played," said Sel, allowing light beams to phase through its body.

"Never has a Lum realm god been killed by a realm god from Sel. I will not die by your hand. Your ultimate goal will never be reached," said the Great Goddess, shaping the light released from her hands into a conscious shield.

"You're merely a stepping stone. My goal goes far beyond your death!" exclaimed Sel, firing spectral blasts at the arrogant goddess.

Lum teleported around, firing beams of light while dodging the blasts.

"You can't hit me when I'm in this form, but I can most certainly injure you!" Sel's spectral energy jutted out as wings. "Prana Pilfer." The wings separated into hundreds of hands all of which tore at the goddess' energy body.

"This power...it's beyond that of Sel," she said, trying to sway the hands with a spontaneously generated current of wind.

"You're only just beginning to comprehend the forces you are dealing with! Dark Conduit!" yelled Sel, sending dark energy out as a ray from each spectral hand.

Lum created a multilayered shield and teleported around while adding more layers to it. "DIVINE-RETRIBUTION!"

The shields emitted inner light, which magnified through each shield and tore through the constant rays of dark energy.

"Haha! That's it, keep wasting your energy," said Sel, his pupil turning each time the realm goddess teleported.

Lum pulled a sword of light from her chest. "You can't stay in that form forever," said the goddess, soaring through the spectral arms and slicing through the darkness.

"I can, but you can't," said Lord Sel, ramming into the arrogant goddess. "*Sel Blast!*" The Dark One released an explosion of Sel energy at point-blank range.

The black energy ate at Lum's armor until it was no more.

"I have all the land to pool energy from," said Lum, raising her hands.

Light particles came out as strands and fastened themselves around Lum.

The moment Lord Sel came out of his phase form, Lum teleported up to the dark god. "INSTANT KILL." Her finger shot into Sel like a bullet and sent the Dark One flying toward the light barrier encircling Samsara.

The overwhelming light energy formed a forest in the air.

"Your creations are mere fuel!" Sel fired beams into the trees and then sent the energy charged projectiles flying at the goddess.

Lum teleported directly in front of her sworn enemy, throwing his assault off-guard. "You cannot escape this place," she said, pressing her nemesis against the barrier.

"Watch me." Sel's spectral aura gripped the goddess' arm, pressed it to the barrier, and twisted it, curving the barrier till it split open.

"I won't let you escape!" exclaimed Lum, pooling her energy into the barrier.

"Oh, I don't care about that!" Sel slammed into the realm goddess at point-blank range. The Dark One gripped the not-so-Great Goddess with outstretched spectral hands, rendering her teleportation worthless.

Beams of dark energy shot out from the Dark One's sides, crashing against her beams of light.

After slamming her against the mountainside, Lord Sel dragged the realm goddess inside Samsara where Atlas, Etaf, Riufen, and the Duke stood waiting.

Dark energy crept out from the walls and sealed the entrance.

"Cut off from outside energy and not enough in you to fight back. You're trapped in your own realm. Ah, this has worked out splendidly. Losing Evol and Tcetorp has sapped away so much of your strength," said Sel, circling around his prey as she slowly rose to her feet.

"I'll need to be sparing from here on. EAWDAT AN-NUR." Lum's aura was sucked into her body. The light faded, revealing the familiar form of Sefiwah.

"What!? You were her? Of course you were! Sefiwah's love of the color white, her obsession with protecting Kaity, your instant kill move, the white cloud that was supposedly the Revive Artifact—it's all starting to make sense now," said Sel with a wide grin.

"You're still alive, sister," said Atlas, looking at Lum.

"As are you," said Lum, taking a stance as the Dark One approached.

Atlas stepped between them. "I stayed behind so that I could finish you, Sel."

"Sorry, I'm busy now. I'll play with you once I'm done," said Sel, pushing aside Atlas with a large spectral hand.

Lum sped up to the Dark One, stabbing her light-coated fingers into the realm god like machine gun fire.

"Eheehee, trying to tickle me?" asked Sel, gushing out dark energy from each stab.

Lum cringed in pain but kept up her assault. The light that poured from her wounds shaped into daggers before piercing into the root of all evil.

"You don't get it." The attacks phased through Lord Sel. "I've already won. Dark Apocalypse."

Sel beams shot out randomly from the walls.

"Please, my lord, get us out of here," said the Duke, leaping aside once its strings indicated an incoming projectile.

"Yes, go home," said Sel, forming a portal.

The Duke and Riufen entered before the portal closed.

Lord Sel turned to the goddess, his eye pulsing with energy. "Sel Beam!" The Dark One's souped-up beam split as it fired out, allowing for Lum to deflect it with arched shields of light. It took a few moments before the God of Destruction realized he had been sliced in half.

The Destiny Sword sped right through the dark god's split body.

Etaf teleported up to the sword and grabbed Sefiwah. "I live to serve you." The Goddess of Fate formed a portal of light, and the two of them went in.

Lord Sel's halves sped toward the portal only to be held back by Atlas' Chaos Chains.

"No! No! No!" Lord Sel slammed its spectral hands against the ground. "I don't feel like dealing you with you right now." The Dark One glared at Atlas and then pooled the energy from its barrier inside its body. The energy came out as a Sel portal. "Damn it. To think things were going so well up till now. That Etaf has become far more than a mere nuisance." The God of Destruction vanished in a black portal.

Chapter 132: Sellum

Previously: Kaity and Kanasta took a stand against Efil.

"Escape this place. Find someone who can heal my brother," said Kanasta.

"We're doing this together," said Kaity, opening fire on the goddess.

Efil aged the bullets into dust before they could hit.

Kaity raised her sniper rifle when an armored figure appeared in front of her.

"Efil, stand down," said the armored man.

"Who are you?" asked Efil, walking up to the intruder.

Light and dark energy came from the armored figure's palm, forming into a barrier.

"I am one who observes the realms but cannot end conflict himself."

Efil dropped to her knees and cried.

"Can you save my brother?" asked Kanasta, looking up at the divine being.

"I already have."

Kaity dropped the capsule.

Wires grew out of it and formed into the black-skinned Exp.

"Devlin, you're alive?"

The observer formed a Lum portal. "Enter and you will be reunited with your allies."

"Thank you." Kanasta hoisted up his brother and entered the light portal.

Sellum dispersed the portal once Kaity came near it.

"I need to go to. They need my help."

"I'd like to talk with you," he said, forming a special portal by mixing Sel, Lum, and Absence energy together.

"Where are you from? Sel? Absence? Lum?"

"I watch over all three realms. I am Sellum," he said in a deep deity voice.

Sellum was eighteen feet tall and clad in golden armor. White and black energy was bursting out from the gaps in the god's shell. The Lord of God's helmet was oval-shaped and had a yin-yang pattern divided by a thin line of Absence energy. A clear aura coated the god's entire body, destroying any light or darkness that escaped from beneath the god's armor.

"I don't understand, but it doesn't matter. If you're so powerful, then you can rescue my team, right?"

"Your allies are safe. Please, follow me. I insist," said Sellum, gesturing to the portal.

Kaity looked around, realizing she was trapped. "Alright, but only because you saved Kanasta," she said, walking in with him.

They were instantly brought to Sellum's throne.

Sellum turned around and created two chairs with Lum energy. "Sit, if it pleases you."

Kaity sat catlike on the top of the chair, gazing around at the stars above her. "What is this place?"

"It's where I monitor Sellum and the Milky Way Galaxy." Sellum gestured to the planets revolving around the circumference of the room.

"You're g-g-god?" asked Kaity with a blank look.

"I can't imagine the source of all creation being limited to the maintenance of a single galaxy. I am called the Lord of Gods, but it is an empty title. I'm the current manager for Sellum and the Milky Way. Nothing more."

"That's still...something else."

A pink bunny with big eyes and soft fur leaped onto Kaity's lap.

"Ah, seems Bobby has taken a liking to you," said Sellum, patting the bunny's head lovingly.

"Why is he pink?" asked Kaity, scratching behind his ears.

"That is beyond my knowledge," said Sellum in a stoic voice, rubbing the bunny's belly.

"So, God, why did you call me here?" asked Kaity, her legs trembling.

"Sellum, not God. First things first. Please, accept this." Sellum bent over with both arms outstretched and offered her an artifact.

Kaity took it and then looked at him precariously. "What do you want?"

"You are on Lum's side, correct?" asked Sellum.

"Yes," said Kaity, her gaze fixed on him.

Sellum sat down in the adjacent chair. "What do you think of her?"

"I don't think she'd want me telling you that."

"I know she incarnated to watch over you as Sefiwah. Just as I know Bob did the very same."

"What? Bob was watching over me?"

"In a sense. Now, tell me more about Lum or, rather, about Sefiwah," said Sellum leaning in and folding his hands.

"She is my companion. I would trust her with my life," said Kaity.

"That may not be the wisest decision," said Sellum.

"Excuse me?"

"Sefiwah and Bob both have their reasons for monitoring you."

"Enough."

"What?"

"I know what you're trying to do. You're trying to turn me against Sefiwah. It won't work, so don't waste your time."

"I am merely speaking the truth."

"Say what you have to say. Then you have to answer my questions," said Kaity, leaning in close to him.

"To put it bluntly: Sefiwah is using you," said Sellum, his gaze unwavering.

"Empty lies," said Kaity, turning away from his eyes.

"She is using you to fight Sel for her."

"She's scared. I felt it. She just wants someone to stand by her, and she doesn't want to lose me."

"There's no denying that. You are in grave danger. It's only a matter of time before Sel comes after you," said Sellum, grabbing her arm.

Kaity pulled out from his grip. "Why me? Why does he want to kill me? He has some personal vendetta against me when I haven't done anything to him. Was it a past life or is he mistaking me for my mother?"

"It's neither. Sel is jealous; plain and simple. He covets my title."

"Okay, but what does that have to do with me?"

"Sel harbors deep resentment for you because you were chosen to be the next Sellum."

"Wh-what? Slow down. I'm what?"

Sellum pulled Kaity out of the chair with a hand of light. "One day you will monitor this realm," he said, gesturing to the swirling planets around them.

"You're not making any sense. I didn't ask for this. Who would pick me, an assassin, to be the next god of the afterlife?"

"I did. And I chose wisely."

"Why me? You don't know anything about me," said Kaity.

"I know enough. Though I chose correctly, it is not fair that I forced this burden upon you." Sellum placed his forehead to the ground. "I apologize for all the suffering it has caused you and for all the loss you will experience," said Sellum in a cut and dry voice as his tears formed a puddle.

"What are you talking about?"

"I am the reason you were targeted by Sel. I do not ask for forgiveness. I only want you to know my apology is genuine," said Sellum, tears leaking out from his mask.

"Why make me Sellum? What do you want from me?"

Sellum stood up, burned away his tears with Sel energy, and turned to Kaity. "You have made peace with the Exps. I need you to lead the Freedom Forcers. But that's not all. I need a new God of Sel and Lum to monitor the realms. Lum and Sel have acted against both me and the balance of Sellum."

"What did Sefiwah do to you?"

"Lum created you to kill Sel because she is not allowed to. Kaity, I've told you all I can. I need to know, will you help me replace Sel and Lum?" asked Sellum, staring past her eyes and into her soul.

"I would sooner tear out my own heart than hurt Sefi-chan!" Kaity's claws jutted out.

"Your birth was just a means for Lum to gain footing in her feud against Sel."

"What does that even mean?"

"Sefiwah is your mother."

"That's right. She's like a mother, a friend, a partner, but above all, she's my soul mate."

"She's more than that. She's family."

"All the Viper Squad members are my family. They are all irreplaceable," said Kaity firmly.

"You two are closer than you realize."

"I don't care if you are god. You don't know more about her than I do."

"Sefiwah gave birth to you. She is your biological mother," said Sellum in a stoic tone, slamming the table.

Kaity's plasma claws jutted out and pressed to Sellum's armored neck. "My mother died," she said with furious eyes.

"Your mother faked her death, and then she joined Kanasta's team as Sefiwah. It was the best way to keep watch over you after what happened," said Sellum, suddenly crying.

"She was dead," said Kaity softly.

"Death is not a difficult thing for a god to stage."

"You're sure?"

"I was there with her. I'm absolutely positive."

"Then she's alive, really?" asked Kaity, tearing up.

"Alive and in danger."

"You have to help. You can defeat Sel, right?"

"It's not my place. But I will aid you in my own way."

"And how is that."

"By sharing with you the secrets she keeps."

"I know she somewhat resembles my mom, but they look different. She's not my mom. But Mom's alive. You said so, right?"

"I do not lie," said Sellum with eyes of conviction.

"Why would my mom even fake her death?"

Sellum bowed. "I apologize. I overstepped my boundaries. I only wanted to warn you that Lum is using you and your allies to fight her war."

"And I refuse to believe that."

"Who ordered Efil to kill Kanasta?"

"Etaf did! She spoke on Lum's behalf. Sefiwah wouldn't do that. She loves him like a brother."

"Lum wants to be the only one you care about. Then she has full power over you, my heir."

"Teleport me back!"

"Very well. I enjoyed our talk. I hope you got something out of it."

A white portal appeared and Kaity walked through it.

Sellum fell to his knees, tears leaking out of his mask. "I've put her through so much."

The woman in the mourner's veil approached from behind him.

"It's as we discussed. As long as you intervene on my behalf, we have a deal."

"When can I see him?"

Sellum created a portal to Absence.

"Thank you."

"There will be a time when I can free him, but for now a visit is all I can offer."

"I just want to speak with him," said Casey, crying with joy.

They walked through and approached Absence.

"I need to speak with Zenero," said Sellum.

"I cannot do that, Great Swami!" exclaimed Absence, placing his head to the ground in apology.

"Why not?" asked Sellum.

"I want to keep my title!"

"I forgive you for your past mistake," said Sellum, placing his hands atop Absence's shoulders.

"Your forgiveness is heartily received, Great Swami," said Absence as he bowed repeatedly.

"This is of the upmost importance. I need to speak with him. If he does escape, you will not be held liable."

"Understood, my Lord! Everyone, clear out!"

Sellum looked around, seeing no souls in the immediate area. "It's all clear."

Absence took out a marble. "**Revert!**"

A clear prison folded out from the orb.

"You condensed the prison. I am impressed," said Sellum, pride emanating from his otherwise stoic posture.

Inside the prison were billions of compacts, each separated in different compartments.

"Follow me, Great Swami!" Absence led Sellum down to the seventh floor of the prison. There was only one compact on this floor. It was encased in a wall of Absence.

"Very thorough. Well done," said Sellum, rapidly clapping.

Sellum and Absence coated their bodies in a clear aura and entered. The woman in mourning had to wait outside the wall.

Absence picked up the compact. "**ᖇᘏᘏᖇᕇ**."

A naked man with long white hair formed in front of them.

"Zenero!" exclaimed Casey.

Zenero spat on Sellum's face. "What do you want?"

"To complete a deal," said Sellum.

Zenero's eyes shot open as he noticed the woman.

"Darling, is it really you?" asked Zenero, almost rushing into the Absence wall.

Absence grabbed Zenero's arm, holding him back from obliterating himself.

"It's really me," said Casey in tears.

"I must keep an eye on the Freedom Forcers. I will return shortly. If these two cause you any trouble, inform me at once," said Sellum.

"Understood, my Lord!" exclaimed Absence.

"Also, I think the prison needs more protection," said Sellum.

"Understood, my Lord."

Sellum vanished.

Previously: Aisha was brought to the Observatory and seated herself atop the throne.

"Dear friend, I have found the accursed scripture," said Thunder.

Aisha turned her attention to her ally. "Then the rebellion was a success. Destroy it. Leave not a single page intact."

"It's made of pure light. How shall I go about destroying it?" asked Thunder.

"I leave it in your hands."

"Understood." Thunder approached a miniature volcano and shoved the corner of the blasphemous book inside.

The book was unaffected.

Thunder pulled out a dagger and repeatedly stabbed the book.

"Stand at attention. There's someone here," said Aisha, pointing to an approaching figure.

"How did you get here? What are you here for?" asked Thunder, holding out the dagger.

"I should ask you the same thing," said Lum, walking toward them in a daze.

"I am the Great Goddess herself. Remove yourself from my presence and you shall be spared," said Aisha.

"One more step and you're dead," said Thunder, whipping out a crossbow and aiming it.

The Great Goddess stepped forward, grabbed the arrow, and tossed it at Aisha.

The ex-Imam shielded her chest with her arms.

"Get out of my chair," said Sefiwah.

"It's her! Lum is real! Thunder, this is it. Take her down. She is weakened. All your training has been for this moment!" exclaimed Aisha, standing on the throne.

Thunder nodded and stepped in the realm goddess' path. "For your blasphemy against my people, against Allah's scripture, and against Allah, I sentence you to death."

Lum zoomed up to the nuisance.

Thunder held up her niqab as a shield, dodging the hand strike that pierced through. Approximating the goddess' location, she fired four arrows into the cloth.

Two of the arrows missed; the other two found a home in the goddess' chest.

Droplets of light came from the wound.

Lum collected the droplets on her fingers and flung them at her attacker.

The droplets unleashed their potential once hitting the cloth, growing out from the other side as pointed branches.

Thunder sliced at the branches as they continuously expanded.

"I have more power in a single drop of my blood than you humans do in your—what's this?" Lum stopped in place.

Her human attacker's form was revealed once the cloth fell.

Thunder's body had been heavily modified. One arm had sharpened thorns coming out and the other had just ignited itself. The warrior's fingertips were purple, likely concealing pockets of poison beneath. Hooks came out from her feet like talons, gripping the ground.

"It's over, false god. Thunder willingly underwent modifications throughout her body. Demon blood flows in her veins. Heaven's Thunder is a living weapon designed to kill angels and goddesses. She is the embodiment of Allah's wrath," said Aisha.

"You've given up everything for this woman? Why?" asked Lum, taking steps toward the demon.

"The woman on that throne is no longer the Imam. It is not for Aisha that I do this. It is for Allah!" Thunder rushed in, firing out the spikes on her arm.

Lum caught one, coated it in Lum energy, and used the newly formed rock to deflect the other projectiles. "I overpowered that demon's corrosive influence over your daughter. Fatima is now mine to control." Lum teleported the young angel in front of her.

Fatima was wounded by Gimpy's energy, and her eyes where pure white.

Lum slammed the rock against the girl's head. "I can kill her or free her, depending on how earnestly you plead for repentance."

"I'm sorry. I never should have left you alone," said Thunder, reaching out to her daughter.

"That's right. You abandoned her for the sake of your rebellion. You have no right to call yourself her mother anymore," said Lum, picking up the girl from the back of her neck and steadily approaching.

"It's true. I am a weapon for Allah's Jannah. And Fatima is now your weapon," said Thunder.

"You do understand. Remove her from my kingdom, angel. Killing is beneath me," said Lum, releasing her weapon and turning away.

Thunder rushed after the goddess only to be intercepted by Fatima. She swiped the angel's legs and kicked her aside. The hooks on the sides of her arm shot out and pierced into the goddess' back.

"I changed my mind. Having a mother and daughter fight is too cruel." Lum's aura traveled up the chained hooks as a thin vine.

Thunder sliced the vine with her dagger.

It was in vain. The vine crawled up the dagger and pierced Thunder's skin.

"WHITE-GENESIS."

Vine's came out from Thunder's pores and bloomed into flowers.

"If it must be done, it should be gracefully done," said Lum, walking up and caressing the white petals.

"Murderer!" Aisha tore off her niqab, set it aflame using her fallen comrade's arm, and captured the goddess within. "Die! Die and Allah will take over this world. No god with form is fit to rule the heavens!"

Water burst out, dousing the flames.

Aisha tore out a spike and repeatedly jabbed the goddess' head until she felt it burst open. Once the deed was done she fell to her knees and sobbed.

Sefiwah's hands removed the cloak.

Rather than blood, Lum's split open head emitted light. The pure white light soon healed the wound it emerged from.

"My time as an assassin was not all wasted."

Aisha grabbed her naked chest as blood leaked out.

"Thunder deserved a quick death. Not you. Grovel. Beg and plead. My merciful spirit may spare you yet," said Lum, looking down at the wretch.

"Fatima is her daughter. Please, bring her back to the way she was. Use whatever power you have to restore her identity," said Aisha, looking up in tears.

"Thinking of the child when your own life is slipping away." Lum pulled away a tear. "We should have been on the same side."

"Does that mean you'll do it?" asked Aisha, seeing the goddess for the first time as an individual.

The Great Goddess approached the angel and placed her hand on the girl's head.

Light seeped back into Lum's arm, coating her body in a thin aura.

The light left Fatima, revealing the girl's amber eyes.

The girl looked around in a daze. Once she saw her mom, she tore at the flowers.

"It's no use. She's in Soul Storage now. Having her reincarnate would only bring Lum more trouble in the future."

"What did you do to her?" asked Fatima, wiping away the corrosive blood off her arm.

"She chose that herself. Living every moment in pain for the sake of liberating Lum. Thunder is a greater rebel than I could ever have been," said Aisha.

"Great Mother!" Fatima rushed to the Imam, trying to lift her off her feet.

"It's too late for me. But it doesn't matter. Thunder succeeded. This is a victory for Allah," said Aisha, looking up at the darkness-coated lump clasped to the fallen warrior's chest.

"What do I do?" asked Fatima in tears.

"Only you can find that answer," said Aisha, fading away with a smile.

Fatima broke down in tears.

"Take as long as you like. I'll send you back when you're ready," said Lum, struggling to hold back her tears.

"You changed me. I'm not even human anymore, am I?" asked Fatima, tearing at her light wings.

"You're so much more now," said Lum with a smile as Fatima's wounds healed themselves.

Meanwhile: in Absence, the realm god looked out at his protectors. Warriors made visible only through their aura armor were sparring all across the land.

Limit approached his lord and bowed. "I would like to make a recommendation for the new first guard and guardian."

"You've already found a pair suitable for the position? I'm impressed," said Absence.

"They are quite skilled at combat and offer something new to our pantheon," said Limit.

"Please, reveal them to me," said Absence.

"Crystal, you heard him," said Limit.

"Just for the record, I'm not sure recruiting them is a good idea.

CRYSTAL CRUMBLE."

The barrier concealing the candidates shattered.

The Führer of Fortune and the Baroness of Blades were revealed, already bowing to their new king.

Absence tried to mask his surprise, but his open jaw gave it away. "What are their qualifications?"

"The Baroness of Blades is a skilled warrior who seeks a cause to fight for. She has been working alongside this gentleman as a commander for Sinner's Fury, a now defunct rebel army in Sel. I have had the honor of fighting her. Devotion and dignity are the power behind her strikes."

"I understand why you have chosen her. Now that Needle has left, we need a voice from Sel in the pantheon. Balance must be maintained. Tell me about the other one."

"The Führer of Fortune is loyal to Sel's people. He has a deep understanding of all seven regions, both regional and realm politics, was once a leader of a rebel army, and is a brilliant tactician. I nominate him as the new First Guardian."

"They're both demons! They cannot be trusted!" exclaimed Tcetorp, rushing in to see the commotion.

"They offer new insight into our pantheon. I accept. However, since they are from Sel, they cannot be first. Occupy, Void," said Absence, turning to his warriors.

"Yes, king of kings," said Occupy with a reverent bow.

"Void is now the First Guardian. You are the First Guard."

"If you say it, then it is so," said Occupy.

"The others will all move up as well. Führer, Baroness, you will take your place as the fifths. Understood?"

"I heartily accept," said the Führer.

"My blades shall take up Absence as their new cause," said the Baroness.

"Balance is our mission. If we fight for Absence, we go against that which it stands for. An old adversary taught me that. Continue training."

"Wait. Please, tell me what the third condition is. What must I do for you so that I may return to Lum?" asked Tcetorp.

"Fight with us to defend this realm. If the realm god of Absence, Sel, or Lum falls, you will be granted leave to your realm. I cannot return you until this conflict is over. Do you accept?"

"Absence has taken up demons as gods."

"Do you accept or not?"

"Urgh! I don't have a choice. I will defend Absence so that Lum may be protected from Sel's advance," said Tcetorp, glaring at the demons.

"Glad we have reached an understanding. It is likely that Sel has already made plans to attack us."

Kanasta and Devlin came out of a Lum portal and dropped onto a white grass bed.

"You're safe," said Kanasta, embracing his brother.

"What happened?" asked Devlin, noticing he was in his Exp form.

"Efil had all but destroyed you."

Devlin turned to his brother. "You saved me."

"Not alone. A god came and intervened. Kaity and I were ready to fight Efil to the bitter end. We'd likely be gone if not for him."

Devlin grabbed Kanasta's hand. "Kaity was protecting me?"

"We both were."

"She risked her life for me? Why?"

"Kaity kills to keep her precious ones safe. It's who she is," said Kanasta.

Demonica landed before them. "Alright, chat's over." She pulled Devlin aside. "We're being called upon."

"He isn't going anywhere," said Kanasta, whipping out a canister filled with light.

"Do you really want to die?" asked Demonica with a crazed look.

"Stop it. I'll come with you. Before we go, can you have your gimp put my skin back on?" asked Devlin.

"So you figured it out." Demonica snapped her fingers, signaling Gimpy to dress up her man.

Devlin fixed his hair. "So, what does Bob want?"

"You're going to tell Lord Sel how you failed to capture Efil," said Demonica, poking her man's cheek.

"My brother nearly died," said Kanasta.

"I doubt it," said Demonica with a smile.

"No point in discussing it. Let's go," said Devlin.

Demonica formed a portal to the Core.

Devlin and Demonica arrived, face-to-face with the God of Destruction.

"Where is Efil?" asked Lord Sel, gazing into Devlin's eyes.

"Shut up," said Devlin with a glare.

"Um, what?"

"I know the truth."

"You mean about Kaity?" asked Sel.

"What?"

"Oh nothing."

"I mean about my powers! There is no God of Ruin! You lied to me!" yelled Devlin, pinning down the god with his wires.

"You weren't able to kill Etah. If you had, you would have become a proper god."

"Don't make excuses! That armor was just a means to control me. Well now it's gone! I'm free!"

"You know, I went through a lot of work making that armor. I think it took a permanent toll on my Sel powers," said Sel, passing through the wires and circling around his pawn.

"I'm done following your orders!"

"Such a shame. Kaity will be so sad to hear that. Demonica's been looking for an excuse to torture her. Congrats. You just threw away her only protection," said Sel with a crimson gaze.

"I've had enough of your empty threats! I'm joining the Freedom Forcers. Together with Kaity, I will take you down and become a real god!"

"You think they want you back? They won't trust you. I've painted you a permanent enemy in their eyes."

"I'll prove my worth. I'll earn their trust. I know your plan. Soon, they'll all know."

Lord Sel turned to Demonica. "Is he asking me to kill them all? That's sure what it sounds like to me!"

Demonica shrugged.

"You still have a use for them or else they'd be dead despite our deal," said Devlin.

"You think you're so clever. Next time you decide to betray someone, make sure you have an escape plan. You're trapped here, fool!" exclaimed Lord Sel, releasing his black aura.

Devlin peered past Sel and smiled at Demonica. "Is that what you think? I have a Lum sword with me!" He waved Bravery until a light portal formed.

Sel's pupil lit up. "Splendid! Most splendid! I should have known better. You're a clever, clever boy. Go on, you've earned it," said the dark deity, shooing its student away.

Devlin entered the portal.

"Should I have stopped him?" asked Demonica.

"He's still in his rebellious phase. Let him have this victory. We have more important things to attend to."

"Then what is the next stage of the plan?"

"We still need to capture Efil, but just in case we can't, I have a back-up plan," said Lord Sel with a devious grin.

Sneak Peek of Book 4, *Destruction, Creation, Absence*:
Resurrection of the Exps

In the Core, the woman in the veil approached the God of Destruction and bowed. "Greetings, Lord Sel."

"We can skip the pleasantries, Casey. What do you want? Spit it out," said Sel, not even looking at her.

"It would be easier to defeat Sellum if we had Zenero's help."

"Zenero, eh? Hmm, are you sure?"

"Yes. He's the only one to have ever defeated Sellum."

"There were likely others in the past, but who knows who they are? You make a good point, but bringing him back would be quite risky."

"What risk can he pose to you?"

"I would say you're obviously kissing up, but you make a point. I can handle him if he gets rowdy. One slight problem: I don't know where he is. I thought he may have been in the Elysium Asylum, but I didn't sense his presence there."

"He is locked up in Absence."

"Is he now? Well then, it's too much of a hassle to get him out. Not worth the effort, sorry."

"If I capture Efil, will you free him?"

Sel turned around and floated up to Casey. "You're offer is rather enticing. But how will you capture the Goddess of Life? My dear Demonica was overwhelmed by her power. I would have helped if I wasn't busy fighting the Great Goddess herself."

"My powers are not affected by time. I will capture her."

"Such conviction! Splendid! We have a deal!" exclaimed Lord Sel, gripping her hand and shaking it with his spectral energy.

"Thank you."

"But once he is free, you will make it very clear that it is his duty to help me take down Sellum."

"I doubt he'll need much convincing."

"Good point. Pleasure doing business with you. Send her to Lum," said Lord Sel, turning to Demonica.

"It is done," said Demonica with a snap of her fingers.

"Now then, moving along. Riufen, Gladius, get over here!"

Riufen approached Lord Sel. He turned to Demonica.

"Where is Devlin-sama?"

"He's busy—who cares? I've chosen you," said Sel.

"You have? Chosen me for what?"

"I'll let you think about it. You know, you caught my interest the first time we fought back in Devlin's lab. Ever since, I was shaping you into my warrior. There were times where it may have seemed that I was disappointed in you—and, well, I was. But I never gave up on you. You're so very special."

"You honor me with your words," said Riufen his voice quivering with reverence.

"That's why I've decided to make you immortal."

"Immortality is the bane of my existence. I will never have an honorable death. Even so, you cannot give me what I already have."

"You aren't immortal. I could destroy you, so could Demonica. There's quite a few who could. I already killed you once, remember?"

"I cannot forget."

"What makes a swordsman immortal? I've been asking myself this for quite some time." Sel manifested the Atma Blade. "The answer: it is their bond with their blade that gives them life eternal. At least that's the poetic poppycock explanation."

"It makes sense to me. A warrior aligned with his blade cannot be struck down."

"Oh, but you can. That's why I've decided to fuse your souls."

"You can fuse souls?"

"Why yes, of course, the Atma Blade is made up of my essence after all," said Sel.

"I would be honored if you could join Gladius' soul with my own," said Riufen.

"Now it won't be quite so easy. You must share a strong bond and both be willing to join together. Plus, it will take time—my time, that is." Sel shoved the Atma Blade through the samurai.

Riufen fell to the floor, unconscious.

Lord Sel pierced the spectral blade through Gladius, absorbing his soul as well. "If all goes according to plan, then the spirit of the warrior and his blade will be forever entwined," said the God of Destruction as the two souls mixed.

"Riufen is already powerful. This is unnecessary," said Gladius.

"In order to kill Sellum, I will need a Lum and an Absence realm god capable of breaching his defenses. I've chosen Riufen to be my Absence. Without true immortality, he stands no chance of taking down the current ruler of Absence."

"So then who will be your Lum?" asked Riufen.

Sel's pupil contorted into a mischievous smile. "I've already chosen, but it's a secret. Victory is all but certain now. With Efil and the realm gods at my command, Sellum will fall and I shall rise anew."

Book 4, *Destruction, Creation, Absence*: Resurrection of the Exps

The Freedom Forcers regroup to uncover what happened to their comrades who went through the Portal to Earth. They know they will need to recruit new allies in the fight against the God of Destruction. On Earth, Senator Jo John sends out Exp Hunters–special troops designed to kill Exps. Sellum takes the rebel Exps under his wing, but masks his true intentions. Lord Sel raids the prison of Absence to free Zenero, the only one who has ever defeated Sellum. Whether the Dark One succeeds or fails with the break out, Lord Sel is determined to battle Sellum. To attain victory he sends out his strongest warriors to usurp the realm gods and gain power over destruction, creation, and absence. Will Sellum, the Lord of Gods, be overtaken by the machinations of the God of Destruction? The thrilling conclusion to the *Resurrection* arc will bring this answer to light.

Coming Summer 2018.

About the Author

Alexander McCarty is an animal born on Earth who actively seeks freedom for his fellow animals. At age five, once he realized that the chickens he loved and the chickens he was eating were one in the same, he became an ovolacto-vegetarian along with his nine-year-old brother. In middle-school, he decided to make use of his free time by writing a book. At the age of twenty-one he met vegan activist Gary Yourofsky and vowed to live vegan alongside his brother. They have since dedicated their lives to animal liberation through educational activism. Alexander recently graduated with a bachelor's degree in Religious Studies, and holds certificates in Jainism, Asiatic Studies, and Spirituality. He is now a full-time writer and is also the president of Sphere of Compassion Inc. He runs SOC with his brother, a company whose purpose is to spread innovative media and promote a vegan worldview. When he isn't writing, he is watching anime, reading, or playing videogames. He listens to any and all comments, suggestions, reflections, and criticism.

Please contact me with a link to where you placed a review for any of my books, and I will answer any single question as one of my characters for **FREE**. If you do a review (and point out where) in addition to submitting fan art, I will write a **FREE** short 2–4 page story (with my characters) in a scenario of your choosing. =(:3)*
Bloggers who wish to review my book may request "Review Copies" of *Exp 8: Rebellion of the Exps* at the links below.
authoralexandermccarty@gmail.com
alexanderjmccarty@facebook.com

Find Solace by Following Your Morals

Many of us believe it is fundamentally wrong to take what isn't ours and to kill for reasons of pleasure. "My rights end where another's rights begin" is a general consensus of belief for most humans. This moral foundation is the reason why we outwardly oppose dog-fighting, animal cruelty in general, and other forms of victimization that are performed for the sake of pleasure. We would not stand by while someone was beating a dog, a pig, or most any animal, because we see the violence. The problem is, through the media, traditions, and our own unwillingness to examine our choices, most of us engage in animal cruelty on a daily basis.

When we purchase an animal product, we are effectively paying someone to exploit (and inevitably kill) that animal and its kin. If we wouldn't buy dog meat, why would we pay for the flesh of other animals or their byproducts? We are well aware that all animals experience a spectrum of emotions and a desire to live, much like the companion animals we live with. Sadly we have been fooled into believing that the exploitation we participate in is natural, normal, and necessary. Only necessity matters. Millions of humans are living healthy without eating or purchasing products derived from animals. This means that the only reason we keep eating animal products (and continue buying them) is for our own fleeting pleasure. While this revelation is disturbing, which I was all too aware of when I realized it, that does not in any way undermine its truth.

If we understand animal cruelty is wrong and we realize that the cruelty we are participating in (often on a daily basis) is for reasons of pleasure, then our only option is to stop exploiting animals by living a vegan life. Veganism is not a matter of belief, it's simply a matter of following the morals we already hold dear. If you truly believe that your moment of enjoyment (from consuming animal products) is more important than the life of the individuals that were exploited, then you are part of the moral minority. The majority feels that you need a compelling reason to harm someone (human or non-human). Thus our morals invariably mandate we live vegan. Living vegan doesn't make you a hero to the animals, just like buying fair-trade clothing does not make you a hero to exploited workers; it is simply a matter of treating them fairly. When we live by our morals we find an inner solace that cannot be attained through other means. When we follow our beliefs, we are being true to ourselves and being fair to others.

Below are some links to places where we can get informed and get involved.

http://www.adaptt.org/

www.serv-online.org

http://www.abolitionistapproach.com

veganeducationgroup.com